I0665573

MY GRUMPY WOLF

SHELLEY MUNRO

MUNRO PRESS

My Grumpy Wolf

Print ISBN: 978-1-99-106384-7
E-book ISBN: 978-1-99-106376-2

Editor: Evil Eye Editing
Cover: Kim Killion, The Killion Group, Inc.

Munro Press, New Zealand.

First Munro Press electronic publication May 2025
First Munro Press print publication May 2025

DEDICATION

For Paul, my husband, partner in crime, and fellow adventurer.
Every day is a good day.

INTRODUCTION

He refused to fall in love...

Maia is excited to score a rugby contract to play for a women's team, and when it places her in the same small country town as her childhood crush, she isn't sure what reaction to expect. But it certainly isn't his grumpy rejection and watching Henry's back as he flees her presence.

Wolf shifter Henry lost his mate when a madman murdered her, and he isn't about to risk his heart again despite the attraction simmering between him and the younger, sunshiny-bright Maia. The age gap is too large. He's best to continue his solitary life rather than gamble with love.

In a shocking twist, someone attacks Maia, and Henry finds he can't ignore this beautiful woman who brings out his protective instincts. He can't walk away, even though history seems to be repeating itself. She needs him, and he's falling in love. And that's where his problems begin...

PROLOGUE

H enry enjoyed the local Middlemarch school visits to his
kennels. The students loved the dogs he trained for security
work. The dogs' presence was also an excuse for shifters to explain
sightings should a human see a leopard or wolf running through
the countryside.

But this classroom interaction had him edgy as hell.

It was the girl.

She hadn't taken her gaze off him since she'd spotted him on her
arrival. The kid said little to her classmates, didn't laugh or giggle
with them. She wasn't the child asking countless questions.

No.

Instead, she gawked at him, her forehead furrowed in
concentration.

Henry's best friend, Gerard, hadn't noticed, but the girl gave
Henry the willies. He was positive he hadn't seen her before.

Maybe she was the niece old Mrs. Ramsey had taken in after the kid's parents had died in a car crash. Yeah, that'd make sense.

She'd crept closer while he'd been busy thinking, and he started. *A kid. Get it together, man.*

She was twelve years old and harmless. For God's sake, he'd been in the military and was a big man who shifted to a wolf. Capable of looking after himself. So why was this kid scraping his nerves the wrong way?

He dragged in a lungful of air and froze.

No!

No. No. No.

That couldn't be right.

The girl was twelve and as flat as an ironing board. She was a child. *A child.*

She couldn't be his mate.

Hell, his wolf was playing nasty tricks on him. His mate had died almost three years ago. Jenny had been Henry's mate, and her ex had murdered her, sending him into a tailspin.

He breathed again, taking care to keep the inhalation shallow.

"Mister, could I buy a dog from you one day? They're beautiful."

Henry cleared his throat, prepared to respond. Nothing but an unintelligible croak emerged, and he scanned for the teacher. Where the hell was she when he needed her?

"Gerard?" He raised his voice so his friend would hear him over the excited kids and equally animated dogs.

"Yeah, mate."

"Could you answer this kid's question? I need to leave. Now!"

He was a dirty old man. That's what he was. *A dirty old man.*

Gerard sent him a glance, and what he saw must've alarmed him. He hurried to Henry. "I've got you."

"Outside." Even as he gasped the explanation, he pushed past the girl, holding his breath to avoid more of her scent.

Unbelievable. Nature playing a nasty trick on him.

He brushed off a parent and a teacher. Henry was sure they considered him rude and taciturn. He knew people gossiped about him, but his loyal friends were all that mattered.

Henry hit the door and pushed outside.

"Hey, mister," the childish voice carried after him. "You didn't answer my question."

"Speak to your parents about a dog," he snapped, wincing at his harshness, but this was self-preservation. "Go back inside. The teachers want you within sight."

Gods, why was fate such a cruel bitch? He broke into a run, barely clinging to his control. His bloody wolf wanted to rub against the kid and inhale her scent.

That would *never* happen.

Henry ran faster, ghostly images of Jenny chasing him. By the time he reached the native bush surrounding their property, he was sprinting. He could no longer see or hear the child, but she was in his mind's eye.

Dammit, fate was diabolical.

He burst into the trees, an uncontrolled shift brutally reshaping his bones, the rent of fabric jarring and echoing his mental state. Henry fell to his hands and knees and prayed no one had witnessed this fall from grace. He bore impressive control, but not today.

Henry lay on the forest floor, exhausted and shocked, the damp earth and dead leaf litter pressing against his belly. Long minutes later, he rose on trembling legs and untangled pieces of clothing from his legs and arms, tossing them aside.

His wolf wanted to return to the child.

No way.

Since this was the last school visit of the year, the girl wouldn't cross his path again.

Henry forced his wolf to travel deeper into the bush, upping his pace and racing into the dark, shadowed areas beneath the trees.

Almost three hours had elapsed before he headed home. This time, his pace was slower, his thoughts less frantic.

He had a plan. He'd avoid town and stay away from gatherings because he couldn't run into the child again—not if he wanted to preserve his sanity.

When Henry arrived home, the school kids had left, and the parking area in front of their security business was empty. London, Gerard's wife, had gone to a Feline Council meeting, and Henry's stepfather and stepmother were away for a long weekend break in Queenstown. Only Gerard was around to ask probing questions.

After grabbing clothing, Henry headed out to his dogs because time with the animals relaxed him. He used to have a Jack Russell, but Geoffrey had died at the ripe age of sixteen. That dog had been his savior after Jenny's death, and his passing had left a yawning hole.

When he entered the kennels, the dogs grew alert. A pup whimpered. Henry attempted to settle his angst because it wasn't their fault his mind was fucked.

He scratched a dog behind an ear and petted one of the braver pups from the latest litter. The young female dog would be huge when fully grown, but now she was a playful, handful of chubby puppy. He crooned to her and, at that moment, made an unusual decision. He'd keep this one since she displayed bravery. His wolf hadn't bothered her, but then she'd taken her cues from her mother and the other adult dogs. They had to overcome their instinctive fear of shifters as part of their training. He always researched the families, and they could only adopt the dogs on the understanding that they would treat them with kindness. Every owner of his dogs understood that ill-treatment would earn a visit from Henry, and it wouldn't go well for them.

"Henry, is that you?" Gerard called from the doorway.

"Yeah." Henry braced for an interrogation. "Thanks for taking over. I had to get out. It felt as if someone was smothering me."

"A panic attack?"

"I shifted. That helped."

"You ran off on that kid. Did she say something? She was an intense wee thing. I could feel her sorrow. The teacher told me she is an orphan, and her aunt isn't a demonstrative woman. She took her niece in out of moral obligation. Can you imagine what it must be like for a young kid losing her parents?"

Henry could but didn't want to feel sympathy. He had no desire to feel anything.

"Maia is staying with the aunt until she can take her place at a boarding school in Auckland. At least her parents organized her education because Mrs. Ramsey is a strange duck. She told the teacher that attending a private school was a waste of good money. The teacher believes Maia will thrive at the boarding school and make friends."

Her name was Maia.

Henry's entire body stalled, his mind lingering on her expressive face and big blue eyes.

"Henry?"

Gerard's sharp tone jerked him back. He flinched and shook himself, a chill running down his spine, before intense heat took over and made him sweat. Henry slid his hand over his clammy forehead.

"Thanks for covering for me. Appreciate it." Nonchalantly, he smoothed his fingers over the pup's head and smiled on receiving a sloppy lick. Unlike his life, animals were uncomplicated.

At least the kid was leaving Middlemarch, and he wouldn't have to sneak around town to avoid running into her. That was great news.

Gerard joined him beside the pen. "The kid wants a dog, but I can't see her aunt getting her one. It's a shame since she'd benefit from having a pet."

Given what Gerard had told him, he agreed. But it was none of his business. He glanced at his watch. He'd let the older dogs out before dinner. Maybe he'd shift and play with them, exhausting himself so he slept tonight.

"I'd better give the dogs a run before I cook the evening meal. Does Matthew still require a quote?"

Gerard nodded, his entire face brightening when he spotted a car coming down the driveway. "London's home early. Meet you after dinner to work on the quote."

Henry nodded, but Gerard had already loped off to meet his mate.

A kid.

No way. Not gonna happen.

He'd pulled himself together after Jenny's death. He was an ex-soldier and mentally strong. Yeah, he'd get through this, and no one needed to know how much that orphan girl disturbed him on every level.

CHAPTER 1

NINE YEARS LATER

Maia Jacobs parked in front of the farmhouse her aunt used to own, which now belonged to her. She climbed from her car and inhaled the fresh country air. Notes of pine and dry tussock grasses filled her lungs, along with a hint of animal manure from the nearby paddock.

She spun in a slow circle, trying to take in everything about the buildings and surroundings. True, the house required work, and the lawn needed mowing, but after years of standing still, she was on the path to achieving everything she wanted.

Maia seized her overnight bag and, by city-girl habit, locked her vehicle and skipped to the door.

Long grass edged the footpath, the riot of greens brightened by the weeds bearing sunshine-yellow flowers. Everywhere was long and overgrown. The trustee had warned her, but Maia had no qualms about her purchase. She wasn't afraid of hard work and had two weeks before she needed to report for rugby training. A grin surfaced at the thought, and she bounced in delight.

She'd scored a contract with the Dunedin women's rugby team. An actual contract when her aunt had accused her of being an unnatural tomboy. Yep, they were paying her to play sports—not a huge salary because she was still unknown, but her writing income made up the difference.

Middlemarch was an hour's drive from Dunedin, and the airport was handy if she needed to travel for personal reasons. Her grin widened, and she pinched her inner wrist.

Yep, pain.

Yep, wide awake.

She had a contract!

Apart from the once cherished lawn and gardens, now overgrown, Maia noted the sun-bleached net curtains screening the windows bore rips. These were things she could fix. All she needed was a bed, a workable bathroom and kitchen, and a place to sit her laptop so she could continue with her other passion: writing urban fantasy.

A *boo hiss* on the accountancy degree her aunt had forced her to acquire. She'd used her trustee powers to ensure Maia behaved. Maia had learned young to placate her aunt and stage her protests in other unseen ways.

It gave her great satisfaction to know her aunt would spin in her grave because Maia had purchased her former home, and she'd done it with writing proceeds. She'd never used her accounting degree; it would be a fiery day in hell when she succumbed to the dark side of ledgers and numbers.

No more spreadsheets or budgets for her.

"Not unless they're my own," she muttered, and even then, she might hire the chore out to a local accountant.

Maia fished the keys out of her pocket and found the right one for the front door. It turned stiffly as if the house bore her aunt's anti-Maia tendencies.

A grunt slipped free at that. *Wow! Over dramatic, much?* That was her writing self, allowing her imagination free rein. Once the lock yielded, she had to use her shoulder to shove the door open.

A musty, damp smell greeted her, but Maia refused to let the property's deficiencies get to her. She could fix the cosmetic stuff, and that was all it was, according to the building inspector who'd reported on the house before she signed the deal.

Her aunt hadn't left the property to Maia, even though Maia was her last living relative. She'd never approved of Maia's father and, heck, had the elderly woman clasped her resentment tight to her bosom. Aunt Beatrice had left her home to charity, even though she'd known Maia had wanted it.

Yeah, her aunt had held a mean grudge, which had lasted until death. Maia grimaced, memories of tetchy orders and demands for Maia to do as she was told and obey her betters.

An old wound. Best to lance the lingering sore and let the past go.

Her aunt was gone, and her current trustee had handed over control of her parents' estate when she turned twenty-one. Not that Maia needed the money. She was doing nicely with her writing and now her rugby contract. Yep, no financial problems. Self-sufficient, that was her.

She loved her life.

Maia set her bag at the entrance and stalked along the creaky hall to explore and run a mental list of the essential tasks to slot into her coming week. The kitchen was as she recalled—the old yellow lino on the floor faded and cracked. She twisted a tap, and water spilled into the sink. As she went back out, she flicked on the light switch. Yes, she had power.

"Groceries." She noted the time. Huh! She'd need to hustle if she wanted to grab food and go for a run.

Maia speed-walked along the passage to the end bedroom—the one that used to be her aunt's. The photos on the website had shown it empty, and she hoped that was still the case. Her furniture wouldn't arrive for a few days, but she had a roll mat and her sleeping bag. It would do.

The bedroom was empty but also dusty, with an impressive display of spider webs. At least she'd brought a broom and basic cleaning materials with her.

She completed her tour with the bathroom. Basic but serviceable.

Maia grabbed her bag and placed it in the bedroom. She unloaded her cleaning supplies, sleeping bag, and roll mat but left her laptop and box of research books in the trunk.

Ten minutes later, she pulled up near Middlemarch's supermarket and hurried inside to grab a few basics. If the selection was limited, she could stock up on groceries when she reported to the rugby administration in Dunedin.

The supermarket shelves were well stocked, and the prices weren't too bad. Maia filled a basket with milk, wholemeal bread, a bag of apples, two cans of baked beans, a dozen eggs, sliced ham, and a small packet of cheese. She lined up behind a stooped gray-haired woman and a freckled teenage male, waiting patiently for her turn at the checkout.

"Good afternoon." The attractive woman behind the counter had long black hair drawn into a ponytail and was of Indian descent. Her accent was pure Kiwi. "Are you doing the Middlemarch Rail Trail?"

Maia shook her head. "No, I purchased Beatrice Ramsey's property."

"Wow! Welcome. We'd lost hope of anyone buying that old house. It didn't come with sizeable land, which put off prospective buyers. I'm Ambar." She held out her hand, her smile as bubbly as her explosion of words.

"Maia Jacobs." Maia didn't intend to explain her relationship to her aunt. It was enough for her to grapple with without nosy questions from outsiders. "Do you live in Middlemarch?"

"Yes," Ambar said. "My brother and I moved here from Auckland several years ago."

"I don't suppose there is a gym?"

"No, most locals are farmers and don't need get-fit equipment." Ambar paused and brightened. "Isabella runs a regular boot camp. If you're interested, the details are on our community noticeboard near the door."

"Thanks. Can you recommend places to run where I won't be in danger of speeding cars?"

Ambar's nostrils flared, and she sucked in a deep breath before replying. Strangely, her shoulders slumped a fraction, but her smile never dimmed. "The main road is out, but some side roads are less traveled. You could run from your place, do laps around the rugby field, and return home. Isabella does most of her boot camp at the school fields."

"Thanks," Maia said. "That will suffice until I familiarize myself with the area."

"Are you a fitness freak?" Ambar asked.

"I'm a rugby player. Our season starts in April."

Ambar's eyebrows lifted. "A professional rugby player?"

"Yeah, I've signed a contract to play for the Dunedin team."

The door opened, the tinkling bell signaling a new arrival. A woman with long, straight brown hair and a freckled face pushed through the door.

"London," Ambar said, and genuine pleasure shimmered in her voice. "This is Maia Jacobs. She's new to the area. Beatrice Ramsey's place."

The slightly plump woman turned blue eyes on Maia and extended her hand. "Welcome. I'm so pleased someone has purchased the Ramsey property. Maia, I hope you'll be happy there."

"Maia is a rugby player," Ambar said.

London's mouth opened a fraction, and her freckled nose wrinkled as she gestured at her curvy body. "Rather you than me. I'm not built for sport."

Maia laughed, charmed by the honest reaction. "Me neither until a university friend dragged me to rugby practice. They were short of players and drafted me before I knew what hit me. I enjoyed it, and the physical exercise balanced out keyboard time for my degree."

"What sort of degree did you do?" Ambar asked.

"Accountancy."

"That's more my scene," London said with a laugh. "I do administration work plus design stuff for several online clients."

"No offense, but I find working with numbers boring. I finished my degree because of family pressure, but rugby is my passion." She didn't mention her writing because that was private. She wrote under a pen name because she hadn't wanted her cantankerous aunt to discover her moneymaking hobby. A moot point now.

"Are you in a hurry?" London asked. "I'm heading to Storm in a Teacup for coffee. I can introduce you to a few other locals."

"Is Isabella there today?" Ambar asked. "I was telling Maia about Isabella's boot camp."

"She was when I popped in to see Saber," London said.

"Sure." Maia blinked. She hadn't meant to agree, but it would be fantastic to meet locals.

Maybe she'd see him.

A frisson darted through her body, and with the ease of practice, she shoved it away. She'd been a kid, and him an adult. The man was probably married with six children. "I have perishables."

"I popped in to get milk and won't stay long," London promised.

"Sounds great." Maia waited while London purchased six

three-liter bottles of milk. "Wow, big family?"

London chuckled. "No, we have three families sharing a residence. We have private apartments within the house but have communal meals. It sounds complicated, but it works for us."

Maia nodded, understanding because at least two girls she'd played rugby with in Auckland were solo mothers, and they'd shared with other single mums. It was a cost-effective way of housing a family and paying bills. "I'll meet you outside." She picked up her bag of groceries. "Nice to meet you, Ambar."

"Are you single?" Ambar asked.

"Yes, but I'm too busy for a man." Maia glanced at the boot camp flyer. *Huh. Worth checking out, since she enjoyed varying her training.*

"Try two," Ambar muttered.

That's what Maia thought she heard before the door closed. She'd parked in the shade and placed her shopping in the passenger side footwell, frowning as she did so. She hoped Ambar and the other local women didn't decide to fix her up with men. Not interested. Maia had done the dating thing, and it never worked for her. The men never measured up to...

And there she went again. She refused to dwell on the grumpy man who'd ruined her for others when they hadn't exchanged more than a few words.

Yeah. How whacked was that?

Once again, she pushed the pesky man from her thoughts.

"I'm ready," London said.

"You have an English accent," Maia said.

London winked. "Noticed that, did you? Came here on holiday, met Gerard, and fell in love. Middlemarch people are lovely. You'll see. They welcomed me when I first arrived."

"I'll be commuting to Dunedin for rugby and traveling for games, so I won't spend much time here during the season. I have two weeks before training starts."

15

"Why Middlemarch?"

"It's handy to Dunedin—an hour by vehicle—and living in the country appealed. Real estate is cheaper here than in the city. After living on campus, I craved a less frantic life." Free of nosy people who wanted to know why she was spending so much time using her computer.

London nodded and gestured at a store. "That's Caroline's shop. She designs and sells gorgeous clothes. She also has fantastic knitwear a local girl makes. I buy tons of my clothes from her. If she doesn't have what you want, she'll make garments to order."

"Evening wear?"

"We're casual around here, but she's talented and capable of producing formal gowns."

Maia considered that. Maybe... "We have a formal prize giving, and finding something decent to wear is always a drag."

London scanned Maia. "You're tall, and that's an advantage with clothes."

London walked through an open gateway and onto a footpath leading to an old house someone had converted into a cafe. Rose bushes edged the path, and the heady scent perfumed the air. Several hanging baskets of purple and white blooms hung from hooks on the verandah. London opened the door, and the hum of masculine voices floated to them.

"Gerard must've finished his job early." London burst through the doorway and hightailed toward a table with two men.

Maia scanned them and the cafe. It was bright and colorful and full of a decadent cinnamon scent that made her tummy sit up and take notice. A blonde woman operated the till, and Maia caught glimpses of another working in the kitchen.

"Maia." London gestured for her to join them.

Without warning, Maia's skin prickled. The man facing her had shaggy black hair and pale eyes. Green, she noted when she forced her body into motion. He smiled.

"My husband, Gerard Drummond. This is Maia Jacobs. She purchased Beatrice Ramsey's place. I ran into her at the supermarket and invited her for a coffee."

The other man turned, slanting his body while London made introductions.

Maia froze, her mouth turning dry as shock pummeled her. *The first day. Why did it have to be her very first day in Middlemarch?*

London introduced the other man. *Henry Anderson.* She'd already known his name and where he lived but stupidly hadn't connected the dots. She heard the introduction through an echo chamber and stood like a ninny, with her mouth wide enough to entice intrepid bugs.

Even as shock pummeled her, she cataloged his appearance. He was still big and muscular—solid—but he'd seemed a giant when she was a kid. Now, his dark blond hair was long enough to pull into a ponytail and expose his face's hard angles. His chocolate-brown eyes flared with the same shock that struck her like a fist.

He paled and shoved away from the table. Without a word, he strode from the cafe and disappeared, leaving her gaping. That answered one question: He wanted nothing to do with her, and she'd made a colossal mistake in purchasing a Middlemarch property.

CHAPTER 2

N o! No, this was not happening.

Once Henry's brain had added two and two, he'd had a few moments to take in the face that haunted his dreams. The mature version was attractive, with glossy chocolate brown hair and the same bright blue eyes that pierced his soul. She'd grown into a tall woman with big bones, but not overweight. Her body appeared toned and muscled, reminiscent of a soldier.

What was she doing in Middlemarch? Wait, London had said she'd brought Beatrice Ramsey's place. Beatrice had been her aunt.

Outside, Henry broke into a run, his heart pounding, his body trembling. Where was his—crap! He'd driven to town with Gerard. His shoulders slumped as he slowed his steps and his brain came online again. Why the hell had he run? Now Gerard and London would ask nosy questions. Why hadn't he done the polite thing, smiled, and pretended he was meeting her for the first time?

Henry snorted. Yeah. Because that was too easy, and he liked to do things the hard way. London would tease him, and she'd tell his stepdad and stepmum. He reached Gerard's truck and leaned against the passenger door.

"Crap." He swept his hands across his face.

He'd panicked like this when he'd first met Maia. She'd been an intense kid, and she'd wanted a dog. The same dog he'd retained even when he'd had several people interested in purchasing her. He'd almost sold the dog, and at the last moment, he'd told the prospective buyer he'd decided to keep Juno.

"Henry." Gerard's voice had his head jerking.

He said nothing, remaining silent. Hell, what could he say when he'd acted so rudely? She'd think he was a nutcase. *He was a nutcase.*

"You haven't had a panic attack for years." Gerard's gaze was watchful. "What triggered it? We have to work out what starts these so we can help you."

Henry swallowed hard. Oh, he knew the cause of his panic, and it was more outright fear. Back then, during the school visit, his reaction had made sense because Maia—her name was Maia—had been a kid. Twelve years old, which made her... He did the mental math and came up with twenty-ish. Still too young for him to act on his instincts.

"No idea," Henry said, lying through his teeth. "The walls were closing in on me, and I had to get outside."

His wolf released a mournful howl that ripped through his mind and had him swallowing again. They were both fucked. He shuddered, still smelling her honey scent.

Gerard's gaze was shrewd and assessing, and Henry hoped his friend hadn't put the clues together. It was the girl—the impossible woman who was way too young for him.

"I'll go for a walk. That should calm my wolf." *Liar, liar.* It had nothing to do with his wolf. It was him as a whole.

19

"I'll call you when I'm ready to leave." Gerard returned to the cafe.

Henry stared after his friend and grimaced when his belly released a protesting grumble. He'd intended to grab a sandwich or pie. Looked like he was heading home—once Gerard finished—and from memory, there wasn't much in the fridge. There'd be time to shop at the supermarket. Focusing on that might shift his thoughts from the woman.

The store was empty of customers, and Ambar was stacking goods in the far aisle. He grabbed a basket and filled it with bread and sandwich makings. After pondering the pantry contents, he added a packet of pasta, a pack of bacon, and a bottle of cream. A sandwich would satisfy his immediate hunger, and he'd cook pasta later. He'd learned to cook during his teen years and found the activity relaxing. Yeah, he'd offer to cook dinner for Gerard and London. That might get him out of prying questions.

He didn't want to talk about this. Couldn't talk about it.

Middlemarch was a small town, and he'd run into her. *Maia.* A shudder jolted him, and every muscle tensed. *Every muscle.* He panted, trying to control his wayward body.

Ambar popped her head around the corner, a box of cornflakes in hand.

"Something wrong?" she asked.

"No. Work problem," he amended when she appeared doubtful. Henry focused on putting one foot in front of the other and his grip on his shopping basket at a reasonable tension. His gaze lighted on beer cans, and he scooped up a six-pack as he walked past. A little alcohol would relax him. *Or not.*

Henry stopped at the checkout counter and stacked his items on top. "I'll grab a bottle of wine." He snatched a bottle of sauvignon blanc from a display and returned.

Ambar scanned the items, and Henry packed them into a box—one of the many Ambar and her brother Rohan kept for their customers' use.

"Did you meet Maia?" Ambar asked.

Henry flinched.

"Did she tell you she's a rugby player? A professional rugby player. She's signed with the Dunedin women's team."

"No, we didn't chat. I left after introductions to get groceries for dinner."

"Pasta, tonight?" Ambar asked.

"I like pasta."

"Me, too. Anyway, I liked Maia. It's nice to have someone new around."

Henry paid for the groceries and retreated as fast as he could. Ambar wasn't a gossip, but she did like to talk. Rohan said it was because their parents had drilled the art of small chat into them to grow their business. It had worked for their parents, and Rohan and Ambar had continued the habit.

Henry's phone beeped, and he pulled it out to see a text from Gerard. He tapped a reply to say he was on his way.

"Thanks, Ambar. Gotta go. Gerard is waiting for me." And with a quick wave, he left before she quizzed him about the new arrival.

Gerard was leaning against the driver's door when Henry approached the vehicle.

"Are you all right?" he asked, his gaze probing.

"Yes. No. I don't know!"

Gerard's eyes widened a fraction before a grin curled across his face. "Which is it?"

"I'm fine." Henry stomped to the passenger side. He placed the groceries in the rear and climbed into the front.

"Where did you go?"

Henry knew what his friend was asking but played dumb. "I purchased groceries since the fridge is bare with Dad and Megan away."

Gerard nodded. "What did you decide we'd have for dinner?"

21

"Pasta. Garlic bread. Wine. Beer. Depends on what is in the pantry, maybe a dessert. Megan made lemon ice cream before she left."

"Sounds good," Gerard said as he started the vehicle and pulled out onto the main street. "I'll help."

Henry whipped around to focus on his friend. "Why?"

"No reason."

"You're gonna interrogate me."

"Maybe." There was a teasing note in Gerard's voice.

"No matchmaking." Henry made his statement firm and decisive, so there wasn't a shred of wriggle room for Gerard to slide away from future responsibility. "Tell your delightful minx of a wife that if she tries to maneuver me, I will move out."

That made Gerard jerk his attention from the road. "You wouldn't."

"I mean it, Gerard. My mate died, and I've lived with the dull pain ever since. It feels like a blunt knife shoved into your guts." Henry recalled the instant of happiness he and Jenny had experienced before her ex had snatched her away. "I hope you never go through the same ordeal."

"We want you happy." Gerard had lost his teasing edge, his green gaze drilling into Henry with compassion.

Henry didn't want people to feel sorry for his loss. He was fine. He had family and friends, and if he wanted feminine companionship, he could travel to Queenstown. He hadn't yet because it was a temporary fix even if the bars and eateries bulged with single tourists, happy to share their time and bodies.

"London misses Jenny," Gerard said.

Henry didn't reply. What could he say? He hated to stress his friend. "Tell London I'm fine."

"Your Dad and Megan worry about you."

"I'm an adult. The four of you need to stop treating me like an invalid. I. Am. Fine."

Gerard drove for a few minutes longer in silence.

Henry shot him a suspicious glance because he knew Gerard. Along with Sam, their friend who lived in Christchurch, they'd gone through a war together. They were tight and would do anything for each other. It was that part that made Henry pause. "What have you done?"

Gerard stopped in front of their house. Henry opened the door, and his barking dogs welcomed him home.

"Gerard?"

Gerard sighed, the sound harsh and weighty. "It wasn't me. It was London. Know she does it from a place of love."

"What did your mate do?" Henry didn't hide the chill or the anger in his voice. He was tired of people thinking they knew better than him.

"London invited Maia for dinner."

Henry cursed under his breath, the muscles of his shoulders tensing. "Why?"

"Maia doesn't know anyone, and London wanted to welcome her." Gerard paused and shot a glance at Henry. "And I'm sorry. I think a little matchmaking was going on when she invited Maia."

Henry groaned.

"Sorry," Gerard said. "I'll tell London not to do it again without asking you first. She was extending a welcome because she liked Maia."

Henry's gut tangled in knots. He'd have to face this head-on. He couldn't run from this dinner because London and Gerard would question his reasons. Yeah, his wolf wanted the younger woman, but no way Henry would let his animal half lead him by the nuts. She was too young, and while she mightn't be a virgin, his experience was worlds ahead of hers. Yeah, he'd cook this stupid dinner and act polite.

"One dinner. That's all. You will help me make it. One sign of blatant matchmaking, and I'll leave. Tell London. I'm serious

23

because I don't need help. I have my love life handled."

"You're not seeing anyone."

"London doesn't know that."

"I can't lie to my mate."

"You will if you don't want me to leave. I don't want London, Megan, or other well-meaning females interfering in my life."

"Yeah, I get it. I wouldn't like anyone managing me."

"Thank you," Henry said.

He climbed out of the vehicle, collected the box of groceries he'd purchased, and stalked into the house. He left the groceries in the kitchen before seeking refuge in his bedroom. Henry sank onto his bed and rested his head in his hands. What the hell was he going to do? He doubted his ability to sit through a dinner with the woman. He took his trembling hands away from his face. "Hell," he muttered.

He stood abruptly and decided to spend half an hour with his dogs. He'd shift and play. That always calmed his wolf. Then he'd shower and start dinner.

He could do this. He *would* do this, and once this day was over, he'd take off a few days and drive to Queenstown because his control was at an all-time low. The last thing he wanted was to make a mistake that he couldn't take back.

CHAPTER 3

A s Maia parked in front of the sprawling house, she recalled the school visit to the kennels. She'd been a traumatized kid, living with an aunt who was full of rules and resentment. The dogs impacted her that day. Seeing Henry had made her heart race. His obvious caring for the animals had meant something to her, and a tiny part of her had looked forward to seeing him again.

Okay. Big fat lie.

He'd made a significant impression on her—this big, burly man with the gruff expression. From a child's perspective, he'd seemed a giant. Heck, he was still big. Not overweight, but solid. He still didn't smile, but something intangible about the man drew her.

She grinned, recalling his hasty departure. London and Gerard had gaped after their friend, dark-haired Gerard shaking his head when Henry had muttered something about dogs and fled. He'd run away when she was a kid. Looking back, she could see that now.

A sigh escaped. Accepting their dinner invitation hadn't been a sensible idea when Henry lived in the same residence. She might be savoring a sandwich and a glass of wine at home, pondering her urban fantasy idea. Maia still wasn't sure why she'd agreed after initially saying no thanks.

She pulled a bottle of wine from her shopping bag. She'd intended to drink it over several nights as a treat for words written, but she couldn't arrive empty-handed.

On the plus side, she'd spoken to Isabella, who had agreed to help her train with sessions twice weekly. With Isabella, she'd learn the area's geography and the best places to run.

Maia straightened, locked her car, and marched to the front door. The door flew open to a beaming London. A delicious scent of herbs and bacon wafted in the air.

"Come in," London said. "Dinner is almost ready. I hope you're hungry."

"Starving. Something smells delicious and much better than sandwiches."

"Henry is a superb cook." London started to say something, frowned, and stopped speaking. "This way," she said, her smile a little overdone.

Maia's stomach did a swift somersault before settling in an uneasy quiver. Yeah, this was a bad idea. Henry had run from her, yet she'd still accepted London's invitation. She hesitated a beat longer before sighing and following her new friend.

London led the way from the tiled entranceway, with its ornate umbrella stand and lacy green plant on a pedestal table, along a short passage. Maia noted paintings on the walls but didn't linger to study the sea landscapes. A door to the right opened into a massive kitchen. A table, already set with cutlery, glasses, and plates, sat near several glass doors. It looked as if they opened onto a terrace, which would be pleasant on a sunny day. A long freestanding counter acted as a breakfast bar, while the workspace was immense. The fridge was a monster, and the massive gas cooker intimidated her.

Maia could cook and attempted to prepare healthy meals, but these appliances were too large for her needs. She smothered a quick laugh because she doubted her kitchen floor would stand the weight. Her gaze drifted to Henry, who stood at the stovetop, his back to them as he stirred a sauce.

"Maia has arrived."

The broad shoulders stiffened.

Maia frowned. What was wrong with the man? More importantly, why did he always flee from her?

"Henry." London's sharp voice held a warning.

He turned, fleeting anger crossing his handsome face before his expression blanked. "Hello, Maia," he said and returned to his sauce.

London huffed while Maia hesitated on the kitchen threshold.

She handed the bottle of white wine to London. "My contribution."

"Thanks." London's smile was stiff. "Gerard had a last-minute phone call. He won't be long. Would you like a glass of wine?"

"Sounds lovely." Maia experienced an urge to rile Henry, but manners won.

"Take a seat at the breakfast bar. You can chat with Henry while I grab beers for the guys." London glared at Henry's broad shoulders as she left.

He heard but only thumped a wooden spoon against the pot in silent reply. Maia flinched and wished she'd stayed with her initial—albeit polite—rejection of the dinner invitation. But her curiosity about Henry had overruled her common sense, and yes, she should've known better. *Hindsight and all that.*

Men didn't fit with her world. Not with the constant training and travel to play other teams. Samuel, her boyfriend of six months, had accused her of seeing another man. He'd been so

27

pissed he'd punched the wall. A man with difficulty controlling his temper wasn't the one for her, and they'd parted not long after that when he'd aimed his temper and fists at her. Not a circumstance she wanted to dwell on.

Her gaze went to Henry, and she decided to clear the air while they were alone.

"Henry?"

He tensed but turned to face her, his expression grim. *Oh heck.* What had she done to ruffle him? Yeah, she felt this weird draw, but she'd met him twice, and they'd barely spoken.

"Have I upset you?"

His intense gaze drilled right through her. It made her edgy. A touch neurotic.

"No."

She waited for him to add information, but no more words were forthcoming. They stared at each other.

"Then why are you behaving as if I'm the enemy?"

"It's not you," he said, his husky voice stirring nerves and increasing her uneasiness.

"Then what is it? I'm sorry I accepted London's invitation. I don't want to make you uncomfortable. Look, tell London something came up, and I had to leave."

"Tell London what?" London asked.

Henry's features tightened before blanking into an enigmatic mask.

"I've received a text message and can't stay for long. It's an internet call with an overseas company for a sponsorship deal." It was all true. Maia had a scheduled online meeting at ten but had ample time.

"But you can stay for dinner?" London asked, her brow furrowed.

"Yes, thank you. I could assist with the dishes," she said, smiling. "Although I bet you have a dishwasher somewhere in this mammoth kitchen."

"The dishwasher is called Gerard tonight," Gerard said, appearing in the doorway. "The cook doesn't clean up after dinner. London will help, although Henry isn't a messy cook—not like someone else I could mention." He glanced knowingly at his wife.

She giggled. "Yep, guilty as charged. I start out with tidy intentions, but things never go to plan."

"I'll serve dinner." Henry glanced at Maia. His brown eyes flickered, and she blinked, his gaze so fleeting she wasn't sure if she'd imagined the golden light flaring in his irises.

"Your wine is excellent," London said. "I haven't tried this sav, but it's lovely and crisp. Did you get it at the supermarket?"

"I did." Maia accepted the glass and took a fortifying sip. "You're right. We'll have to buy out their stock."

Gerard laughed while Henry didn't react. His was a resting grumpy face, but on the plus side, he was a decent cook, judging by the delicious scent filling the kitchen.

Henry placed a plate of spaghetti carbonara in front of her and set another down for London. Maia leaned forward to savor the creamy bacon and cheesy scent and breathed an appreciative sigh as she straightened.

Henry returned with plates for himself and Gerard and sat beside Gerard. London gave him a funny look but didn't comment.

"Henry, did you hear Maia plays rugby professionally?" London asked.

His head jerked up, and no, it wasn't her imagination. His eyes had flashed golden before he glanced away.

"What got you started playing rugby?" Gerard asked.

"A friend dragged me along one night because I had nothing better to do. They didn't have enough players, and she pleaded with me to participate to prevent their disqualification. She promised I was playing on the wing and wouldn't need to tackle.

All I had to do was run and pretend I was part of the team."

London gave a delighted laugh. "Did it not go to plan?"

"It did not. I had a working knowledge of the game and must've absorbed some rules. One thing I have going for me is my speed, and,"—Maia gestured at herself—"I'm bigger than most girls. After ten minutes of acute boredom, I inserted myself into the game. The team won for the first time, and I couldn't escape after that. My friend nagged me to join, and I've played ever since."

"You must be skilled to play for a professional team," Gerard said.

Maia shrugged. "I love the game. The camaraderie with teammates. The Women's World Cup is next year, and I aim to make the team."

"Wow," London said.

Maia twirled spaghetti on her fork. She closed her lips around the creamy mouthful and hummed approval as tastes and textures hit her senses. *Yum.* She forked up more, only hesitating when she felt the weight of a stare. Her gaze lifted to collide with Henry's. Once again, it was golden and gorgeous. Spellbinding until he blinked. A brown screen came over his eyes, and he focused on his meal.

Maia shook herself. Why did this man attract her? He was grumpy and forbidding. But it was also clear he and Gerard were tight. This strong friendship showed Henry wasn't an arsehole.

"What training do you do?" Gerard asked.

"You mentioned running. Did you speak to Isabella?" London asked.

"Isabella is going for a run with me tomorrow. She'll assess me, and we'll go from there."

"Isabella is a brilliant teacher," Gerard said. "Henry and I attend her boot camp when we can. It helps us keep fit for our security jobs."

Maia nodded, pleased to hear her judgment was sound. Isabella's manner and confidence had impressed her. Maia applied herself to eating while fighting an urge to peek at Henry. The man intrigued her despite his surliness. Perhaps her busy schedule was a blessing. She could avoid this infuriating, grumpy man.

She glanced at her watch when she finished her meal and decided it was time to leave. "Apologies for rushing, but I can help with the dishes."

"No, I'll help Gerard," Henry said. "You go."

Her mouth dropped a fraction before she collected herself.

"Henry," London said in a stern reprimand.

Okay, it hadn't been her imagination. Maia pushed back her chair and stood. "I'm sorry I'm rushing away, but this meeting is important." All true. "Thanks for dinner. It was delicious and much more enjoyable than the sandwich I'd intended to eat."

"You're welcome," London said.

Gerard sent her a friendly smile.

"Henry will see you out," London said.

Henry's big body shifted as if he'd object. Maia caught the tail end of London's glower and suppressed a smile.

"I'm fine. Henry, finish your dinner." Maia aimed a casual glance in his direction. She even curved her lips while her pulse raced, the pace choppy. He had a mesmerizing effect, shoving her off balance. "Thanks again."

To her consternation, Henry set down his cutlery with a clatter. She swallowed, increased her pace, and hoped she didn't look like she was fleeing. She was, but appearances were important.

"It was lovely to make your acquaintance," London said.

"Nice to meet you, too," Maia said.

Finally, she reached the hall leading to the front door. She wondered if Henry might say something, but he remained silent, his strides long as he overtook her. He reached the door first and opened it, standing aside so there was no danger of casual contact.

Maia's quick glance showed a granite-hard face with no evidence of softness or friendship. Confusion engulfed her, followed by a blast of anger.

"What crime have I committed to make you treat me like the enemy? We don't know each other."

Henry winced before even that emotional flash fled. "London is—never mind. Good night."

Angry at the man, she strode into the evening air. She whirled to unleash her tongue and tell him it was rude to pre-judge someone, but he clicked the door in her face.

She raised her fist to pound on the door before good sense overcame her. Fuming, she stomped toward her car and made a silent promise to avoid the impossible man in the future.

CHAPTER 4

Guilt assailed Henry as he waited until the rumble of her departing car ceased. He'd acted rude, and that wasn't him. London's fault. He might've held it together better if his friend's wife hadn't surprised him with her non-subtle matchmaking. His breath came in quick pants, each laden with the essence of Maia—her rich, honeyed scent that called to him.

He banged his forehead against the door, not hard enough to make a noise—that would attract London and Gerard—but enough to break him from the Maia spell.

Finally, he opened the door and headed toward the kennels. His dogs didn't judge or have unrealistic expectations of him. All they wanted was food, exercise, and companionship—a scratch or two behind the ears. Affection.

Jenny had died, and he didn't think he had the strength to try again when life was so uncertain. No, it was better to remain alone.

He had friends and his dogs. He didn't need more than that.

Footsteps from behind had him stiffening. He cursed under his breath and prepared for the conversation he didn't want to have.

"Henry?" Gerard's voice didn't hold anger, and that was something.

Luckily, Henry's stepdad hadn't witnessed his rudeness, sparing Henry from his wrath on Maia's behalf.

His problem, as he saw it. If he gave into this insidious need, disaster would ensue. Maia was still so young. He did the calculations again in his head. Yeah, maybe twenty. He was so much older in years—even if he didn't look it—and in life experience. No, Maia was better off without him in her life.

"Henry, talk to me. What's going on?"

"You'll tell London."

Gerard's hand closed around Henry's biceps and dragged him to a halt. "You're my friend. If you tell me to keep this to myself, I will. If you don't trust me, call Sam and Lisa. Talk to them because it's obvious you need to speak to someone. You're twisting yourself up inside. I don't need to use my shifter senses to see this. Even London has noticed. She sent me after you."

Henry groaned, his thoughts in turmoil. "Please don't repeat this to London. I don't need the extra pressure of her poking her pretty nose into my affairs."

"She doesn't do that."

"She does. I love her like a sister, but the woman likes to mend things. I don't want anyone to fix me. Everything is fine."

"But that's the thing. It's not," Gerard said, his tone even. "I'm your best friend. Your business partner. Look, I won't force you to confide whatever is bothering you, but you're behaving strangely. London has noticed. She'll want to set the problem right no matter what you do. Why don't you take time off? Go to Queenstown and let off some steam."

It was on the tip of his tongue to tell Gerard everything, but at the last moment, he rejected the idea. London would wriggle the truth out of his friend. Gerard couldn't help himself because he loved his mate and would do anything for her.

His chest expanded with his deep breath, and the cool air wiped away Maia's scent and lingering presence. "You're right. I should get away for a few days." *But he didn't want anyone except Maia.*

"I can feed and exercise the dogs. We have nothing urgent with security. I've got a couple of quotes. Wait, one quote is in Wanaka. Could you do that one?"

"No problem." Yeah, this was a good idea. He could do the job and perhaps some cold calling while there. They could always use more business.

"I'll tell London you're not feeling well and have a headache."

"Yeah, she's bound to believe that." Henry didn't hold back his sarcasm.

Gerard laughed. "Which is why it is the perfect excuse."

Right. He had a headache, but it had a name: Maia. And he had no bloody idea what he'd do to shift the pain that assailed him. He rubbed his chest, but the pressure of his fingers did nothing to ease his inner turmoil. He had a mate—a potential mate, he corrected himself. There were dozens of single men in Middlemarch who'd sell their souls to find a perfect-for-them woman.

"When you return, we'll help with the mid-year Christmas floats. Dad and Megan offered to help, but Saber and London need more volunteers," Gerard said, dragging Henry from his inner torture.

Henry was used to Gerard referring to Jacey as Dad. He and Gerard were as close as brothers, and his stepfather was the father figure for both of them.

"Christmas." Henry wrinkled his nose, but keeping busy would keep his mind off Maia.

Maia fumed during her drive home. Henry was strange, and she hated the constant urge to be in the same place as the moody man. That piece of stupidity would wear off fast if he continued his surly behavior. She disliked grumpy men. Life was way too short to frown.

A sudden smile formed as the thought popped into her head. Her father used to say this when she'd had a bad day. It was over ten years since her parents had died in the vehicle pile-up on the Auckland motorway, but she missed them every day. She wondered what her mother would think of her playing rugby and laughed aloud. Her mother would worry she'd become a tomboy. Her father had been a massive All Blacks fan, New Zealand's national rugby team, so he might've encouraged her.

She'd never know.

Great, she was doubting herself. That big oaf's fault.

Maia pulled off the main road and turned into her driveway. She frowned when she coasted to a halt in front of her house. When she'd left, the porch light had been on because arriving home in dark, unfamiliar surroundings creeped her out. It wasn't now. She fumbled in the glove box for her torch.

Maia grabbed her handbag and climbed out of her car. After locking it, she scanned the torch over the footpath before her. A tiny gasp escaped, and she came to an abrupt halt. Her heart hammered faster as her brain tried to understand what she'd seen.

Was that blood?

She inched forward, her heart thumping so loud it was deafening. "Oh!" The sound was a soft explosion of air as she stared at the defined footprint on the path. The footprint in blood. Maia swallowed and sent the torch light ahead. Nothing out of place on the porch, and the front door remained shut.

Maia retreated to her car and locked the doors. Her urban fantasy heroines might be kick-butt and strong. They might act brave, but neither were they stupid. Creating intelligent heroines was part of her brand, and they had a lot in common with her.

She called the cops.

It didn't take long before a sleepy feminine voice answered. Maia cleared her throat and introduced herself. "Hello, I'm Maia, and I've moved into a property on March's Road. I had dinner with Gerard and London Drummond. The porch light—I left it on, and I thought the bulb had blown. I found my torch and..." She paused, aware she was blabbering instead of stating concise facts.

"Yes." The female cop sounded more alert now.

"I found a bloody footprint on the footpath leading to my front door."

"Are you somewhere safe?" the cop asked, a sharp note in her question.

"I'm locked inside my car."

"Excellent. Stay there and remain on the line. I won't talk to you, but I'll hear if you need me urgently."

A clunk sounded on the other end of the line, and Maia tried to calm her racing pulse. A prank meant to scare the district newcomer. Nothing more. Maia reached for the lock before her commonsense reasserted itself. While it might be a creepy prank, it might not be. Ten minutes wasn't too long to wait to appease her curiosity and answer her questions.

About six minutes later, she spotted flashing headlights. She held her breath and let it ease out when the vehicle turned into her drive. A man and a woman exited the marked police car.

The woman came to her window, and Maia opened the door.

"Maia, I'm Laura, one of the Middlemarch cops. This is Jonno, my husband, who isn't a cop and will stay with you while I investigate." There was a soft, masculine growl, and Laura laughed. "Where did you see the footprints?"

"Straight ahead on the path. Do you have a torch?"

"Yes," Laura said. "Did you see or hear anything after you contacted me?"

"No, but honestly, my heart was beating so loud I might've missed someone creeping around. Is this a practical joke?"

Laura frowned. "Possible, but if that were the case, I would've thought I'd receive more calls because people usually share a good prank. Stay there, and keep the door locked. We'll be back in a few minutes."

Maia had no trouble following the cop's instructions. Laura seemed competent and had an edge that suggested she had the mental toughness necessary for the job.

The flashlight beam bounced across the path, although Maia was too far away to see the blood. The pair halted about a third of the way to the house before approaching more cautiously, their strides slower. Maia's hands fisted, and she focused on breathing, running through the same exercises she did on game day to conquer her nerves.

The house had appeared secure when she arrived, and she'd seen no evidence of intruders. She'd left the house locked tonight. No, this must be a nasty trick meant to scare her.

Well, consider her unnerved.

The pair took the two steps to the entrance, the flashlight piercing the darkness. Maia wished she was closer because now that the local cop was here, anger, frustration, irritation, and a hundred other emotions pumped through her, reactions that she'd no doubt use later when her heroines were detecting or fleeing monsters.

The flashlight beam traveled over the verandah to the right of the door without pause before shifting to the left. The round of illumination slowed before the cop aimed it at something. Maia couldn't see what from where she stood, and impatience sizzled low in her gut. This was her home, and someone had come here intending to scare her.

She'd get security lights installed—the type that came on when something moved to set them off. That should deter any would-be tricksters or persons intent on burglary.

The pair returned to Maia, this time with long, hurried steps.

"It might be a prank," Laura said. "But someone has gone to a considerable effort to scare you. There's a mannequin on your porch with a pool of blood beneath it and a knife protruding from the head. We think the blood is animal in origin. Do you have any enemies?"

Maia scowled. "I don't know anyone here apart from London, Gerard, and Henry. Oh, and the woman in the supermarket."

"Ambar?"

"That's her name," Maia said. "What about smartarse teenagers? Isn't that more likely? Few people know I've purchased a house here. It's not a secret, but apart from my close friends in Auckland and the management at my rugby club in Dunedin, I haven't given out my address."

Laura nodded. "We'll walk a circuit of your house, but there are no signs of anyone else here."

"Thank you for coming so quickly," Maia said. "I'm sorry I've wasted your time."

"You did the right thing. It's my job. I can also put out the word that this sort of prank is unacceptable."

"If that's what it is," Laura's husband said.

"You think it's something else?" Maia demanded.

"We have no way of knowing why someone did this. We're not jumping to conclusions." Laura's warning glance at her husband was fleeting, but Maia heard the nuances in that silent exchange.

Laura wasn't confident this was a prank. The thought chilled Maia's bones, and a shiver ran through her. While she loved writing her dangerous and adventurous tales, she didn't want to live the same experience.

"I'd suggest you invest in security lights," the man said.

"It's on my list. It makes sense to increase security since I'll be away a lot playing rugby."

Laura's eyebrows shot up. "You play rugby?"

Maia nodded. "I've signed with the Dunedin franchise."

"Congratulations," Laura said. "You must do a lot of training. You should get in touch with Isabella."

Maia grinned. "Already done. Ambar recommended her, and I spoke to Isabella at the cafe."

Laura's husband sent her an appraising glance. "Isabella teaches self-defense to the local ladies. Get her to show you a few moves. She's an expert and knows what she's talking about."

It was the most he'd said since their arrival.

"Thanks, I'll do that."

Laura's husband hadn't finished. "Gerard and Henry are security specialists, and I highly recommend them."

Maia's mind ran straight to Henry, and it was difficult to suppress a scowl. Stupid her. She wanted the stubborn man. Annoyingly, every time she thought about him, her mind darted straight to sex. Maybe she should've hooked up with someone before she left Auckland. But a part of her had hoped she'd see the fascinating Henry again.

The grumpy man.

Maia shook herself. Nope, she needed to stay away because he'd made his thoughts clear.

"I'll talk to them," she said, reminding herself to investigate other security avenues. She'd taken basic maintenance courses, so she didn't need to count on others. That had been one valuable thing her aunt had taught her.

Laura nodded in approval. "We'll walk around the house."

"I'll come with you," Maia said.

Laura sent her another searching look before glancing at her husband. He shrugged.

"Stay close," Laura said, and it was an order.

Maia nodded and fell in behind. She followed Laura, and Laura's husband took up the rear. It took long seconds for Maia's eyes to adjust to the darkness. She blundered after Laura, her feet crunching on gravel until the long grass masked her clumsiness.

"Someone has walked around your house recently," Laura said.

"Tonight," Laura's husband said in his deep voice.

"I haven't explored the gardens yet," Maia said, a thread of tension running through her. "When I arrived this afternoon, I checked the house's interior. Nothing more."

Laura shone her flashlight from left to right, and Maia spotted the path through the long grass. When Laura shifted the torch to scan the house, she noted the windows were intact. Laura turned a corner to the rear. A rotary clothesline, the lines droopy, sat at the end of a narrow path, and farther away, a water tank. Maia lurched forward, her foot catching on a broken slice of the pavement before she regained her balance.

A hand grasped her forearm, steadying her.

"You okay?" a masculine voice asked.

"Wasn't looking where I was going," Maia murmured. "Sorry."

He released her. "No problem."

Laura cursed, attracting their attention.

"What—?" Maia started before she spotted the reason for Laura's consternation.

Someone had tagged her house, the words *Die Bitch*, difficult to miss.

CHAPTER 5

Maia gaped, trying to wrap her head around what she was seeing. She could count the number of people who'd known she was moving to Middlemarch on one hand.

"I don't understand," she whispered.

Laura patted her on the shoulder. "I'll take photos tomorrow morning when the light is better. We might discover clear footprints since it rained two days ago."

"Thank you," Maia said, still eyeing the words written in blood-red paint.

Laura continued their walk around the house, her pace slower now that they'd discovered the graffiti. When they arrived back at their starting point, Laura turned to her. "All the windows and doors appear secure. If you want, we can walk through the interior before we leave."

"Thanks. I'll sleep better if I'm certain no one is skulking in the wardrobe. They can't hide under my bed because my furniture hasn't arrived yet."

Laura laughed while her husband released a chuckle.

"Fair enough," Laura said.

Maia retrieved her handbag from her vehicle and locked it before walking up the footpath.

"Step over the blood," Laura instructed. "I want to take more photos in the morning."

Maia suppressed a shudder. "Are you sure the blood isn't real?"

"Animal blood," Laura's husband said, his tone positive.

"Someone killed an animal to scare me?" The creature must be dead, given the amount of blood on her footpath.

"Not necessarily," Laura said. "There are places to get blood. A butcher or a farm."

"Oh," Maia said in an understatement. If someone was trying to scare her, they were succeeding.

The three searched the sparsely furnished house, looking inside wardrobes and behind the plastic shower curtain. Maia searched the compact laundry. Thankfully, they didn't discover a single bloody footprint or any other sign that someone had broken into her home.

"Call if you need me," Laura ordered as she left. "I'm ten minutes away. I'll come around nine tomorrow morning to take more photos and do another walk around."

"Thank you," Maia said, grateful because the police weren't always prompt in the city.

"Lock the door after us," Jonno said.

Maia rolled her eyes. "You don't have to tell me twice. It was at the top of my to-do list."

Laura chortled. "A woman who doesn't take crap. I like it."

The pair left, and Maia locked the door, still trying to understand why someone was taunting her. None of her friends who knew her plans would pull this stunt. She frowned as she ambled to the kitchen to make tea. But Samuel...

Every muscle in her body pulled tight, and tension locked into place in her chest. Her ex-boyfriend hadn't taken their breakup well. At first, everything had gone well between them. They'd had rugby in common and were both rising stars. Then Sam had suffered an injury during a hard tackle, and she'd discovered his nasty side. She'd stuck with him through his physiotherapy and rehab, telling herself it was frustration making his temper fray. He didn't mean the wounding words. But when he'd used his fists, she'd told him to take a hike. One punch was the only free shot he'd get.

Maia reached for the kettle and clenched her fingers when she noted the distinct tremor. Sam hadn't taken rejection well and had made her life hell, spreading vicious rumors when he'd understood she had no intention of reconciliation.

If there was one thing her aunt had done, it was to help her grow a hard outer shell. That had come in handy with Sam.

Perhaps she should've mentioned Sam to Laura, but the unexpectedness of the situation had shaken her. Tomorrow, she decided, when Laura returned to take photos. She plugged the kettle in and flicked the on switch, letting it do its thing while she searched her box of supplies. Too much caffeine this late at night wasn't sensible, but she doubted she'd sleep with dozens of questions lurching around her head.

First, she'd check on Sam's whereabouts. One of her friends would know. She picked up her phone and scrolled through her contacts, pausing at one before deciding on her second choice. She didn't want news of this communication to reach Sam. Bryce wouldn't blab because he and Samuel had their problems.

The kettle whistled, steam billowing above the spout before the power clicked off. Maia chose a peppermint tea bag, shoved it in her favorite travel mug, and topped the container with water. Immediately, the scent of peppermint rose, and her muscles relaxed at the familiar ritual.

Maia pressed call and listened to the ringtone while she waited for Bryce to answer.

"Maia? Is something wrong?"

A burst of music and loud voices told her Bryce was at the corner pub for the one beer he allowed himself after training. Maia closed her eyes, comforted by her friend's caring. "No. Well, nothing life-threatening. Do you know where Sam is tonight?"

"We finished training an hour ago. Why? Has he done something?" Bryce's voice hardened into protective.

Maia allowed herself a smile. She almost wished there was a romantic spark between them, but they were better friends than lovers, and both knew it. "Not if he was at training."

The background noise faded, replaced by the honk of a horn. "What's going on?" Bryce's voice was sharp, demanding answers.

"Someone tagged my house," she said, choosing her words carefully because she didn't want Bryce to race to her rescue. She didn't require a man for security. No, she wanted a man for vigorous, hot, sweaty sex. Her mind slid to Henry with his stern face and his narrowed gaze. His muscular body. A sigh escaped, and she shut down that yearning. Given his reaction to her today, there was no chance of friendship, casual or otherwise.

"Did you report it?"

"Yes." She hoped the curt note in her voice let him know precisely how insulted she felt at his question.

"Right. Sorry. You're the smartest woman I know. Of course, you reported it. What did the cops say?"

"It's pitch black in the countryside. She took photos, checked the perimeter, and searched my house to make sure I didn't imagine monsters under the bed. Not that I have beds at the moment."

"She?"

Maia laughed. "Yeah, she arrived with her big, protective

husband."

"Damn, I miss all the kick-arse women. They get snapped up quickly. I guess I'll have to continue my search. Are you sure—?"

Maia cut him off with a laugh, glad she'd called him. "Quit being a goof. Laura said she'd return in the morning and inspect the evidence in daylight. You're one of the few people who know where I've moved, so I don't understand why someone would target me."

"Did the tagging occur before or after you moved in?"

"After, which makes it feel more personal."

"What did the taggers write?"

"Die bitch."

Bryce sighed. "Who have you pissed off?"

"I've been keeping my head down." She'd had a writing deadline. "I had to pack my stuff and organize shipping. Then there was the legal stuff, quotes for insurance, and a hundred and one other things, including training."

"Which is why you called to check on Sam."

"Yeah."

"Well, unless he organized someone to do his dirty work, that arrogant prick is in the clear. I can't see it though. Sam takes pleasure in the personal approach. Nah, he wouldn't hire someone to mess with you."

Maia pushed out a breath. An understatement, not that she'd tell Bryce. "Yeah, he's more likely to take a direct approach and tell me to my face."

"You mean the man lacks finesse."

"If Sam isn't responsible, I don't know what's happening. My gut tells me this is more than a stupid prank, which was my initial conclusion." Maia yawned, the audible sound reaching Bryce.

"Try to sleep. Call me tomorrow and let me know what the cops say. I'll monitor Sam, but he has a big game in two days. I doubt he'll be traipsing around the country to get back at you."

"You're right. His love for rugby is as huge as his pride. I do need to go to bed. Moving the length of the country is tiring."

"And you miss me," he teased.

"True," she said with a smile. "I'll call tomorrow. Thanks for talking me off the ledge."

Bryce snorted. "What ledge? You sound like your normal self. You're always calm and level-headed. Don't forget to call me." He hung up abruptly, making her chuckle.

They held an ongoing contest over who hung up first without being rude. Maia set down her phone and took a sip of tea, the tension she'd experienced earlier a mere shadow. She checked the time and resolved to write before climbing into bed.

Maia retrieved her laptop and set it up at the kitchen table. The wooden chair wasn't ideal, but her desk and ergonomically designed chair would arrive tomorrow with the other basic furniture she'd purchased before leaving Auckland.

Minutes later, she was deep in her world of witches and dragons and magic-wielding sorcerers with evil on their minds. The words flowed, but gradually, the discomfort of aching muscles seeped into her consciousness and interfered with her progress. She raised her hands above her head, hoping to unkink enough to finish the chapter.

Muttering in frustration, she stood and prowled the length of the kitchen before noticing the quietness compared to the apartment where she'd lived in Auckland. The tap at the kitchen sink dripped, and the old refrigerator hummed and clacked in a haphazard rhythm. No traffic sounds cut through the countryside. No arguments from the couple next door in their on-and-off relationship. No loud screams of make-up pleasure.

She recalled the weeks spent in this house with her aunt and the frightening timber creaks during the night. The first time she'd heard the sound, she'd rushed to her aunt's bedroom—a mistake she'd never repeated after the older woman had sternly told her there was no such thing as monsters. She was weak like her parents. If she didn't use her brain, she'd end up dead like them. Her aunt had held no softness, no compassion as she'd dragged Maia back to bed and told her not to move until morning.

Maia rubbed her arms, hugging herself and recalling those pincer hands bruising her flesh. Aunt Beatrice had been a cruel woman, disappointed in love and life, and she'd allowed that emotion to fester, making herself and everyone around her miserable. As an adult, Maia understood this, but she remembered the terrified child she'd been, missing her parents and thrust into another life. Aunt Beatrice had hated her. In hindsight, she'd been lucky her parents had arranged for her to attend a boarding school. Maia had found friends and made her own family.

A foreign sound came, and she listened closely, frowning. What was that noise? And why was the hair at her nape standing on end? She took two steps toward the door before good sense kicked into gear. Roaming outside wasn't sensible, given what had happened tonight.

A pained whimper cut through the silence, and Maia stiffened. What the hell? She was moving before the thought even registered. As she approached her front door, she paused again, her hand on the lock.

The cry repeated, and the terror in that sound had her unlocking the door and bursting outside. It was an animal of some type, and Maia couldn't stand by and do nothing. With her heart pounding, she listened and orientated herself. There! Over to her right in the long grass, near the big totara tree.

Maia took off at a run, her eyes rapidly adjusting to the darkness. The sounds came closer together, and the fear tore at her heart. At the base of the tree—a trap that held a tiny white animal. Blood flecked its fur, and its cries were pitiful. Maia slid to a stop by the trap and crouched. It was a tiny puppy and in a bad way.

"You poor thing," she whispered, tears coming to her eyes. Her hands hovered above the puppy as she hesitated, unsure where to start with the complicated trap. "There should be a special place in hell reserved for those who hurt defenseless—" She broke off on sensing someone behind her.

Stupid. So stupid.

She'd done the one thing she'd promised Laura she wouldn't do. Maia rose from her crouch and whirled, but it was too late. The blow on her head had her seeing stars, the ripple of pain instantaneous. A powerful strike on her hamstring caused her to fall, and she thumped her skull against the tree trunk. Maia breathed hard, her leg and her head a fiery blaze of pain. Her vision turned black at the edges, overtaking her in a wavelike surge, and she fell into unconsciousness.

CHAPTER 6

Henry answered the late phone call with a scowl. He'd just returned from a long run with his dogs, and sweat coated his body. He plucked his phone off the dresser, about to bark a complaint, but clacked his teeth together on seeing it was Laura, one of the local cops.

"Laura. Something up?"

"It might be nothing, but my spidey senses are tingling, and I've learned to trust them. Have you met Maia, who purchased old Mrs. Ramsey's house?"

"London invited her to dinner tonight," Henry said while his stomach tied into knots. Had something happened? While he was trying to keep his distance, this was his mate. And no, he wouldn't claim her, but that didn't mean he wanted something bad to happen to her.

"She mentioned she'd met London and Gerard."

"Get to the point," Henry snapped, too worried to bother with niceties.

"I got a call out earlier. Someone left what looked like bloody footprints on her front path and deck. We discovered tagging at the rear of the house. Jonno couldn't smell anything off. Several human scent trails, but the real estate agent had prospective buyers through the house, and I don't know if Maia had servicemen in before she moved. Didn't ask because I didn't want to create questions in her mind. I'm heading back tomorrow to take another look in daylight."

"Why are your spidey senses tingling?" Henry demanded, losing patience. He wanted facts.

"Maia was ready to write this off as a teenage prank. I wasn't convinced, especially when I saw the tagging at the rear. It felt personal as if someone had a hard-on for Maia. I suggested she contact you and Gerard to ask about additional security."

"What did she say?"

"She said she would."

The tightness in Henry's chest released.

"She doesn't have close neighbors, and I'd feel better if she had decent security."

Henry nodded, even though Laura wouldn't see his agreement. "She mentioned at dinner she's a professional rugby player and will be away during the season. A security system is wise."

"A rugby player." Laura's astonishment rang out, making Henry's lips twitch.

He was glad no one witnessed his humor, but her awe poked at his funny bone. "Yes, she's not petite and has excellent muscle tone."

"You looked at her muscle tone, did you?"

Now Laura was laughing at him. He redirected the conversation. "I'll tell Gerard to expect her."

"Thanks. Appreciate it and don't think I didn't notice your

subject change. You like her."

Henry hung up, hesitated. Then he pulled on a clean T-shirt, tugged it over his head, and grabbed his car keys. With his phone in hand, he headed out. When he arrived at her house, he had no idea what he'd do, but harassment wasn't right. He might want to distance himself, but he didn't want anyone to hurt her.

The roads were quiet this late at night, and the darkness was absolute. A sliver of moon hung in the sky, and his wolf was conscious of the lunar cycle.

When he neared Maia's property, he slowed and parked on the gravel shoulder at the entrance to her driveway. He hadn't seen a single vehicle, but the second he alighted from his truck, his gut twisted, and every sense screamed caution. An ex-soldier, he'd learned to trust his instincts. He slid through the darkness, his footfalls silent. For a long moment, he debated whether to shift to wolf but decided it was best to remain in his two-footed form in case he ran into Maia.

He inhaled and tested the air but smelled nothing except the hedges and the long grass surrounding the house, plus a hint of cow manure from the neighbor's paddock. An owl hooted its mournful cry, and another answered, then something else jerked him to a stop—a smell, a noise. His wolf tensed beneath his skin.

Danger lay ahead.

Henry breathed in, and this time, the metallic scent of blood carried in the breeze. Laura had mentioned blood. He paused, using every one of his senses to read the situation. That pitiful cry, full of pain, came again, and Henry cautiously stepped forward. He thought it was a crying animal.

A mewl came from his left, away from the house. Since he couldn't sense anyone else, he increased his speed and headed toward a totara tree. The blood scent intensified, as did the whimpers.

Henry cursed and broke into a sprint. Maia lay unmoving near a tree trunk while a white puppy struggled in a cruel trap. Henry swore again and retrieved his phone to ring Laura.

"Laura, I'm at Maia's house. Better call Gavin. She's unconscious."

"On it." Laura hung up.

Henry ran his eye over the puppy, his muscles tensing. *The bastards.* He loathed abuse of any kind and wouldn't act civilized if he discovered those responsible for this heinous act. It was still alive, but first, Maia. With his heart in his throat, he scrambled to her side and crouched. His breath whistled between his teeth when he found a strong pulse. He used his phone torch to check her more closely. Judging by the blood coating her hair, someone had struck her on the head. Henry didn't want to move her before Gavin examined her. Whatever had happened, she'd been lucky.

Henry turned his attention to the puppy. His jaw set as he unraveled the intricate trap. Whoever had made the thing hadn't wanted the puppy to escape, nor had they wanted Maia to free the animal too fast.

The puppy trembled, and she emitted a pained whine that tore at his heart. His wolf growled, low and vicious, and try as he might, Henry couldn't make him stop. His hands shook when he finished freeing the puppy. It was a tiny thing of indeterminate breed, but Henry thought it was part terrier. Thoughts of Geoffrey, the old Jack Russell he'd inherited from Lisa's neighbor, flitted through his mind. He missed that dog.

A vehicle approached, but he relaxed when he spotted Laura's police car's flashing lights. A second car followed.

Henry let the puppy right itself. He didn't think it would flee since it was so weak, so he stood to greet Laura. Gavin, the town's vet and shifter doctor, trailed her. Gavin had brought one of his mates, and Henry nodded at Charlie, Middlemarch's other cop.

"What the fuck?" Gavin said, his eyes on the quivering, distressed puppy.

"I don't know for sure because Maia is unconscious, but my best guess is she investigated the crying puppy. Either she stumbled, or someone thumped her and left. I'm betting on the second option."

"You didn't smell anyone around?" Laura asked, in full cop mode.

"No," Henry said, his chest tight. Someone had attacked his—

He cut off that thought with the ruthlessness of a desperate soldier under fire.

"Look after the puppy," Charlie said to Gavin. "Laura and I will check on the woman."

Henry bristled at the impersonal tone, or rather, his wolf took umbrage. He locked down his beast and stood back to give Gavin room. "I'll pay costs and adopt her once she recovers."

Gavin curtly nodded. "I'll do everything I can to save her. She's a puppy."

Henry turned to Laura. "I want in on this investigation."

Laura opened her mouth to argue as he'd known she would, but something in his expression must've persuaded her otherwise.

"She has a lump on her head, but her breathing is steady. She should come around soon," Charlie said, confirming Henry's assessment.

"Laura, now you're here, I'll do a circuit and try to find a scent trail," Henry said, his tone brooking no refusal.

She acknowledged his suggestion and strode over to join Gavin.

Anger and agitation rose in Henry. Someone was after Maia. While he might want to keep his distance, he wouldn't let anyone hurt her. He shuffled through the possibilities as he disrobed. Once naked, he called up his wolf and let the pain of the shift rush through him, the scant moment of disorientation familiar and comforting. His wolf had a better sense of smell, and he got to work, highly motivated to find a scent that might help him discover the person responsible.

With nose to the ground, it didn't take long to sift through the different layers. The green of the long grass. The damp soil beneath. He glimpsed something shiny in front of him and paused. A sweet wrapper with a distinctly minty scent. The grass appeared trampled as if someone had lingered. Waited to ambush Maia when she left her house.

Henry used his nose to decipher other scents. Once confident he'd caught the trail, he expanded his search, following the trampled path through the grass and the waft of peppermint. The path wound to the rear of the property before leading to the neighbor's paddock and over the fence. Henry jumped the top wire, giving the dozing herd of cattle a wide berth or as much as the trail allowed him. It led to the far side of the paddock and a side road. Henry located the spot where the trespasser had parked their car. They were long gone, but he'd monitor this farm track in case they returned.

Henry trotted back to Maia's property, taking the fence without pause. Once he reached his clothes, he shifted and rapidly dressed.

"How's Maia?" Worry stabbed Henry in the gut, and he had difficulty tamping down his wolf's panic. His wolf wanted Maia nearby, and Henry cursed softly because he wanted the same thing. Damn it. He couldn't catch a break.

"Charlie carried her to the house. Gavin went with him and took the puppy. I elected to wait to learn if you'd found anything."

"I followed the trail to a side road." Henry jerked his thumb in the direction he was talking about, and Laura nodded. "Flat grass and a trace of oil where a car had parked, out of sight behind a hedge. I discovered another peppermint wrapper, so I think our culprit dropped it during their wait."

Laura jerked. "Where?"

"Back near where we found Maia." He didn't mention the puppy, but his wolf released a growl of anger.

"We'll bag it in case we can find prints."

Henry gave a curt nod, even as he castigated himself. He

should've thought of that, but fury rode him because someone was messing with his—with Maia.

"This way." With long strides, he returned to the spot and waited while Laura crouched to study the candy wrapper.

"It might hold a print." Laura pulled a plastic bag from her trouser pocket. "Worth a shot."

Henry waited for Laura to finish. "Do you want the wrapper from where they left their vehicle?"

"Show me," Laura said.

Henry wanted to see Maia. Instead, he forced himself to lead Laura away from Maia's home.

They approached the house twenty minutes later and found Charlie waiting on the porch.

"Maia is conscious but didn't see who hit her. She heard the puppy, and the sound was so heartbreaking she went outside to investigate. She discovered it in the trap and tried to free it when someone attacked her. A thump over the head laid her out, and she doesn't know what happened after that. She seemed surprised to see us and asked about the puppy."

Henry pushed past Charlie before he thought better of it. Laura and Charlie exchanged a loaded glance as he passed, and he groaned inwardly. At this rate, he'd have his friends gossiping about his weird behavior. But he couldn't stop himself from checking on Maia. He wanted to see her big blue eyes staring back at him. He wanted her to look at him with wonder, silently communicating messages he didn't think she realized she was sending.

Yeah, he wanted her, damn it.

And that was the fuckin' problem.

CHAPTER 7

Maia lay on her mattress, devoid of energy and as weak as the softly whimpering puppy that the vet was checking over in the room next door. Her heart twisted with sympathy, although she knew from experience the man had gentle fingers and a fantastic bedside manner. She'd liked Gavin on sight.

A sound from the doorway caused her head to turn, and she immediately tugged the sheet to her chin.

Henry stood there, a fierce frown etched into his face. She half-snorted a laugh because, really, did the man have other expressions?

"What?" Her weird obsession with this man unnerved her. She hadn't understood it as a child and didn't understand it now.

"Why did you go outside?"

Indignation rose in her, burning away her anxiety at him seeing her this vulnerable and in her flimsy nightgown. "Did you see that puppy? Hear it? You love your dogs. You would've gone outside." Her defensive words spewed, and she tensed, her chin rising defiantly.

He blinked once, and a tic burst into motion on his jaw when he gritted his teeth, but he didn't argue. She'd been right and challenged anyone to ignore that tiny puppy. Whoever hurt it needed to be locked up and the key lost. She'd show them suffering if she ever got her hands on them.

"Going outdoors at night wasn't a smart decision. Charlie said you saw nothing. What about smell? What did you hear?" Henry glanced at her in clear expectation.

Her body went rigid, and she blew out a noisy breath of frustration. He wasn't wrong, but she challenged anyone to ignore the puppy's cries. She'd do the same again. Then, his silent demand for answers intensified. His questions ran around inside her head, and she tried to recall the moments leading up to her falling and thumping her head on the tree. A shard of pain speared through her skull, striking her temple, and she prodded the area with careful fingers.

"My focus was on the puppy. By the time I realized someone had sneaked up behind me, it was too late." She scowled, thinking back. Her assailant hadn't made a sound. They hadn't uttered a word. They'd merely acted, striking her head and the back of her thigh. "I didn't hear anything." *Apart from the sickening crack when the person thumped me on the skull.*

She barely suppressed her shudder. "But I smelled something," she said, the memory drifting to her slowly.

"What?" Henry demanded.

"I smelled mint, which is weird."

"Ah."

"Ah, what?" She wouldn't allow him to pat her on the head, figuratively or physically. She was an adult, and she'd been looking after herself for a long time.

"I followed their trail from where they'd attacked you to where they'd parked their vehicle. I picked up two candy wrappers that smelled of mint."

"Where did they park?" Maia's pulse jumped up a gear. She'd wanted a fresh start and to be close to Henry, although she'd admit that gem under pain of death. Maia hadn't even understood the impulsive urge that had sent her back to Middlemarch, but the instinct had felt right, and she'd gone with it.

"Beyond the neighbor's paddock, there's a service road, and they parked out of sight."

"They've been watching me." Someone had planned this carefully. "I haven't sensed anyone following me around. I haven't been in Middlemarch for long."

"No, if I were a gambling man, I'd say you brought your assailant with you," Henry said.

"You think it's someone I know?" Apart from Bryce and her teammates at Auckland, she didn't have any close friends. Bryce was like a brother, and she and her teammates were sisters. They'd done everything together, shown in their play on the field—they'd moved like a well-oiled machine. She refused to suspect one of them.

"Yes, I think you know them, but it might not be a close friend. It's someone on the peripheral, and you've upset them," Henry said. "I'll get you to write me a list so Gerard and I can do a quick background search."

"You're not prying into my friends' lives," Maia said. "I trust each of them implicitly."

"What about fans? Does your team have fans?"

Maia snorted. "Of course we do. They're enthusiastic but civilized. I can't imagine any of them would hurt me."

"What about boyfriends? Lovers?"

"None of your business. Stop bothering me. I'm tired."

"You'll need someone to stay and wake you every few hours."

Her mouth opened and closed because Gavin had told her that, and she'd intended to ignore his advice. She didn't know anyone here enough to ask them to stay. Besides, she was too tough to die and add pissed on top of that. The person who'd assaulted her was a coward. She frowned, trying to recreate her memories of what had happened. Yes, the person who'd thumped her had taken care not to get in her line of sight, and they'd disappeared quickly. She recalled legs clothed in black trousers or perhaps sweat pants, and then blackness had overtaken her.

"Will the puppy be okay?" she asked rather than admitting Henry was right.

A muscle in his jaw twitched, and his hands balled into fists at his sides. "Gavin thinks if she makes it through the night, she'll pull through."

Henry was as angry as she was about someone injuring a defenseless puppy. "What will happen to her?"

"I told Gavin I'd take her."

"Good. That's good." Suddenly, she felt exhausted, and her eyes fluttered closed. She forced them open, but it was a losing battle. Fatigue weighted her limbs, and her entire body ached. Then there was her leg. She was more worried about that because the injury might interfere with her rugby training. Gavin had told her the cut was superficial and the bruising might bother her for a few days, but it shouldn't prevent her availability for the first match of the season. Something to be thankful for, at least, although she wished she understood why someone had attacked her.

Henry sat on the floor next to her mattress. It was too much effort to order him to leave, and she closed her eyes again. The truth—not that she'd ever admit it to anyone—Henry made her feel safe. He had all those years ago, which was why she'd plucked up the courage to speak with him. Right now, she didn't want to delve too deeply into the emotions that went into her decision. She let the healing sleep take her and trusted him to keep watch.

Henry scanned her pale face and the freckles dotted across the bridge of her nose. Without her beautiful blue eyes to distract him, he noted other details. Her skin bore a tan from spending time outdoors, while her lips were pink and plump. He ached...

No! No, he couldn't do this. It was wrong. There were too many years between them. His life experience compared to hers. Yet he didn't rise or attempt to leave the bedroom. He stayed and quietly watched the woman who'd wormed into his heart.

A mate.

He sighed loudly, but she didn't wake. A tiny frown etched into her smooth forehead before it evened out. Yeah, he could run, but since she seemed determined to stay, he couldn't keep avoiding her. It wouldn't work, not when London had taken a liking to her. His stepfather and Megan would like her, too, and his dad was cannier than most. He'd see through Henry's denials.

He scowled because there was no decision. Someone wanted to hurt his mate, and he couldn't let that happen. Not again.

His thoughts stuttered, and his frown grew fiercer. He hadn't saved Jenny. What if he couldn't protect Maia? What if she died?

The low rumble jerked him back, and this time, he rose abruptly and left the room before he woke Maia. He found himself in the kitchen and poured a glass of water while he tried to think.

He'd have to catch and stop this person before they harmed Maia. They'd be back. He sensed it in his gut. They'd planned how to get her outside, even though she'd already called the cops. Yes, they'd gone to a lot of trouble. He needed a list of Maia's friends and acquaintances, but right now, he could start filling the gaps in his knowledge by researching Maia. It was no longer time for avoidance.

Maia was his mate, and while they mightn't have made promises, she understood this too on a subconscious level.

Henry found a seat in the sparsely furnished room. Maia had a laptop open but powered down. Henry hesitated for a moment and fought against prying into her privacy. He glanced over his shoulder, but the house remained silent. His gaze shifted back to the laptop, and he sighed, knowing only one course of action existed. Time to snoop and learn more about this mate of his.

A soft chuff echoed through his head, his wolf in total agreement.

Henry switched on the laptop, and it opened to a password screen. He swore softly, irritated on one hand yet pleased on the other. Security was necessary, and it was surprising the number of people who didn't bother to protect their information.

He didn't enter a password but pulled out his phone and started a basic internet search for Maia Jacobs. His brows rose when he encountered several stories about her rugby successes in Auckland and a recent newspaper article about her signing with the Dunedin club. Apart from this, Henry found little else on her. Her social media presence was basic, and what she had was out of date.

So he'd use the old-fashioned method. He'd ask Maia herself and get to know her. From there, he could extend his searches. There was also the possibility that whoever had attacked her was staying locally. That was another avenue to check. Henry noticed an hour had passed. It was time to check on Maia. Gavin had told him to wake her every three hours and make sure she made sense when he spoke with her.

Henry padded down the passage and stopped in the bedroom doorway. He'd left a light on in the bathroom, which spilled into the room, allowing him to see Maia. At some point, she'd kicked off the covers, and her nightgown hid little from his gaze. She was solid but still shapely and feminine, and she'd fit in his arms perfectly.

A rugby player. He shook his head, marveling at the thought. Someone to run and train with. Henry forced himself to stop thinking about the future, but his gaze strayed to her again, and his muscles tensed because he wanted to touch her.

No! That wouldn't happen.

It was bad enough that there were so many years between them, but no way would he act like a creeper. She'd had enough bad luck tonight. He swallowed hard and sternly informed his wolf they would cover her and wake her. Nothing else was going to happen because of her injuries. If they took the next step, there would be plenty of communication, and they'd get to know each other better.

His relationship with Jenny had moved at warp speed, and maybe if he'd gone slowly, he might've noticed not all was well in her life.

Swallowing, he reached for Maia's shoulder. Her skin was warm beneath his fingers, but he shoved away that thought. *Impersonal. Slowly, remember?*

"Maia. Wake up, Maia." When she didn't respond, he shook her. "Maia, it's time to wake up."

Henry frowned when she didn't stir.

"Maia."

She jolted awake, her blue eyes flying wide. Fear slid across her face, and she opened her mouth.

"Maia, it's Henry. We're in your bedroom, and I'm waking you as per Gavin's instructions." He spoke soothingly, his heart jolting rapidly because he hated to scare her. She'd been through enough tonight.

"Henry?"

To his relief, the tenseness seeped from her body, and she fell into his arms. Henry hesitated before he gathered her closer and held her. He didn't dwell on his wolf's soft sigh, how she felt pressed against him, or how being in the same room was like coming home. Instead, he let her take her time. He inhaled the fruity scent of her hair and the floral scent radiating from her skin. It was subtle and perfect.

Maia stirred, and he made himself pull away.

A shudder ran through her, and she swallowed audibly. "Every time I shut my eyes, I see that poor puppy."

"Gavin will look after her, and once she's better, I'll give her a safe home."

"I'd adopt her, but I'll be away playing rugby. It wouldn't be right to have a pet, no matter how much I'd like one."

"You can spend time with her once she's better," Henry said, working on his gentle voice. "Tell me more about your rugby."

"I'm lucky," she murmured, her focus on her hands, one of which bore blood.

Henry cursed inwardly because he should've washed her hands and face. She didn't need reminders of the attack. He'd seen a stack of facecloths earlier. After wetting one with warm water, he returned to the bedroom and sat on the bed to cleanse the dried blood from her hands.

"I should shower."

"No! Gavin instructed me to monitor you. If you want a shower, I'll have to watch. I'm not ready for that."

Her gaze jerked upward, and her mouth dropped open before a slow grin crawled across her lips. "Do I scare you?"

CHAPTER 8

H enry's expression! She snorted out a laugh and immediately wished she hadn't. Pain seared through her head, and she couldn't help but wince. "Ow."

"Head sore?" Henry asked, his horror wiping clean from his features.

"Yeah." Maia didn't know why, but victory flooded her. A sense of winning a battle. He was in the same room. She couldn't say if it was willingly, but he wasn't trying to slide out the door. And he'd touched her. Her heart beat a little faster as she realized that. This weird urge she experienced every time she saw him had a sexual component. There was this attraction simmering between them. Her gaze flew up to meet Henry's, and he didn't seem surprised. He already knew, and this was what he'd been fighting.

Maia opened her mouth to demand answers but changed her mind. She needed to think about this and analyze the situation because it wasn't like she had time for romance.

"Stop looking at me like that," Henry said, his tone harsh.

His touch on her arm was gentle, though, contradicting his attitude. She knew without a doubt he'd never hurt her physically. However, emotionally, it was another matter. Yeah, this was a situation she needed to contemplate.

Maia forced herself to frown at him and thought she did a pretty good job of acting puzzled.

Henry grunted and jumped to his feet. "You should try to sleep."

"I'll feel better after a shower."

"You're as weak as that little white puppy," Henry said. "The last thing you need is a fall. You might miss the entire rugby season if you knock your head again."

That truth gave her pause. "A quick shower," she said because she felt grubby. The blood, grass stains, and perspiration made her skin itch. "I'll leave the door open and promise to call if I can no longer stand."

"That is not giving me confidence."

Maia thought for a moment. "What if I use a chair and sit in the shower? I have a plastic chair in the kitchen."

"That at least sounds sensible. Stay there while I organize it."

Maia held back her amusement until he left the room. She'd think she'd ruffled his feathers if she didn't know better. The man was back in mere minutes, slinking like a soldier.

"Don't think I didn't see your triumphant smile. I'm only agreeing because you're acting stubborn. The quicker you shower, the faster we'll sleep."

"I don't have another bed." The second the words left her mouth, she castigated herself. *Way to go, Maia. Can you be any more obvious?*

"Don't worry about me. You're the one who requires sleep." He carried the chair into the bathroom and returned. "Everything is ready. A brief shower. Do you have fresh clothes?"

Maia gaped at him. "You're not my father."

"I'm your keeper," he snapped. "I'll be in the kitchen. Holler if you need me." Henry stomped out of the bedroom, and she stared after him.

"Wow." This man's temper was all over the place.

"You're not moving," he called.

Maia lifted her right hand in a rude gesture before gingerly rising. Good grief. Her legs trembled, and the low-level headache returned, making her wince. Henry was right—not that she'd admit that to him, but once she was clean again and dressed in a T-shirt and sleep shorts, she'd feel better. A warm shower would help her relax, and hopefully, she'd fall asleep.

She limped into the bathroom and limited her shower to five minutes. Henry had been correct. Her legs would've given way. As it was, her thigh ached where her assailant had struck her. She had a team meeting tomorrow, and the last thing she wanted was any weakness for the coaches to seize upon and sideline her. Yes, healing sleep and a reassessment tomorrow.

When she entered her bedroom, she found Henry had straightened her covers and left her a cup of herbal tea, two painkillers, and a glass of water. Henry was gone, but she sank onto the mattress and sipped her tea before picking up the tablets and downing them with a swallow of water.

Five minutes later, she closed her eyes. She woke again in daylight, and the night's events came rushing back. Aware of a pressing need for the toilet, she swung her legs to the floor. To her immense relief, her thigh wasn't too bad, and her headache had subsided.

Maia stumbled to the bathroom, alarmed when her balance didn't seem right. After taking care of business, she returned to her bed and sank down.

"You're awake."

She glanced up to see Henry in the doorway.

"How are you feeling?"

"I thought I was fine, but my balance is off, and my head is throbbing."

"Concussion. You'll need to take it easy. No screen time or reading until your headaches retreat."

"I'm supposed to report to my new club to pick up my uniform and training schedule. It will look bad if I don't." She bit her lip, aware panic was pushing her.

"I'm sure they'll understand if you explain."

"But I have to meet my teammates. I'm the newbie and can't let them see any weaknesses."

He shot her a funny look. "This isn't war, Maia."

"No, it's a competitive game. I'll start on the bench and must play myself onto the team. I can't no-show."

"You won't be any use if you fall face-first in front of them either."

Maia bit her lip because he was right. She needed to be smart, damn it. "I'll get dressed. Do a little gentle walking and see how I go. We won't train today, and there's nothing strenuous. I might manage as long as I'm careful."

"You can't drive." Henry met her gaze in a challenge.

Damn. He was right again. How could she manage this? Attendance was non-negotiable. Management—they'd want to see their investment.

"I'll drive you. I'd like to check out your team."

She gaped. "You can't think they have anything to do with last night?"

"No, but I'm still interested in seeing them."

"Why?"

"Never mind why. If you want to attend your meeting, the only way is with me."

Their gazes locked in a silent battle, and despite the throb in her head and the sluggishness of her muscles, Maia had never felt more alive. Something about the grumpy, determined man got to her.

"You'll stay in the background," she said, but it was a question.

"I'll drive you to Dunedin and wait. You can tell everyone your vehicle is with the mechanic for repairs. I'll wait in my vehicle and look harmless."

Maia barely prevented her snort of disbelief. This man would never fade into the background. He was too big, but she sensed this was the best deal she'd get. "Very well."

"What time is your meeting?"

"I need to be there at 9:45. We have fifteen minutes to grab our uniforms, and the meeting starts at ten."

Henry checked the time. "I'll sort out breakfast."

A vehicle sounded outside.

"That might be my furniture."

"I'll take care of your visitor. You get dressed." He disappeared with silent stealth. Not a single floorboard creaked beneath his weight.

Maia stared after him before she gave her head a brisk shake. A mistake because the pounding in her skull increased. She gingerly touched the spot and found a lump. Henry was right. She should stay in bed, yet if she missed this meeting, she'd be at a disadvantage.

It took a few minutes before the worst of the aching subsided. She decided another quick shower might wake her and was thankful to find the chair still sitting in the stall. When she had the time and the money, she'd rip out this shower and put in something more modern. This step into the shower was dangerous, especially if she was carrying an injury.

Half an hour later, Maia felt one hundred percent better, although she moved slower than usual. Voices came from the kitchen, and she discovered it was the cops she'd met the previous night. And to her delight, her furniture had arrived.

"We're here to take your statement and see if we missed anything during our previous visits," Laura said. "How are you feeling?"

"My head is pounding. I'm hoping there are painkillers left because it's hard to think."

"You should've stayed in bed," Henry said with open disapproval.

"I'm not a child," she snapped before taking a deep breath. "Sorry. You're not meeting my best version."

"Understandable. You haven't had the greatest start in Middlemarch," Charlie said, speaking for the first time.

"I don't understand why. I've only met a few locals and made no friends when I lived with my aunt. Not that I tried."

"Losing your parents traumatized you," Henry said. "That was understandable."

Maia didn't reply, but she had been grieving. Her home life with her aunt had proved difficult. It wasn't until she arrived at boarding school that she'd rebuilt her life and engaged with the outside world.

"Coffee?" Henry asked.

"Yes, please. My coffee machine and pods are in one of those boxes over there. Laura, Charlie, would you like coffee?"

"Yes, please. We'll walk around your house and take more photos first. See if we've missed anything," Laura said.

"The milk is in the fridge." Maia took a seat at the small wooden table. She moved her laptop aside and stacked her notebooks to make room. "I'd like one of the purple pods with steamed milk, please."

Henry sent her another enigmatic look before sauntering to the boxes to search for the coffee maker. It didn't take him long to plug in her machine and load the capsules. He even proved a dab hand at steaming milk, which surprised Maia.

He set the perfect cup of coffee in front of her before starting on two more. When the coffee was ready, Laura and Charlie tromped inside, the bottom portion of their trousers damp from the morning dew.

Both removed their boots before entering.

Henry handed over their coffee. "How is the puppy?"

"Gavin said she's a fighter, and he's certain she'll pull through. She's a cute pup," Charlie said.

"Yeah," Henry said. "Did you find anything?"

"Two more mint wrappers. We missed the graffiti on the side of your car last night," Laura said.

"Really?" Maia straightened, the coffee sloshing over the brim of her cup. She wiped up the puddle with her sleeve before it reached her laptop. "Will it wash off?"

"You'll need a new paint job. Are you insured?" Charlie asked.

"Yes, but that's not the point," she said, anger coating her words. "What have I done to cause this harassment?"

"We won't know until we catch the culprit. It could be any number of reasons." Laura sent her a sympathetic smile. "This is more than a nuisance crime. The viciousness of the attack worries me. Maia, is there anyone in Auckland who might've followed you here?"

"My ex-boyfriend. We didn't part on cordial terms, but I called a friend. My ex was in Auckland last night."

"He might've organized someone to do this," Henry said.

There was something in his expression that gave her pause. Henry looked as if he wanted to take on the world on her behalf, and no one had ever done that for her. It had been her on her own, struggling for everything she wanted. A warm sizzle started in her chest, and she didn't take the time to identify the emotion. She merely held it close and treasured the unfamiliar reaction.

"Will you help me arrange alarms?" she asked.

"Already done. Gerard will be here soon with the supplies we need. We'll set up cameras, and if this person returns, get them on video. We'll organize your furniture for you too."

Maia wanted to protest, but she'd already decided to organize greater security measures. Henry had merely preempted her request. "Thank you."

He gave a clipped nod in response. "No problem. Are you ready to leave?"

"As soon as I change my jacket," she said, staring ruefully at the coffee stain. Her new washing machine hadn't arrived yet, and she had limited clothes. "Laura, do you have everything you need?"

"Yes. I'll check with the owners of local businesses and ask if anyone spotted strangers lurking where they shouldn't. You didn't spot anyone following you yesterday?"

"No." Maia managed not to shake her head. "Why would I? It's not as if I expected anything like this."

"We'll watch now," Henry said. "We're off to Dunedin so Maia can attend a team meeting. If anyone follows us this time, we'll notice."

CHAPTER 9

Surprise flitted across Henry's somber face when she directed him to an unassuming gray building on the outskirts of Dunedin. She could've told him women's rugby didn't grab the same attention and advertising dollars as the men's game, but that might've come across as complaining. She wasn't that person. Maia was ecstatic to have a career playing the game she loved. And she had her writing as a backup. Living the dream, as Bryce would say.

"This is us," she said, glancing at her watch. At least her headache had settled since breakfast.

"What position do you play?"

"Given my build, I have a forward position, but I'm lucky enough to have a turn of speed." She grinned. "That surprises most people."

He shocked her with a return grin, and her breath stalled. When he smiled, his eyes glittered, and the harsh lines of his face relaxed, turning him into a handsome man. That, coupled with his quiet confidence, would turn any woman's head.

"I've never paid attention to women's rugby. We have a successful local rugby team. They'd be happy for you to train with them when you're around."

Maia doubted this because many disapproved of women playing a contact sport. "I'd better get moving." She took a steadying breath and gave a self-conscious laugh. "Nerves. I shouldn't be apprehensive, but I don't know the team members."

"You'll be fine. Can you manage without limping?"

"I'll try. Honesty is best, but my intuition tells me I should keep the attack to myself."

"I'm a believer in gut instinct." Henry's gaze caught hers and held for a long, pulse-pumping moment. She broke the connection first and reached for the door.

"I should come with you."

"No, your presence will invite questions."

Maia climbed out of the vehicle and followed two laughing women into the squat concrete building. Butterflies danced around the pit of her stomach, but she forged onward. She wanted this, and a large part of her desire stemmed from her aunt, who'd always told her she couldn't. *"Don't do that. Young women can't do that."*

The elderly woman's querulous orders and demands had always brought out Maia's determination. *Talk about character building.*

Now that she was out of Henry's sphere, she assessed her aches. Her thigh throbbed, but she'd suffered worse. Her headache was more problematic, but the first round of training didn't start until next week. Hopefully, she'd improve by then.

Through the open door, she noted women crowded around tables, the buzz of chatter filling the air. A pretty brunette looked up from assessing a pile of blue rugby shirts.

"Oh, hey! You're Maia Jacobs, right? The new girl."

"That's me," Maia said, immediately drawing attention.

"I'm Amanda. The team captain."

"Pleased to meet you," Maia said. "I'm excited to be here."

"We're the lucky ones." Amanda introduced several other women bustling around the piles of uniforms.

Maia committed names to memory, thankful she had a knack for this. The squad, including her, totaled twenty.

"Grab one off each pile," Amanda said. "If your size isn't available, make a note on the sheet on the table. It's all very scientific."

Maia joined the line and grabbed items and a gear bag. The other women chatted, throwing jibes and one-liners, while Maia experienced new-kid vibes. A few tried to include her, but she didn't understand the inside jokes because she hadn't spent years playing through the different Otago grades.

Once she reached the end of the line, her arms full of clothing, she hesitated.

Amanda tapped her on the shoulder. "The coaches and management want to discuss our training schedule and season expectations."

Maia shoved the clothing into the gear bag and fell into step with Amanda. She'd seen her play in Auckland once. She was a talented player—athletic and a skilled kicker. On the day Maia had watched her play, she'd nailed several penalty goals.

The two coaches, one male and one female, and Seth Davies, the manager Maia had already met, were waiting for them. Everyone slid into seats, and she followed suit.

"Does everyone have their uniforms?" Seth asked.

Maia scanned the bulging gear bag at her feet. *Yep, all done.*

The man scanned faces and stopped when he came to her. "Ah, Maia. Excellent. Everyone, this is Maia Jacobs, our new number eight. She brings a lot of skill and speed to our forward pack, and we expect great things from her. Maia, I need you to complete some paperwork once the coaches finish here."

She gave a swift nod and turned her attention to the coaches, who started discussing training and the schedule of matches. The coaches didn't introduce themselves, but it didn't matter. Rose McDonald was an ex-Black Fern player, and Cameron Doige had coached the Hurricanes in Wellington—both top-notch coaches.

"Since our first match is in a fortnight, we're bringing forward our training. Meet here at five on Thursday. If you don't attend training, we won't consider you for the game," Cameron said when a few grumbled. "We'll also have the planned training session on Wednesday. Anyone have injuries?"

Maia hesitated, then told the truth. "I tripped over my own feet and hit my head yesterday. The doctor says I have a mild concussion. I'd intended to speak with you after the meeting." She pulled a face—a comical one, she hoped, because everyone was staring at her with varying expressions ranging from dismay to horror to grins.

The manager shared a speaking glance with the coaches before turning to her. "Maia, we'll catch up once we finish here."

Maia's stomach flipped, and the sensation didn't come close to anticipation. No, dread slithered through her, given the silent exchange.

Henry didn't stay in his vehicle. He tried, but his foot jiggled, his wolf whined, and he couldn't get comfortable. He watched the women arrive in groups of two or three. They seemed a tight-knit bunch since loud laughter and greetings rang out when the different groups interacted. They vanished indoors, and Henry climbed from his vehicle and prowled the crammed parking lot, scanning the different cars. Some were almost new with gleaming paint, while others were beat-up economy-sized cars covered with scratches and dings. None appeared out of place, and they were all empty.

No one had followed them. He was positive of that, but the person who'd bashed Maia might know her schedule. Henry would quiz Maia about the possibility.

The ex-boyfriend.

His mind stalled at that point.

He wanted to push Maia away, but the idea of another man in her life... It bothered him big time. A growl echoed through his mind.

Long strides took him around the compact parking lot and back to his vehicle. With his restlessness assuaged, he'd double down on background research. He'd start with Maia and her family.

Maia had a basic social media presence that she rarely updated, but he'd follow up on her friends. She might appear in their photos. Yeah, he'd do that and go from there.

He'd already memorized the names from her informal interview with Laura. He'd start with Bryce, the guy she'd mentioned. According to Maia, they'd dated and decided they worked better as friends. No spark. But what if this man had unrequited feelings for her? Maia's friend-zoning might cause him to snap. Yeah, he could understand the urge to get closer to Maia.

Bryce was an accountant, the same as Maia, but he'd taken a job at a prestigious Auckland firm. He had several social media accounts, and Henry discovered photos of the man with Maia. None of them appeared loverlike, but Henry scowled anyway. They had their arms draped around each other, hamming for the camera. They looked young and carefree, making him feel like a cranky old man.

Then Henry came across a recent post of Bryce with another woman. Susan. The photo resembled the ones of Bryce and Maia. A romantic couple? Heck, Susan could be his sister. He followed links and no, Susan wasn't Bryce's sister. She'd posted a photo of the pair on her page at an annual charity ball. Relief slapped Henry because they appeared close in this one. *Bryce and Maia weren't together.*

Henry discovered more photos. They were lovers. Something about the eyes and tender expressions. Satisfaction filled him on seeing this proof until he followed a link from a group photo to find one of Maia with a blond man. A handsome dude. Preppy type, yet he possessed some muscle, so he wasn't a nerd. He held Maia close, his grip possessive.

Henry located more photos—one at a rugby match, showing Maia's face speckled with mud after a game. In contrast, the dude was spotless, and the camera had caught the man's mild distaste. Maia beamed, full of suppressed excitement and triumph. Other shots showed them at charity balls, university functions, and at a pub. He released a heavy sigh. Maia had told Laura he was an ex-boyfriend. Could he be harassing Maia? Henry's fingers danced over his keypad as he deep-dived into the dude's background. Also an accountant with a bigwig Auckland firm. He lived in a luxury apartment and liked to run.

Henry would've done more research, but women exited the building. He shoved his phone away and paid close attention. They exited in twos and threes, carrying bulging bags. At a guess—their uniforms. The exit slowed, and Maia didn't appear.

A half-hour ticked away, and instinct prodded him to find her. Before the thought formed, he jumped out of his car and was halfway up the steps to the building entrance. Amused despite his worry, he forced himself to slow and took a deep breath before he entered the building. Just inside the door, he inhaled again, his wolf locating the faint trace of Maia. Without hesitation, he turned to the right and followed the scent trail. Then he heard her laugh and shout a cheerful goodbye before her footsteps headed toward him.

His heart fluttered—man, there was no other word for it. Henry shook from his stupor and resumed walking toward Maia.

His mate.

Damn it, she was young, but she *was* his mate, and he couldn't step back and let her go now that someone was attempting to harm her. And yes, he'd been going back and forth about this since he'd heard from Laura. Hell, it wasn't like him to act indecisively.

Maia walked toward him and cocked her head as if silently asking him why he'd come inside.

"Hi," he said, forcing himself to meet her gaze when his every fiber longed to study her and commit her image to memory. Not gentlemanly to ogle a woman, so he held strong. "Everyone else left, and I wondered what was keeping you."

She pulled a face. A slight limp was evident now, and he frowned but didn't mention the hitch in her step. "They asked if everyone was fit. I told them I tripped, and the coaches and manager asked me to stay and chat."

"You didn't tell them what happened?" Henry asked.

"I did once we were alone. I thought it best not to tell everyone my problems."

"What did they say?"

"The manager wants to talk to Laura." She slid him a sidelong glance as he opened the door for them to exit the building. "I got the sense they thought I was exaggerating."

"They thought you were lying?"

Maia shrugged. "My explanation seems fanciful."

"You could've shown them the lump on your head. How is the headache?"

Maia snorted. "Rose, the head coach, looked, and the throbbing seems to have settled."

"That's good. What will they do about security?"

"No problem, according to them," Maia said. "Yes, someone attacked me, but in Middlemarch. Whatever happened has

79

nothing to do with the rugby club."

Yeah, Henry understood their perspective. "What about training? Will this impact your place on the team?" He tugged the bag she carried, and she released it.

"They've arranged an appointment for me with the team doctor." She checked the time. "My appointment is in an hour. The medical center is on Edwards Road, close to here. Is that okay?"

"Have you seen much of Dunedin? I'll give you a tour."

Maia beamed, and Henry stared back, delighted at her approval. He opened the passenger door and waited until she'd settled before shutting it again. Once inside the vehicle, he said, "We'll drive around the Octagon and past the railway station before we head to the doctor."

"My aunt brought me to Dunedin when we visited the lawyer. I was too young to understand, but she tried overturning my parents' wills. She disagreed with them sending me to a boarding school."

"That must've been hard. My mother died when I was young, but my stepfather was a rock. He remarried a few years ago, but we're close."

"You're lucky. Do you see him often?"

"He and Megan live on the same property as me."

"Oh, right! London chatters a lot, and it was hard to remember everything. That must be nice. My aunt was my only family member. I made lasting friendships at school, though. I don't see them often because we went in different directions."

"Gerard and Sam are my best friends. We were in the army together. Sam lives in Christchurch with his wife."

She turned wide eyes toward him. "How long were you in army?"

"Almost ten years. Gerard, Sam, and I left around the same time. Sam had fallen for Lisa, and Gerard and I were looking to set up our business. We ended up in Middlemarch. What happens after your medical?"

"The doctor needs to clear me for training. Gavin told me the headaches would subside in time and that I shouldn't try to play too early. I've had head knocks before, and Gavin is right. Recovery takes time."

Worry seeped through Henry. She spoke casually, but rugby players made the news a lot these days. The lasting effect of head injuries—it wasn't great.

"Do you wear a helmet?"

"Some players wear headgear, but that's to prevent cauliflower ears."

"Cauliflower ears?"

"Yeah, the ears become misshapen. It's common in wrestlers. At least I can grow my hair long and cover any problems."

Her cheerful unconcern had him shaking his head.

"This is The Octagon," he said, indicating a left turn. "Its name comes from its distinctive shape." He drove slowly so Maia could see everything.

"Oh, that's the Robbie Burns statue."

"It is." Henry drove around again, enjoying Maia's wide-eyed interest. "We'll park at the railway station. There's time for a quick look and a coffee before we head back for your appointment."

An hour later, Henry paced the dingy waiting room. The young receptionist kept sneaking glances and averting her gaze. He should have taken a seat, but concern unsettled him. What the hell was taking so long? He paced another circuit and was preparing for a third when movement from behind had him whirling. Relief flooded him.

It took him seconds longer to realize Maia's dejection. A scowl dug into her pale features.

"What's wrong?"

"I need a minimum of two weeks off, and if my headaches have

81

disappeared, they'll manage my return to the team. I'll mostly warm the bench."

Henry tugged her to a halt. "You're alive. Things could've turned out worse."

Tears filled her eyes, and Henry yanked her closer, wrapping his arms around her trembling body. He breathed in her scent, and his wolf rumbled his satisfaction. This was their lady, theirs to protect, and Henry was determined to do everything possible to keep her safe.

Henry pulled back and used his fingers to wipe away her tears.

"Excuse me, Miss Jacobs. The doctor wants me to rebook you in two weeks."

Maia stiffened, her shoulders slouching, and Henry sensed her frustration. He fished his keys out of his pocket and handed them to her. "Wait in my vehicle. I'll get your appointment."

"But you don't know when I'm free."

"Maia, don't worry. We'll sort it together." He gave her a gentle nudge. "Go. I won't be long."

By the time Henry reached his vehicle, Maia was sound asleep. The vehicle remained unlocked, which wasn't great security, but she looked peaceful. She'd be safe now because he wouldn't countenance anything else.

Chapter 10

The mandatory two-week stand-down upset Maia. She tried writing but couldn't focus, her thoughts like a scattered flock of pigeons. So, instead of working, she unpacked her boxes and set about making her new bed, positioning her couch to her satisfaction, and organizing her office.

That was the first day of the enforced two-week break before Henry arrived.

"Henry?" She stared at the man darkening her doorway, her gaze fixing on his bag. "Why are you here?"

"You can't stay by yourself. You turned down London's invitation, so I'm here."

"I'm not a child."

"Not accepting help is a juvenile act. Besides, Gavin gave you the same instructions as the doctor. If you want a full recovery, play by the rules despite your frustration."

"I know." Maia glared at Henry. She didn't want this man in her private sanctuary. "Where will you sleep?"

"I have a sleeping mat in my vehicle, but we should hash out my stay first."

Her brows rose. "I can persuade you to leave?"

"No."

A snort escaped her, but staying alone had made her jumpy and frayed her nerves. "Only for tonight," she said.

"For at least three nights until we install the alarms and the security system is online."

Maia considered his request. "All right. Thank you. I don't have much food. I'd planned to do a larger shop after the meeting."

"London made a stew and sent potatoes, carrots, and leeks with me. We won't starve."

Maia glowered. He'd neatly maneuvered her into agreeing with his plan. "I don't like bossy men."

"What?"

"Nothing. I'm going to unpack more boxes before dinner."

"Anything I can help with?"

"No!" Heat gathered in her cheeks, but she maintained his gaze. He unsettled her. She wanted him gone. "I might as well unpack. Once I can train, I'll be busier and won't be at home."

Henry didn't respond, but his expression tightened, and his eyes turned flinty hard.

Maia turned away from his disapproval. He was not her boss. She'd had enough of that as a child. She headed to the room she intended to use as an office. The doctor had told her she should experience daily improvements but to avoid electronic screens and television. She'd asked him about computer work, but he'd intimated it might slow her recovery. She could take a few days off. Her deadline was self-imposed, and her editor would understand if she was late with her manuscript. She'd flick him an email at the end of the week once she knew her recovery pace.

Meantime, she'd jot plot notes and plan more than usual. Hopefully, she could nail down her story in bullet points and hasten the writing process once the doctor gave her medical clearance.

She pried open the flaps of another box of reference books and piled them into an empty bookcase. Lots of books on human sexuality, a few on grammar, and several travel guidebooks.

"Why are you reading books about human sexual behavior?" Henry's eyes bugged out before he narrowed his brown gaze on her. "What's with the oral sex manual?"

"None of your business." Using her hand, she nudged him across the threshold. Then she shut the door in his face.

He muttered something guttural under his breath, and she grinned. That would teach him to act so nosy. Maia returned to unpacking and emptied three more boxes before stopping because the ache at her temples was bothering her. She found Henry working in the kitchen, bits of wiring and tools littering the counter.

"I'm going for a nap," she said and stalked to her bedroom.

When she woke again, a rich tomato scent drew her toward the kitchen. Henry stood at the stove with a tea towel draped over his right shoulder. He stirred several times before knocking the spoon against the pot's side.

"You're awake. How's the head?"

Maia started, her pulse lurching. How had he known she was there? She hadn't made a sound. "It's fine."

Judging by the rich scent of tomato, garlic, and herbs, the man was a whizz in the kitchen.

Maia didn't have to think hard about the last time a man cooked for her or went to this effort without a big production because it was never. Her ex had always taken her to expensive restaurants and made a huge deal out of his generosity in paying for her meals. He'd even ordered for her as if she were some nincompoop without a single thought in her pretty little head.

He hadn't liked people learning about her rugby interest either. She'd always been a student or an accountant.

Maia's jaw hurt, and she realized she'd started scowling. One of Henry's brows rose in silent question.

"Sorry," she said, knowing she'd need to explain her grimace. "Dreadful memories."

Concern rushed into his features. "Did you dream about the attack?"

"No," she said, deciding to give him honesty. "A memory of my ex-boyfriend. He preferred me to have a feminine career. He believed in traditional roles for men and women. I met his parents once, and my ex hardly let me speak. He told his parents I was shy and took a while to warm to strangers."

"That's not true," Henry said. "You were fine with London, Gerard, and the other locals you met at the cafe. I saw you chatting with girls on your team before you entered the meeting."

Maia shrugged. "That wasn't more than a hello to my teammates. To be honest, they seem standoffish. A new person coming into a team always treads on toes. It's the nature of the business because you're stepping into a position another woman covets. That sort of thing can't be helped. Others have received a game day position, and I haven't, and vice versa. It's the coach's job to pick the best player."

"Do you think your ex-boyfriend would attack you? Or perhaps someone on the team?"

Maia shook her head, refuting the suggestion. After she'd told Samuel they were finished, he'd made out their relationship had left him dissatisfied. His ego wouldn't allow her to reject him. According to him, he was the one discarding her. He'd informed her they were over because she didn't follow his instructions. As if! Simple decision on her part, especially since his moods were erratic. She never knew which Samuel to expect.

"No, my ex was in Auckland. As for my team, the coach explained they'd ensured cover for every position if someone was sick or injured. All the girls know this—they're fools if they don't accept it. Besides, injuries happen. We get switched to a different position."

"Take a seat," Henry said when she took a breath.

"Sorry. Short answer: I doubt any of my team is responsible." She dropped into a chair. "Times are tough right now. People are stealing trolley loads of groceries from supermarkets. It was a random attack—a burglary gone wrong."

"You forget the graffiti left behind," Henry said.

"Oh, yeah."

"I talked to Gavin. The puppy is doing better today, and I can pick her up in the morning."

Maia recalled the puppy as a blur of white. That was all she'd seen before she'd blacked out. "It's unbelievable that someone would hurt an animal."

"Gerard is watching my dogs while I'm away, but we could bring one here. While someone is threatening you, it'd make sense to have a dog around."

His offer had her tearing up. "You'd do that for me?"

"It's no big deal."

But it was a terrific offer. A kind one. Maia jumped out of her chair and threw her arms around Henry's neck. She pressed against him and kissed his cheek. Henry tensed. It took her long moments to comprehend his discomfort. Seconds later, the length of the kitchen loomed between them.

Maia blinked because she'd never seen a man move so fast. Henry stared back, almost in shock, his vibrant brown eyes full of golden flecks.

She broke the strained silence. "What is wrong with you? I don't have cooties. I was trying to say thank you for your generous offer. What was wrong with that?"

"I don't like being touched." Henry gave her his back and checked on dinner.

Maia didn't believe him. It was something else because he kept running from her. She surreptitiously sniffed herself. Not body odor. "You keep running from me. Why? What have I done to you? " She glowered at him. "You ran from me during the school visit. I remember because you practically sprinted away."

"No," he said.

"Yes," she insisted, seeing it now that she'd spoken the words aloud. "Something about me repels you."

Henry stared at her for a moment longer before he whirled away and exited the kitchen. The slam of the door said it all.

He'd run from her again.

CHAPTER 11

"She's a lot younger than you," Gerard said with a hearty chuckle full of implications.

Henry's mouth flatlined, and he glared at his best friend. He wasn't a coward.

"Coward," Gerard taunted.

Henry's scowl deepened, digging into his cheeks and his forehead. Damn it. He shouldn't have come home in this state. Instead of returning to base, he should've gone for a run to burn off his angst. Now, they sat in their office, drinking beer while he spilled the emotions he usually kept tucked close.

"She's an exceptional woman. Do you want one of the Mitchell cousins or local men to grab her while you run away? Invite her to dinner. A date. You have the inside track. Instead, you're behaving like a teenage boy. I've never seen you like this before." His brow crinkled. "Not since..." His expression froze, and his gaze shot to

Henry.

"She's my mate," Henry said through the knot in his throat.

"But Jenny—"

"Yeah." Henry closed his eyes, that knot growing larger. His mind darted through his memories. Jenny's face didn't hold the same definition, and he cursed at the realization. Maia's visage came to the forefront instead, superseding Jenny. Henry wanted to hate Maia for this.

It wasn't working.

"It's possible to have two mates. Dad did. Your mother before he fell for Megan. Why is it so impossible for you to have another mate?"

Henry wiped his hands over his face and met Gerard's gaze. "She's so young."

"Too young," Gerard said, his green eyes narrowing.

Henry could see his friend's brain ticking over and slotting facts together.

"Maia was present during the school trip. I remember her because her big eyes were full of tears after you left. You knew then."

"Yes."

"Hell," Gerard said in an understatement. "No wonder you've been out of sorts since Maia arrived." He tapped his fingers on his desk. "She's how old now?"

"Still too young," Henry said in a curt voice.

"Exactly how old?"

"I don't know."

"You should ask."

"Doesn't matter," Henry snapped. "The age gap is too big."

"What does Maia think? Have you asked her? The mate bond must be tugging her too."

"We're poles apart in age and experience. Maia won't be in Middlemarch much once she heals and returns to training."

"Minor problems. Besides, how will you cope with seeing her with another man?"

"I'll... I don't know." Henry wanted to snarl, but Gerard wasn't saying anything he hadn't told himself.

"Talk to her."

"I can't lay this on her when she knows nothing of shifters. And someone is trying to hurt her. She'll think I'm the one who's crazy."

"Ask her out on a date. Take things slow. Get to know her as an adult instead of telling yourself she's that kid who drew you years ago. Henry, she *is* an adult. She might not have the same years as you, but she's mature. You could have a sensible conversation without feeling like you come from different generations."

Henry groaned even as he allowed Gerard's wise words to sink into his beleaguered brain. Maia intended to make Middlemarch her permanent home—at least for the near future. He had two options: he could stay the hell away from Maia, which wasn't going well, or... Yeah, he needed to go with his second recourse and embrace the chance of a mate.

"What's happening inside that thick head of yours? You can't walk away from Maia, not if it means you have a mate. I know you're lonely. It can't be easy when your friends have partners. Your dad."

"That's the part that gives me hope." Henry ran with honesty. "I do feel lonely and left out, which is why I spend so much time with my dogs. They give me simple companionship. Maia is more—hell, she comes with complications, yet I can't stay away. Not when someone means to hurt her."

"Sounds as if you've made your decision. Your heart, at least. It's that clever brain of yours creating roadblocks. Give the girl—the woman—a chance. My bet is she'll surprise you."

"Maybe." Henry swallowed a mouthful of beer, savoring the amber liquid instead of using it as a prop.

"You should go home now," Gerard said.

"I am home."

"Your place is with Maia. If you're to have any chance of a future, you need to keep her safe."

Henry drank the last of his beer. "You're right. I might park a distance from her house, shift to wolf, and do a circuit. That way, I can tell Maia no one is loitering outside." He changed the subject. "I can pick up the puppy tomorrow. She's recovered well, but Gavin said she's skittish."

"Not surprised. You keeping her?"

"One more makes no difference. Maia said she wanted a dog but can't have one because she travels often. I might take one of the older dogs to her place. She can keep it while she's at home, and if she needs to be away, she can drop them back with me."

"Look at you thinking of the future," Gerard teased.

"Please don't tell London. I don't want her sticking her nose into my business. She'd mean well, but I need to do this at my pace."

"Got it. I'll run interference. I won't lie to London, but I will ensure she and Megan don't pressure you. Neither are stupid. They'll notice your behavior."

"My behavior?"

"You're lacking your normal confidence, and your temper is running hot when normally you're Mr. Cool, and nothing rattles you."

Henry frowned, not liking this. Yeah, he'd noticed his mood swings. God knows what Maia thought. "I better go."

"Take one of your dogs. Let Maia think that is why you left her house."

Yeah, that wouldn't work, but taking the dog might help. At the very least, it would distract Maia.

"Thanks for the advice."

"Any time. You can always talk to Sam if you want impartial counsel. If Maia is playing up that way, go with her and take an extra day to visit Sam. Sam and Lisa would understand, especially if the person responsible for the graffiti keeps hassling Maia."

"That's a pretty decent idea."

"I know," Gerard said smugly.

Henry rose.

"Keep me in the loop. If anything happens, I'm nearby. Dad and Megan should be home in a few hours. Dad will help."

"I know. Thanks."

"Should I tell Dad what is going on?"

Henry considered this and nodded. "Please. Tell him I'll talk to him tomorrow, but yeah, tell him what's going on and not to tell Megan if he can help it."

Gerard's eyes gleamed with silent laughter. "I've got your back."

Henry left with a wave and headed out to his dogs. He wanted to decide which of his dogs would work best for Maia. After a quick exercise run, rough and tumble, and ear rubs, he chose Juno. If she didn't work out, he'd try one of his other dogs, but Juno was older, well-mannered, and adaptable. She was intelligent, and she'd quickly learn Maia's routine.

An hour later, he set off with Juno riding shotgun, her eyes bright with anticipation. Henry parked on a quiet side road near Maia's house. He exited his vehicle and let his night vision kick in, listening carefully for any out-of-the-ordinary sounds. He heard nothing but a lone owl perched in a pine tree.

Satisfied no one lurked nearby, he let Juno out and stripped. He didn't bother locking his vehicle but placed the keys beneath an old log a few feet from where he'd parked. That done, he shifted, letting the change slide over him. The familiar pain-pleasure of the morph flared under his skin and through his muscles. Hair sprouted on his body, and he arched forward, landing on all fours. Henry took a few seconds to let the exhilaration of his expanded senses roar through him before he signaled Juno. Like the well-trained dog she was, she trotted after him with a soft grunt. They'd enjoy this run across the paddocks. It would serve two purposes. He'd reassure himself Maia's stalker wasn't lurking in the darkness, and it would allow Henry to calm and center himself.

He owed Maia an apology. This time, he'd change how he interacted with her—starting with friendship and going from there.

They trotted around Maia's house, finding nothing out of place. Perhaps the graffiti was a one-off thing. He hoped so, but his gut told him otherwise. He and Juno loped back to his vehicle, and the owl hooted twice before taking off to arrow through the sky and disappear into the gloom.

Henry shifted and retrieved his keys before dressing. When he stopped at Maia's house, the outside light blazed, and the three sensor security lights he'd installed at the front flicked on, illuminating a large area. Excellent. That would make any would-be thieves or intruders think twice before proceeding. Juno followed him up the three steps to the door and sat at his side.

When he tested the front door, he found it locked. Maia had listened to his lectures on security. He knocked three times and waited, hearing Maia's light footsteps as she approached the door.

"Who is it?"

"Henry." Approval filled him, along with relief. She'd taken his advice on board and was taking care of security.

"Do I know you?" she asked after a long pause.

Henry stiffened. She intended to let him inside, right? Perhaps he needed to ask since he'd left abruptly. He'd run. Hell, she probably suspected he was a fruitcake.

"Yes, I'm the idiot who left without telling you why and behaved as if I had a fire lit under my butt."

"Ah! That Henry," she said, humor lurking in her voice now.

Henry's breath puffed out in relief. This was fixable as long as he stopped repeating the same mistakes. Since he was older, he should be the mature one, but he was striking out big time.

That had to stop.

It *would* stop.

He'd act his age and ask her out to dinner. He'd take her somewhere outside of Middlemarch. Maybe to Naseby for dinner and a visit to the curling rink. Or they could tramp part of the Rail Trail and have a picnic lunch. These thoughts flashed through his mind while he waited for Maia to open the door.

His brows rose. "Are you going to make us stand out here all night?"

"Us?"

The door cracked open, and Juno went on alert.

"Yes," Henry said, his mouth twitching.

"Gah!" she muttered. "Why didn't you tell me instead of letting me behave like a moron?" The door flew open, and a frown dug into her cheeks until she spotted Juno.

"A dog?" Her gaze shot to his, her entire expression a question.

"Juno is one of my dogs. I thought you might like her company while you're at home. You can drop her back with me when you need to spend time away from Middlemarch."

Maia's face lit up. "Really?"

"Yes." Henry held himself stiffly, frightened to move because the impulse to embrace her almost overwhelmed him. Then it was too late. Maia hugged him. He breathed in her decadent scent of soap and floral shampoo and felt her muscles press against him. Without volition, his arms wrapped her body, tugging her closer. He buried his face in her hair, immense satisfaction filling him with a sense of lightness. Happiness he hadn't experienced since Jenny.

She stepped back, beaming, and Henry's arms fell to his sides. "What commands should I use? I presume you're training her as a security dog?"

"Juno is my star pupil. I've brought food, a leash, and a bed for her to use. I'll grab them now. We've already walked around your house, so she's familiar with her surroundings."

"I didn't hear you."

"We were quiet in case you were asleep."

"Can I help you carry her supplies inside?"

"I've got it," Henry said before running through the commands he used. "I use hand signals because dogs are visual learners, and a security dog is often in a situation where it's impossible to give verbal commands."

"Should I show Juno around inside?"

"Do you intend to let her have the run of the house?"

"Yes," Maia said without hesitation.

"Then that's a good idea."

Henry had a spring in his step as he went outside to retrieve Juno's supplies. Maia had hugged him, and he'd managed not to embarrass himself. Things were looking up.

Maia waited until Henry's footsteps faded before signaling the massive, shaggy black and brown dog. To her delight, Juno followed without hesitation. She entered each room and let the dog sniff to her heart's content before moving on to the next.

In her bedroom, she stroked Juno's silky ears. "He's letting you stay. I hope you're okay with that. We'll have fun together. You can train with me. I'd love the company."

"What about my company?" Henry asked from the doorway.

"You want to run with me?"

A strange expression flickered across his features before he replied. "Yes, not that you'll be running for a few days. Your head is aching again. I can tell."

"Smartarse," she said without heat. "I took a painkiller half an hour ago. I need to write and powered up my computer, but my eyesight seemed blurry."

"Let me see your eyes." Henry peered into them until she felt uncomfortable. "They look all right, but you should head to bed.

Have you eaten?"

"I had soup and toast. Tomato," she added, giving him a little attitude because she wasn't a kid. "How old are you?"

"Thirty-six." He paused, that strange expression flickering over his face. "You?"

"Almost twenty-two."

"Older than I thought."

"Are you trying to insult me?"

"No," he drawled. "I thought the gap was larger."

Maia tried to decipher the man's thoughts. He remained deadpan, so she asked the question. "Meaning what?"

"Once you're feeling better, can I take you to dinner? We could visit Naseby or one of the other nearby towns."

Maia gaped, still unsure of what he was thinking. But he wasn't running away, which was unusual. He'd left every time they'd met. What had changed? While she puzzled, Juno ambled over to Henry and nudged him. He ran his hand over her head and spine, and the dog leaned into him with total trust.

"I'd like that," she said, not giving herself a chance to overthink. "I never had a chance to explore Middlemarch when I was here as a child." Besides, having Henry along would help her stop glancing over her shoulder, searching for possible attackers. And on that note, the back of her thigh had started to ache, and if she didn't sit soon, she'd fall.

Henry smiled wide and bright, stealing her breath. Before she could comment on how good a smile looked on him, he said, "No more computer work. You need to follow the doctor's instructions."

She sighed, thinking of her next deadline. She could make up for the time lost, but it would mean late nights. "I will. The sooner I get better, the sooner I can train and aim for a place on the starting team."

"You'll get there. You don't want to push too hard."

But she did because she needed to prove they hadn't made a mistake signing her. This injury was annoying, and she wished a horrid fate on the person who'd conked her over the head.

She drank a glass of water and prepared for bed. Henry had left Juno's bed in Maia's bedroom, and she heard Juno settle in with a doggy sigh as she slipped into sleep.

A shout woke her, and she lay in bed, every sense screeching at her to run. Maia leaned over and pressed the base of her lamp to switch it on and nullify the scary shadows. Juno sat in her basket, but she'd heard the noise, her ears pricked toward the door, muscles quivering. She released a tiny whine, the sound almost covered by another shout. Had that been Henry?

Maia slid her legs off the bed. The last time she'd heard a sound like this, someone had struck her over the head. Was she gonna be that stupid heroine who crept down into the cellar?

Why, yes. Yes, she was.

A snicker escaped, the burst of humor giving her a bravery boost. She grabbed her dressing gown and belted it before she grasped Juno's collar and crept out to face her fears.

Chapter 12

The terrified shout repeated, and Juno growled, her muscles bunching as she scrambled down the passage, dragging Maia after her. Maia stumbled after the powerful dog. Had someone broken into her house? No, the alarm would've gone off, and Henry was a soldier. Every bit of research she'd done for her writing indicated military men slept lightly. The cries had held anguish that tugged her heartstrings.

Maia paused in the doorway of her spare room, but Juno didn't hesitate. She burst inside, looking neither left nor right. Taking confidence from the dog's behavior, Maia followed, the light coming through the single window letting her see Henry on his sleep mat. He was tossing and turning, his moans painful to hear.

What did she do? Should she wake him?

Judging by Juno's reaction—yes.

Maia edged closer and used her voice rather than trying to touch him. She didn't want him to throttle her before he was fully awake.

"Henry?"

His reply was another of those heart-rending cries.

She took a half a step closer. "Henry!"

Juno barked.

Henry shot upward and was off his bed in seconds, his eyes wild and his face etched into savage lines, she could see even in the darkness. Two seconds later, she dropped onto his bed, the air leaving her lungs with a whoosh, a heavy body pressing her down.

A hand gripped her hair, yanking until her scalp stung.

"Who are you?" he growled. "What do you want?"

Juno barked louder than she had before.

The grip on her hair released, and the weight bearing down on her lessened. Henry froze, and Maia hesitated. Did she fight for freedom, start shouting and screaming, or use her voice?

She opted for the third choice.

"Henry." A noticeable tremor tinged her words, and she cleared her throat to try again. "Henry, it's me. *Maia.*"

Henry went rigid. Strong fingers curled around her shoulders and turned her body. "Hell," he muttered and released another string of curses that made her blink. "Did I hurt you? Fuck, of course I did. I'm so sorry. Why are you in my bedroom?"

Maia huffed out a laugh. "I think you'll find this is my bedroom. My house, my bedroom."

"Don't be a smartarse. You get my point."

"You were shouting. I thought someone might've broken into my house."

"So you came to investigate?"

"Juno came with me." She met his gaze. "I'll admit it mightn't have been the smartest idea, but I won't ignore someone in trouble because what kind of person would that make me? Besides, Juno led me straight here."

"I could've hurt you a lot worse."

"But you didn't."

Henry's gaze swept down her body, making her aware her robe had come unfastened and the T-shirt she'd slept in was short and form-fitting. Yet, she didn't move. This grumpy, complicated man drew her, and it was time to show no fear. Besides, he'd asked her out on a date, which showed interest from his side.

She cleared her throat. "Kiss me."

His brows drew together.

"In all the romances I've read, the hero would kiss the heroine at this stage, and things would progress from there. I wouldn't oppose action in that direction."

Henry blinked, and his mouth dropped open. She wanted to laugh but sensed this might make him dig in his heels or flee again.

"What do you mean?" he asked hoarsely. "Spell it out for this dim-witted male."

She made a scoffing sound. "You're not stupid. You know what I mean."

"Why?"

"I'm attracted to you. These days, women can do the asking."

"And you're petitioning for..."

"Henry!" The man needed a good shake. "Please, kiss me."

He dithered as if trying to make up his mind. Exasperation curled through her, and she rose, stepping into his personal space. Again, she wanted to laugh at his deer-in-headlights stare. She edged closer. Until now, she'd kept her gaze on his face. Now, she wished she'd sneaked a glance at his torso because standing this close to him made her feel feminine and even dainty. He was a big man with prominent muscles and didn't spend his days lolling about eating pizza.

"This is a mistake." His words were low, tortured.

"Why? I repeat, you asked me on a date. Did you not intend to kiss me good night?"

He flinched when she placed her hands on his shoulders. "You don't understand."

"I'd like to, and that counts for something. I might be young in years, but I've been on my own since my parents died. While I had adult supervision, I learned about independence and aiming for my goals." She paused because she'd spelled out her wants. If he intended to run again, let him. She wouldn't force herself on him. She wouldn't inflict herself on anyone.

Maia straightened, meeting his gaze and silently reinforcing with her expression and posture that she was serious. It was weird how his eyes glowed golden—a little freaky, even. It reminded her of the other-world characters she wrote.

"I hope you don't regret this." He waited for a beat as if he thought she might object.

Not gonna happen.

When she thought he might seize her and act as a caveman, he did the opposite, delightfully surprising her. He tugged her nearer until her breasts flirted with his chest. She wasn't wearing a bra, and her T-shirt was no barrier. Her nipples grew hard, and a shudder worked down her body. She drew in a sharp breath, and that was the moment he claimed her mouth. His lips were soft against hers and cajoling rather than demanding.

Maia's eyes drifted shut, and she pressed closer, enjoying the gentle kiss that weakened her knees. Her stomach fluttered, and she never wanted this kiss to end.

But it did.

Henry gentled his hold and placed more distance between them even though they remained touching.

"You didn't scream."

"Why would I? I asked you to kiss me."

"True, but my mind keeps telling me you're a kid. No, wait," he said when she protested. "It didn't feel as if I was kissing a child."

"I should hope not."

Before she could summon more indignation, he kissed her again, and this one contained more passion. It was a lover's kiss, and Maia wrapped her arms around his neck and held on tight as she enjoyed the slant of his firm lips across hers. Henry cupped her head with one big hand, controlling the kiss. Those flutters in her stomach deepened as he varied the intensity. He didn't thrust his tongue into her mouth but paused, going slowly when she opened for him. Their tongues tangled, and she moaned, relishing this new intimacy.

Her nipples brushed his pectoral muscles, the slow drag adding another layer to the pleasure blooming inside her.

Henry drew back, his golden gaze intense and mysterious. "Fuck."

Maia grinned. "Yes, please."

Henry scowled. "That's not amusing. What about your head wound?"

"It's a bit funny." Her grin widened, and she winked. "My head is fine as long as we don't get too adventurous. If I'm experiencing pain, I'll tell you. I want to be clear. I'm happy with this interaction between us. Just so we're extra transparent, I want more kissing, and I'd like to advance to sex. Hot, toe-curling sex. Got that?"

"Half of the population of Middlemarch heard you," Henry said drily.

"Excellent, because I don't want misunderstandings between us or Middlemarch residents. We're going to date, just like you said. I refuse to hear you mention my age again."

"Are you always this bossy?"

"When I know what I want."

"Interesting." Henry entwined his fingers with hers and directed her toward his sleep mat.

"My bed would work much better."

Henry paused, tilting his head as if considering her suggestion. "A double bed."

"Queen size," she corrected.

103

"Well, in that case," he said, lifting her effortlessly into his arms.

"You don't intend to argue?" she asked as he carried her down the passage to her bedroom.

"Right now, I want to kiss and touch you. Maybe tomorrow. You might come to your senses by then."

"Huh! I doubt it. Something about you gets to me. No other man interests me in the same way." When he didn't comment, she continued. "You attracted me when I was younger, but I didn't understand. Something compelled me to speak with you, and you ran away." She hadn't meant to sound accusing, but that's what emerged in her words.

Henry reached her bedroom and released her, holding her upright until she stood firm.

"You terrified me," Henry said. "I can admit that now, but I was running scared. You still terrify me, but I've stopped arguing with myself."

"You promise?"

"If I take a backward step, you can call me on it."

She beamed at him. "Done deal. So what next? More kissing?"

"What if you have doubts? Second thoughts?"

"Don't think so." The memory of meeting Henry all those years ago had stayed with her. She'd seen his panic before he'd fled and felt the rejection, but she'd remembered him during the intervening years and thought of him often. When she met him again, those memories surged back along with frustration at him for rebuffing her again. He'd spotted her in the cafe and practically sprinted out the door. That wouldn't happen a third time.

"I'll say this once, Henry. You don't get another chance if you run from me again. I don't need that kind of negativity. The aim is to play rugby and give it my full attention. I won't be home much, but spending time with you and having fun when I'm here would be fantastic."

His brows drew together, and the ease in his features dissipated.

"I'd be your boy toy while you're at home?"

"Not so much of the boy," she purred.

"I'm not willing to be a plaything for your convenience," he snapped.

Maia paused and cursed inwardly. She shouldn't have tossed a careless joke when he was so skittish. "Henry, when I'm not in Middlemarch, I won't have the time or inclination to date or spend time with men. My rugby career comes first, along with my other commitments."

"What other commitments?" he asked, suspicion coloring his tone.

Maia hesitated before deciding if she wanted Henry in her life, nothing but total honesty would do. "Those reference books you saw in my office..."

His brow creased, and a flash of confusion crossed his face. "The books on mythology, the sex guides, and the travel handbooks?"

"I have those because I write when I'm not playing rugby. I write fantasy with a dash of romance, and the books are research."

His brows rose. "The sex guides?"

"Yep, those too. Some of my characters are sexual, and reading a book on human behavior or about sex can spark ideas I can incorporate into my writing."

Instead of giving her a hard time about the sex guides, which was where she thought this conversation might head, he changed tack. "Do you write under your name?"

"No." She hesitated again before giving him the absolute truth. "I started writing when I was young after attending a creative writing class during the school holidays. My aunt hated me. She thought my mother wasn't good enough for her brother. She refused to have me stay during the holidays, so I remained at my boarding school when the other students went home. The creative writing class helped me fill my days. I enjoyed it, and I wrote and entered competitions. In one, I caught an editor's eye and, from there, published my first book. I'd started university, and the money I earned came in handy. The company my editor worked for ended up absorbed into another. My editor lost her job, and I didn't get another contract, but she suggested self-publishing. Long story short, that's what I did, and my series found an audience. I didn't need to go through my aunt to request money from the trust my parents had set up for me. She rejected my requests and told me to get a job to pay for luxuries." Maia couldn't prevent her derisive snort. "As if a new pair of jeans and athletic shoes were luxuries when I grew out of my clothes."

"You sidestepped my question about your name."

"My aunt wouldn't have approved of me writing books, so I chose a pen name and have used the same name ever since."

"Which is?"

"Never mind," she blurted. "I don't want you looking up my books."

"My stepmother writes romances and is quite successful. She was a sports journalist and wrote to fill the travel hours. Now that Dad and Megan have a kid, she writes while Levi is at school. London is in charge of her admin stuff, which frees Megan up to do more writing."

"Is Megan self-published?"

"Yes, so London is familiar with formatting, writing blurbs, and promo stuff."

Maia felt her eyes widen while shock at Henry's ease with writing terms kicked her in the gut. Wow, he wasn't lying or making up stories to impress her. Not that he struck her as that type of person.

"London might help you because your writing time will be minimal with your rugby."

"Is this a sneaky way to learn my pen name?"

"Perhaps." His answering grin was beautiful, and her knees went a little weak before she shored them up.

"London has experience in all things writing?"

"Megan writes romance while you said you write fantasy. The basics must be similar."

"Let me think about it. In the meantime, I'd prefer you keep this revelation to you and me. I only told you because I wanted to give you honesty. No secrets between us."

A strange expression darted across his face. "Thank you. I won't say a word. Most people don't know Megan writes books, so I'd appreciate it if you don't mention it—unless you decide to work with London."

"Fair enough. Now that the truth bomb has struck, where were we?"

Henry's eyes gleamed, and he seemed more relaxed than she'd ever seen him. He scooped her up and had her airborne before she had time to let out a surprised *eep*. With silent grace, he caged her body with his so fast she gasped.

"Wow, someone is in a hurry."

"We've established we're dating and not seeing other people when we're in different parts of the country. We've kissed. Next up is hot sex," he whispered.

Maia shuddered, weirdly turned on by his strength and how he tossed her around. No sly digs about her weight, which was refreshing.

She wasn't overweight and knew it. She'd told her ex so and proved it to him in the gym during a hand-to-hand combat session. Maia had kicked his arse, and he'd never forgiven her for showing him up amongst their friends.

"Hey." Henry clicked his fingers next to her nose, grabbing her immediate attention. "What were you thinking?"

"My ex."

"That's not complimentary to me."

"My ex is an arse, which is why he belongs in the past. Believe me, you are ten times, twenty times better than my ex."

"Pleased to hear it." Henry claimed her mouth with a possessive kiss that zapped every thought from her busy mind. Every muscle relaxed as the pleasure of his touch, his dominant mouth, rolled over her. Her heroines wanted this type of kiss, and Maia soaked up the sensations. This man. So sexy and confident now that they'd drawn a line regarding their relationship.

Henry's lips slid down her neck and sucked—a light draw of her flesh that had her sighing. Her arms tightened around his neck before she decided it was time for her to explore the sculpted muscular body that pinned her to the bed.

CHAPTER 13

Henry lifted his head to stare at Maia. There was nothing childlike about her. She was mature with hidden depths. Right now, his cock throbbed, his body onboard with taking this to the logical conclusion.

Without warning, thoughts of Jenny bombarded him, and Henry wavered. He couldn't tell Maia about mates. Not yet. He and Jenny had jumped into their physical relationship. He hadn't had time to tell her they were mates before her ex-husband had murdered her.

And he'd ached ever since, a part of him missing until Maia's return to Middlemarch.

He wanted to go slow this time if only to protect his heart.

Maia bit his earlobe. "If this is you having second thoughts, think again. We will strip to bare skin and share our bodies, and you will enjoy yourself. Hear me?"

Henry fingered his abused ear and scowled. Maia bore a determined expression, and he understood there was no stopping this train before they had sex. *Made love.* It would be making love to his mate. No going back after this step. Jenny flitted through his mind again as he remembered the completeness.

His wolf took that moment to whine and remind him of how great it was being with the one person who fulfilled them. It was true. He recalled the emotions and the protectiveness he'd felt. But along with that had come anguish when he'd lost Jenny. It had felt as if someone had ripped out his heart. He'd barely functioned. He mightn't have survived if it hadn't been for his friends and dad.

The truth—Maia terrified him, or rather, the idea of accepting and losing her. He didn't think he could repeat the experience and survive.

But his wolf made stepping back and moving stealthily challenging, preferring to leap into the future. What if he lost Maia? While she seemed definite that she wanted him, that age difference came into play. He aged more slowly than a human.

Hell, that age thing again.

His wolf growled a low, menacing rumble that signaled Henry exactly what his wild half desired.

Maia.

"Henry!" Maia snapped.

Henry started, his gaze snapping to Maia's bright blue eyes. "What?"

"Sex, remember? Have you forgotten what to do? Do you need one of my manuals?"

He scowled, and when her grin widened to mocking, he stopped it dead by kissing her. He grasped her T-shirt and ripped it off without pause.

"That was unexpected. What other moves do you have?"

Henry let his wolf's growl rumble up his throat. He didn't say anything else but ran his gaze down her body, and when he noted the pair of lacy panties she wore, he ripped those off, too.

"Next time, remind me to remove my clothes before bed. You're hard on apparel."

"You're assuming there will be a next time. I might decide I don't like a lover overseeing me."

"Huh, it seems you require direction since nothing is happening. You're running hot and cold. Very confusing."

His wolf growled at her challenge, and indignation filled Henry. "We met half a minute ago. Maybe I like to savor every moment."

Her blue eyes gleamed with intelligence and humor, and she opened that luscious mouth to spout more wisdom, another complaint, or dig at his masculinity. Henry stopped her words before they formed. He kissed her and squeezed her nipple, giving her a sharp jolt of pain.

"Oh!"

Satisfied by her reaction, he lifted his mouth momentarily and, when she didn't complain, settled in to taste her. His hands wandered and smoothed over her bare hip. Each kiss and touch had satisfaction roaring through him. Part of this was his wolf, but a decent slice came from his human side.

Maia was all curves and tan skin. Her breasts were paler, and they filled his hands. He could feel the muscles in her arms and legs, yet she was sleek, and they fit together perfectly.

Henry set about learning what she enjoyed most. He started with her breasts, kissing and exploring with his tongue, tasting her flesh. Her fingernails dug into his shoulder blades, and she wasn't careful about it as she arched against him. He'd wear the marks from her touch for several hours, which gave him tremendous satisfaction.

He adjusted their bodies until the bulge of his cock lined up with her clit. Feminine arousal dampened his boxer briefs, the spicy scent of her thrilling him. He groaned when she kissed his neck and dragged her nails down his back. He thrust against her, letting her feel the drag against the heart of her.

"Yes," she murmured.

But he wasn't ready for that yet.

He moved down her body, kissing, nipping, and using his tongue in random order. Her legs parted for him, and he lifted her, setting his mouth on her sex and sucking. She bucked, crying out at the direct stimulation.

"You taste amazing." He stared up at her and knew she'd see his wolf. His eyes would appear more amber than brown, but he couldn't find it in himself to care. He placed a lazy kiss on her inner thigh and used his tongue to tease her and stoke her need higher.

She trembled, her legs tightening around his shoulders, her hips lifting into his touch in a silent plea. He didn't try to extend her pleasure. Not this time when desperation roared through him. He fluttered his tongue against her swollen flesh, her groan the sweetest music.

Maia came apart, her body tensing and bucking as his touch became too much for her. Henry gentled his contact and watched the color rise up her throat and the relaxed pleasure of her expression, snatching every moment in his visual camera to remember later.

He'd given in to her, but a tiny part of him felt manipulated—by his wolf and this marvelous miracle of a woman who was his mate. He'd been fortunate to have a second chance, and this was not the moment to thumb his nose at this gift.

Henry valued her honesty and wished he had the same backbone. He should have told her about his otherness but hesitated when their relationship was beginning and so much else was happening in her life.

A new career. A new home. A new relationship.

Maia opened her eyes, and he sucked in his breath on seeing the vibrant blue. She glowed with inner beauty, and again, he couldn't believe his luck in finding another mate. Some men went through life never finding their perfect fit. Most settled and were happy enough with their life, their wife, and the children who came along.

He rose up her body and kissed her deeply before sliding into her body with one seamless thrust. "Heaven," he murmured against her ear.

"You're not wearing a condom."

Henry froze, his horrified curse ringing out. "Fuck, Maia. I'm so sorry. I didn't think."

"As long as you're clean, we're good," she said, her gaze searching his. "I'm on the Pill."

With devastation still reverberating, Henry blurted out his closely guarded secret. "I haven't had sex with anything but my hand for years."

"What?" Now she sounded uneasy, and he thought disbelief echoed in her startled question.

But it was the truth. After Jenny had died, his happiness snatched away, he'd fallen into depression, and it had taken him months, hell, years to gather the strewn pieces of his life. Something else he should've told Maia.

"Why?" It was a sharp demand for information.

"My girlfriend was murdered, and it destroyed me, especially since the local cops decided I was the culprit. And now, someone is trying to hurt you, and it's hard." He went for the simple truth without giving too many details.

"Murdered! How long ago was this?"

"It was before you came to Middlemarch to stay with your aunt."

"I see."

Henry doubted that. Not in a million years would she understand why he'd kept away from the opposite sex. At first, it was because he was mourning for Jenny, and after he'd met—a tepid word for the way Maia had exploded into his life—he hadn't

113

wanted another woman. His wolf had wanted Maia and that couldn't happen when she'd been a child. Hell, the idea was repulsive and had messed up his head for ages. Henry snorted. He wasn't sure he had his head on straight yet. How could it be when he was balls-deep in Maia?

"You will explain more fully tomorrow. Right now, I'm permitting you to continue. One orgasm is not enough."

"Greedy."

"Demanding. I want to make sure you deliver."

Henry leaned down to kiss her, smiling against her lips. This woman challenged him, and he liked it.

"Start moving, Henry, before I go insane. I need to feel that magic again."

"Yes, ma'am."

She rolled her eyes and kissed his neck, using her teeth to show her displeasure at the *ma'am* part of his compliance. He jolted, his wolf's yip of pleased approval echoing through his mind. *Sassy mate.* His animal half adored her cheek and demanding ways.

Henry pulled back before surging into her clinging warm heat again. Sweet heaven.

"That's better," she purred. "Much better. I heartily approve of a man who can take direction."

Henry laughed, his chuckle loud and carefree. "You'll be the death of me, sweetheart."

"Sweetheart. I like that one much better than ma'am. And really, you're complaining because I tell you what I want? You should give me hints so we have a fantastic time together every session."

Henry spluttered out another laugh, then groaned when she tightened her inner muscles around his shaft. "Too much of that, and I won't last." The truth—he was dangling by a thread now.

"No problem. You won't leave me hanging because you've got skills." She purred the words and lifted into his stroke, her eyes closed and her expression serene.

Henry's smooth thrusts faltered while he tried to control the laugh threatening to burst from him. "I can tell you're going to be a handful."

"Most men like a challenge."

It made Henry think of her past lovers, which was dickish because he'd had other lovers before Jenny. "I can see that the only way to shut you up is to kiss and keep you busy until you're incapable of speaking."

Her *huh!* got trapped against his lips as he increased the pace, rocking into her with intent. Her flesh tightened, and seconds later, she exploded, her scream of enjoyment almost deafening. Henry grinned, taking that as permission to seize his pleasure. He pulled back and plunged into her decadent warmth, his entire body shuddering as he lost control and nipped her neck, her groan dragging his common sense back. He smoothed the mark he'd inflicted on her with his tongue, thankful he hadn't bitten her too deeply. God, he had no control around her. Zilch.

Henry tried to slow, but he was past any semblance of humanity. He and his wolf were on the same page. They wanted to dominate her and seize the pleasure Henry had denied them because Jenny's death had changed him.

He thrust and rocked and let the sensations build while enjoying her floral scent and his as they combined. Her smooth skin beneath his fingertips enthralled him, and her snug grip...

He exploded before he could finish that thought, pouring himself into her. His heart thumped, his breath coming in heavy pants as if he'd been running for hours. Aware he was crushing her, he turned their bodies so she lay atop him. Their closeness was perfect—his wolf demanded it, so he allowed his animal half his way because he enjoyed this lazy, pliant Maia. Her breasts flattened against his chest, and this gave him the opportunity for more touching. He ran his hand down her spine and let it come to rest on her rounded arse.

"Nice," she murmured. "I bet you'd give a great massage."

"I've never given anyone a massage," he said, surprised.

"It will be a first, then. Excellent." Maia sounded sleepy, but he didn't mind if she drifted off. He was supremely comfortable with her in his arms and was content to savor this moment.

The other stuff would need to wait.

He'd made love to her now, and there was no way in hell he could give her up. She was his mate, and soon, she'd understand all this entailed.

CHAPTER 14

Maia woke slowly, warm and rested after her best sleep in ages. She yawned without opening her eyes and stretched. When her arm collided with flesh, memories flooded back. *Henry.* They'd made love last night and very early this morning. She smiled and turned toward him, giving him a sleepy nuzzle and kissing his neck.

"Good morning. How do you feel?" His formal demeanor and tense muscles had her waking fast. Surely, he didn't have regrets?

"I feel fantastic," she said, speaking clearly and connecting with his gaze so he could see she was happy with the status quo. *Ecstatically effervescent.* "I hope we'll have a repeat soon. Often."

He didn't reply, but he kissed her so she took that as a promising sign.

Maia slipped out of bed, gingerly testing her leg. It was much better, and her head wasn't throbbing so far. "Do you want a mug of coffee and something to eat? I can do eggs and toast."

"Thank you. May I use your shower?"

Still so polite. So formal. "We could shower together. You start the shower while I hunt up some towels. I won't be long."

Henry rose and wandered from the bedroom, giving her an excellent view of the beautiful, muscular buttocks she'd enjoyed touching last night. She sighed in cheerful appreciation. On hearing a shower blast, she lurched into action. She did *not* want to miss showering with Henry. Her headache was minimal to her relief, and she navigated the passage with scarcely a limp. Per the doctor's instructions, the heat pad she'd applied had helped a lot. Optimistic about her recovery time, she found a box of towels and lugged it to the bathroom. A job for today. She'd line the shelves and get her bathroom organized. Her carton of toiletries and shower gels was around somewhere. The gels were her treat and the scents always helped her to wake in the mornings.

Maia pulled aside the curtain and stole a peek at Henry. So sexy. *So tempting.* He was washing himself with brisk and economical moves. She slipped under the steamy water and pressed against him. Instantly, his arms came around her, his erection prodding her stomach.

"I should do something about that," she murmured.

"You don't have to," Henry replied, smoothing his hand down her back.

"I want to touch you this way," she said, kneeling in front of him. Water poured over her head, but she ignored it. A quickie since the floor was hard on her knees. She grasped the base of his cock with her hands before she opened her mouth and sucked him inside.

"That feels amazing," he whispered.

She grinned around his shaft and used her tongue and lips to drive him crazy. He angled his body so the water wasn't bombarding her while she teased him, taking him as deep into her mouth as she could. His groan made her work harder, and soon he trembled. He pulled back without warning, his seed striking her chest. Maia blinked since she'd happily swallow but seeing the satisfaction on Henry's face clued her into the why of his actions. She didn't mind, feeling a little possessive herself. It was why she'd bitten his neck, and he'd enjoyed it since he'd gone crazy.

Henry helped her to stand, his expression impassive.

"A mark of possession?"

"Yeah. Sorry."

"It's okay," Maia said. "I understand. Besides, I bit you last night." She peered at his neck and frowned. "I thought I'd bitten you hard enough to leave a mark."

A smile flashed. Disappeared. "You can bite me anytime, but I don't bruise easily."

"Oh, that's disappointing."

Henry kissed her hard, passion instantly flaring between them. He pressed her against the shower wall and parted her legs with a well-placed knee. His teeth scraped the tendons of her neck, and the slight hint of pain had an equal slice of pleasure roaring directly to her core. Wow! *Just wow.* There was something about this man that made their lovemaking magical. She had no idea what it was, but it was clear the Middlemarch single ladies were blind. They should've snapped up Henry while they'd had a chance. It was too late because she had no intention of letting him go.

Cavewoman, much? Yeah, she'd own that.

The way Henry looked at her, touched her, sent an answering possessiveness through her. She was his. He might be grumpy. He might be a loner, but the man had hidden depths. Henry had a soft heart he kept carefully concealed and was loyal to his friends. They were also steadfast to him. That was obvious in the close friendship he had with Gerard. He'd mentioned another friend. Army buddies, so the strength of the friendship made sense.

And she needed to quieten her busy brain and focus on his

SHELLEY MUNRO

touches. Confidence shone in every firm stroke while the passion simmering between them flared into fiery pleasure. He cupped her breasts, kneading and testing their weight, lighting bursts of excitement. One of his hands moved then, sliding down to her hip and holding her firmly.

"I can't wait to get inside you again," he whispered, his breath hot against her neck.

"Do it. Do it now," she encouraged, full of delicious anticipation. Oh, yeah. That eagerness bubbled in her belly and filled her with happiness.

Henry needed no further urging, and he guided his shaft, pushing smoothly into her. A unified groan filled the air, and thankfully, Henry didn't linger or tease. He shunted in and out of her, his talented fingers caressing her clit and sending her over the edge faster than she could believe. His thrusts became faster, a deep growl emerging from him before he stilled, planted balls-deep inside her.

They stood silent and still as the water poured over them, cooler now.

Maia yawned, and Henry nuzzled her neck. He slipped out of her and stood back. She wobbled slightly, and his arm snapped out to hold her upright.

"It's still early. Why don't you wash and go back to bed? I'll take Juno outside and join you soon."

"Sounds like a plan."

The minute Maia hit the mattress, her eyes closed, and she drifted to sleep. She woke suddenly, panic flaring through her until she realized the gaze she felt belonged to Henry.

"Is something wrong?"

"Laura called," he said, and she belatedly realized he'd partially dressed.

Maia frowned, not having to feign her confusion. "I didn't hear the phone."

"It was on vibrate."

"Oh, there's a problem?" The chill in his voice and the deadness in his brown eyes made her arms and legs prick with foreboding.

"After your attack, Laura and Charlie canvassed the local bed-and-breakfast places, the motels, and the Airbnbs."

"Did they find something?"

Henry glowered at her. "Your fiancé."

Maia jackknifed up and grabbed at the covers when she remembered she was naked. She lifted them to her chest. "What are you talking about? I'm not engaged to anyone. Men are too much damn trouble." She sprang off the bed and stomped toward her shower. She turned it on cold to scare away her lingering lethargy. Right now, she needed her A-game.

When she entered the kitchen fully dressed fifteen minutes later, Henry leaned against her counter, his hands cupping a mug. Damn, she needed to sort out more furniture. Maia stalked to her coffeemaker, grabbed the first coffee pod to hand, and shoved it into the machine.

"I don't have a fiancé. What is this person's name?"

"Samuel Rattray."

"My ex-boyfriend. We broke up about two months before I left Auckland. I'm insulted that you'd think I'd cheat if I were in a relationship. I'm not a cheater!"

Henry grunted, but his posture relaxed during her haranguing speech.

"You don't know me well, but you didn't think to give me the benefit of the doubt or at least ask me before hurling insults against my good character?" Her coffee was ready, and she grabbed the mug. "Where is he? Is Samuel still in Middlemarch? I thought he had a rugby game in Auckland."

"He's telling everyone you're getting married in three months."

Maia held her temper with difficulty, telling herself that if she were in Henry's shoes, she'd feel betrayed. That kept her from throwing her hands up in disappointment and stalking off.

"Where is he staying? I don't know what game he's playing, but I'll enlighten him quick-smart."

"He's staying at the Middlemarch Bed-and-Breakfast."

"Middlemarch is a small town. He could've asked around and found me easily. Why would he wait until Laura discovered him?"

"I wondered that."

She snapped a glower in his direction. "It didn't make you doubt his reasons for arriving in Middlemarch? He could've told me he wanted to speak to me in person."

Henry grimaced but, as usual, didn't give away much.

"Where is the Middlemarch Bed-and-Breakfast?" Maia grabbed her car keys off the hook near the door. She had things to say to Samuel and didn't care if she created a scene.

"Laura says he's at the cafe eating breakfast."

"I bet he's entertaining the locals, telling them about the horrid way I've treated him when all he wants is to love me and make me his wife."

"Do you think he was the one who attacked you?" Henry asked.

"No idea, but I intend to find out."

Juno and Henry followed her outside.

"Give me the keys," Henry said. "I'll drive."

"Thank you, but I don't require your help. I. Need. Space."

Henry halted abruptly, and for an instant, she swore hurt flickered across his handsome face. She cursed under her breath and stomped to her car. It inclined at a weird angle. Good grief! She stomped around the front of her car to the passenger side that still bore a tag. Yep, her tire was as flat as her kitchen floor. A twinge in her thigh suggested her clomping wasn't helping her leg.

"What's wrong?"

"I have a flat tire."

"Please let me drive you to the cafe. We can fix your tire later."

Maia heaved out a breath of frustration. He was right. Yes,

Samuel had riled her, but there was no point in acting like a moron. The local gossip vine would light up at her expense, all because she'd injured Samuel's pride and walked away.

"I'd appreciate a ride."

Henry plucked his keys from his pocket. A suspicious thought slid into her mind. "Did you make my tire go flat?"

"No, I did not," he said with a dignity that was the opposite of his expression.

Henry didn't give the impression of a petty man, and really, why would he flatten her tire? He was strong enough to physically stop her if he objected to her leaving to harangue Samuel.

The drive to the cafe was silent since they'd left Juno. Maia observed the cattle paddocks and the scattered sheep grazing on the far slopes. She recalled the piles of stones littering the hills from her childhood. They reminded her of a giant's building blocks and scattered the region like discarded Lego pieces, strewn where they'd fallen in stacks or singly. The grass on the hillside was tussock, while the fields nearer the river were green and heavily farmed.

"What made you choose Middlemarch for your business?"

"Gerard and I wanted a town with a community feel, and here, we're close to Dunedin, but we're also relatively close to the tourist hotspots in the south. We figured we'd get business from wealthy owners of holiday homes in the area, which has turned out to be true." He shot her a curious look. "Why did you decide to purchase a property in Middlemarch?"

"I liked the idea of sticking it to my aunt and imagined her rolling in her grave yet unable to stop me from turning her house into my home," Maia said. She didn't mention the other reason because she'd barely admitted it to herself—Henry had been a draw card. If he'd been with another woman, she would've backed off.

Maybe.

The surge of jealousy that rippled through her told the truth.

She would've fought for Henry and was unsure what this said about her character. Was she turning into a stalker? One of those obsessed women who did horrid things to get their way? She shook her head in denial—a sharp jerk that had Henry turning to her with raised brows.

"Something wrong?"

"No." Yes! She was subconsciously skulking after Henry, even though he'd rejected her. She got the age thing, but she was an adult with a mind of her own. And she was tipping over into the creepy, criminal side. "Henry, despite your grumpiness, I like you. I don't know what Samuel wants, but we're no longer together. I am interested in you. Surely, I can't be plainer than that. Playing games isn't my way. Unless it's rugby. Understand?"

While she'd been spilling her heart, they'd entered the business center of Middlemarch. A grandiose term to describe the small country town, but it was busier than she remembered. A group of six cyclists pedaled down the road and pulled up outside the supermarket. Charlie drove past in his police vehicle and waved before turning into a side street.

Henry parked near Storm in a Teacup. He took her hand in his. "I'm sorry for acting like an idiot. I'll try to curb my craziness in future."

"And that, right there, is why I'm with you and not Samuel. You apologized, and your words show me you're willing to meet halfway."

Henry tightened his grip momentarily before releasing her hand. "Laura is waiting."

"Is Samuel in trouble?"

Henry's lips curved into a wry smile. "I suspect you'll be his worst problem. Laura is monitoring him because she's suspicious of his sudden appearance. I'd bet my mind has turned the same corner as Laura's. We're wondering if he had anything to do with the attack."

"Samuel is vindictive when he doesn't get his way."

They walked past the rose bushes at the cafe's entrance and stepped onto the wooden verandah. Henry opened the door for her, and a bell tinkled. Maia scanned the cafe and spotted Samuel sitting at a corner table, a half-eaten breakfast in front of him. He half-stood on noticing her arrival and noticeably bristled when he registered Henry.

"Henry, could you order me a coffee, please? I want to deal with Samuel."

Henry hesitated before giving a curt nod and detouring to the service counter.

Maia crossed the distance between the door and Samuel's table on shaky legs. While this setting was safe, she hated to add extra fuel to the local gossip vine. Samuel was forcing this confrontation on her, and her temper strained at the leash.

"At last," Samuel snapped. "I thought I'd have to send the police to retrieve you."

CHAPTER 15

M aia gaped, shock at his frigid attitude batting away her doubts. Her spine stiffened, and she yanked out a chair at his table. "What the devil do you mean?"

Samuel's hand shot out and captured her wrist, his grip an unbreakable band. Not that this brute force stopped her from attempting to free herself.

"Release me, or I will scream. Loudly."

"I don't like games, Maia. Where are they?"

"If you'd tell me exactly what you mean, I might help. Right now, I'm clueless."

"You took the Greek myths and legends books."

She didn't bother to hide her confusion. "You gave them to me."

"On the understanding we'd stay together. You grabbed the books when you left."

"I did," she said, not grasping why he was so angry. She'd left the larger, more expensive items he'd given her behind because she didn't think it was ethical to take them.

In her peripheral vision, she noticed Henry take a seat with Laura, and she silently thanked him for his support.

"I want them back," Samuel said in his high-handed way.

"Why didn't you call me? Why travel from Auckland to Middlemarch?"

He shrugged, his dark blond hair flopping over his eyes. He shoved it back and glared at her. "You aren't taking my calls."

True, because he'd harassed her, demanding another chance.

"You could've contacted Bryce and asked him to message me. When did you arrive in Middlemarch?"

"Yesterday. I want my books."

"You can have them. I'll deliver them."

"I'll come with you and collect them now."

"No."

Fury slid over his face, and he leaned closer to snarl at her. "Don't test me, Maia. Trying my patience never ends well."

After the last loud fight that had turned physical, Maia had packed and left, bunking with Bryce until she'd purchased her Middlemarch property.

Another thought occurred. "Why tell the police I'm your fiancé?"

His mouth twisted. "You could be. Say the word."

"No. Thank you," she added in the interest of tact.

"You've replaced me." Samuel's gaze darted over to Henry before settling on her again. The twist of his lips wasn't attractive despite his blond handsomeness. He resembled a thwarted child.

"Henry is an old friend. I've known him for years."

"Ah, yes. How did you afford a property? It seems substantial and worth decent money."

"What do you know about my property?" she demanded, suspicion leaping to the fore.

Samuel picked up his knife and fork. "Bryce told me."

"Bryce wouldn't tell you shit."

"Watch your language," he snarled.

What he meant was that he disliked her standing up to him. He liked his women subservient. "I repeat, I'll deliver your books."

"That makes no sense. Let me collect them now."

"You don't care about the books. They're an excuse to get me alone and salvage your pride. Not happening. This meeting is over." She sprang to her feet. "Stay away from me. I don't want you in my life. I thought I'd made that clear."

"Don't walk away because you won't like the consequences."

Good grief. What had she seen in this man? Luckily, she'd wised up and terminated their relationship because it hadn't been great for her mental or physical health. She sent him a sweet smile—one bearing the sting of a wasp. "I'll courier your books to you. Don't contact me again."

Maia took two steps before Samuel grabbed her. He yanked her arm, and she stumbled, knocking over a chair. The cafe fell silent. Maia was strong from her strength training in the gym but temper had given Samuel an edge. He dragged her back to their table.

Henry started toward them, but Laura was quick. She darted around Henry and placed herself between him and them. Maia gave a silent shake of her head, and Henry stilled, although his expression screamed murder. A low growl had her head whipping to her right, and she half expected to see a dog, but four men eyed proceedings.

Okay then. She'd officially entertained the locals. Samuel's hand whipped out, and he slapped her across the face. Shock accompanied the loud crack. Silence. Then pain. Chairs scraped the wooden floor.

The men at the table to her right moved in concert, and they, along with Henry and Laura, surrounded them.

"This is a private matter," Samuel snapped.

"You're under arrest for assault." Laura whipped her handcuffs off her belt.

Samuel bellowed as Laura wrenched his left arm behind his back. He cursed and struggled, but two of the four strangers grabbed and held him for Laura to finish cuffing.

Henry walked straight to Maia and gently tilted her head. "He didn't break the skin, but your cheek will throb. Come with me, and we'll get ice."

"I didn't think he'd wallop me in public," Maia said.

"But he has hit you."

"Once, and I struck back. Bryce told me Samuel's black eye was award-worthy. I'm not proud of the physical violence, but I wasn't intending to be his punching bag. He has a filthy temper and a set of rules longer than his arm. None of his directives applied to him."

Laura and the two men dragged Samuel from the cafe. He kicked and shouted, pretending to be the victim.

Two men approached them.,

"Did Emily get you some ice?" The man's dark eyebrows drew together, his green gaze laser sharp.

"Not yet," Henry said. "She's busy with customers."

"I'll grab some," the other man said and disappeared behind the counter.

"Maia, this is Saber Mitchell. Emily, his wife, owns this cafe," Henry said.

"Pleased to meet you, Maia," Saber said, assessing her and her injuries. "Are you all right?"

"Mainly embarrassed that Samuel created a gossip-worthy scene," Maia said.

"Don't worry about it," the man who'd retrieved the ice said. He handed it over, wrapped in a tea towel, ready for her to hold to her face. "I'm Felix, Saber's brother. Tomasine, my wife, is working out the back. She prepared the ice pack." He grinned. "My attempts wouldn't look so pretty."

"I hear you had trouble at your house," Saber said. "Was it him?"

The thought had crossed her mind, but despite his short temper, Samuel wasn't sneaky or the type to skulk. Samuel preferred the direct approach. Instant gratification. She couldn't see him gaining pleasure from scaring and taunting her.

"It's possible. But he is direct. Samuel is more likely to confront than use clandestine methods. I could be wrong. He might've changed or could've paid someone to harass me."

Henry's phone rang. "Yeah?" His gaze settled on Maia. "Yeah, we'll be there soon. What? Yeah, that'll work." He hung up. "Laura asked if you could give her an official statement. She suggested a restraining order."

"Sure, we can go now," Maia said, removing the ice from her cheek.

"Laura recommended we let him stew in custody for a few hours. We'll get another coffee and one of Emily's famous cheese scones."

"Join us," Saber said. "I'd like to show we're decent people in this town."

Maia laughed and was pleased to note it sounded more her. "I've met Emily. I know the residents are welcoming."

"Well, then," Saber said. "You'll have no problem having coffee with us. Joe and Sly should be back soon, so you can meet more of my brothers."

"How many of you are there?" Maia asked.

"Five," Saber said, his eyes twinkling. "We all have children, so there's a lot of Mitchells in Middlemarch."

"If you hang out with Henry long enough, you're bound to meet my daughter Sylvie," Felix said. His features were more rugged than Saber's, but their black hair and green eyes made their relationship obvious. "She works with Henry, training his dogs. She's off to university in Auckland next year. I still don't know how she got old enough."

Henry urged Maia toward the larger table where the men had sat. "I didn't ask about your coffee preference earlier. What would you like?"

"An Americano with a dash of milk," she said. "Are the cheese scones that good?"

"They are," Henry said. "Laura ordered me to get scones for her and Charlie. She had to leave before the first batch was out of the oven."

Henry waited until she'd seated herself before he strode to the counter to place their order. Saber and Felix joined her, and not long after, the doorbell jingled. The two men who'd helped Laura entered the cafe and beelined for them.

"Joe, Sly, this is Maia Jacobs," Saber said. "She plays rugby."

Maia shot him a look, and Saber laughed. "Emily told me she'd met you and everything she learned. It's a small-town thing."

Maia smiled at the two arrivals, tall with black hair and green eyes like their brother's. If they moved seats, she'd get confused since they were identical. "Pleased to meet you. I moved here to take up a contract with the Dunedin women's rugby team."

"I heard you suffered a concussion during the attack," Saber said.

"Yes, not the best timing. I can't play until the team doctor clears me. I know it's for my health, but it's frustrating when I'm eager to start."

"Understandable," Felix said. "To change the subject, what are your plans for the land attached to your property?"

"I haven't thought that far ahead. I know nothing about farming, but I wanted the property."

Felix exchanged a look with Saber. "We could do with additional grazing for our alpacas. Would you be willing to lease the land to us?"

"The fences aren't stock-proof. My aunt's health meant the property deteriorated toward the end. How about this? Repair the

131

fences, and you have two years grazing rights. My rugby means traveling often, and I won't have time to deal with it. If you prefer a written deal, fine, but truthfully, the land would've become a problem."

Saber extended his hand. "Are you happy to shake on the deal?"

"Absolutely." Maia took his hand to seal their gentleman's agreement.

Maia enjoyed meeting other locals who came up to say hello. Choosing to confront her here had been a big mistake for Samuel, considering the cafe was the town's heart. After leaving, Henry gave her a town tour and introduced her to everyone they met until names stuffed her head.

Maia recognized Samuel's furious shouts when they entered the police station.

"Thank goodness you're here." Charlie stepped away from the desk when she handed over the scones. "That man is driving us crazy, saying he must leave because he's playing in an important rugby match tomorrow. We'll be pleased to get rid of him."

"He should've thought of that before he caused trouble," Maia said. "My walking away from him hurt his pride. He thought he could snap his fingers, and I'd return to Auckland with him as his fiancee. The books were an excuse."

"What if he's lying about the game and doesn't leave Middlemarch?" Henry asked before she could.

"We suggest a restraining order. If he ignores that, we can add additional charges. He's an idiot to hit you in public. Joe and Sly did witness statements for us. Saber offered if we needed another."

"I want to press charges. He's a spoiled brat who thinks his parents' wealth gives him rights."

"Excellent. This way," Charlie said.

The formalities didn't take long, and they left the police station less than half an hour later, with Samuel's curses ringing in their ears. He wasn't happy, and Maia wondered if he'd get his father involved. She'd met his parents once and hadn't envied Samuel their unreasonable expectations. Yeah, she'd never told Samuel she'd overheard his mother telling a friend Samuel was playing with Maia and would soon see sense. Heck, his parents had rivalled her aunt, which had brought out her empathy.

That sympathy bubble had burst quick-smart.

"This isn't your fault," Henry said as they left the station.

"I know." Maia thought back to the time she'd spent with Samuel. "I think he was telling the truth. An attack isn't his way. Samuel is a loner. He has lots of acquaintances but no one close. His parents taught him to distrust, and he always questioned me about what I was doing or where I'd be. His possessiveness drove me crazy, and when it spilled over into physical abuse, I decided enough. No, Samuel came to Middlemarch because my leaving stung his pride. I'll discuss it with my friend, Bryce, but my guess is Samuel wanted to end our relationship on his terms, not mine." She glanced out the window. "I'll deliver the books to Laura, and Samuel can take them. Where are we going?"

"We're stopping by Gavin's surgery to pick up the puppy. He can check your head wound. How's your headache?"

"The light is hurting my eyes, making my head pound."

"Grab the pair of sunglasses in the glove box."

She fumbled with the latch and rifled through before pouncing on a leather case. Maia slid the glasses on with relief. "Isn't Gavin a vet?"

"We don't have a doctor's office in Middlemarch. Gavin is the nearest thing we have, and we trust him implicitly."

Well, that made sense. Vets trained as long as doctors did, and while they couldn't prescribe drugs, they had a vast knowledge of bones and muscles.

Henry parked and aided her exit from the vehicle. She would've objected, but her head and leg were aching. Now was not the time to reject help.

"Ah, excellent timing," Gavin said.

Maia smiled at the dark-haired man while his green eyes assessed her. "Why do so many Middlemarch residents have green eyes?"

Gavin chuckled. "It's the Celtic blood. Many of us have roots in Scotland."

"Oh." She removed the sunglasses and winced at the bright light in the surgery.

Gavin noticed. "Sit," he said, pulling out a chair. "Your head giving you problems?"

"The doctor says it's the concussion, and the headaches will tail off given time and rest. It's challenging because I need to do computer work. Working on a screen makes the pain worse."

"Your doctor is right. You need to rest your brain after a knock. Research has shown that ignoring the problem or repeated knocks has repercussions in later life." He glanced at Henry. "There is a drug I could suggest—"

"No drugs." Maia sprang to her feet. "We have random testing, and anyone positive gets benched. A repeat offense can lead to a contract cancellation. I've worked hard for this and don't intend to lose my contract through stupidity. Pretending innocence is not an acceptable excuse."

"It was a suggestion," Gavin said in a mild voice. "The drug, however, would show up during normal medical tests and raise questions."

He glanced at Henry, and Henry's cool demeanor surprised Maia. Shouldn't he act indignant on her behalf?

"The puppy has recovered well but gets anxious around unfamiliar people. She's easily startled. You'll need patience and avoid rapid movements," Gavin said.

Henry's icy expression faded, but unspoken communication winged between the two men. Maia shot a glance from one to the other. Her head pounded. She'd think about it later.

"I intended to put the puppy in a box, but she became agitated and wouldn't stop yelping. It might be best to carry her. Cuddle her and speak calmly. She might cry, but Henry, you're good with dogs. They trust you."

Again with the subtext. Maia would ask Henry later.

The puppy must've heard them coming. She cowered in the corner of her cage, her entire body shuddering. Maia's heart broke. It would take time, but Henry was a natural. He'd gain the puppy's confidence.

"I'll let you get her out of the cage," Gavin said. "Maia, you need to sit. At least let me look at the knot on your head. How is your leg?"

"I thought it was improving, but it's throbbing now."

"Have you tried heat pads or ice? Either might help."

"I've used heat, and that helped. The doctor said it's badly bruised. There's nothing broken, although it's swollen," Maia said.

The puppy squeaked, cowering, but Henry drew her out of the cage. "Shush, little girl," he crooned, gently stroking her head. He opened his shirt and pressed the puppy against his chest before redoing the buttons. Her whimpers gradually ceased, and Gavin smiled.

"Well done. I've given her antibiotics for the cuts on her belly and front leg." He retrieved a white container and gave it to Maia. "She'll be stronger after the antibiotics course finishes and the chances of infection decrease."

"Thanks, Gavin," Henry said. "Send me the bill."

Gavin nodded and held the door open. "Maia, try more heat pads on that thigh. At the least, it will help with the swelling."

They drove home slowly since Henry couldn't fasten his seat belt with the puppy inside his shirt. She'd calmed considerably.

"She's asleep," Henry murmured.

"Good. She deserves peace and a happy life."

And so did she. But her gut insisted Samuel hadn't attacked her, which meant someone else had.

Chapter 16

"If we believe Samuel and he didn't attack you, then who? I don't buy the local kids. I can see them breaking into a house, the graffiti because some are wild, but I doubt any would've tortured this puppy," Henry said, pulling into Maia's driveway, his mind working in tandem with hers.

Maia hobbled from the vehicle, smiling when she heard Juno's welcoming bark. "Will Juno tolerate the puppy? What are you going to call her?"

"I'll see how her personality develops unless you have a suggestion."

Henry stroked the tiny head, whispering to her, and Maia's heart flipped. For a large man, he was gentle. Juno trusted him implicitly. His passion for the dogs and their confidence in him had attracted Maia's attention as a child.

Maia pulled out her keys to unlock her front door, then stopped, her heart leaping with alarm. "Henry."

"What?"

"I one hundred percent locked the door. It's not locked now." She opened it, and Juno bounded outside.

Henry tensed. "Stay here while I do a circuit of your house."

"I'm coming with you. Besides, Juno seemed fine when we arrived. Wouldn't she have acted anxious or barked more?"

"Yes," Henry said grimly. "Let's go."

Maia followed Henry, her gaze darting back and forth, but nothing seemed out of place except her door. She recalled locking it.

"Does someone else have your key?" Henry asked when they'd done a circuit of her house and found nothing unusual.

"I have two house keys on my keyring. I've been meaning to separate them." She pulled out her keys to show him, then stared in consternation. "My spare isn't here."

"Did you have them during the attack?"

"I grabbed them to unlock my door to get outside. Oh! You think whoever attacked me took my spare while I was unconscious?"

"That's exactly what I think." Henry sounded grim and pissed. "We'll change your locks this afternoon."

"Perhaps they were watching and saw us leave."

"Yeah. The alarm didn't go off, which means no one entered your house."

Maia bit her lip. "It wasn't Samuel. He was in the cafe."

"Exactly, so either he organized this, or it's someone else entirely."

"I don't think Samuel would do that. He prefers to control every situation, which is why my leaving him cut so deep." She scowled. "Why is this person hassling me?"

"I don't know, but they were lucky Juno didn't crash through the door and take them out. She would've tried."

"What should I do? I can't keep looking over my shoulder." The throbbing in her skull took on a deeper intensity, and she lifted her hand to massage the nagging pain. "I have no idea what this person wants or what imaginable crime I've committed to earn this attention."

Henry reduced the space between them. He embraced her carefully, the puppy between them. His silent comfort made her wilt, and her fight seeped away. She had deadlines and needed to train. She'd worked hard to get this contract, determined to succeed because her aunt had told her she was useless and unworthy, that her parents would've been ashamed of her. Part of her worried her little-girl memories of them weren't accurate, her views from the lens of a child rather than the adult she'd become. No! She refused to let her persecutor sway her for the same reason she'd forbidden herself to succumb to her aunt's machinations.

Her parents had chosen a school for her and set up the trust, making some matters non-negotiable. They'd cared enough to do this should anything happen to them. They'd loved her as much as she'd loved them.

"Maia, I can't be here with you all the time. What would you say to staying with me? There's always someone around. We have excellent security. Give yourself time to recover from your concussion." He drew back a fraction when the puppy whimpered. "This puppy will require patience and constant attention until she gets comfortable. It would help me if you could watch her."

Maia wanted to argue, but he was right. She would constantly look for threats. "Just until I recover and can play again." She didn't verbalize her fears that this might set her back and that she'd remain on the bench.

"Good." He grinned, and her breath caught. "I didn't think you'd agree so easily. Just so you know, I'm inviting you to stay in my apartment. I have a spare room."

Her brows rose, her spirits lifting. "And if I want to share your bed?"

His smile broadened. "I'd love that. We can set up a workspace once you're healed."

"Thank you." She glanced at her front door and barely suppressed her shudder. "Do you think this person is following me around? Watching me? I didn't notice anything."

"Neither did I," Henry said, his manner turning grim, "but that's something we should consider. I'll call Laura and she can question Samuel if he's still at the station. You pack your bags. We'll organize new locks for your front and rear doors. Your window locks require replacement."

Maia hesitated before nodding. "Let me know the costs, and I'll reimburse you."

"You don't need to pay. We have the materials in stock."

"It's important to reimburse you. For me, I mean."

He stared for long seconds, measuring her determination. "Okay, but you get parts at cost. My labor is free."

She lifted her chin. "In exchange for helping to look after the puppy and cooking and cleaning during my stay."

He capitulated immediately. "Deal, but your headaches need to subside first. I can tell you're in pain. You pack while I scout around and check on your car. I'm also curious to learn if the vehicle parked in the lane. I'll take the puppy with me and leave Juno with you. Lock the door, okay?"

"I will." It was an easy promise. The thought of someone creeping around her house was bad enough, but entering her property, presumably with malicious intent, left her shaky.

Henry kept his shit together until after he did a quick scan inside

Maia's house and left her packing a bag and Juno watching over her. She'd given him the key, and he locked the door after telling her he wouldn't be long.

The puppy had gone to sleep, pressed close to his chest.

His wolf's growl built inside his chest until his entire body vibrated. He wanted to shift, to track. He wanted to pounce and bite and rip this imposter into pieces. They were threatening his mate! The growl finally emerged in a low rumble that surged up his throat. The puppy stirred, and Henry strode down the driveway, the rapid steps helping him tamp back his anger.

"Shush, little one," he murmured.

When Henry reached the sideroad, he scanned the crushed grass. If he and Laura hadn't bagged every sweet wrapper, it would've been difficult to tell if a vehicle had parked here today. He discovered a paper cup that had recently held coffee. It was from a fast food chain, the nearest in Dunedin. Of course, that didn't mean much. It could've come from anywhere, but there was another sweet wrapper.

Henry plucked his phone from his pocket and called Laura.

"Henry, what's up?" she said, brusque as if he was interrupting her in an important task.

"The front door of Maia's house was open when we arrived and one of her keys is missing. She locked the door when we left. I watched her do it. Also, I'm at the site where we think the culprit parked. There is an empty coffee cup and another sweet wrapper."

"It's not Maia's ex unless he has someone helping him. I'll ask and watch his reaction. Did they do any damage inside?"

"We left Juno at the house because we weren't expecting to be away for long. We think Juno scared the person off. Nothing else appears out of place apart from Maia's flat tire. There's no further damage that I can see."

"Leave the cup and the sweet wrapper in situ, and I'll collect them later after I finish processing Samuel. Charlie and I hadn't had our morning tea break, and we get mean if we don't refuel."

Henry suppressed his chuckle. Good on them. He hadn't taken to the arrogant man either. "Maia is staying with me while she recuperates."

"Excellent idea. Text me if you find any damage, and I'll take photos when I remove the cup and wrapper."

"Thanks, Laura." He shoved the phone back in his pocket and returned to the house. He did a circuit and breathed a sigh of relief when he discovered nothing out of place. It hadn't escaped his notice that Maia was barely holding it together. He suspected her head injury bothered her more than she let on, and he was pleased she'd agreed to stay with him.

He knocked on the door and called out when he unlocked it, not wanting to take her by surprise. She appeared in the kitchen with an overnight bag, three books, and Juno on her heels.

"Did you find anything?"

"Someone parked in the sideroad again, but other than that, everything is fine."

Maia nodded. "I need my laptop and notes. These are the books I need to deliver to Samuel. If I've forgotten anything, I can pick it up later."

With every door and window locked, they climbed into Henry's vehicle.

Henry detoured back to town and gave Laura the books to give to Samuel before heading to his place. Everyone was home when Henry pulled into his regular parking spot. While he'd kept Gerard appraised of what was happening, his other family members were clueless, and he steeled himself for teasing.

After letting out Juno, he circled his vehicle and grabbed Maia's bag and laptop. Maia exited, carefully holding the puppy. The main door opened, and his stepfather stood in the doorway, a welcoming, if quizzical expression on his face.

"Son, how are you?"

Henry grinned, especially when Jacey's gaze zoomed to Maia and back to Henry. "Dad, meet Maia. She's staying with me to recuperate after a head knock. Maia, this is my stepdad, Jacey Anderson."

She stuck out her hand, and Henry caught the moment extra awareness entered his father's gaze. A wolf like Henry, Jacey could smell their interwoven scents.

His dad's mouth twitched, but he said nothing to make Maia uncomfortable. His father would have questions because bringing a human into a shifter household posed difficulties. They'd need to take care Maia saw nothing incriminating.

"Come in," his father said.

"Thank you, Mr. Anderson."

"Call me Jacey," his dad said, drawing her inside. "We're having a late lunch in the kitchen. Come and join us."

"Sure, Dad," Henry said, the twinkle in his stepfather's bright blue eyes confirming the upcoming teasing. Understandable, since he never brought women home. "Let me get Maia settled and her belongings stowed. Can you mind the puppy for us? We won't be long." He took the puppy from Maia and handed it over to his dad. "She's nervous because someone abused her."

"I could have kept her," Maia protested.

"She needs to become used to all of us," Henry said. "We want her to gain confidence."

Jacey stroked the puppy's head, and she settled quickly under his calming influence. His werewolf heritage eased the puppy's fears, but Henry could hardly tell Maia that. Not yet. He wanted to make this a permanent relationship and hoped Maia felt the same.

"She might want a toilet break," Henry said.

"I'll take care of it while you get Maia sorted." His stepfather's brows rose with silent questions, and Henry shook his head. He received a quick nod of acknowledgment, telling Henry his stepfather understood. Curtail all shifter talk and behavior for now.

Henry guided Maia down the passage, not stopping to say hello to his family. A sense of urgency drove him—a compulsive need to see Maia in his rooms amongst his possessions. Perhaps the wolf in him pushing the mate bond? He wasn't sure and merely followed his instincts.

Henry opened his suite door and ushered Maia inside, his breath easing out when no one came chasing after them.

"This is beautiful," Maia said, her surprise evident. "I didn't expect this gorgeous teal focus wall."

"London helped with the decor," Henry said. "I told her what I wanted—comfortable furniture and open spaces. I wanted stained wood floors, and she suggested the enormous rug."

"It's so tidy."

"Army training. Gerard is the same."

"Which is your room?"

"We're still sharing?"

"Yes."

The faint band of pressure around his chest dispersed, leaving happiness in its wake.

"This way." His steps were lighter as he guided her to his bedroom. Henry's room was at the rear of the house with views over the valley. He'd chosen floor-to-ceiling windows to enjoy the view, but no one outside could see him. A sliding door opened onto a private verandah with a wooden table, bench seat, and two matching chairs to relax in while savoring nature. Juno was already there, snoozing in the sun. Two steps led down to a grassy plateau where he'd sometimes play with his dogs or let them run around while he watched. It was also the site of his vegetable garden.

His bed was massive since he was large and enjoyed his comfort. The covers were cream, while his pillows were a steel gray. He also had a gray rug draped across the end of his bed, which his mother had purchased during her travels before his birth. His mother had

143

been a keen photographer, and he'd framed three of his favorite photos of him in his wolf form and him and Jacey, also in their wolf forms, in a forest. They hung above his bed.

"Which side of the bed do you sleep on?" she asked.

"The middle," Henry replied.

"Works for me. I'll take this side. Bathroom?"

"Through that door over there." His gaze affixed to her arse, faithfully outlined in tight black denim. Ah, this woman. Despite already making love with her, he wanted her with an intensity that vibrated through him. Not that he could act on that need now. His dad and the others would expect them and...

"Wow! I love it." Maia appeared in the doorway. "Your shower is decadent. I'll disappear in there and never come out. And your hot tub. That must be amazing, sitting in that and watching the view."

"We get stunning sunsets. The hot tub is the perfect place to relax and enjoy them."

"Ooh! I can't wait for that. The heat should help my leg. Where is your kitchen?"

"This property comprises three accommodation suites and a shared kitchen and den—where we ate dinner the other night. We take turns cooking, and that's where we entertain if we have dinner guests or visitors. Our suites are private, and we've decorated them to suit our individual tastes."

"How does that work for you? Most people wouldn't want to live so close to their parents."

"Gerard and I set up the business, and Dad came to help. We work well together, and the housing situation suits us. Gerard is my best friend. The soundproofed suites are entirely private. Once I step into my room, I don't hear or see anyone. We've lived here for a few years, and it works."

Maia smiled, her blue eyes as bright as Jacey's. "I think it's fantastic."

Henry reached for her hand. "How is your head?"

"The pain is a dull ache. I'll take another tablet to help shift it."

Henry leaned closer and kissed her. A hurried press of lips, but he was aware of the ticking time clock that was his nosy family. Smiling, he drew back and maintained the clasp of their fingers. "Let's go."

CHAPTER 17

U pon entering the kitchen, they found Jacey, Megan, London, and Gerard seated at the table, enjoying pikelets with jam and cream. A large, bright yellow teapot sat in the middle of the table, along with a milk jug and a sugar bowl. Everyone turned as one, and Maia's steps faltered. Henry tugged her to an empty seat.

"You've met my stepdad, and you know Gerard and London," Henry said. "Maia, this is Megan, dad's wife." He dropped into the seat beside Maia. "My stepmum."

The blonde woman snorted. "London mentioned a new arrival, and I've been looking forward to meeting you. Congratulations on your rugby contract. Your family must be proud of you."

Maia's answering smile suddenly didn't fit her mouth. "I...um...don't have any family left. My parents died years ago, and my sole remaining relative—an aunt—died last year."

"I'm sorry to hear that," Megan said. "I was a rugby commentator, so I'm interested in your rugby career."

"How did you and Henry meet?" Jacey asked.

"Dad," Henry rumbled. "We met years ago. Maia went to school in Middlemarch."

"Oh," Megan said. "That's nice."

There was a long pause that turned a little uncomfortable, puzzling Maia. What had created this weird vibe? She cast about for something to say, but Gerard spoke first.

"Have you decided on a puppy name? You know Levi will take charge the moment he gets home from school. He'll want to play with him or her."

"Her," Henry said. "She's nervy and not up to rough play yet. That's why Maia is staying with me. Someone attacked her, using this puppy as bait. For now, we decided it is best if Maia doesn't stay alone."

"You poor thing," Megan said.

"Oh, Maia. That's scary," London said.

"Thanks for having me," Maia said. "Since the attack, I've jumped at every noise, which isn't conducive to recovery."

"Would you like a cup of tea?" Gerard asked.

"Yes, please." Maia caught silent communication between Gerard and Henry and thought Henry seemed grateful for the interruption. Then she intercepted Jacey and Megan's sly grins and understood. They were ready to tease Henry, and Gerard had stepped in to divert them. Given the older couple's gleefulness, this was only a temporary cease-fire.

"You didn't mention the puppy's name," London said.

"Because she doesn't have one yet," Maia said. "We're waiting to see if she shows her personality."

"You need a name that means white," Jacey said. "Something like Bianca or Alba."

"That's not a bad idea, but Bianca might be difficult to shout quickly if she's naughty." London studied the pup, curled into a tight ball in a makeshift bed in a box. "Alba is easy to say. What do you think?"

"I like it," Maia said.

"Alba it is then," Henry said.

Maia accepted a cup of tea and a pikelet. After the kerfuffle with Samuel and at home, she and Henry had missed lunch. Emily's cheese scone seemed a long time ago and hunger gnawed at her. London shunted the cream and jam toward her and refilled her own cup.

"Henry said your team sidelined you until you recover. I'm sorry to hear that, even though it's the best thing," London said. "You can't fool around with head injuries."

Maia slathered raspberry jam on her pikelet. "I need to recover fast. I'd hate to lose my contract."

"When I first met Gerard and Henry, my sister's ex was stalking her," London said. "I know exactly how you feel, but you're safe here. Nobody will get past our security."

"Thanks," Maia said simply. Losing her fitness was another worry. Every time she moved too fast, her head thumped. She could hardly train when she felt like that.

Megan seemed to read her mind. "I've been attending Isabella's yoga class. We do gentle stretching, which might help with your fitness. The next class is a few days away on Thursday."

"Thanks," Maia said. "My friend, Bryce, swears by the stretching class he takes. He plays rugby for his local club."

Henry listened to Maia, Megan, and London discuss training and stretching, a sense of buoyancy filling him. He enjoyed seeing her interaction with his family. His good humor evaporated when he heard the front door open, and seconds later, a blond wolf slunk into the room.

He nudged Jacey. "Levi is home. He needs to stay in two feet."

Jacey was in motion before Maia noticed the new arrival, and Gerard, seeing the problem, went into diversion mode.

"What are you doing with the land that comes with your house?" he asked.

"Felix Mitchell is grazing it for me."

Levi must've smelled the puppy because he gave a yip of excitement and shot past Jacey, avoiding Henry's outstretched hand. The boy loved animals and helped Henry to train his security dogs. He was a natural.

"Oh," Maia said. "Where did he come from?"

"Levi must be home and let out a pup," Jacey said with admirable calm. He stepped forward, grabbed Levi by the ruff, and exited the kitchen with long strides, Henry on his heels.

Damn, this wasn't how he'd wanted Maia to learn about his dual identity. They needed more time. *He needed more time.*

Jacey took Levi to the kennels before he set him down. Juno arrived, and the other dogs let out a friendly chorus of welcoming barks. Henry opened doors to allow them into the exercise area before he returned to Jacey and Levi.

"Shift," Jacey said in a stern voice.

A tremor went through Levi as if he'd suddenly realized he'd messed up. Henry felt sympathy for the boy because he recalled the energy that had sizzled through him when he'd been younger. His enthusiasm sometimes meant he'd forgotten the rules.

"Levi," Jacey said, a faint edge to his voice, but when he met Henry's gaze, he winked.

Levi shifted, the process taking long minutes because he was a child, but finally, he stood pale and naked in front of his father.

"Where are your school clothes and your bag?" Jacey asked. "Your mother will be cross if you've lost them again."

Levi shook his head, his blond curls bobbing while his blue eyes held a trace of pleading. "I left them by Henry's car."

"Did you test the air for strange scents before you ran inside?"

149

Jacey asked.

Levi gave a solemn nod. "I smelled family and Henry's lady and a puppy! Is the puppy for me to play with? Can we run together?"

Jacey's brows rose, his gaze connecting with Henry's. Humor lurked in his dad's eyes. "Henry's lady, huh? I got that scent, too. Wanna explain, son? Especially the bit about knowing Maia from years ago."

Henry didn't bother with evasion, but he did glance at Levi.

"Levi, why don't you get dressed and take your bag inside? You can say hello to the puppy. Her name is Alba, and she might be frightened because someone was mean to her and she got hurt. She needs you to move slowly and talk softly until she trusts us," Jacey said. "Can you do that?"

"Yes!" Levi bounced on his toes, his grin broad and his expression one of excitement.

Jacey's hair might be gray now, but Henry saw the resemblance to Levi. "Go along now and remember to stay in two feet while Henry's lady is staying with us. She doesn't understand shifting, and we don't want to scare her."

"Okay!" Levi raced away, leaving silence apart from the odd yip or bark from the exercise paddock.

"What's up?" Jacey asked.

"Maia has trouble. Someone graffitied her house and tried to enter. We think Juno scared them off. They've also attacked her, using the puppy to lure her outside."

"She's your mate."

"Yes." Henry closed his mouth, but he needed to tell Jacey what was happening with him and Maia. "I met Maia when she was a child on a school trip to visit the dogs."

"Ah! You recognized she was your mate, and it scared you rigid. Now everything makes sense. I thought you were mourning Jenny, and you were, but Maia threw you a curveball."

"She was a kid! Even now, there's an age gap between us."

150

"I haven't seen her before. How is that?"

"She spent a few months in Middlemarch before she went to a boarding school in Auckland. She recently returned and purchased Beatrice Ramsay's property."

"Ah."

"She told me she wants me," Henry blurted.

"And knowing you, you tried to fight that. Can't fight nature, son. I tell you this from experience." He sobered. "Few shifters are lucky enough to have two mates. She seems like a nice girl. Treat this as a gift. You feel something for her. Otherwise, she wouldn't have taken on your scent."

"But she's still young. She should be traveling and exploring life. Living it instead of settling with me," Henry said, the words painful even if they held the element of truth. She'd barely left university and had her entire life before her.

"Have you asked what she wants?"

"She says she wants me." Even now, this bewildered him. Her certainty that they belonged together.

Henry was afraid. *There! He'd admitted it.* With someone intent on causing trouble for Maia, this situation tossed him back into the past—Jenny's murder and the horrid aftermath of jail and depression.

"I worry about history repeating itself if the person harassing Maia has something worse in mind. I'm not strong enough to face that again."

"Aw, son." Jacey embraced him, sharing his strength and force of character. "When your mother died, I thought my life over, but my responsibility for you pulled me through the dark times. Then I met Megan, and my life took another turn. Now, I have a larger family: two sons who make me incredibly proud. I have a mate who challenges and loves me despite my faults, and through your friendship with Gerard, I have a third son and a daughter. I feel exceptionally rich to have you all in my life. Your mother wouldn't have wanted me to live my life alone. She told me so before she died, even though it wasn't something I wanted to hear. London would tell you her sister wouldn't want you to live in misery. You need to embrace this miracle."

"And if something happens to Maia?" Henry asked in a hoarse voice. "How do I keep going?"

"First, we know someone is after her. Are Laura and Charlie aware of the problems?"

"They are."

Jacey nodded approval. "You were right to bring Maia here. It will allow her to settle and give you time together. You'll see if she fits. I like her, Henry. You can be a grumpy sod while she is a ray of sunshine. She'll pry you out of your rut."

"Thanks, I think."

Jacey clapped him over the back. "I'll help you feed the dogs, and we'll go inside and relax with our family. Movie night tonight."

His dad was right. When he and Jacey reentered the house, the three women were chatting while preparing dinner. Levi was holding the puppy, stroking her while doing his reading homework with Gerard.

Henry's gaze went straight to Maia. She appeared relaxed and happy, laughing as much as London and Megan.

"Dad, we're having pizza tonight, and then we're watching a movie!" Levi shouted.

The puppy yelped, and Levi immediately soothed her, calming her before Henry could chide his younger brother for shouting.

"Hey, what did I say about using your inside voice?" Megan said.

"Sorry." Levi went back to his reading aloud.

The evening gave Henry a glimpse of an enticing yet scary future. He had to remember Maia was safe with his family, and second, they knew someone was messing with her. They wouldn't let down their guard.

During the movie, Henry wrapped his arm around her

shoulders, drawing her against him. She settled without complaint, and Henry spent the entire time savoring her warm weight against him. Maia yawned as the closing credits ran, and Henry stood.

"Good night," he said. "Maia needs her sleep."

"I can stay up longer," she protested.

"No, Henry is right," Megan said. "You need to get on top of your headaches, and sleep will help."

"Good night," Maia murmured, her protests ceasing.

Henry directed her out of the den toward his room. He shouldered open his bedroom door and closed it after them.

"They're right. I am tired," Maia said with a yawn.

"Then come to bed."

"It's still early," she complained.

"I want to be with you," Henry said, halting further protests by kissing her.

"Mmm," she said. "Perhaps I'm not as tired as I thought."

Henry drew off her sweatshirt and the T-shirt she wore beneath. Soon, she was naked, and he lifted her, carrying her to the bed. He scrambled out of his clothes, tossing them on the floor, which he wouldn't normally do. Right now, he craved touch. He wanted Maia in his arms. Reassurance they trod the same path.

Maia ran her hands over his shoulders and kissed his neck. Every part of him pulled tight at the innocent touch on his marking site. If Maia had been a wolf, this was where she'd bite to claim him as his mate. Eventually, he'd claim Maia in this manner once he'd told her about his otherness.

"I like your muscles," she said with another yawn.

"I like your curves," he countered, and she laughed.

They kissed lazily, their mouths mating and tongues tangling as their passion rose. Henry caressed her body, savoring every possessive stroke while his inner wolf reveled in touching and taking on her scent and her taking on his.

Their lovemaking was languid, with no urgency, just a shared need for each other. After ensuring she was ready, he grabbed a condom from his nightstand and rolled it on.

"Thank you," she said. "I'm on contraception but appreciate the extra safeguard."

He kissed the tip of her nose. "Protecting you is no hardship. I want you to return to the team and earn your place in the starting fifteen. We want nothing to impede that." And he meant every word. No matter how careful a couple was, an accidental pregnancy was always a possibility. He didn't want that for them. He wanted Maia to follow her dreams. It was the least he could do.

Henry parted her legs with his knee and kissed her deeply before he situated himself and pushed inside her searing heat. He set a slow pace, savoring her and the way she clung to him, making him feel as if he were the most important man in her life.

The only man.

His wolf's growl rippled through his mind, loud and possessive. For a moment, he wondered if the sound had been audible when Maia's nails dug into his shoulders. She trembled, and his strokes faltered.

"Henry, don't stop. Please."

His next kiss was fierce and full of yearning. He wanted this woman at his side. Maia was determined, and his grumpy nature didn't faze her. She challenged him, made him want more. She filled the dark places in his soul.

He resumed his rhythm, taking cues from how she moved against him. He kissed her neck, his teeth grazing her skin, and this time, it was he who trembled when she dragged her tongue over the mating site. He wanted to claim her with every fiber of his being. Henry forced himself to lift his head and kiss her shoulder instead.

He'd never dishonor himself in that way. Maia needed facts and, at the right time—the truth.

"Henry, where is your mind drifting? Focus." Her eyes were

enormous and almost black in the room's darkness.

"I don't want to lose you," he confessed, because that was the root of his thoughts. He'd lost Jenny and couldn't lose Maia to a madman as well. "Recent events have me concerned."

"They disturb me too, but let's make love and forget our problems."

He kissed the spot between her eyes where worry dug into her forehead. "Sorry. I won't let it happen again."

"See you don't."

Henry claimed her mouth, kissing her slowly and thoroughly. She sighed, her fingers digging into his biceps. He surged into her, this time allowing the sensations to sweep him away. Her touch. Her heat. Her decadent scent. He adored everything about this woman, and she seemed to return the sentiment.

His measured thrusts into her body stimulated her pleasure. This time, they both shuddered, and Maia gasped. Her warm flesh clung to his cock, clasping and clenching as she hurtled into pleasure. She arched into him, letting him slide deep, and then he was gone too, incinerated and turned inside out, his growl of satisfaction more wolflike than he preferred.

Maia stilled against him, and Henry tensed, waiting for questions. Instead, Maia laughed, her body shaking against his.

"You've been spending too much time with your dogs. You even growl like them."

Henry released a relieved sigh and gave in to the urge to kiss her again. He couldn't get enough of her mouth. Long moments later, he separated their bodies and rose to deal with the condom. When he returned to the bed, Maia was sound asleep. Her lips curved in a soft smile, and her hair fanned across his pillow.

She looked like a perfect angel. His angel—as long as he didn't make any mistakes.

CHAPTER 18

The next morning, Maia bubbled with energy, her headache absent. A glimpse of her watch shocked her. Nine. She never slept this late.

The entrance swung open, and Henry stepped in, holding two mugs.

"You're awake. How do you feel?"

Once she sat up and propped a pillow behind her, he handed her a mug. Tea, she discovered when she took a cautious sip. She smiled at him. "I feel great. The world doesn't seem so fuzzy, and I don't have a headache. I could train today."

"No," Henry said without hesitation. "Take off the week. Don't push too hard or too soon. We can go for a walk this afternoon. Gentle exercise is better."

Maia's instinctive protest subsided. "You're right," she said with a heavy sigh. "But I worked hard for this contract. I feel like it's slipping from my grasp."

Henry sat on the bed, his expression full of sympathy. "We'll walk to Sutton Salt Lake. Have you been there?"

"No."

"Excellent. We'll take two or three dogs and put them through their paces. Maybe do a little kissing and cuddling because it's a quiet place."

"Kissing and cuddling, huh?"

"Yeah." He rose. "What would you like for breakfast? We had scrambled eggs and bacon, and I kept some aside for you."

"I'd like that." She hadn't eaten much, hadn't wanted food. Today, she did.

"Get dressed and meet me in the kitchen."

"Where is everyone else?"

"Levi has gone to school. Dad and Gerard are installing a security system. London is at a meeting, and Megan is in her office writing. She writes in the mornings when Levi is at school."

"You should've woken me."

"You needed sleep. It's helped since you've lost your pinched look. Ten minutes," Henry said and exited the room.

Maia finished her tea. Henry was right about pushing her training. She'd have less chance of making the starting team if her stupidity sent her backward.

She showered, then dressed in jeans and a long-sleeved shirt to combat the cold, the last of summer vanishing into autumn.

Breakfast was delicious, and she enjoyed every mouthful. She spent the morning pottering around with Henry, helping him with his dogs and on a security job. Although the lure was strong, she kept away from her laptop and resisted reading or anything that might make her headaches and blurry vision return.

That set the pattern for the next week, and finally, it was time for her doctor's appointment. She sat in the team doctor's surgery with Henry at her side. She'd asked him to come at the last moment. He'd looked surprised but hadn't argued. She'd wanted someone to hear the conversation. Maia had no idea why, but she'd followed her instincts.

"Ah, Maia. You're looking much better. How are the headaches?" The doctor appeared in his late thirties with short black hair, probing brown eyes, and a calm yet impassive manner.

"I haven't had a headache for days," she said.

"Blurry vision? Nausea?"

"None. I'm feeling good."

The doctor gave her an assessing glance. "I'll clear you to train, but it should be non-physical. Begin slowly and use honest assessment. If any symptoms return, cease activity and come to see me again. I'll let the team know they can ease you back into playing after another week. The coach knows what to do. You'll play for short bursts and not for the entire game. The object is to get you back to full fitness without setbacks. Do you understand?"

"Yes," Maia said.

"Excellent. Call if you have questions. Your coaches and manager know the program for players recovering from a concussion."

Maia stood, pleased with the positive outcome. "Thank you."

She and Henry left the surgery.

"Do you need any supplies while we're here? There's a mall nearby where Megan and London stock up."

"I'd like to purchase a decent coat—a waterproof one for our walks."

"Let's go, then."

During the next week, Maia kept in contact with her coaches and attended their first team game as a spectator. It rained for the entire match, and she was pleased with her new coat. It kept out rain and cold, as did Henry, who created a barrier.

"Your thoughts?" she asked after they said goodbye and headed to Middlemarch.

"My honest assessment?"

"I expect nothing else."

"Your team isn't playing as a unit. They're talented players, but they're not gelling. They didn't pass the ball. It's like they're worried a teammate will score instead of them."

"And because they're not team players, only the opposition are scoring."

"Exactly." Henry cast her a sidelong glance. "Why are you asking if you saw that?"

"I wondered if it was my imagination or if I truly was seeing the problem."

"It's the first game. The players need more time."

"Perhaps," Maia said.

"Are you attending training next Tuesday?"

"Yes, I'm ready to go. Eager." She slid him a look. "I should move back to my house. It's time to attack the lawns and make the place presentable."

"Already done," Henry said, sparing her a glance as he navigated traffic. "Jacey, Gerard, and I mowed your lawn yesterday. I meant to tell you, but we got distracted. I enjoy having you in my bed. Are you sure you need to leave?"

"Megan and London are probably tired of having me around."

"They like you."

"The funny stuff has ceased. You haven't discovered more sweet wrappers?"

"Not a one, and I've been looking. Laura and Charlie do drive-bys."

"They do?"

"They're excellent cops and care about Middlemarch's residents."

"My time at Middlemarch wasn't happy as a child. My aunt—she hated me. Resented me, but everyone has made me welcome."

"Why? You were just a child."

"My aunt and her mother disapproved of my parents' relationship, and they tried to break up my parents. My mother was pregnant when she married my dad, and his family accused my mother of trapping him. I don't know how much of what I heard was true, but my aunt became bitter. After my parents died, she took her frustration out on me. My dad had possessed money and put it into a trust for me. My aunt couldn't touch it, and once she learned that, she made my life hell. I'm grateful to my parents for their foresight. The money provided me with an excellent education and kept me, mostly, out of my aunt's clutches. But the way my parents constructed the trust, she had a say in what courses I took, and she pressured me to take accountancy. I have a degree I don't use because I hate spreadsheets."

Henry looked askance as he turned onto the main road. "But she left you her house?"

"She left it to charity, and they put it up for sale." Her grin felt decidedly impish. "I bought it because I imagined her spinning in her grave. That makes me petty, but she made my life hell."

Henry barked out a laugh. "I'm surprised you wanted to return to Middlemarch."

"A little was revenge, but once I received my contract and needed to find somewhere to live, I thought of Middlemarch. It's an okay commute, and the countryside appealed. When I looked at the properties for rent and sale, I saw my aunt's house. I made an offer, and they accepted. It had been on the market for six months, and they were glad to be rid of the house. I got a fantastic deal."

Silence fell between them, and Maia stared out the window at the passing scenery. The shopping center gave way to warehouses, then private residences. Soon, they were driving through the green countryside with hedges obscuring the view.

"When considering Middlemarch, I thought of you and your dogs." She frowned, recalling the slight yearning that had twisted her heart. It hadn't been like her to sign the contract without a viewing, but since it passed an inspection, she had. The house's condition hadn't been terrible. Sure, the kitchen needed remodeling, but it was liveable.

"I'm glad you came," Henry said, breaking into her musing.

"The first time you spotted me, you ran away." She studied him, fascinated when a faint tide of red swept up his neck. Maia thought he'd ignore her comment, but he slowed the car and pulled over on a wide shoulder.

"You're much younger than me. You're at an age where you should go to parties, interact with different people, and learn what you want from your life. I'm past that stage." He closed his eyes as if steeling himself to continue. "I'm happy with where I'm at with my business and my life."

"But you're lonely."

"Yes, but that's not a good reason to force you into a mold of my design."

Maia chortled. "Listen to yourself and credit me with intelligence. Middlemarch is full of smart women creating opportunities for themselves. Megan writes her books. London has her online admin and her committee work. Isabella is a powerhouse and does varied things from personal training to fitness classes and helping Caroline in her dress shop. Then there's Emily with the cafe. Emily is one with her finger on the pulse. That husband of hers might be big and strong, but he's putty in her hands. Those are a few of the local women I've met, and I wouldn't call one of them dull or stuck in a mold."

"I want children," Henry said.

"So do I, but not right away. I intend to play rugby as long as I can and my dream is to play for the Black Ferns. My plan is for about five years of rugby before any children. You'll still be young enough to run around with your sons and daughters. Jacey is a fantastic father, and there's a huge age gap between you and your stepbrother."

Henry released a chuckle and shook his head. "Levi was a surprise for Dad and Megan. Not planned."

"But everyone in the house loves that little boy. He's blooming. Our kids would do the same."

"I'd like to think so." Henry restarted his vehicle.

Maia stared. There was something he wasn't telling her. She considered pushing, but something pulled her back. Now wasn't the time. Their relationship was new, and she learned things about Henry every day. No, she'd bide her time and let events fall as they may, even though her curiosity would turn rampant. She liked puzzles, and solving them was her specialty.

CHAPTER 19

The first training session with her team was strange. The girls acted standoffish. Maia shrugged it off and continued the drills, listening to the coaches' advice and learning their different plays and set pieces. The team captain played the same position as Maia, but Maia was flexible, not minding where the coaches put her.

After a two-hour session, which Maia was pleased she'd come through easily, the two coaches called them together.

Cameron took the lead, reading from his clipboard while Rose jogged toward her car. "Our next game is on Sunday afternoon in Wellington. I'll read off the team and the three reserve players."

Several girls, including their captain, let out celebratory cries when Cameron called their names.

As Maia expected, she was on the bench. The doctor wouldn't clear her for an entire game for a while.

"If I read out your name, drop by the coaching office before you leave, and we'll issue your travel documents and schedule. Superb session, everyone. You're working together. That's what we need on Sunday. If you see an unmarked player in the clear, pass. None of this ball hogging." Cameron's mouth firmed as he scanned faces. "This is a team game. There is no *I* in team."

Once the coaches left, some grumbled about his comments.

Maia ignored this while wishing the girls were more accepting of the new kid. Her Auckland team hadn't been this cliquey and had socialized off the field. Maybe she would invite everyone to her place for a barbecue and drinks. If she asked, perhaps they could try the obstacle course London had told her they had used for a zombie run. Yeah, she had plenty of room, and the girls could stay the night if they wanted.

She'd ask Henry for his opinion and speak with Isabella and London. She could invite her Middlemarch friends. Use the party as a housewarming exercise.

Maia trailed the team into the dressing rooms. Steam, floral shampoo, and feminine chatter filled the air. Maia decided to shower later and changed into warm track pants, a dry T-shirt, and an old university sweatshirt before packing her dirty clothes.

"See you on Sunday," she called, smiling brightly.

A few girls shouted farewell, but the majority continued talking amongst themselves. Maia maintained her pleasant expression and left, making her way to the coaches' office.

"Maia, wait up!" someone called.

She turned to spot two teammates.

"Congrats on making the team," one said, her brown eyes full of sincerity. She ran a hand through her short black curls. "I played like crap last week, so I'm not surprised I'm staying home. My frustration with the team erupted."

"I watched the game," Maia said cautiously. "We didn't look like a team."

"It was a shitstorm," the second woman said. She had long red hair in a tight braid. She played in the winger position, her speed impressing Maia. "The coaches will knock us into shape. Especially since they've shown they intend to pick the team on form."

"I'll be glad if I get playing time. The team doctor wants me easing into games," Maia said.

They reached the office, and the first woman waited while Maia and the redhead collected their travel details.

"Jan, you played well on Saturday and deserve a place on the team," Rose said as she handed over an envelope. "Maia, you've obviously followed the doctor's instructions."

"Thank you," Maia said, accepting her envelope. "I'm looking forward to moving past the concussion restrictions."

"No headaches?" the coach asked.

"Not for the last week."

"See you at the airport," the coach said.

"I'll be there," Maia said.

"We're going for coffee," Redhead said. "Do you want to come?"

"Thanks, I'd like that." These girls were extending friendship, and she needed to reciprocate. They walked to a cafe near their training ground. The girl behind the counter greeted them with familiarity, and Maia figured they were regulars.

"We'll take our usual," Redhead said.

The girl turned to Maia. "What would you like?"

"I'll have an Americano and one of those date scones." She paid for her order before joining the two women at a table near the window. "I should confess I've forgotten your names," she said.

The two women laughed.

"I'm Jan," the redhead said.

"Rebecca," the dark-haired woman said.

"Someone said you live at Middlemarch," Rebecca said, interest in her voice. "How come there instead of moving to the city? You came from Auckland, right?"

"I have family ties in Middlemarch, and my boyfriend lives there." It gave her a thrill to claim Henry as her boyfriend.

Jan nodded. "That makes sense. How long is your commute?"

"Around an hour, depending on traffic. Travel times in Auckland are much worse, so an hour doesn't seem bad."

"Middlemarch is small, right?" Rebecca asked.

"Yep, a country town. Lots of single farmers looking for lovely wives," Maia added with a wink. "I was thinking I might invite everyone for a barbecue. What do you think?"

"That's a marvelous idea, especially since some team members act like mean girls. You have done nothing wrong. Don't let them get to you," Jan said.

"All I want is to play rugby," Maia said. "I love the game. The girls are stupid if they think they can win games by playing individually."

"Preaching to the choir," Rebecca said. "I'm looking forward to seeing if we improve after training today. It felt better. What do you think?"

Maia shrugged. "Training differs from game time where the opposition is unpredictable."

"True," Rebecca said with a glance at her watch. "I'd better get moving. I need to pick up my daughter from daycare."

"And I'd better get to the supermarket," Maia said. "If I don't stock up on groceries, I'll go hungry. Thanks for inviting me."

"Good luck for the game," Rebecca said, standing. "I intend to work hard to make the team for the next game." With a wave, she and Jan left.

Maia arrived home almost two hours later and found Henry and Juno waiting.

"Hey, how did training go?"

"I'm on the team," Maia said, allowing her excitement to show. "I'll be coming off the bench and won't be on the field for long, but I made the team."

Henry wrapped his arms around her. At that moment, she finally felt as if she'd arrived home. She pulled back to beam at him. "I'm glad to see you, but why are you here?"

"If you're determined to stay, I wanted to change the locks and beef up your window security."

"As long as you charge me for doing the job," Maia said.

"You qualify for special rates." Henry's voice was flat and determined. "Pay for the materials, and we'll call it quits."

Juno nudged Maia's leg, her eyes beseeching, and Maia ruffled the dog's ears. "All right, but I owe you dinner. Whatever is your favorite, I'll cook for you."

"Roast beef," Henry said. "With roast vegetables, Yorkshire pudding, and lots of gravy. And a dessert. Something hot with custard or ice cream."

"Wow, a man with opinions," Maia said, not bothering to hide her amusement.

Henry didn't crack a grin, his visage shaped in his usual stoicism.

"That's a deal. You'd better show me what you've done. Let me unload my groceries first." She'd bought fresh fruit and vegetables along with two steaks, a chicken, and a piece of salmon. This time, she'd purchased cans of food and packets of pasta she could use for meals during a time crunch.

Henry made light work of her bags of groceries and lingered in the kitchen while she put away the perishable items.

"I'll leave Juno with you. You'll find a bone in the bottom of your fridge, a bag of dry food in your laundry, and her dishes. I left a couple of toys since she loves to play."

"She has made that clear," Maia said with a laugh. "Thank you. I won't turn down your offer since she's brilliant company."

"I wish you'd stay at my place," he said, pinning her with his brown gaze.

"Henry, nothing has happened for over two weeks. No one has spotted loitering strangers, and I want to work and renovate the

167

interior. Besides, you're away for a job. Your family doesn't need me loitering when I have my house." It was an old argument that had run its course, but she needed to solidify it.

Henry's displeasure dug into his features, but he didn't argue. Wise man because she was obstinate and determined to get her way.

"Let me show you what I've done." He pulled a set of keys from his pocket and handed them over. "I've changed the entire lock. These are the keys, and might I suggest you separate them?"

A flush filled her face at her rookie mistake. "I won't do that again. Why don't you take the spare? We'll be together often, so you having a key makes sense."

He nodded before pointing out the chain he'd installed. The windows' locks made outside entry difficult unless someone broke a window.

"Thank you," she said, truly grateful because she'd feel safer when alone. "What time do you want dinner? I wouldn't mind a training run first."

"Would you like company?"

His phone rang, cutting in on her reply. Henry frowned as he checked the caller ID and answered. It was a work call, and she meandered to the kitchen to finish unpacking her groceries. Afternoon sunshine lit the kitchen. Plants would look fab on the windowsill. Herbs because she loved Italian dishes and fresh basil made them sing. *Plan*. Maia hummed as she stacked cans in her cupboard, enjoying the minor act.

"Maia, I'm sorry, but an urgent job has come up, and I need to sort it out tonight. Can I have a raincheck on dinner?"

"I understand work comes first."

With two rapid steps, Henry crossed the room and pulled her close. His mouth crashed down on hers, and his arms tightened as he kissed her passionately. Maia groaned, leaning into him and relishing being the focus of this intensity. A whirlwind storm of emotion.

When he lifted his head and released her, her knees wobbled. Maia lifted her hand to her tingling lips.

"Wow," she whispered.

"Look after my rugby girl." He brushed his knuckles across her cheek before striding from the room.

Juno drifted to the door, and Maia slowly followed. She waved goodbye and decided a run would settle Juno, and after a shower, she'd work on her book.

Later that night, Maia sat watching television with Juno sprawled at her feet. She'd chosen to watch the BBC version of *Pride and Prejudice*, a show she'd seen countless times, but she enjoyed the witty banter.

She was about to watch the third episode when a foreign sound intruded. At first, she thought it was the nearby cattle, but the noise moved location. Juno bounded up, her head cocked. She barked when a loud groan broke the silence.

Maia's pulse jumped, and her fingers curled into the chair cushions. "That is not a cow."

The wail, which sounded ghostly, came from a different direction, and fear spiked in Maia. This time, she wouldn't go outdoors. With a trembling hand, she dialed Laura. To her relief, the call connected immediately.

"Laura, It's Maia Jacobs. Someone is outside my house, playing spooky moans."

"Stay on the line. Charlie and I will arrive soon. We'll come in silent and block the lane where the person has been parking. If we're lucky, they'll think they're safe there."

"We hope it's the same person," Maia muttered. It had never occurred to her she'd have problems when she moved to Middlemarch, and she was an author who enjoyed writing and reading creepy scenes.

"Did you call Henry?" Laura asked.

"He's away on a job."

"On my way. Can you still hear the noise?"

Maia jumped when a throaty laugh cut through the air. It was spooky, and the hairs on her arms and legs stood to attention. "Y-yes. It sounds like a creepy clown from a horror movie."

"Almost there," Laura said, her manner calm.

Maia inhaled sharply but couldn't prevent the tremor that sped down her body. She was so tired of this...this stalking. It would be a relief to fly to Wellington and avoid her problems. At least for a day.

"I'm pulling up in the side lane now. Charlie's already here. Hang tight. We'll be with you shortly." Laura disconnected, and Maia listened to the tone for long seconds before tucking away her phone.

The clownish cackle repeated, and Juno barked, her attention fixing in a different direction. Maia listened intently and started when a crash came from the rear—a window breaking. She swallowed hard. Instead of investigating the broken glass, she crept to her front entrance and unlocked the door but left the security chain in place.

She couldn't see anyone. Juno scratched at the door, clearly wanting to go outside. Laura appeared in Maia's thin line of vision. Maia removed the chain and opened the door. Juno sprang out and sped into the darkness before Maia could restrain her.

"Is that one of Henry's dogs?" Laura asked.

"Yes."

The clownish noise pierced the night, and Laura frowned. "That sounds like a horror movie."

"That's what I thought," Maia said as the evil laughter tailed off.

Juno's bark cut the taut silence. A masculine shout.

Laura glanced at Maia. "Stay there, and if you see anyone, lock yourself inside." Then she sped into the darkness, the bob of a torch showing her progress.

"They went that way!" Charlie shouted.

Maia watched the torchlight veer to the right. Seconds later, a car engine roared.

"Damn it, they've gone." Laura sounded nearer. "Did you see them?"

Laura and Charlie came into sight, and Maia straightened.

The clown cackled its evil laugh.

"Where the hell is that coming from?" Charlie demanded. "It's damn creepy."

"That's what I said," Maia muttered. "I heard a crash from the rear of the house. A broken window."

"Stay there while we check it out. Shout if you see anyone," Laura ordered.

"You'll hear me scream," Maia said dryly. "Half of Middlemarch will hear me. Did you see where Juno went?" Maia was worried about Juno. She'd hate to tell Henry she'd lost his dog. His favorite.

As if she'd sent a message, Juno appeared from the darkness. She ran to Maia, and Maia petted her, full of relief.

Laura trotted around the corner of Maia's house. "Can I check your window? It's too dark to see the damage." Laura's tone had her warning antenna pinging.

"What's going on?"

"Not sure yet. We need light."

Maia led the way to the rear bedroom. Her steps slowed, and she halted in the doorway, reaching around to flick on the light. Her gaze went straight to the broken window and she let out an *eep* of alarm before her eyes and her brain caught up.

The upper torso of a skeleton, decked out in a clown's costume and curly red wig, was halfway through her window. It even had a red bubble nose on its leering face.

She took an involuntary step back. "Who does that?"

"They appear to be working to a theme," Laura said. "The laughter was evil-clown from a horror movie. I'm impressed. This prank shows planning."

"Laura," Maia chided. "They scared me half to death."

"You didn't see anyone?"

"No, the creepy music started. It moved, which means someone had a portable speaker and wandered to give me a surround sound effect."

Laura snorted. "That's one way of putting it. Charlie, you still out there?"

"Yeah. Do you want me to pull it out?"

"Let me take photos first." Laura whipped her phone from her pocket. She snapped several shots before shouting at Charlie to do the same.

Once they'd taken evidence, Charlie pulled the clown skeleton back through the window.

"Let's get the entire effect," Laura said, and they headed for the front door.

Maia opened the door to find Charlie leaning against a verandah support, his arm around the clown skeleton and wearing a broad grin. "How do you like my mate?"

"Not much," Maia said. Someone wanted to scare her. "He'd look better dressed in a tutu."

Laura let out a laugh. "We don't have any use for it; we have evidence photos. Why don't you use it as a scarecrow?"

"I could have fun with the skeleton. Could you take a photo of me and the clown so I can send it to Henry? He won't believe this. Actually, on second thought, could Laura be in the photo too? Then Henry will believe me when I tell him I did everything right."

Laura nodded approval. "I like to keep two steps ahead of my husband."

Maia led the way inside. "We should take this inside in case the person is watching."

"I agree," Laura said.

"Would you like tea or a coffee before you head out?" Maia ran her hand over Juno's shoulder, and the dog leaned into her. Juno seemed calmer now, which told Maia the person had left.

The two cops shared a glance.

"That would be great," Charlie said. "Why don't we do the photos first?"

To Maia's surprise, their photo session was fun, and the chuckles and laughter dispelled her residual fear. Once they were done, she sent the photo to Henry and told him she'd call in the morning. She also added she'd had an issue but Laura and Charlie were here.

"Henry will call and demand answers, but I'll sort out a hot drink. Tea or coffee?"

"Tea for me," Laura said. "If you have peppermint, great, but normal tea is fine."

"I'll take the same," Charlie said. "Either peppermint or regular. I bet you get that call from Henry in five minutes flat."

Maia's phone chirped. "Henry," she said.

CHAPTER 20

"Henry, we're flying back immediately after the game, and I won't be alone. Besides, nothing has happened since the skeleton."

"No headaches or concussion-related problems?"

"Not a one. I've attended three training sessions. My coaches seem pleased with my progress."

Her words didn't appease the big man.

Maia reached over and placed her hand on his knee. "Give me a goodbye kiss for luck. I'll see you later tonight."

"Please watch over my rugby girl." He jumped out of the driver's seat and rounded the hood to stand by her door. When he opened it, he said, "I want a proper kiss."

Maia climbed out straight into his arms. Their lips met, and he kissed her—an incredibly sweet kiss that had her wanting to beg him to come with her. Except he couldn't, and they knew it.

"Play smart. Look after your head," he ordered. "I'll be waiting in the terminal when the plane lands."

"Thank you." She gave him a swift kiss before grabbing her gear bag. "I'm nervous even though I won't play for long."

"You'll do fine," Henry said in a gruff voice.

With a wave, she shouldered her bag and hoofed it to the terminal entrance. As she'd expected, she found her team members and coaching staff gathered in the terminal.

"Ah, there you are, Maia," Seth, the team manager, said. "We're boarding in thirty minutes."

Maia accepted the boarding pass. She smiled at the girls standing around her. Some met her gaze, but few returned her friendly smile. Her stomach plummeted, and disappointment spread. Being the new girl wasn't easy, but she hadn't expected overt hostility. No, that wasn't the right term. The girls were more standoffish.

"Maia!"

Maia turned to spot Jan and smiled.

"Are you nervous?" Jan asked.

"Yes," Maia said.

"I'm petrified. I've been to the restroom twice since I arrived," Jan confessed. "It's always like this before a game. If I'm not panicky, that's a bad sign."

"It's my first chance of game time for a new team. I'm ultra anxious." Maia scanned the other girls, who were all chatting while waiting for the last two players to arrive. "Is it me, or are the girls acting aloof?"

"A bit of that and game nerves. We played badly last week, and the coaching team has shown they will reward form players. That brings pressure and competition for team spots."

What Jan said made sense. She would've asked more questions, but the two tardy players arrived, and they moved to the boarding gate as a group. The flight was uneventful, and Maia spent her time proofreading one of her manuscripts on her e-reader before she sent it to her editor.

A bus waited for them at the airport, and as Maia expected, the place they were playing was off the beaten path. Spectators stood around the edge of the field instead of sitting in a stand. The changing rooms were drafty, making Maia glad she'd donned her playing gear beneath her tracksuit before leaving home and didn't have to strip and get cold. She'd bet the showers had limited warm water, and there'd be a battle royale to get to them post-game. She'd shower at home.

Game time arrived, and the two teams jogged onto the pitch. Maia sat on one of the deck chairs provided for the coaches and trainers and wrapped a coat and a blanket around her knees. The charcoal gray sky told her she might end up playing in the rain.

The referee's whistle blasted, signaling the start. The opposition kicked the ball, and everything turned to custard. Their player—Maia couldn't remember her name—dropped the ball, knocking it on and giving the opposition team an advantage.

Rose, sitting beside her, cursed softly, not taking her focus off the run of play. Maia groaned because the girls were fumbling the ball like rank beginners. Nerves? Or pressure? Maia didn't know, and that was up to the coaches to fix.

The opposition team capitalized on their mistakes and scored a try in the corner, to the delight of their supporters. They cheered and banged a drum in celebration. The kick to convert the try hit the upright and bounced off. The spectators groaned and shouted encouragement.

In the next set of play, Jan caught the ball, dodged a tackle, and fended off another player before going down. Her run steadied their team, and they played better, stringing together runs that took them close to their goal line.

"That's more like it." Rose jotted in her notebook.

Maia saw their players relax after several better passages, but her team got sloppy instead of focusing and working out how to get through the opposition. Amanda threw a pass that telegraphed her intentions. One of the opposite players intercepted the ball and charged toward the goal line, dotting down beneath the posts.

"And it's a try to the Wellington Ravens," the commentator cried.

Maia gave a silent groan, but the two other bench players weren't as tactful.

"Wow, she's always telling us how talented she is, and she makes a rookie error," one whispered to the other.

"These things happen," Maia said crisply. "We make mistakes. The challenge is to pick yourself up instead of spiraling into pity, losing your temper, or blaming someone else." At least Jan was playing well. One player, however, couldn't win by herself. Jan did everything right, passing when necessary and taking the ball to ground when required.

Unfortunately, the other girls held grudges, and tempers ramped up. When the first half drew to a close, Rose and Cameron held grim expressions, and Rose had written screeds in her notebook. She gestured for Maia and the other two players to follow her.

Maia steeled herself to listen to a blasting from the coaches, and as soon as they reached their dressing room, the concise bullet points dissecting their first-half game came in quick succession. They were playing as individuals rather than a team. Their ball handling was sloppy. They were letting the opposition rattle them. Set-piece play had gone by the wayside. They were kicking too much and needed to hold the ball.

"Megan and Harriet, you're on for the second half."

The two players who'd sat with Maia stripped off their gear and ran outside to warm their muscles before they jogged onto the field.

"Kathy and Wilhelmina, you'll come off. Everyone else—watch

177

your ball handling. Use kicking as a last resort, and start playing together. Pass the ball if you can, but use our set plays if you need to take it to ground. Jan and Zara, good game. Keep up the excellent work. Maia, I'm going to sub you on with about twenty minutes to go."

"Okay," Maia said, excited to have confirmation she would play. Getting the first hit-out behind her would be reassuring. Then, she could focus on improving and slotting into the team.

"I'll give you instructions once the second half begins," the coach said.

"Yes, Coach," Maia said.

The break went fast, and soon, the two teams trotted onto the field. The referee's whistle blew, and the game commenced.

"Oh, heck," Rose muttered. Beside her, Cameron bit out a pithy curse.

Maia gaped at Amanda, their captain, who'd thrown a punch.

The referee sounded his whistle and plucked a red card from his pocket. Amanda scowled and stood her ground until Jan nudged her. Amanda stomped to the sideline where the coaches, Maia, and the two substituted players sat.

"Go to the dressing room and get changed," Rose said, her mouth set in disapproval. "Once you're done, come and join us." She turned her focus to the game in a firm dismissal.

Despite being short one player, the team started playing better with Jan issuing orders. They attacked and beat the opposition team back to their goal line.

"She's leadership material," Cameron murmured to Rose.

"Yes," Rose said. "Maia, start your warmup. We'll sub you in ten minutes."

Maia did some light jogging on the practice field next door. She stretched her limbs, and when the coach signaled her, she ran over and stripped off her tracksuit pants and jacket.

"Go in at number eight," the coach said. "Tell Liz to come off."

Maia nodded, pleased to play in her favorite position, and waited while Cameron signaled the referee that he was sending on a substitute player.

"Which number is coming off?" the ref asked as Maia trotted past.

"Number eleven." Maia ran over to Liz and told her the coach wanted her off.

Liz cursed and stomped to the sideline. Maia didn't comment but secretly thought the coach had made an excellent call. Liz's shirt appeared pristine, and she'd done little to help today. A few players were having worse games than the previous week, and Maia had no idea why when the coach had considered them skilled enough for the team.

She disregarded the thought and immersed herself in the game. Her initial contact with the ball passed without incident, and her nerves settled. It was a blast, and now that Jan was directing the game, the girls played with alertness.

The referee blew his whistle. A penalty for their team. Maia glanced at Jan and received a quick nod. She tapped the ball and started running, with Jan shadowing her. They surprised the opposition when they'd dithered through the rest of the game. Maia fended off an opposition forward and flew past with Jan still backing her and in the clear for a pass if Maia got tackled or blocked.

Her heart pumped, and her muscles strained as she sped toward the goal line. Then she was there and dived, dotting the ball down as a forward tackled. Too late! They'd scored.

Maia rolled away and sprang to her feet. In the next second, Jan and Zara had her in a fierce hug. The official raised his hand to signal a try.

Zara took the kick, and the ball floated through the goal uprights.

Yay! They were on the scoreboard.

The next fifteen minutes passed rapidly. Her team took heart from scoring and lifted their game, making excellent runs toward the opposition's goal.

The Wellington team scored a field goal, and Maia's team went into a quick huddle.

"Let's make the coach proud and try one of our set plays from the kickoff," Jan said.

Maia suggested one, and the girls nodded, each knowing their part.

Zara kicked off, placing the ball in precisely the right place. Their forwards rushed the receiving player, and the ball flew free. Maia seized it and set off toward the goal line. There was no one in front of her. She couldn't be this lucky. She didn't hear the referee's whistle and sprinted for the goal line. Then she was over in the corner. Not an easy kick. Since no one tackled her, she rounded and ran across until she could dot down under the goal.

The referee's whistle was the sweetest music. Although they wouldn't win today, they'd made the score more respectable.

Zara slotted the conversion, then the referee blew the final whistle.

Maia shook hands with the opposition players, congratulating them, while Jan and Zara did the same. Some of her team just walked off the pitch, making for the dressing room.

"Huh," Jan said, glancing after them. "Looks as if they're intending to have hot showers."

Maia left the field with Zara and Jan.

"Great game, girls," Rose said. "You did well, considering you played the last twenty minutes with one player down."

Maia noticed Amanda hadn't reappeared. Maia couldn't say whether she was embarrassed, but that sort of behavior was stupid. Amanda's punch had allowed the opposition team a penalty from which they'd scored, and Maia's team one player short. It would be interesting to see how the coaches handled this and if they stood her down as punishment.

The dressing room wasn't a happy place when Maia entered with Zara and Jan. They heard shouting and abrupt silence when they entered. Not one girl looked at them. Amanda picked up her gear bag and sauntered past.

Maia glanced at Jan and shrugged. Zara queued for the shower while Maia quickly washed with a flannel before dressing warmly.

Half an hour later, the team boarded their bus and headed for the airport. No one said much, and Maia wondered if she'd erred in taking the Dunedin contract. But no. Jan and Zara were great. So was Rebecca. She'd go ahead with her plan to invite the team to a barbecue once they won their first game. Amanda wasn't working as captain. They needed someone else. Jan, probably, since she'd had the girls playing more cohesively.

"We have an hour before we need to get to the gate," Rose said after she'd checked them in. "Don't be late because I'm not running around looking for you."

Jan wandered over to Maia. "Zara and I are going to grab a coffee. Want to come?"

"Sounds good."

"You played a fantastic game," Maia said once they'd settled at an empty table with coffee and a cake each. "I didn't like to say anything in the dressing room because the atmosphere was oppressive. Is it always like that?"

"Our team used to be superb. We played and socialized together, but the older players left, and the dynamics changed," Zara said. "It will come right. It always does. The coach just needs to get the right balance of players."

Maia blinked because, from where she sat, their team was a hot mess. She texted Henry before boarding the plane, letting him know they were on time and they'd lost the game.

A return text came. **How did you go?**

She understood what he meant. **No problems**, she texted back before pocketing her phone.

Maia sat with Zara and Jan on the flight home. They'd attended the same school as Rebecca and had come up the ranks together.

The plane landed, and Maia grabbed her bag. It didn't take long to deplane, and she spotted Henry easily.

"See you at training," she said to her new friends and with a wave, headed for Henry.

Henry didn't strike her as a demonstrative man, but he surprised her, grabbing her in a hug. "I was worried. I'm glad you came through the game unscathed."

She squeezed him tight in return. "What's for dinner? I'm hungry, and I can't wait to grab a shower."

"Didn't you have one after the game?" Henry asked.

"The showers were busy. I washed as best I could and dressed warmly. I am not used to the colder weather."

"Megan invited us to dinner," Henry said. "You can shower in my rooms and grab my clothes if needed."

"Are you sure?"

"If you're tired, we can stay the night at my place. I'll make sure you don't get cold."

His wink had her grinning, and she was still smiling when they left the airport for Middlemarch.

CHAPTER 21

"What are you doing today?" Henry asked, his deep rumble puffing warm air against her neck.

"I didn't know you were awake." Maia turned to face him and, on impulse, kissed his nose. "I need to work on my manuscript and get in some training. I'll hook up with Isabella if she's free. What about you?"

"I have a job in Roxburgh and a quote near Gabriel's Gully."

"Gabriel's Gully? That's where they first struck gold in New Zealand."

"Correct. You could join me, and we'll have lunch somewhere," Henry said.

"I'd love to, but I must train if I want to play a bigger part in next week's game."

"I understand." Henry checked the time. "It's my turn to cook breakfast. Levi is an early riser and creates havoc if he's unsupervised. Last week we had breakfast cereal over the counter and floor."

Maia laughed and rolled over to get out of bed. Henry stayed her with a hand on her bare hip.

"A good morning kiss, first."

Maia's thoughts turned to morning breath, but after dreaming about Henry for so long, she wasn't turning down a kiss. She sank into his embrace, and it ended way too soon.

"Any sore muscles after playing?"

"Nothing too bad, but I'll have a hot shower before I dress."

Henry stole another kiss and slid out of bed. He dressed with efficiency and slipped from his apartment. Maia stared after him, a tiny smile playing on her lips. She was halfway—no, maybe three-quarters of the way to falling in love with him. Every additional detail she uncovered intrigued her. There was a lot to like about the somber man.

After her shower, Maia changed into leggings and a long-sleeved training shirt. She pulled on thick socks to combat the cold. These chilly temperatures were not to her liking, and right now, she'd prefer Auckland's winter rain. She called Isabella and organized a training session before she found London and Megan in the communal kitchen, the men and Levi long gone.

"I'm running home to take care of business stuff before I hook up with Isabella," she said.

"Is that safe?" Megan asked. "Henry told us you had to call Laura and Charlie again."

A shudder ran through Maia. "Creepy clowns are best in a movie, not breaking into my house." She still had the skeleton and had decided to visit Caroline at the dress shop for help. "I'll take Juno. Besides, I'll have my phone."

"Henry won't approve." Megan took one look at her face and backpedaled. "Ah, not that he should tell you what to do."

"Exactly," London said with a grin. "Megan means we'll worry about you, given the things that have occurred."

"I'll keep the doors locked and have Juno inside."

"Ring us once you reach your house," Megan suggested.

"I can do that." Since she'd been alone for years, having people worry about her was agreeable. "Where will I find Juno?"

"I'll show you," London said.

Ten minutes later, she and Juno were on their way. Maia jogged slowly because, despite the hot shower, she sported a few ouchies. Now that it was later, it was a magnificent autumn day with a crisp blue sky overhead. The sun shone warmly on her back, and each breath emerged with a puff of steam. They followed the road, and her steady pace got them to her property faster than she'd envisioned. Her steps slowed when she neared her house, and she carefully scrutinized the vicinity. Nothing appeared out of place.

The big dog whined, its ears pricked.

She glanced at Juno. "I should check around the house before I declare everything normal."

She backtracked and walked a circuit of her section, pausing frequently to listen. When she saw nothing unusual, heard nothing except a cow mooing and birds tweeting, the tension that had invaded her body eased back.

Maia unlocked the front door and stood aside for Juno to enter. The naked skeleton stood in the kitchen corner, and she scowled since it still wore a clown costume.

"Let's get you a bowl of water and a treat then I'll get to work." She had two hours and fifteen minutes before her appointment with Isabella. Maia powered up her computer and immersed herself in a fae battle in an enchanted kingdom where everything was suspect.

A knock at the door had her head jerking upward. When the knock repeated, Maia cautiously approached her door. She peered outside to see a woman, her face obscured by pink flowers. Maia glanced at Juno, but she didn't bark or growl.

Maia opened the door.

"You are at home. I wasn't sure whether to leave the flowers or not. The order didn't specify. Are you Maia Jacobs?"

"Yes," Maia said, eyeing the flowers. Samuel had always apologized with flowers, and given that thought, she wondered if Laura was monitoring his whereabouts. She'd told Maia she didn't think he was responsible for Maia's problems, but she was keeping tabs on him through her police contacts.

"Then these are for you." The woman thrust the flowers into Maia's hands and retreated to her courier van.

A white card nestled amongst the pink flowers and green foliage. Maia marched into the kitchen and deposited the flowers on the table. Juno barked.

"Ah, yes." Maia returned to lock the door. "Thank you for reminding me."

With the door bolted, Maia plucked out the card. The flowers were charming, their perfume decadent. They'd look beautiful on the side table, but she wanted to know the sender. Henry struck her as practical. Organizing a courier to a country address would've been expensive.

She ripped open the envelope, annoyed to find her hands trembling. Three kisses in bold black writing were on the card. Nothing else. Maia shot the flowers an aggravated look and left them where they sat before returning to work. Unfortunately, her concentration had gone AWOL.

Maia made a cup of coffee and read her emails, answering fan letters before moving to her business email account. She'd underestimated how long these admin duties took and needed to look at hiring outside help, especially since rugby took more of her time.

London was the solution, especially since she already worked for Megan. She'd understand Maia's needs and require minimal training. Yes. She'd speak to London. Maia dealt with the three remaining emails.

She had time to visit Caroline's shop. The skeleton caught her eye, and she paused. Yeah, it might be easier if she took the skeleton and explained what she wanted.

"You want to what?" Caroline eyed the skeleton dubiously ten minutes later.

Beside her, Isabella cackled, the blonde personal trainer holding her side as if laughing were hurting her.

"I want you to design outfits for my skeleton. I'm going to stand him outside on my verandah," Maia said. "It will be a statement."

Finding Isabella here had been a surprise, but she remembered London or Ambar had told her Isabella helped Caroline during her free time.

"I thought a pink tutu would be fun and maybe a cowboy or no! A Mexican cowboy with a sombrero. A sixties housewife vibe might be fun, too, and I'll need a Christmas outfit."

"You're serious," Caroline said.

"As a heartbeat."

Isabella chortled again, laughing long and loud before controlling herself. "You should help, Caroline. You were wondering what to do with the scraps of material you have. Designing skeleton outfits might be fun. You'll need a Halloween costume."

"And maybe one for Valentine's Day and King's birthday. I thought I could post them on my social media pages." Maia didn't reveal she'd post under her author pen name, with no mention of her location.

"All right," Caroline said. "If you're pranking me, there will be trouble."

"No, I'm deadly serious. I'd also like you to design an evening dress for me. Something formal yet pretty to wear at an awards dinner."

"I'd love to," Caroline said, whipping out a tape measure. "I'll take your measurements now. Can you leave the skeleton?"

"Sure," Maia said.

She and Isabella walked out of the dress shop together.

"Laura told me your stalker dressed the skeleton as a clown."

"Yeah. I left the outfit at home."

"Creepy. How did the game go yesterday?"

"Despite the loss, my performance satisfied me. I evaded most tackles."

"Excellent. We'll continue with stretches and keep the workout light until your doctor clears you for vigorous activity."

When Maia arrived home, two parcels and a balloon bouquet sat on her doormat. The pink helium balloons danced in the breeze.

She edged past to unlock her door and peered inside. Juno greeted her, and Maia let her outside. Juno trotted around the lawn, sniffing until she found the perfect spot. With her business tended, Juno returned to Maia's side. Maia started to go inside but caught a white flash on the tree trunk several feet away. It was the same tree where she'd found Alba.

Maia took one step in that direction before reconsidering. She called Laura.

"Problem?" Laura demanded.

"I'm not sure. I've been out, and there are parcels and balloons at my door. There's another object fastened to the tree where I found the puppy. It seems innocuous, but I thought I should contact you. I wasn't expecting any deliveries."

"Touch nothing. Charlie's doing a coffee run. We'll be there as soon as he returns."

Maia left the parcels and the balloons where they sat and ushered Juno inside. She walked to the sink and poured herself a glass of water, her attention out the window. When she glanced back at her glass, she dropped it with a shriek. It shattered in her sink, splashing red liquid over her T-shirt. That was blood pouring from her tap. For a long moment, she gaped before turning the tap off with shaky hands.

"Well, I won't be drinking that water. Juno, we're checking the windows and doors to ensure everything is locked tight."

Laura and Charlie arrived, and she met them at the door.

"I've put your number on speed dial," Maia said.

Charlie's laugh faded. "Is that blood?"

Maia led them into the kitchen and turned on the taps. Red water gushed from the cold tap while the hot tap ran clear for long seconds before turning a faint pink.

"That's disturbing," Laura said, staring at the sink.

Charlie stuck a cup underneath the tap and sniffed the contents. "It doesn't smell like blood."

"You're on tank water," Laura said. "I remember seeing the tank out the back. We'll check it out. What else?"

Maia turned off the taps. "I received flowers before I left this morning. When I returned, the balloon bouquet and the other things were at my door. There's also something attached to the tree. After I called you, I checked the windows and rear door. I was going to have a shower next." She shuddered. "So glad I had a glass of water first."

Laura grimaced. "Ugh, showering would've been creepy."

Juno nudged Maia's leg. "Juno didn't seem worried when I let her out, but she probably barked when someone delivered the items to the door."

"Stay put. Charlie and I won't be long."

Maia watched Charlie and Laura photograph the items at the door before cautiously opening them. She sighed and checked her kettle. She had enough uncontaminated water to boil for a cup of tea.

"Juno, what is going on?" she asked as she pulled a mug from the cupboard. She dumped a heaped spoon of masala chai tea leaves into her green teapot and, once the jug boiled, poured the water over them.

Troubled, she plonked her butt on a stool at her kitchen counter and stared moodily out the window, watching Laura and Charlie by the tree. They were in an intense discussion, and Laura gestured toward the house. Charlie snapped several photos of the white thing—Maia presumed a note—attached to the tree. He plucked an evidence bag from his pocket before carefully removing the object and placing it inside. Meanwhile, Laura disappeared around the side of the house.

Maia stood to grab milk and added a little to her mug. She reclaimed her seat and poured a cup of tea. It was weak, but she desperately needed a hot drink to chase away the chill in her veins.

She couldn't stay here tonight, and it irked her that someone was driving her away from her home.

Maia stewed and sipped the tea, the tang of ginger, cloves, and black pepper hitting her palate. By the time Laura and Charlie appeared, Maia felt marginally calmer.

"Learn anything?" she asked.

"The cards on the items at the door say the same thing. The time is coming... It looks as if someone has tampered with the food items. We'll take them for testing. I don't think we'll get fingerprints, but we'll try. As for your water tank, the red is a combination of blood and food coloring," Laura said.

"Blood?"

"An animal is floating in there." Laura took a deep breath, and when she spoke again, her voice was frigid. "It looks like a possum that someone hit on the road."

"I agree," Charlie said, grimacing. "It looked flatter than it should."

Maia's phone rang, the screen display showing an unfamiliar number. "Hello."

A clownish laugh rang out, and a creepy voice crooned, "The time is coming, coming, coming!"

CHAPTER 22

I f the person tormenting her had wanted to freak Maia out, they'd done an excellent job. Even now, the following day, she was jumpy and constantly scanning her surroundings.

Maia couldn't focus at training, but to her surprise, the coaches chose her for the starting team for their home game in four days. Rose and Cameron were determined to play those who were in form. A thrill went through Maia. This was fantastic news.

Their coach continued reading out the names. "Jan, Zara, Rebecca."

Rebecca released an exuberant cheer.

"Thanks, Coach. I won't let you down," Rebecca said.

"See you don't," Rose said. "Jan, you're the captain. Amanda, Cameron and I want to speak with you privately once we finish here. Wait outside my office."

"Questions?" Cameron asked.

"What time do you want us to arrive at the venue?" one girl asked.

"One hour beforehand," Rose said. "Anyone late will go to the bench. Everyone, apart from Amanda, will get time on the field. Please bring your best game and impress us. If you need any further encouragement, the Black Ferns coaching staff is coming to watch this game."

Excited chatter burst out.

Rose smiled. "I thought that might please you. See you on Saturday."

Maia walked to the changing rooms with Jan, Zara, and Rebecca. Their excitement was infectious, but she had to force her smile. Somehow, she'd gained a stalker. A chill ran down her spine, and cold sweat covered her body. Her mind kept coming back to the why, and she was clueless.

"Earth to Maia," Jan said, nudging her arm.

Maia blinked at her new friends. "What?"

"You'd better not zone out like that on Saturday," Jan teased. "The coach doesn't give second chances."

"Sorry, what were you saying?"

"We're going for coffee at the cafe. Did you want to come?"

"I'd like to, but I have a water problem at home and need to get it sorted."

"The woes of a property owner," Rebecca said, full of sympathy. "I can't stay for long either, but I'll eat a scone on your behalf."

"Gee, thanks," Maia said when the other girls laughed as they entered the changing room.

"See you at the game," she said, zipping up her gear bag after her rapid clothes change.

"Bye, Maia," Jan said. "Coffee. Next time."

"Deal." Maia forced out a laugh that sounded surprisingly natural. With another wave and a smile at several other girls on her team, she exited the building. She thought for a few minutes, her mind going to Samuel. Without giving herself time to think, she dialed his number.

"Maia?" It was easy to discern his surprise.

She didn't bother with niceties. "Samuel, someone is stalking me. Is it you? Have you organized someone to harass me?"

"No! No to both questions."

She heard the honesty in his voice but poked a bit harder. "You came to Middlemarch."

There was a long pause. "Maia, I'm sorry."

She snorted inwardly, having heard his apologies before.

"I can be a dick sometimes, but it's not me this time. I'm dating someone else. I like her, and the parental unit approves."

Once again, she thought she heard truth in his words. "Okay. Thanks for speaking with me."

"I hope the cops discover the culprit. Maia, I'm not responsible."

Maia hung up, glad she'd made the call, although she was certain neither Laura nor Henry would agree with her actions.

When she arrived home, four vehicles were parked in front of her house. Maia stared at the youngsters kicking a soccer ball around her front yard, their high-pitched shrieks full of laughter and carefree fun.

She climbed out of her car, and one boy gamboled over to her. Levi.

"Hi, Levi. What are you doing here?"

"Dad and Uncle Gerard and Mr. Saber are fixing your water. We're watching the front of your house in case someone bad comes."

"Oh." Intense gratitude had tears welling in her eyes, and she blinked hard to clear her vision. "I can see you're doing an excellent job. Would you and your friends like juice and cookies?"

Levi nodded vigorously.

"Let me talk to your dad first, then I'll get your snack. Keep playing and guarding my house, okay?"

Levi jumped in the air, and when he landed, he loosed a shout resembling a wolf howl. Maia grinned and trotted around her house to the rear. She came face-to-face with Jacey. He looked scary but relaxed when he saw her.

"A birdie told me you might be working on my water problem," she said.

Jacey squeezed her in silent commiseration. "I'm glad you're staying with us while Henry is away. Whoever is doing this is unpredictable. No telling what they might do next."

Maia agreed. "How bad is the tank?"

Jacey's eyes flashed with anger. "Along with the dead possum, they tipped in bottles of red food coloring. We've emptied the tank and scrubbed it clean. Depending on what they used, we might need to empty the tank again."

"The dead animal?"

"Gerard buried it. At least it was already dead when someone tossed it into your tank." His jaw tightened. "Whoever did this is a disturbed person."

And she needed to be extra careful about security. If this person grabbed her, there was no telling what might happen.

"I promised Levi and his friends I'd give them juice and cookies. Is there anything you need me to do?"

"No, sweetheart. We have everything under control."

"Thank you." Maia returned to the front, unlocked her door, and let Juno out. The big dog licked her hand and immediately rushed to play ball with the kids. She chided herself for not doing that first as she turned off the alarm.

"Maia!" a shrill voice piped behind her.

She whirled to face the door.

Levi cocked his head, his forehead furrowed in a frown. "Did you not scent me?"

"Ah, no," she said, confused by his words. The boy didn't smell any worse than the others.

A gaggle of boys and one girl stood behind him.

"They don't believe you play rugby."

"I've come from practice. I can show you my muddy clothes and boots."

"That's not proof," the girl said.

"Tough sell, huh?" Some of Maia's gloom lifted. "I guess the only way to prove it is for you to see me playing. You'll have to ask your parents, but I have a game on Saturday."

"She has real boots with spikes," Levi said. "Dad said she isn't playing much right now 'cause someone hit her and gave her a concussion."

"Why didn't she scent them?" the girl demanded.

"That's enough of badgering Maia," Gerard said. "She might decide not to give you cookies."

There was a chorus of protests.

"You okay," Gerard asked. "I didn't call Henry, but you should tell him."

Maia sighed, knowing he was right. "Maybe when he gets home."

Two days later, in the early evening, Henry walked into his suite and smiled. It smelled like Maia. It smelled like home in a way it hadn't before. He found Maia in his lounge with her laptop on her knee. She was staring outside into the darkness, her mind far away.

"Hi, honey. I'm home," he said from the doorway.

She let out a screech, almost dropping her laptop. Wide blue eyes stared until her initial alarm subsided, and she recognized him.

"Maia?"

"Henry," she said, standing on noticeably wobbly feet and setting her laptop aside. "I didn't hear you come in."

"What's going on?" he said. "What haven't you told me during our phone calls?"

"I didn't want to worry you. Let's get a drink, and I'll tell you everything. And I need a hug. That would help big time."

Henry drew her against him, savoring her scent and her softness. He'd missed her and worried about her the entire time, thoughts of how he'd failed Jenny and repeating mistakes never far from his mind. She trembled, and anger built in him, but he kept it contained. His wolf struggled against his grip, wanting out. He wanted to rip and tear and destroy the villain persecuting their mate.

Instead, Henry kissed the top of her head and pushed her away with a smile. "Let's get that drink. What would you like?"

"Red wine, please."

Henry led her back to the chair she'd been sitting in when he arrived. He grabbed a beer for himself and poured a wine for Maia.

He sat opposite her and waited. She swallowed before she described the events of the past two days. Fury pulsed through Henry, although he hid his anger from Maia. None of this was her fault; she was suffering enough without him adding to her burden.

"The good news is I've made the starting team for our game on Saturday."

"Congratulations." She worked hard and deserved this chance. "Has the doctor cleared you?"

"They're still managing my playing time. It will be another week or two, depending on how I get through the next match. London and Megan are coming to watch me play. Will you have time to see the match?"

"I wouldn't miss it." Henry's phone dinged. "Dinner is ready."

"Oh, I meant to help with dinner prep," Maia said. "I didn't realize how much time had passed."

"You have a lot on your mind."

"Henry, what am I going to do? I can't live this way. It's impossible to concentrate on writing and difficult to focus on training. I keep wondering what will happen next. It's making me jumpy."

Henry set his beer aside and took her wineglass before tugging her to her feet. "You need to eat. You look as if you've lost weight. Other than that, we take one day at a time. Did Laura find any sweet wrappings?"

"I don't know."

If he got his hands on this person... "Did Laura check on your ex?"

"Yes, she has a friend keeping tabs on him. Samuel is attending a training camp right now. Bryce is there, too. A group of ex-soldiers runs it, and they confiscate phones. The camp is in the middle of nowhere, according to Bryce. Moewai. It's near Eketahuna. I don't think it's Samuel. I...ah...called him and asked him if he was responsible. He said no, and I believed him."

"You called him."

"Yes." She lifted her chin and met his gaze without flinching.

Okay. He hated that, but a part of him could understand Maia's need for answers. At least she hadn't approached the bastard in person. He ignored the internal growl from his wolf. "What does Laura think?"

"She is leaning toward an unknown person."

Tension slid through Henry, but he did his best to hide his concern. Maia was freaked enough now. He guided her toward the door. "Let's go eat."

Dinner, family-style, was a lot of fun. Everyone chatted about their day, including Levi. He told them about his rugby team and how hard they were practicing.

"I'm driving to Dunedin to watch Maia play," Henry said. "Anyone else want to come?"

"Megan and I are going," London said immediately.

"Can I bring my friends?" Levi asked.

Jacey grinned. "Looks like the entire family is going along with extras. I can't wait."

CHAPTER 23

G ame day arrived. The morning was frosty, but the sky was clear, and by the time Maia's team ran onto the field, the sun shone. It was the perfect day for playing rugby.

The loudspeaker crackled as the commentator introduced the team.

"Number eight, Maia Jacobs."

A loud cheer came from the sidelines, and Maia grinned and waved at Henry and his family. Wow, Saber Mitchell and his brother Felix had brought their families.

"Go, Maia!" someone shouted.

Tears pricked Maia's eyes as she spotted Isabella, her husband, and their son. As she scanned faces, it felt as if half of Middlemarch had come to watch her play. Her heart beat faster, and her hands trembled, but her smile was full of happiness. No one had ever supported her like this before.

"Quite the cheer squad," someone muttered, their tone snarky. Maia frowned, but the caustic player now wore a bland expression. She met Jan's gaze, and the other woman shrugged. Maia let the sarcasm wash over her. She felt fit and was ready to give one hundred percent effort.

The whistle blew. Maia focused and fell into the zone. Rebecca, Jan, and Zara were in top form, and they played more like a team.

Maia hooked the ball from the back of a scrum and fed it to the backs, the speed taking the other team by surprise. Jan crossed the line to score.

Maia leaped at her friend and hugged her hard. "Great job."

That was the first of their three tries. When the halftime whistle blew, they led 21-3.

"Excellent," Rose said. "More of that, please. Maia, you're off. Yvonne, you'll take her place." She mentioned two other position shuffles and offered advice. Then it was time for the second half.

Maia took the empty seat next to the reserves.

"How's the head, Maia?" Cameron asked.

"I feel great." And it was the truth.

"You played an excellent game. Check with the team doctor next week," Cameron said. "If you're not experiencing side effects, we can get you signed off to play a full game."

"Thank you," Maia said.

"Excellent game, but don't get comfortable in my position," Amanda said with a smile from the seat beside her.

Maia laughed. "I won't." The team was still playing well, although their backline had a hole, the player out of position. If she could see it, she was sure the opposition could.

Yep, they'd seen it, and one of their forwards surged through and scored a try.

Finally, the end whistle blew.

"A win. Not pretty, but we'll take it." Rose stood. "Good game, Maia. Keep that up. We'll see you at training next week."

Maia rose. "Thank you."

"Amanda, I want you to come to training. Make sure you get the sign-off from the anger management people; otherwise, you can't play once your stand-down period ends."

Amanda gave a stiff nod. "I let down you and the team. It won't happen again." With a wave, she set off for the car park.

Rose and Cameron followed Amanda off the field, and Maia jogged over to Henry and her cheer squad. Henry came to meet her, sweeping her into his arms. Levi was a few steps behind.

"Maia, you do play rugby," Levi said.

"I told you."

She turned back to Henry, but Levi tugged on her jacket.

"Maia," he said. "Will you help me train?"

Her gaze met Henry's, and he gave a tiny nod, telling her this would be okay with Jacey and Megan. "We can arrange that." He was still young, but she'd already noted how active the boy was. She thought he might keep up during a run.

"Yay!" Levi shouted and ran off to tell his friends.

Henry slipped his arm around her shoulders, and they ambled to their Middlemarch cheer squad.

"Maia," London said. "You were incredible. So fast!"

"That's my doing," Isabella said smugly, making everyone laugh.

"We're going for pizza," Jacey said. "Do you want to come?"

"Tell me where, and I'll meet you there. I need to collect my gear, and hopefully, the water is still hot."

The dressing room had emptied fast, and two shower cubicles were free. The girls looked almost ready to leave. Maia glanced down at her muddy knees and decided she might as well shower, even if the water was cold.

She set out her spare clothes and grabbed her towel and shower gel before stripping rapidly, aware of the ticking clock. The water was lukewarm, and she lathered up a washcloth with her orange-scented shower gel and washed away the mud. A loud crash made her jump, but she relaxed when no further noises sounded. Someone had dropped something. The wooden floors in here echoed badly.

She dried off with equally brisk efficiency, wrapped her damp towel around her, and after collecting her shower gel and washcloth, she exited the shower. Wow, everyone had left already. She hustled over to where she'd left her clothes and paused.

They were gone.

Everything.

Even her dirty gear.

Maia gawked at the empty cubicle. The empty bench. She checked her bag, but not a stitch of clothing lay inside. Her dirty boots sat underneath her bag, but even her socks had vanished.

She plucked her phone from the side pocket, thankful she still had a way to communicate her problem. Strange. The last remaining girls had left while she was in the shower. Was this a prank on the new girl? She called Henry.

"Hey, sweetheart."

Her stomach curled at his lazy greeting. "Henry, I have a problem."

"What?" The word emerged crisp and alert, and she imagined him straightening, his attention laser-focused.

"I took a quick shower, and when I returned, my clothes had disappeared. Every. Single. Item," she gritted out. "Everyone has left. When I find out who is responsible, I'm gonna speak my mind. This is beyond childish. And they took my playing uniform. I don't know if I can get another set." Aware she was rambling, Maia shut up, but she wanted to hit someone.

"Just a sec."

She heard him speaking to someone.

"Isabella has a spare set of clothes."

"Thank you," Maia said. "I'm gonna need an enormous glass of wine."

"We can do that. I'll drive Isabella over. Five minutes."

Maia spent her waiting time pacing, trying to work out who had done this. It had to be a team prank, didn't it?

A shudder worked down her spine. She'd been alone in the shower. Vulnerable.

A crash sounded, and she whirled toward the exit, prepared to run or fight. Do something. Another thump echoed through the changing rooms.

"Maia, are you here?" Henry sounded panicked.

Maia hitched her towel tighter and hurried to the entrance. "What was the banging?"

Isabella stood beside Henry, her beautiful eyes narrowed in anger. "Someone locked the door."

A frigid blast swirled through the opening, and Maia shivered.

Isabella thrust clothes at her. "Get dressed while Henry and I scout the area. If I find anyone skulking behind the trees and sniggering..."

She didn't complete her sentence, stalking from the changing rooms, but Maia got the gist. Isabella was infuriated on her behalf.

"Are you okay?" Henry asked, his brown gaze full of unconcealed emotion.

"Cold and angry that one of my teammates did this. It couldn't be the person messing with me at home. Could it?"

"I don't know, but you need to lodge a complaint with your team management. You're lucky they didn't take your phone."

"You would've come for me," Maia said, feeling this in her gut. "But you're right. As soon as I'm dressed and warm, I'll call the head coach. Rose can get things started."

"I'll be outside with Isabella. No one will get inside without us seeing."

"Thanks." Maia tugged on a pair of track pants and the matching sweatshirt Isabella had given her. Instantly, she felt warmer, but she couldn't stop shivering.

She scooped up her remaining possessions, packing them away in her gear bag. Thankfully, her pair of runners remained tucked under the seat where she'd left them, and she pulled them on. Henry and Isabella were waiting near the door, holding a hushed conversation. They broke off on noticing her.

"Did you want to go straight home?" Henry asked. "Everyone will understand if you do."

"No," Maia said. "I value everyone's support, and I want to thank them for coming to watch my game. I'm not letting this ruin my day. Besides, I want wine. I'm back from concussion problems, and that's something to celebrate."

"Let's go." Approval shone in Isabella's eyes. "They have a pizza calling my name."

The three of them walked into the restaurant. Levi spotted them first and let out a shout of welcome.

Henry chuckled. "My brother does nothing quietly."

"He's a kid and a boy. Noise goes together with those two things," Isabella said drily. "Kian thumps and hollers a lot."

No one blinked at her casual dress, everyone greeting her with smiles and hugs. After being alone for so long, she found emotion getting to her because this felt like a family.

Jacey had saved chairs, and Maia slid into one next to London. The children were sitting at a nearby table, engrossed in their pizza and chatter.

"Despite what you and Laura had concluded, I was sure the culprit was your ex-boyfriend, and he arranged for someone to persecute you while arranging for alibis for himself," Henry said and pulled a face. "History giving me tunnel vision. Now, I think this might have something to do with your team."

Everyone looked at Maia.

"Why? What reason could they have? We're a team. I'm a stranger, but I'm gradually winning the girls over."

"But, Maia," Isabella said. "Only someone in your team would know the inner workings of the after game routine. You weren't that much behind the other players. Why did the entire dressing room empty while you were showering? Unless you had a really long shower."

"The water was almost cold," Maia said. "I was five minutes tops because I hate cold showers."

"How many teammates were still in the dressing room when you arrived?" Jacey asked.

"Maybe five. It surprised me. Usually, there's a line for the showers."

The server arrived bearing two large pizzas, cutting into the conversation. At the next training, she'd ask questions, as would the coaches and team management once she'd made a formal complaint.

Megan and London handed out pizza slices, and everyone fell upon their meal as if they were famished. Maia savored the meaty, cheesy goodness as she tried to make sense of events.

The kids drifted over to their parents, and they cut the conversation short, but whoever was doing this was escalating. It was obvious the perpetrator was capable of violence. Torturing a puppy wasn't normal. This situation had gone beyond a prank, and she refused to ignore what had happened today. As soon as she got home, she'd call Rose. If the other girls hated her for it, then so be it.

CHAPTER 24

Henry pretended he was fine. He ate pizza, joined the conversation, but agitation swept him. What if he couldn't keep Maia safe? And was his new theory right? Would another woman act with such malice? So many questions. They churned through his mind and built fear upon fear, throwing him back to the time of Jenny's murder.

Maia's reentry into his life had plugged the massive hole in his heart, and he'd felt happier. More centered. Whole, but these attacks on Maia were getting to him.

"Henry," Maia said, jerking him back. "I'm heading home now. I want a hot shower and need to contact the coach. That will be a tough phone call because I'm accusing my teammates. No one wants to be a tattletale. I'll have to tell her about the other things happening." She stopped and swallowed hard. "What if Rose doesn't believe me?"

"One, you've reported everything to the police, and two, Isabella and I had to break the door to open it. The broken lock is there for all to see."

Her expression told him she expected drama, and she was probably right. A team game centered on trust and friendship. Those two things made a group into an individual unit. It was no different from his army days. They'd learned quickly if they didn't work together, one or all of them would end up dead.

"I'll follow you home," he said.

"No, stay with your family and friends."

"You are my family," he said with a wolflike growl that had everyone quietening. "If you haven't figured that out now, you're not as intelligent as I thought." *Wow, way to go, loser. That's sure to keep her at your side.*

He watched her carefully, not sure how she'd react. She blinked before poking him in the chest with her forefinger. "Did you growl at me?"

A snicker sounded, but Gerard choked off the sound at a glare from Maia. His green eyes, however, danced with amusement. His friend wouldn't let Henry forget this moment.

"It's okay for Levi to act like a wolf. He's a kid," Maia snapped. "You have no reason to snap and snarl like an animal."

Oh, man. There was a moment of acute silence before everyone burst into chatter simultaneously, trying to pretend they knew nothing about wolves and growling.

The furrow on Maia's brow grew deeper before she shook her head. "I'm leaving now."

"I'll follow you. Please, for my peace of mind, Maia. Jenny..." He shook himself and shut his mouth. Her eyes widened, and he saw the moment of understanding.

"Okay. Will we stay at my place or yours tonight?"

Relief that she wasn't intending to sulk or shut him out had him almost giddy. He gripped the edge of his chair and concentrated on breathing. "Mine, if that's okay. I need to exercise the dogs and feed them when I get home."

Maia nodded decisively. "I'll collect my laptop and a change of clothes from home and meet you there."

Henry didn't tell her that there was no way he'd let her stop by her house alone.

Later that night, he held Maia in his arms. She'd fallen asleep after they'd made love, but his mind remained alert and full of questions. They needed a plan. Maia's coach had sounded horrified, and he'd thought genuine. She'd promised to discuss the situation with management, and they'd take action if they discovered the culprit. Meanwhile, they'd need to tighten security at home. Maia would object, but maybe he could take time off work and surreptitiously trail her. At least then, he'd be nearby should she need help.

A blur of red flashed before his eyes. Hell, he'd been close to Jenny, and her ex had grabbed her so quickly she hadn't had a chance to escape.

He had to do as much as possible to protect Maia and hope that he'd be present when a confrontation came. Not that Maia was useless. She had a good brain and used it. She was a warrior. *His warrior.*

Yeah, he needed to use his brain like Maia had and ask for help. He'd talk to Laura, Gerard, and Isabella. He'd ask their advice and proceed with a plan. His heart told him this mightn't be enough, but it was a start. Other than rolling Maia in cotton wool, there wasn't much else he could do.

The next morning, he put his scheme into action. He spoke with Maia and told her of his worries.

She frowned. "Most of the stuff has happened at home—the attack and the nuisance stuff. Do you think I'm in that much danger?"

"All I'm asking is that you limit the time you're alone until Laura gets a handle on the culprit. They'll make a mistake soon. We have a fingerprint on one of the sweet wrappers."

"We don't even know if they're connected."

"True, but we've found them in several places around your house."

"I'll admit that's strange. Are we sure it's not kids?"

"We're not sure of anything," Henry said. "That's the worrying thing."

"I hate having my routine messed up. It plays with my head. Right now, my focus is on my fitness and meeting my looming deadline with my editor. Mostly, I'm training with Isabella when I'm at home. When I need to go to a team training, plenty of other people are around. I'll come straight home afterward. I'll travel light, leave my gear on the sideline, and tell the coach."

"And if it's raining?"

"I have a waterproof coat I can tuck over my bag to keep out the worst of the rain. And on a game day, I'll buddy up with players I trust. I can't do more than that other than ensure my phone is handy and charged."

Grudgingly, Henry agreed. He couldn't keep her prisoner to soothe his angst. But instinct whispered to him. His grip on his wolf loosened as fear sliced and diced, and his wolf took advantage, pushing out a frustrated growl.

"Will you cease growling?" Maia snapped. "It's annoying."

Henry stilled. His wolf went rigid inside him. And that was the next problem. How did he tell Maia he was a werewolf and all his friends were big cats? He hadn't even told Jenny before she'd died. He hadn't had a chance.

It wasn't something to blurt out on a whim. Before he confessed and potentially placed his family in danger, he had to make certain Maia intended to stay. That he was enough for her.

Yeah. Two massive problems, and he had no idea of how to solve either.

Half an hour later, he followed Maia's vehicle and stayed back so she wouldn't feel like he was crowding her. Worries churned through his mind, his possible failure to protect her uppermost.

She was strong and independent, and it wasn't as if she was stupid about security. Maia was doing everything right, yet his busy brain kept telling him of the things that could go wrong.

Hell, he'd be no use to her if he continued to behave like this.

His phone interrupted his frenzied thoughts. He connected with Bluetooth since he was driving. "Yeah?"

"It's Gerard. We've been making a plan and concluded that Maia needs to continue her everyday routine. She has her alarms and security when she's at home. We'll follow her in our animal forms when she's doing a training run. Set up a roster."

"But what if someone sees? Someone who shouldn't?" Henry asked.

"It's Saber here," Saber said. "I'll discuss it with the council, but London and I agree it's more important to protect Maia. She's your mate, and you deserve happiness. If the worst happens and there's a sighting, it will be an excellent test for our contingency plans. I suggest that everyone with big dogs takes an interest in exercise and the great outdoors. I'll ask Rory Henderson if his pack can help. Wolves will be less obvious than big cats. We'll also notify everyone in the shifter community to watch for outsiders. That will also test our phone tree procedures."

"Thank you." Gratefulness suffused Henry.

"You're an important part of the community," Saber said.

"It's me again," Gerard said. "Are you staying at Maia's place or home?"

"At home. Maia is stopping at her place to collect clothes and her laptop."

"Right, we'll see you later," Gerard said and hung up.

Henry followed Maia into Middlemarch and along the country roads until they reached Maia's house. The first thing he heard when he climbed out of his vehicle was the blare of the alarm.

"Crap," Maia said. "When does this end? I'll call Laura."

Henry prowled toward the house, and Maia grabbed his arm to halt him.

"Wait. Don't go without me. We shouldn't split up. Please."

Henry nodded, and while Maia spoke to Laura, he used his wolfish senses. His nostrils flared as he dragged scents deep into his lungs. Nothing jumped out at him, and his slow scan of the surrounding area showed nothing out of place. Now and then, he caught a hint of pungent turpentine. It was almost metallic and alcohol-sweet. Perhaps paint?

Maia hung up. "Laura and Charlie are on their way. She told me to wait with our vehicles. Five minutes, she said."

Henry cursed inwardly, even though Laura's orders made sense. Once they caught this person, and it was only a matter of time, they'd require evidence to prosecute. He didn't want to destroy proof of the crime.

"Can you see anything? Smell anything? Hear anything out of normal?"

Maia wrinkled her nose. "Apart from the alarm?"

Her sudden grin took his heart by storm. Everything about being with Maia felt right. Their relationship was of limited duration, but maybe he should tell her about his dual nature. There was always a chance she'd reject him, but she wrote fantasy fiction. At least she might be open to the idea.

"Yes, apart from the alarm," he said gruffly.

"I keep getting hits of paint, so art is involved."

"Yeah, I can smell paint."

The lights of a car flashed as it turned into the driveway. A police car.

The car parked beside Henry's, and Laura and Charlie alighted.

"The police car drives here on automatic," Laura said.

"I'm sorry," Maia said.

Charlie grinned. "Not your fault."

"Have you checked the alarm?" Laura asked.

"You instructed us not to touch anything, so we haven't moved," Henry said.

"Huh," Laura said to Charlie. "I didn't think that would work."

"I want this person or persons caught," Henry said. "And I suspect the culprit is long gone."

"Okay," Laura said. "Let's check inside before we walk around the outside. You know the drill."

Once they approached the front door, the damage was clear. Someone had smashed each window on the front and taken to the door with an ax.

Charlie whistled. "Someone is holding a lot of anger."

"I had a problem earlier," Maia told Laura about the changing room debacle.

Laura and Charlie exchanged a glance.

"It might be unrelated," Charlie said.

"Perhaps," Maia said.

Laura nodded. "Let's see if they got inside. Henry, could you turn off the alarm?"

Henry stepped forward. "Do you have your key?"

Maia handed over her keyring, and he unlocked the badly damaged door.

He stepped inside to disarm the alarm, his ears welcoming the sudden silence. The stench of paint was overwhelming. "They didn't get through the door but must've come through a window."

"We'll go first," Laura said. "Keep behind us and tell me if anything is missing or out of place."

"Someone had broken every window, and my door is full of holes. Is that the sort of thing you want me to mention?" Maia issued a harsh sigh. "Sorry, it's not your fault."

"Understandable," Henry said, reaching for Maia's hand and threading their fingers together.

Henry scanned the kitchen. The trespasser had pulled things from cupboards and dropped them on the floor in a heap. Sugar, flour, and macaroni noodles lay scattered on top of cutlery and a blender. Raspberry jam smeared the fridge/freezer doors.

"I hope my laptop is in one piece," Maia said, sounding close to tears.

They remained together, broken glass and other items crunching beneath their feet.

"Do you usually leave this door shut?" Laura asked when they approached the room Maia used as an office.

"Yes, it's my office," Maia said.

Laura nudged the door open while Charlie snapped photos of the damage in the kitchen.

Henry sniffed and caught a familiar sweetness. "Candy wrapper," he said to Charlie. "It looks like the same brand as the earlier ones we found."

Charlie snapped a photo.

"For fuck's sake!" Maia shouted.

Henry's gut roiled, and he hustled to join the women.

"Look what they've done to my laptop."

The screen and keyboard sat on the floor, separated into three pieces. Tears rolled down Maia's face, and he tugged her into his arms, holding her pressed against his chest. Her folders of notes lay in scattered piles, and everything Maia had arranged on shelves and on her desk lay scattered. Red paint covered the wall, the word *thief* prominent against the neutral cream wall.

"A lot of rage here," Charlie said from behind them. He took several photos from various angles.

"Any idea what they mean?" Laura gestured at the word on the nearest wall.

"No," Maia said.

"I'm still thinking it's someone connected to your rugby world," Henry said. "If it was, today's little prank would make more sense."

"You mean the players resent me for joining the team?" Maia said. "I won my spot by playing well and training hard."

"You know that, and we know that," Henry said, "but sometimes disappointment makes people do stupid things."

"Did you report the changing room episode to your team management?" Laura asked.

"Yes, they're going to look into it. My coach muttered something about juvenile pranks. This felt more than that to me."

"I agree," Charlie said, retreating. "Let's do a sweep of the rest of the house."

Henry let Laura and Charlie go ahead before he released Maia. "Do you have backups for your work?"

"I do on the cloud and on a backup device, but that's not the point. I'll have to file a claim, purchase a new computer, and go through setting it up. It's going to take time I don't have."

"We'll talk to Megan and London. They might have suggestions on how to get you up to speed fast."

Tears formed in her eyes, and one ran down her cheek. He thumbed it away, feeling useless and wishing he could make it all disappear.

She made a snuffling sound. "I'm sorry. These are angry tears. I feel like a punching bag, and everyone is taking a free shot."

"We'll sort this out and stop the culprit," Henry promised. No one should have to suffer this level of harassment.

"Maia. Henry." Laura's voice originated from Maia's bedroom.

"I don't want to know what they've done in my bedroom," she whispered.

Henry squeezed her hand, and she lifted her chin. His lady was so brave.

"Let's go," she said.

They walked down the passage hand-in-hand and halted in the open doorway of her bedroom. Henry cursed while Maia released a croak. "How could they?"

CHAPTER 25

"This is one disturbed person," Charlie said, distress coloring his expression.

"Alba?" Maia closed her eyes, but the vision of a white puppy lying on her sheets remained seared to her retinas.

"It's not Alba," Henry said. "This puppy has a patch of brown on its right front leg."

"Call Gavin. The puppy is still alive," Laura said.

Charlie hit a button on his phone and spoke in a low, urgent voice before hanging up. "Ten minutes."

"Maia. Maia!" Laura spoke sharply, dragging Maia's attention from the poor puppy.

"Y-yes?"

"Is anything missing or out of place?" Laura said.

Charlie busied himself, documenting the scene.

"Is that perfume I can smell?" Laura asked, looking at Henry while Maia carefully surveyed her bedroom.

"Yeah, but it doesn't smell like anything Maia wears."

"Maia, do you recognize it?" Laura asked.

"Yes, I do," Maia said slowly, her mind desperately trying to refuse this clue. "I've smelled that perfume in the changing room."

"Which team members?" Henry asked, his gaze intent.

Maia swallowed, betrayal an unbearable weight on her shoulders. "Two of the girls I'm friendly with—Jan and Rebecca."

"That sounds like Gavin," Charlie said. "I'll let him in."

Laura whisked a blue notebook and a pencil from her pocket. "Give me their full names."

"No, I can't believe either would do this." Maia wiped clammy hands on her track pants. "No, they wouldn't. I don't believe it. Torturing a p-puppy."

Henry took her hands. His expression was somber, brown eyes shining with sympathy. "If they're innocent, they have nothing to worry about. Laura needs to eliminate the possibilities. This person won't stop, Maia."

"Henry is right," Laura said.

Charlie rushed into the bedroom, with Gavin a few steps behind him. Maia watched the vet carefully handling the puppy and listened to his gentle voice.

"I have a team sheet in my office containing each player's full name and phone number. It was on my desk."

"We'll give Gavin room and try to find it. Do you have a team manager?" Laura asked.

"Yes," Maia said. "Seth Davies. I have his number in my phone."

"All right. I'll note that number, too."

A sick sensation churned in Maia's belly, and her legs trembled so much she had to clap one hand out to the wall. Ugh! She jerked her hand away and stared at the red, sticky paint. Tears blurred her vision as she puzzled over why someone would do this. That poor puppy.

Jan and Rebecca?

No, she couldn't believe they'd hurt her and the puppies. The vandalism. Numbly, she thought back. No, they hadn't been in the changing room when she arrived because her gear bag had been next to theirs. She frowned. Rebecca and Jan had friends and family watching them, so she'd assumed that had been why they'd collected their gear and left so quickly.

"Maia, we need to find that list for Laura." Henry's voice was gentle and full of sympathy. He understood her inner turmoil.

"Yes, okay."

When she entered her office, her gaze darted to her smashed computer, and anger combined with woe-is-me. She used her T-shirt to mop up her tears. "Um, it was on my desk." She bit her lip at the heap of books, the broken spines and loose pages—research items she'd collected over the years. Some were irreplaceable.

"Maia." Henry tugged on her hand to get her to face him. "This is bad, but it's only possessions. You can replace them."

"I know, but I have a deadline looming, and I have to fix this before I attempt to write."

"Contact your editor. Tell them someone vandalized your office. Say you need more time."

Maia snorted. "It sounds like a dog-ate-my-homework excuse."

Henry snapped a photo with his phone. "Send him a copy of the police report. You can email photos along with the report."

"I... Okay." Then, she nodded more decisively. "Yes, good idea."

"What does this list look like?" Henry asked, his brusque manner helping her to regain her emotional balance.

"It's a single sheet of white paper with a spreadsheet of info."

Henry stepped over a pile of books and papers. "We'll stack your books and see what is salvageable while searching."

Maia crouched beside another haphazard pile, anger zapping when she plucked a damaged book off the floor. She'd liked Jan and Rebecca. They'd offered friendship from the start, but the idea they'd turn around and try to destroy her... No, even though the perfume scent was uniquely theirs, it didn't mean they were the culprits. She racked her brain but couldn't think of anything she'd done that might cause accusations of theft.

She sighed and flattened a piece of paper then set it aside. Worrying wouldn't help Laura get the information. Maia picked up a book on Irish tales and legends and one on Māori myths. Both had broken spines and bore tread marks on the covers as if someone had stomped on them with heavy boots. She placed them into the toss-and-replace pile. The next two books bore splotches of red paint. They went in a separate pile.

"Any luck?" Laura called.

"No." Maia stood. "I'll call my coach and ask her to email you a copy."

Laura produced a business card from her wallet before replying to a shout from the direction of Maia's bedroom.

Maia called her coach. She gave Rose a precis of her day and told her the police wanted contacts for her team.

"Is this connected to the attack?" Rose asked.

"The police think so."

"Are you okay?"

"Yes, I'll stay with friends tonight."

"Sensible," Rose said. "I'll email the list now and mention the situation to Cameron and Seth. Let me know if we can help, but we'll touch base after training on Tuesday."

"Thanks." Maia hung up and forced a smile in Henry's direction. "I need fresh air. The stink of paint and perfume is giving me a headache."

"I'll come with you."

Maia wanted to argue because she needed time to decompress and straighten her head. A stupid thought when someone wanted to destroy her physically and mentally. She hustled outside onto the verandah and inhaled deeply.

Country night sounds were quieter and more subtle than those of the city. Now that she'd been a resident for several weeks, she'd learned to appreciate the call of an owl, the cadence of insects blending with a cow's moo.

But tonight, a discordant unbalance plucked at her nerves. She scanned the front of her house, most of the shadows chased away by lights blazing from her unshrouded windows. There was a prickling. A sense of awareness.

"Henry," she murmured.

His gaze swept the darkness where her house lights didn't penetrate. "Get Laura and Charlie. Inform them we suspect someone is monitoring the house."

Maia darted inside, anger fueling her again. She wanted a piece of whoever had trashed her property. "Laura. Charlie. Henry and I believe someone is watching us. He instructed me to get you."

The two cops burst into action. Instead of leaving via her front door, they exited the back.

"Go right, Charlie," Laura ordered. "I'll go left."

"What about me?" Maia demanded.

"Stay inside."

Before Maia could object, the two police officers disappeared, blending into the shadows. Maia shut the door and locked it. Best to keep up her security so no one could sneak in while everyone was busy.

Gavin was still with the puppy, murmuring while he tended its wound—a deep gash on its left hind leg. Maia hurried to her front door, searching for Henry, but he wasn't there. He'd sent her to do a simple job while he placed himself in danger. Just because he was a retired soldier, it didn't make him invincible.

Maia hesitated before turning off the front lights. It would make her harder to see, and her night vision would kick in better.

"Maia," Henry said as she flicked off the light. "They left two candy wrappers, but I was too slow. They parked in a different place and escaped before I spotted them."

Laura jogged around the corner of the house in time to hear Henry. "How many people?"

Frustration filled his scowl. "The car was too far away."

"Type of car? Color?" Laura barked.

"Black or dark gray. A sedan."

A sick sensation punched Maia in the stomach. Betrayal. Despite their brief acquaintance, she'd believed they were forming a strong bond through their shared love for rugby. "Rebecca drives a gray car. It's that graphite gray."

"Do you know where she lives?"

"Dunedin, near our training ground. We don't have home addresses. Only names, emails, and phone numbers. The coach might tell you, but the players have a right to privacy. I wouldn't like anyone to publicize my address."

"I intended to call your coach in an official capacity," Laura said, "and will explain why I require the details. If she says no, there are other ways to find this woman."

"How did this person find you?" Henry asked.

Maia frowned. "I wouldn't have noticed anyone following me. The management and coaching staff have my contact details, and anyone who has asked knows I live in Middlemarch. It's not a secret."

"Leave this to us," Laura said. "We'll contact you once we have answers. Henry, take her home. Oh, one last question: these candy wrappers we're finding everywhere. Have you noticed anyone from your team eating sweets?"

"No." Maia didn't need to think about it. "Whenever I'm with the other girls, we're sprinting around or completing training drills. It's not the time to eat sweets."

Laura nodded, her gaze thoughtful. "I'll call tomorrow. If I have questions, I'll ask you then."

"Maia, do you need to grab anything before we leave? Backup drives? Valuables?"

She thought about her laptop in pieces in her office, her clothes scattered across her bedroom, splattered with red paint and foreign substances, and shook her head. "My backups on the cloud will be enough. My notebook is at your place. Luckily."

Gavin appeared with the still puppy in a carrier. "If he makes it through the night, we'll be good," he said, his face somber. "I hope Laura and Charlie catch this monster soon. I can't take much more."

"If he survives, I'll take him. The two puppies should be together. Levi won't object to another puppy to play with and look after," Henry said. "I'll call in the morning."

"Talk to you then," Gavin said and carried the puppy to his vehicle.

Maia watched him drive away before stepping closer to Henry. "It has been a long day, and I'm too exhausted to tidy up this mess. I'll face it tomorrow."

Henry lifted his nose and inhaled deeply. "It won't rain tonight."

Maia let out a huff. "Sniffing the air told you that?"

"Yes," Henry said, his brown gaze intense.

"Oh! I need my planner if I can find it. I didn't spot it earlier."

"Let's find your planner and go home."

Home. Henry's words resonated because she felt comfortable at Henry's place. Part of it was Henry, but it was also his family. They didn't treat her as an outsider.

"It's my aunt's ghost causing these problems. Until I moved here, my life was uncomplicated."

"Don't give that old bat powers she doesn't deserve," Henry said in a clipped voice that held a tad of pissed. "You resisted her attempts to break you as a child, and she won't now."

Maia sighed harshly, questioning if staying in Auckland would have avoided this mess. "Did Laura check on Samuel? Just in case."

"If she hasn't already, she or Charlie will. They're excellent cops." He gave her a quick hug before scanning the mess. "Describe your planner."

"It's a hardcover diary about the size of this book." She plucked a book off the floor and held it aloft. "My planner has spiral binding and a dragon on the cover."

Henry crouched by a heap of papers and books. With deft hands, he sorted items into piles. Books. Papers. Others.

With another heartfelt sigh, Maia started searching. Her planner contained her upcoming writing commitments, editing dates, and advertising promo. She could recreate details from her email, but it would take time. The planner also contained details of her training program with Isabella and game days.

After twenty minutes, they had everything in neat piles.

Maia stood and rolled her shoulders before raising her hands in a stretch. "It's gone. My planner was sitting on my desk because I jotted notes and added appointments yesterday."

Henry tapped a message into his phone. "Do you have confidential info in there?"

"The info makes it clear I'm a writer. I try to keep that part of my life private because the last thing I need is a stalker." As she uttered those words, she grimaced. "Perhaps someone has discovered my secret identity."

"Another possibility we need to mention to Laura." Henry patted her shoulder before drawing her into a hug. "Sweetheart, Laura needs to know in case there's a link. We should've mentioned it earlier, but it didn't occur to me." He set her away. "Let's go home."

They walked outside hand-in-hand.

"Have you got your keys? We should lock your doors."

She handed over her key ring and let Henry do the honors.

"I'll need my car," Maia said.

"I'll follow you home."

Maia drove to Henry's place on automatic pilot. She didn't pass any traffic, and apart from Henry's headlights, visible in her rear vision mirror, she didn't see another person. It was a relief. She'd started looking sideways at her friends and doubting her judgment.

Her persecutor had done this to her.

Task achieved.

She officially felt scared.

It wasn't only her safety at risk, but those around her. What if something happened to Megan or London? To Isabella? Or worse, to Henry.

He'd become important. And to herself, she admitted the truth. Part of the reason she'd purchased her aunt's property had been to thumb her nose at her deceased relative, but she'd never forgotten Henry interacting with the other kids. Kind. Strong. Calm. She'd wanted him to focus on her with the same intensity.

And now she shared his bed.

It should've been enough because she was young and wanted adventure. But the thought of having that experience without Henry at her side left a bitter taste in her mouth. She wanted that masculine confidence focused on her.

Yeah, she'd thought seeing him again would slice him down to mere man status instead of the godlike creature of her imagination. Hadn't happened. Henry made her feel as if she could do anything, and not once had he scoffed at her dreams.

Samuel had tried to control her and lost his temper when she wouldn't follow his instructions. He'd treated her rugby like a hobby she'd put away when bored. That was why she hadn't told him about her writing, yet she'd shared with Henry.

Maia pulled into the A & D security driveway and parked in her usual spot.

What she needed to do was to tell Henry precisely what she wanted from her future. Maybe he could be flexible and see a way forward for them.

A forever future.

Maia thumped her head against the steering wheel, then abruptly straightened at a knock on her window. She pulled on the handbrake.

"Something wrong?" Henry asked.

"Feeling sorry for myself. I wish this person would accuse me to my face."

Henry snorted. "They're having fun tormenting you."

Maia's mind zapped to perfume. "I can't believe Rebecca or Jan are responsible. They've been friendly. I can't think of anything I might've done to make them turn hostile."

"Try not to think about it, or you'll send yourself crazy. Let Laura do her thing."

Maia reached into the back for her gear bag. "I should confront them at our next training, or better, discover where they live and visit tomorrow."

"I know what Laura would say," Henry said. "You don't know what you'd find. You might make it easy for them to injure you or worse."

CHAPTER 26

Maia was courageous. Henry liked that about her, although he could see the disadvantages too. Maia wanted to act, and he understood that. No military man enjoyed the hurry and wait of battle, but it was a necessary part of soldiering—considering the angles and making strategic decisions to emerge safely.

But she wasn't impetuous. Maia went the cautious route if she could see the sense in waiting or following instructions rather than racing into danger. That might change because, along with being rattled, anger consumed her.

"What if we're completely wrong, and it *is* something to do with my writing?" she asked suddenly.

"Or it could be a third party who has watched and knows your routine. People often follow habits without noticing."

"I hope they've run out of puppies," Maia said in a dark voice. "That alone shows this person needs containment in a deep, black hole."

"You're not wrong." He'd like to see how the perpetrator reacted to pain. But he didn't mention this. "Want a drink? Tea? Something stronger?"

"Do you have whisky?"

"I have a bottle of Scottish whisky."

Henry directed Maia toward his suite. Every part of him wanted to investigate and find whoever upset Maia. Yet he also wanted to keep her safe. It was difficult to let her out of his sight, but he knew instinctively that smothering Maia's independence was the worst move. It was bloody tricky balancing his fears for Maia and his need to protect her, as he hadn't protected Jenny.

Unconsciously, he tugged her against his side as they entered his suite. He flicked on a light, his gaze instantly assessing for threats.

Nothing out of place.

He consciously relaxed and smiled at her. "I'll get that drink. Do you take anything with it?"

Maia drifted over to his leather three-seater couch and sat with a beleaguered sigh. She pulled a mauve throw rug over her knees. "Three ice cubes."

His brow quirked at her preciseness, but he pulled two crystal glasses from the cupboard and ice out of the freezer. He splashed a generous measure into each glass and handed one to Maia.

"I like it here," Maia said when he joined her on the couch. "I like your suite's privacy and the shared rooms' madness. There's always someone around if I want company, yet everyone does their own thing. My place doesn't feel like home. I'd hoped to make it into a lovely, peaceful haven where I could write and spend time when I wasn't away for rugby. I thought I'd get past the memories of my aunt if I stamped my personality on the place. It was working until this started." She made an air gesture with her right hand, and Henry understood.

All her frustration and anger at the violation of her privacy shimmered in her words.

"Move in with me permanently," Henry said, meeting and holding her gaze. "It will take time to repair the windows and put right the damage done today. Once it's liveable again, rent it. There is a shortage of accommodation in the area, and you'll find a tenant soon enough. Use it as an investment property." He paused, still studying her while anxiously waiting for her reply.

"I'll consider it," she said. "The break-in might be an opportunity to do serious remodeling, but the terrible memories linger. Every time I glimpse that enormous tree in my garden, I see the puppy. When I hang out my washing, I see the tank with that possum." Her hand tightened on the glass. "Everywhere I look, I see clowns and other things."

"Maia, I love having you here with me. I enjoy coming home from work, and you're here. I like spending time with you. My place feels more like a home when you're here." Nothing but the truth. He'd been lonely before. Maia brought contentment he hadn't experienced for years.

She smiled, making her blue eyes sparkle. That smile warmed him inside and out. Now, all he needed to do was tell her he was a wolf who sometimes howled at the moon.

"I enjoy being with you, too, now that you've stopped running."

Henry shifted uncomfortably. "Some people will comment on our age difference. Sometimes, it still concerns me when considering the disparity in our world experiences."

"Just because I'm younger doesn't mean I don't know what I want from life. I don't care what other people think. It's you that matters, and me. No one else." She was so fierce, her blue eyes shooting fiery sparks at him. "Do I want to travel? Yes, but we can do that together. We have things in common. We like living in Middlemarch. We love community. I hope we will have children. I want it all with you, Henry. Everything."

Henry's throat tightened and damned if his eyes didn't tear up at her declaration. He loved spending time with her, and everything about her fascinated him. He swallowed hard, and his lips curved into a smile with minimal coaching. "You're so brave and fierce. So determined. You know exactly what you want and aren't afraid to pursue your goals. I admire that."

Her brows arched. "Enough to kiss me?"

"Oh," he said, his voice no more than a whisper. "I can do better than that."

"Only if you mean it, Henry. I can't take you second-guessing because people make snide remarks."

At that moment, even though he didn't think it possible, Henry fell even more in love with Maia. He set his glass down and took Maia's from her. Seconds later, she sat astride his knees, her eyes wide in surprise. Joy and a hunger to seize everything she'd offered suffused Henry.

He wanted children whenever Maia was ready. He'd love to explore unfamiliar places with her at his side. But most of all, he wanted Maia.

He captured her lips, sipping and tasting her before lust sank its teeth into him. Henry plundered her mouth, kissing her, touching her until his world righted itself and everything was in balance again. He broke their kiss to whip her long-sleeved T-shirt over her head. Her bra disappeared next, and he kissed down her neck, giving in to the temptation to nip. She shuddered and pressed closer, her breasts brushing his chest.

Hell, he needed closer contact. Skin.

He drew back again and peeled off his black shirt, ripping buttons. He ran his hands over her shoulders and down her back, pressing her closer while he licked and explored her breasts. Her nipples tightened in the cool air, and he ran his tongue over one nub before drawing it into his mouth and sucking hard. A groan rumbled from her, and her fingernails dug into his biceps. The sharp pricks into his flesh ran straight to his cock.

Maia shifted on his knees, rubbing against the hard ridge. Henry shuddered, barely controlling himself. No, this wouldn't do. He abruptly stood, holding Maia upright until she maintained her balance.

In a flurry of movement, Henry stripped off her track pants to reveal naked, creamy skin. He tossed the pants away before ripping at his fly. He hauled his jeans and boxers down to his knees, allowing his erection to spring free. Only then did he sit and haul Maia back astride his knees. He skimmed her body with his hands, savoring her soft, fragrant skin. He cupped one hip and explored the folds of her sex, stroking her gently in the way she enjoyed. A whimper escaped her, and she kissed his face, his shoulders as she arched her back to give him easier access.

His fingers slid back and forth, teasing her but not giving her too much friction.

"Henry. Henry." She gripped his shoulders, those fingers of hers digging into his flesh. "Please. I need to come."

He lifted her enough so she could sink onto his cock. She took him slowly, an increment at a time, teasing both of them.

"You feel amazing. I don't think I'll ever tire of this, even when we're old and wrinkly."

He barked out a laugh, amused at the vision her words conjured. "Let's just enjoy now."

"Yes," she whispered, rising before sinking back down and taking every inch of him without warning. She didn't settle but rose and fell swiftly, her head thrown back and her hair waving around her shoulders with each vigorous move.

Henry focused on this beautiful woman who was suitable for him in every way. His perfect match. Each of her frenzied moves drew him deeper, the clasp of her pussy gloving him perfectly. He smoothed his hand down her back and back up before leaning forward to suck one nipple into his mouth. He drew hard. She instantly rippled around his cock, clenching him tighter.

"Touch yourself," he said. "I can't hold on for much longer."

"So don't. This isn't a race. You've shown me that," she replied, tightening her inner muscles.

Henry swore he saw stars, the jolt of pleasure searing his entire body. Maia stroked her clit, and her sheath clenched around him. Henry tried to hold back. He did, but the next urgent rise and drop of her body pushed him over the edge. He exploded, the force of his release stealing his breath and making him realize they hadn't used a condom.

Again.

Maia gasped, her grip on his shoulders tightening to a point shy of pain. She cried out, the minute ripples running through her massaging his cock. When she stilled, he embraced her, satisfied.

His woman.

The one he wanted in his future.

All he needed was to get past this next hurdle.

"We forgot the condom again."

"Doesn't matter," Maia said. "I'm on birth control. I told you this."

"No birth control is one hundred percent effective. I want you to play rugby. You should play and finish on your terms, not because of an unexpected pregnancy. Not that I wouldn't love any child we had, but you should achieve your dreams."

He meant every word. This was a non-negotiable point. He loved her. He did, even though he hadn't told her this yet. She must aim high, and he'd support her every step of the way.

"Henry," she said, closing the distance between them to kiss his lips tenderly. "I appreciate that level of support. I dream of playing for the Black Ferns—seven a side or in the first fifteen. But I don't want to do that forever. Along with my writing, I'd like to find a part-time job in or near Middlemarch. I haven't decided what, but I'm open to possibilities. It's always fun learning new things."

A shiver ran through her, and Henry lifted her off him and

stood. "Let's warm up in bed, and you can tell me more about this mythical job."

"I don't want to lock myself away and write all the time." She slipped into bed. "Adding something different to my routine improves my writing flow and life balance."

Henry hopped into his bed. He'd thought it before and thought it now. Having Maia here relaxed him. He drew her against his chest and flipped the covers into place.

"The puppy is safe, isn't she?" Maia asked. "I'd be heartbroken if she disappeared because this moron got his hands on her again. I meant to call Gavin and ask about security. I can't believe someone would do this to play with my head. It's sick."

"You can't forget this person might injure you—something worse than a knock on the head. So far, they've taunted you, tried to scare you. They might up the ante."

"I know." Maia turned a troubled gaze on him. "I understand, but I can't stop living my life. My training is important. I can't impress the Black Ferns' coaches if I'm constantly warming the bench."

"I get it, and I'm glad you've decided to stay with me. Having you here means more eyes on you. If you're alone, it gives them more leeway to strike."

"I won't go anywhere without company, apart from team training. Our sessions are closed, and I can't expect anyone to sit around waiting for up to two hours. It's winter, and people have commitments."

"All I ask is for you to keep your phone handy. Make sure it's fully charged. Limit your exposure and try not to pattern your days. Run at different times. Write at different times. Don't make it easy for this dickhead."

Henry's phone rang, and he climbed out of bed to rummage amongst the pile of clothes he'd dropped on the floor.

"Yeah, Laura. What's up?" He listened. "Did you believe her?

Yeah. Okay." He hung up.

"Your friend Rebecca reported her car stolen three hours before Laura contacted her. She told her local police she'd parked it in the driveway. Locked. The car had vanished when she went to drive to her parents for dinner. Laura checked with the cops. Your other friend attended a twenty-first in Wellington."

"Back to square one," Maia muttered. "I hate this."

CHAPTER 27

The following day, Maia wandered into the communal kitchen around nine after spending ten minutes speaking with Laura. She'd mentioned her writing and the missing planner. Only London was present, deeply immersed in whatever she was reading, with a cup of coffee sitting nearby.

Maia must've made a sound because London's head jerked up. She smiled in welcome.

"Henry and Gerard got called out on a job. Megan and Jacey have gone on a school trip as parent supervisors, so it's me and you." Her brow puckered. "Henry put me in charge of your security."

Maia blinked.

"Yeah," London said with a twist of her lips. "That was my reaction."

"I have a lot to do and not much time. I promised Henry I'd

take care and not be alone if I could help it. How's your morning looking? Feel like a quick trip to see Laura, a stop by my house for clothes, and a drive to Dunedin? I urgently need a computer because mine is in pieces."

"Henry mentioned someone ransacked your house. Are you intending to move back once everything gets repaired?"

Maia shrugged. "Henry wants me to stay with him. To be honest, I think I might. I've never had a family and like it here. It feels safer with other people around."

"Understandable. We have excellent security, even if you find yourself alone. The dogs bark if visitors arrive. They're used to us, but you'll hear them if someone lurks near the house."

"Good to know. Henry suggested I rent my property and keep it as an investment—at least until Henry gets sick of having me around."

London laughed and picked up her coffee cup to take a sip. "Don't think that will happen. Henry loves you. I've never seen him like this—not since..." She trailed off, looking uncomfortable.

"Since your sister?"

Relief flooded London's face. "I wasn't sure if he'd told you. Yeah, since Jenny. I can see he's protective, and this person harassing you has him worried. It's surprising he isn't dogging your steps and scowling over your shoulder."

"I get the sense he'd like to, but he's trying to give me space. My best approach is to avoid alone time and compromise. Common sense. This person has already injured me and almost destroyed my playing season. I'd be stupid to ignore Henry's suggestions. I won't be the foolish character who blunders about making it easy for the bad guy. So far, I've been incredibly lucky I've escaped worse injuries."

London set her coffee mug down and squeezed Maia's arm. "You're perfect for Henry. As much as I loved my sister, you're an even better match for him. My sister was bull-headed and stubborn. I don't know you well enough to tell if you bear the stubborn gene, but you're determined and have common sense. You're not high drama."

Maia grimaced. "You make me sound like an old maid."

"That's not what I mean. My sister was high-maintenance. In the long term, she and Henry would've butted heads. You're more likely to pick your moments. You're self-sufficient and capable."

"Thank you, I think."

"Why don't you borrow Henry's laptop?"

"I could, but I'd need to upload my software and other files. It's easier to get a new one."

London's gaze narrowed, laser-focused on Maia. "Why do you need special software?"

"I write," she said, observing the other woman. "Fantasy fiction. Under a pen name."

London's brows shot up. "Did Henry tell you Megan writes romances? I do her admin work."

"Henry suggested I ask you for help. With my deadlines and rugby training, I don't have enough time for advertising and promotion."

"I'd love to work with you. I've learned a lot from working for Megan. It won't take me long to get up to speed. What pen name do you write under?"

Maia hesitated and felt heat seep into her cheeks. It surprised her that Henry hadn't asked for more details. No doubt he'd get to it, eventually.

"Maia?" London resembled a reporter after a hot tip.

Maia sighed. "Henrietta M. March."

It took London seconds to get it and for her eyes to open wide in astonishment. "You took your name from Henry and our town."

Maia couldn't maintain London's gaze and the acute speculation she saw on the other woman's face. A clever way to stay close to Henry and keep part of him with her. When she raised the courage to glance at London, the other woman was busy tapping on her phone.

"What are you doing?" Foreboding rose in her. Surely London wouldn't tell everyone her secret. She'd had a huge crush on Henry, and he'd remained tucked away in her thoughts while she'd had boyfriends and dated. No, she couldn't confess that because she'd sound like a nutcase stalker.

"I'm doing an internet search for your books. Holy crap! You're a bestseller. Go you!"

"Writing helped me buy the house and pay for things my aunt didn't approve of before I could access my trust," Maia said. "She forced me to study accountancy, and writing was me thumbing my nose at her. I hate numbers and spreadsheets, but I love writing. I scraped by with my degree, and it drove my aunt crazy when I didn't get a job. She couldn't figure out how I was surviving because she wasn't approving my living expenses."

"She sounds like a bitch."

"My aunt never approved of my father's choice of wife and thought he could do better. Once she decided on something, there was no shifting her. She blamed my mother for the accident. It was a freak thing and no one's fault."

Maia's phone rang. "It's Laura," she said as she answered. "Sure, I need to fill out an insurance claim and take photos. Can I get a copy of your police report to go with my claim? All right, I'll be there in ten minutes. I want to see if any of my clothes are salvageable." She hung up. "Can you be ready in ten minutes? I thought I'd drive to Dunedin from there."

"I'll grab my purse and phone. Let's take my vehicle in case someone is following you."

Maia agreed without mentioning someone determined could observe the house from afar and track vehicle activity.

The interior of her house was as bad as she remembered. In fact, it looked worse in the light of day. Laura and Charlie met them outside, and Laura handed Maia the paperwork for her claim.

"Thanks." Maia unlocked her door and stood aside to let them enter.

"Holy Hannah," London muttered. "Henry mentioned the damage, but I didn't picture this destruction."

"This was my office. They've wrecked my research books. That was my laptop." Maia pointed at the different pieces.

"Someone is angry," London said.

"Yeah. I wish I knew what I'd done." That's what made this so difficult. It stressed her to think she'd agitated someone so much that they sought revenge. "I wonder if I have another relative who thinks my aunt left me this house. Aunt Beatrice didn't leave me anything except a letter stating how I'd disappointed her and she was ashamed of me."

"That's cold."

"It was my father she was angry at, but she aimed her arrows at my mother when she was alive and me once my parents died."

"I never met her but heard she was eccentric and particular with tradesmen."

"That's a polite way of saying my aunt was a bitch. I shouldn't speak ill of the dead, but she made my childhood miserable. Once I turned twenty-one, control reverted to me. After that, I didn't speak to her again, which is sad. She was my only remaining family."

London's face softened, and she embraced Maia in a heartfelt hug. When she drew back, tears blurred her vision. "With Henry, you'll have a happy family and a supportive community. I don't have any family left either, but I don't feel the lack now." She grinned. "I love my life. Let's see your wardrobe, then hit the shops."

Maia and London arrived back from Dunedin early afternoon. As she'd suspected, she hadn't found a piece of usable clothing. The trespasser had destroyed everything he or she could find.

They'd had a monster tantrum and left days of work to clear the mess. She'd be busy and wouldn't have time to think between cleaning, rugby, and writing.

"Let me set up your computer," London said over coffee once they'd unloaded the car. "Give me a list of the software you urgently need, and I'll get started. If you trust me with your passwords, I can get everything done quickly."

Maia grabbed a notebook from her purse and wrote her password for her password safe. She added her cloud name and jotted down the software she required to write. "Those are the main ones. You'll find my passwords in the online safe."

"Easy," London said with a smile.

"How much do you charge? I didn't ask."

"Don't worry about that. You get the family rate, the same as Megan."

A clatter at the door announced Levi's arrival home from school. Accompanied by a friend, Levi entered the room, followed by Jacey.

"Are we too late?" Levi demanded. "Have you finished your training run?"

Maia checked her watch. "In about half an hour, after I've unpacked my shopping."

"Can we come with you?" Levi asked.

Doubt crept into Maia, and she glanced askance at Jacey.

"As long as Maia agrees and you can keep pace with her," he said. "Her training is important and part of her job. You have to be serious and focused. No tearing off to investigate interesting noises or smells."

"We won't do that, Mr. Jacey," Levi's friend said.

"No," Levi agreed. "We want to get faster and play rugby like Maia."

Maia figured if the two boys lagged, she'd do a shorter run than usual. It wouldn't matter for once. She had team training on Tuesday, and a partial rest day wouldn't hurt. "I thought I'd drive down to the rugby grounds and do laps and interval training today, along with some warmup exercises Isabella taught me. Is that okay?"

"Yes!" Levi shouted.

His friend beamed. "Yes!"

"All right, boys. Change into your running gear and come back straight away so you don't hold up Maia," Jacey said.

"That's my cue to leave," London said. "I much prefer my job. You'll have to get Henry to show you the obstacle course. Yesterday's council meeting discussed having a fundraiser where everyone dresses in costumes and runs the course. Some people got excited."

Maia laughed. "Thank you for helping me today and volunteering to set up my laptop."

London waved a hand in dismissal. "Not a problem."

"Jacey, are you sure the boys will be okay with me? What if... What if something happens to them because of me?"

Jacey smiled. "They'll be fine. The rugby field is open ground, and you'll notice anyone lurking. The kids will spot strangers. Just make sure you take your phone. If anything worries you, call Laura or me."

A howl rang through the air, followed by a doggish-sounding yip, and Jacey shrugged ruefully. "Those two are not quiet. If anything, you're doing me a favor by tiring them out. That way, we might manage a movie after dinner instead of active games outside."

"I'll change and meet the kids back here. Won't be long."

Jacey had sounded unconcerned, so she'd take her cue from him.

CHAPTER 28

To Maia's relief, and everyone else's, the following week remained calm and calamity-free, although no one had confessed to stealing her clothes and locking her in the changing room. If all went well this coming weekend, she'd play an entire game. It was an away game, and the team was catching an early morning flight to Auckland.

"A birdie told me they picked you as team captain," Jacey said when the family sat down for dinner the night before the game.

"It's only temporary. Jan and I are co-captains. Amanda, our usual captain, hasn't played for several weeks but will likely take over again. I'm fine with that."

"Can we go training with you again next week?" Levi demanded.

"Sure, as long as your parents approve," Maia said.

"Did you hear the *we* part of the sentence?" Megan asked drily. "Levi means him and his friends."

"Oh." At Henry's slight nod, she said, "I'm fine with you tagging along, but you must keep up. I'm doing road training."

"We can do it," Levi cried. "Tell, Maia, Dad."

"If you and your friends go with Maia, you must be on your best behavior," Jacey said sternly. "Follow her instructions. And I'll need to talk to your friend's parents to ensure they give their permission. Which friends do you mean?"

Levi poured out seven names.

Maia's mouth fell open. She'd resemble a momma duck with a gaggle of ducklings. Jacey and Henry shared a look, and Maia noted Gerard give a slight nod.

"Maia, if you don't mind," Jacey said, "I don't think they'll slow you down. They're around Levi's fitness level. If you're worried, one of us will jog at the rear."

"One of us?" London asked, her brows raised. "I hope you're not including me in that tail-end group."

"No, sweetheart," Gerard said with a grin. "I think Jacey was volunteering himself, plus me and Henry."

"Okay," Maia said. "I look forward to putting you through your paces. We'll run uphill and downhill along the course Isabella planned for me."

"Now, I'm doubly certain I'll be writing and unavailable," Megan said.

London nodded emphatically. "Same."

Maia chuckled. "I love running. It's relaxing and gives me time to plot books or mentally work on gnarly problems." She didn't confess these days she constantly scanned her surroundings and feared she was losing her wits. Last week, she'd imagined a big cat, and it hadn't been an overfed and overindulged house pet. This one had been black. Large. One moment, it had been there, and the next, it had disappeared, leaving her with doubts.

Her imaginary world had imposed itself on reality.

"Are you sure you want to take me to the airport?" she asked

Henry. "I can drive and leave my car at the short-stay car park."

"Maia," Henry said.

"*Uh-oh*," London said. "I've heard that tone before."

Maia rolled her eyes. "Just checking."

"Henry and I have an early meeting with a prospective client. Dropping you at the airport isn't a problem," Gerard said. "Besides, Henry would like a kiss for luck with our client."

Levi pulled a face. "Yuck, swapping germs."

There was a moment of startled silence.

"Levi," Megan said. "Who told you that?"

"Olivia Mitchell tried to kiss me. She pounced when I wasn't looking."

Pounced? Kids differed from when she went to school. Admittedly, she'd attended an all-girls school, and there had been no kissing.

Jacey looked as if he were trying not to laugh. He cleared his throat. "What did you do?"

"I pushed her into the wall and ran away," Levi said and shuddered. He wiped the back of his hand across his mouth. "Her mouth was slimy."

"Did you make her cry?" Megan asked, her voice carrying a steely tone.

"No, she got me back at dodgeball." Levi held out his arm. "I've got a bruise."

"You will do nothing to pay her back," Jacey said, sounding sterner this time.

Levi's gaze darted to his plate, and Maia clapped her hand over her mouth to block her merriment.

Megan's eyes narrowed. "What did you do?"

Maia made the mistake of glancing at Henry and saw he was having trouble not laughing.

Levi hung his head. "She sits in front of me in class. We were painting, and I dropped my pot of red paint."

Megan groaned while Gerard and London were actively laughing, having given up the fight.

"Let me guess," Jacey said. "It accidentally fell all over Olivia."

"Yes," Levi said. "It turned her white shirt red."

"Emily is gonna hate me," Megan muttered.

"She started it. I didn't want her kiss," Levi said.

"Fine," Jacey said. "This is my advice. Avoid being alone with her to prevent any further kisses."

"She kissed Tom last month," Levi blurted.

"I see. London, I think we'll have coffee tomorrow morning. Do you have time to come with me?" Megan asked.

"And skip parenting advice," London quipped. "I wouldn't miss it."

"Ah, Megan," Jacey said.

"No, Olivia can't go around causing chaos," Megan said. "Emily needs to know about her daughter's actions."

"Will she get in trouble?" Levi asked.

"About the same amount you're in for tipping paint on her," Megan said. "Now, eat your dinner. No! Don't speak or you won't go running with Maia."

"Hey," Maia said. "Innocent party here. I didn't kiss anyone or toss red paint."

"You can kiss me," Henry said. "I won't take revenge."

"*Eww!*" Levi said, wrinkling his nose.

Maia chuckled along with the other adults. She'd never experienced this slice of family life and loved every moment. The arguments. The discussions and teasing. The shared laughter. She hadn't meant to, but she was falling hard for Henry and his family.

Henry walked her into the airport terminal the following morning, and once she'd sighted her team, he kissed her. It was an affectionate kiss, but she clung briefly before stepping back.

"Is it weird I'll miss you, even though I'll only be gone for the day?"

"No," he said gruffly, giving her another hug. "Stay safe."

Her brows lifted. "Aren't you going to tell me to play well?"

"You'll give it your everything. That's a given." He stroked her cheek. "I'll pick you up tonight."

"Thanks." His utter confidence in her had her throat tightening with emotion. His entire family believed in her. She stepped away and forced a smile because her emotional maelstrom threatened to spill over. "See you tonight."

"Tonight," he said and left with a wave.

Maia swallowed hard. She loved Henry and felt she had known him forever, which made no sense. She picked up her pace, pushing her frenzied thoughts aside to join her team.

"Is that your boyfriend?" Jan asked.

Maia noticed several girls paying close attention. "Yes," she said, not embellishing her answer.

"Is it serious?" someone else asked. "He's old. Does he have money?"

"Not that old. I met him when I moved to Middlemarch," Maia said, trying not to sound defensive, but it was a touchy point because it worried Henry. Thank goodness they hadn't stated their opinions when he could hear. She'd hate him to decide he was too old for her again.

"But he's rich, right?" another woman asked.

"I've no idea," Maia snapped. "Why would you ask that?"

"Do you call him Daddy?"

Maia didn't see who uttered that gem and was relieved when their coaches approached.

"All right, listen up, ladies," Cameron said.

Maia was glad of the interruption, although knowing her teammates, they'd return to the conversation. She was coming to know her team. Even the standoffish ones were more accepting of her, but someone had stolen her clothes and locked her in the changing room. Now this. Her relationship with Henry was none of their business.

The questions came as soon as they had tickets and passed through security.

Maia forced a laugh she wasn't feeling and raised her hands in a stop signal. "Henry and I are new, and I don't want to jinx our relationship. I like him." She made a buttoning motion across her lips. "No more questions."

"But he's old. Age-gap romances are fine in books and movies, but they don't work in real life," one girl said.

"At least he's experienced," another quipped.

The teasing continued in the same vein, but Maia remained stubbornly silent and mentally pushed away their age-gap comments, even though they worried her. None of their business, and they were wrong. When they tumbled off the plane in Auckland, the women were in high spirits and eager to play the Auckland team.

Maia felt fantastic when she jogged onto the field. The referee blew his whistle, and the game began. It flowed, and it was clear they had gelled; their set-piece plays on point, and everything going well. The tries came quickly, and each successive one spurred her team onward. When the final whistle blew, they'd won by twenty points.

Amanda jumped off the bench and hugged Maia hard, beating the other reserves into squashing Maia by a hairsbreadth.

"That was such a great game. You played so well." Amanda pulled away and hugged the other players, her face ablaze with triumph. "Those girls didn't think you'd win. I played some of them in grades when I was younger. They're arrogant and won't take this well."

Great. Something else for Maia to worry about—pissed rugby players coming at her.

"Excellent game," a woman said from behind her.

Maia turned to spot the other team's captain with her

hand outstretched. She immediately smiled and accepted the sportsmanlike gesture. "Thanks, but you made us work for the win. The game could've gone either way at the start."

"We'll beat you next time," the captain said, grinning.

"We'll work hard to stop you." Maia stepped forward to shake hands with the other team members, who stood behind their captain.

"You played an inspired game," one woman said. "We couldn't keep up."

"Yeah," another agreed. "We'll be more careful next time."

"I look forward to it," Maia said, meaning it. She glanced over her shoulder and found her team gaping in shock. What the heck? Maia glowered at them and jerked her head, silently ordering them to fall into line and act gracious winners. They glanced at each other before slowly moving. Maia puffed out a relieved sigh when she heard murmurs behind her from her teammates.

Most of her team had disappeared to their changing rooms during their last games. Admittedly, it had been cold and raining. If appointed captain again, she'd line up her team and show they were gracious winners or losers. It showed sportsmanship and set a good example for younger players.

After the hand-shaking, the two teams parted, but Maia called her team together. "Thanks for the awesome game. We did everything right today. Let's make it a habit!"

"Yes," Amanda said.

After a moment of silence, the players cheered, everyone joining the celebration.

"Excellent job," Rose said, breaking into their circle. "We still have elements to work on, but you listened at training, which makes me happy. You're working together. Well done."

Rose hurried off to meet with a group of men and women waiting to speak with them.

"We've got four hours before our flight," one woman said. "I intend to go shopping."

"I'm celebrating with drinks. A couple of fruity cocktails," another said.

Maia scooped up her gear bag and jogged toward the changing rooms, hoping to grab a shower. Luck was finally on her side. After showering and dressing warmly, she pulled out her phone and called Bryce.

"Maia! I watched the second half of the game. You were awesome."

She grinned. "Where are you? I have four hours before I have to catch my flight.

"I'm hovering outside the changing rooms and trying not to look like a perv."

"Five minutes," Maia promised, eager to see her friend. She packed her gear and double-checked to ensure she had missed nothing.

She found Bryce loitering outside, but he wasn't alone. He had a redhead with him. Maia managed a smile before Bryce grabbed her in a tight embrace.

"Maia, it's so good to see you," he murmured against her ear. "I've missed you like crazy. Phone and online calls don't cut it."

"Missed you too," Maia said, meaning it. Bryce was her sounding board, and they discussed everything and anything. She pulled back and smiled at the woman again. "Is there something you haven't told me?"

"Yep." Bryce's grin was broad. "This is Sam. Samantha. We ran into each other in the university hall. Literally. I asked Sam out as an apology, and we've been dating ever since."

"Sam, I'm pleased to meet you."

"Bryce talks about you a lot."

"I was going to drag Bryce off shopping," Maia said. "But I won't subject you to that."

Bryce and Sam shared a look, and the intimacy between the pair surprised Maia. Bryce had always flitted from one woman to the next. He had a knack for remaining friends, but none remained in his bed for long.

"As long as you feed me, I'll tag along. Why don't we go to Sylvia Park? That's nearer the airport, but it's a great shopping center, and you should find everything you need. We can eat at the food court."

"If you're sure, that works for me," Maia said. "Bryce?"

"My two favorite women together. What's not to like?"

Bryce and Samantha dropped her at the airport, and Bryce gave her another tight hug.

"I like Sam," Maia whispered. "You should keep her."

"I intend to," Bryce said.

Maia hugged Sam, too, before heading off to join her team. She'd purchased a suitcase and filled it with clothes, so she checked in by herself.

The flight home seemed endless. Maia ached from several hard tackles. It was a minor issue, but she craved a hot shower and Henry, in that order.

She pulled out her e-reader and immersed herself in a book. Once the plane landed, she took longer because she had to wait for her bag. She spotted Henry immediately, and he bore a scowl.

"Sorry for the delay," she said. "Bryce and Sam took me shopping, and I bought a suitcase to pack my purchases inside."

"Who's Sam?" Henry said, his voice close to a growl.

No, it *was* a growl. She glowered at him. "Samantha is Bryce's girlfriend. I hadn't met her before, but I liked her. They watched the game, and we went shopping and had a meal before they dropped me at the airport."

Henry winced. "Someone posted photos of you on social media, and they found their way into my feed. I was jealous because you looked so happy with that guy. I didn't realize it was your friend, Bryce. Sorry. For a moment, I thought it was Samuel."

CHAPTER 29

"I f you think that, you don't know me at all. Samuel is in my past, and I'd be happy if I never saw him again."

Henry read Maia's expression and apologized again. "I'm sorry. I won't make the same mistake again." He didn't mention the nasty posts about their difference in age because they had plain stung. Hell, no wonder he was making a mess of this with Maia. The maliciousness had pushed at his pride and made him question their compatibility and spun him right back to the start of their relationship. The posts had pushed him into panic.

"Make sure you don't," she snapped. "I'll show you the photos Sam took for me. There are also photos of the three of us and Bryce and Sam together." She poked him in the chest. "I have not behaved inappropriately. We tried the dating thing years ago, and it was weird. Oh, I don't care!" And she stalked from the airport with her nose in the air.

Henry took a moment to admire his woman before jogging to catch up. He'd been dumb to let his fears take grip. Everything he knew about Maia told him she was upfront and honest and didn't care that he was older than her. He had to remember that. It didn't matter what other people thought. It was what he and Maia thought that counted.

Yeah, he'd need to do some heavy-duty groveling because he was a dumbass. He joined her, where she'd come to a halt, realizing she had no idea where he'd parked.

"Maia, I apologize again for thinking you'd been cheating. I don't have an excuse. I just reacted. Please, let me take your case for you."

She handed it over. "For the record, the only man I'm interested in is you. I don't cheat. I never have and never will. That behavior goes against everything my parents and teachers taught me."

"Noted," he said. "This way." His phone pinged, and he made a mental note to turn off notifications. He didn't need business stuff in his head when watching out for Maia's safety. This entire situation was frustrating as hell. He'd prefer facing the enemy head-on rather than dealing with a skulking unsub in the shadows.

He placed the suitcase down and unlocked the vehicle with his remote before opening the door for Maia. "You must've done heavy-duty shopping."

"I picked up notebooks and found reference books to replace my damaged ones. I also bought a pair of running shoes and clothes while I had the opportunity."

Henry rounded the vehicle to get in the driver's side. "How did your game go? I saw the result online, but the article didn't say much. Just that your team won unexpectedly against the team leading the competition."

Maia beamed, and every bit of wariness faded into the background. She didn't sulk, and that was lucky for him.

"We had an exceptional game. It was the first time everyone in our team worked together. They passed the ball instead of trying to go alone. Our set pieces worked perfectly, and Jan's kicking was on point. She didn't miss one."

"Your coaches must be pleased. They've looked like they wanted to tear their hair out during the games I've watched."

"Yeah, the win satisfied them." Maia's phone beeped, and she wriggled to get it from her jeans pocket. "What the heck?"

"What is it?"

She handed him the phone, and he saw several photos—some of him and some of Bryce. Maia was the connection in several of the photos. The heading of the social media post said, "Trouble in Paradise?"

"Someone is spying on us," Maia said, her gaze traveling the vicinity. "And trying to create trouble."

Henry started his vehicle and pulled out of the car park. "They were quick to post the photo of our supposed argument."

Maia's brows rose. "It was close to a quarrel."

"But I apologized and meant every word. It won't happen again."

"It better not." Maia glanced back toward the airport terminal building. "I can't see anyone."

"Neither can I." But now that he wasn't so irked with Maia, a prickling sensation made his wolf slide uneasily beneath his skin. Someone *was* watching them, but he couldn't figure out their position.

Never mind. Best to retreat.

"Would you like to stop for dinner or have something at home?" Henry asked.

"We had a late lunch. I'm not hungry," Maia said. "Are you?"

"I'd feel better if we were off the road. I haven't spotted anyone, but the middle of my back is itching."

"Do you think they followed me to Auckland? They must've since they had photos of me and Bryce together. Someone took

250

those photos today."

"Yes," Henry said grimly. His phone rang. "Damn, can you get that for me? I'm waiting for confirmation of a job."

"Henry's phone," she chirped and pushed the speaker button so Henry could hear.

"You like old, rich men?" a low voice growled. "Sugar daddies?"

Henry stiffened. "Who is this?"

"Setting yourself up for pain. She'll find someone richer and move on."

"Who is this?" Maia demanded.

A cackle sounded before the call ended.

"Fuck," Henry said, stunned and uncomfortable at the caller's insinuations.

Maia cursed under her breath. "Don't you dare pay attention to what that...person said. Heck, I wasn't sure if it was a male or a female. You know I don't care how much money you have, right? Henry," she snapped. "I'm with you because you're attractive and sexy, and I have the hots for you. I've dated men my age, and they've all disappointed me. You don't. Got that? Henry!"

"Yes," he said. When he was with Maia, the years between them faded. It was rarer now for him to worry that he was taking advantage as he had at the start. However, this person had a problem and was intent on causing a rift.

"I wonder how they got your number."

"It's painted on the side of my vehicle."

"Right. Could we trace their number? Laura, I mean," Maia said.

"It's probably a prepaid phone. We'll talk to Laura, but I don't like this call, or that someone was spying on us. When is your next game?"

"It's a home game against the Southland team," Maia said.

"We'll make sure Laura or Charlie attends, and I'll enlist other helpers to watch people on the sideline," Henry said. What he didn't say, but it worried him big time. What prevented the unsub from shooting Maia with a rifle from afar?

Henry reported the social media pictures, the nasty posts, and the phone call to Laura while Maia unpacked her suitcase. She'd purchased what Sam called a base wardrobe with pieces that worked together.

While she'd been with Henry, her anger had kept her level, but now that she was safe, a tremor racked her body, and tears burned her eyes. She was trying to hold it together, but these repeated attacks were getting to her. And now, someone was trying to drive a wedge between them. The last thing she wanted was for Henry to panic or get weird ideas in his brain, thinking he knew what was best for her, so she worried.

The only time she forgot was when she was playing rugby. Something about the game's physical nature helped her to focus.

Her phone jangled, the intrusive sound making her start. Maia was unfamiliar with the number, and that made her hesitate.

"No, this is stupid." She scooped it off the dresser and answered the call.

"Yes?"

"Maia Jacobs?" a man asked.

"Yes," Maia said cautiously because she didn't recognize the voice.

"This is Gary Hart. I'm a selector for the Black Ferns. This year, we're choosing forty players, having a training camp, and picking our team from these women. Your skills have impressed us, and we'd like to include you in our training camp. What do you think? Are you willing to attend?"

Maia opened her mouth, but a croak emerged.

"Are you still there?" Gary asked.

"Yes!" Maia blurted. Her end goal was selection for the Black Ferns, but she hadn't thought it would come this quickly. "Yes, I'd love to attend the training camp."

"Excellent." A trace of amusement filled Gary's voice now. "If you give me your email address, I'll forward the details."

Maia rattled it off.

"Right, the information I'm sending covers everything, but please call me on this number if you have questions."

"Thank you," Maia said. "Thank you so much."

"You're welcome, Maia. Keep playing well, and your chances of making the team are excellent."

"Thanks," Maia repeated.

With a resolute click, the call ended, leaving Maia holding her phone. Her dreams were within reach as long as she didn't mess up the training camp.

"Maia?" Henry appeared, concern on his usually stoic face. "Maia, what's wrong?"

She discovered her eyes brimmed with tears. With a shaky laugh, she knuckled them away. "Sorry."

"Don't be sorry, sweetheart." He sat beside her and hugged her to his side. "Tell me what's wrong. I'll help if I can."

She turned a teary smile on him. "I don't know why I'm crying because it's awesome news. A Black Ferns selector called. They're holding a training camp with forty players, and they've picked me to attend. The selector assured me that if I continued to play well, I would have an excellent chance of making the team."

Henry set her on his knee. He nuzzled her neck and held her tighter for an instant. "Maia, that's fantastic, although seeing you play, I had no doubts. You deserve this chance. Did any of your teammates get chosen, or are you the only one?"

"I don't know." She wriggled, repositioning herself so she could see his face. "I nearly let it go to voicemail because I didn't recognize the number. All I did was listen and say thank you. I didn't ask about the selections. We have an extra training session tomorrow. I guess I'll hear then."

Henry stood, setting her on her feet. "Megan and London have finished their tasks and want you to join them for a drink. What do you say?"

"One drink won't hurt," Maia said with a grin.

"Two drinks would be okay," Henry said, "because we're eating too."

Maia let Henry lead her down the passage to the communal rooms.

"Yay, Maia!" London said. "How did your game go today? I know your last training run went well because Levi is still excited. He told us you're the best and did extra training with them because they behaved well. Levi's exact words."

Maia laughed. "They're good kids. Sometimes boisterous, but if that happens, I just up the speed, which usually quietens them down."

Henry vanished into the kitchen, only to reappear with champagne and flutes.

"*Ooh*, champagne," Megan said, her blue eyes twinkling.

"What's the occasion?" London asked.

"Maia has news. I'll let her tell you while I pour the drinks."

Gerard and Jacey walked into the lounge, each carrying a plate of snacks. Levi chased after them, holding a can of soda. Two white puppies raced after Levi, both in excellent health after their ordeal.

"Don't shake the can," Megan said. "Put your drink here. Maia has exciting news."

Levi slid onto a chair. "Sit," he told the puppies in a firm voice. They sat, and he petted them, murmuring soft words of praise.

"What's the news?" London asked.

Maia caught the roll of Henry's eyes when London and Megan checked her left hand for a ring. She waved it in front of them so they could see her naked fingers.

"Bother," London said. "There goes my bet."

"You're betting on..." Maia shook her head. "Never mind."

"What's your news?" Gerard asked as he handed around champagne flutes.

"I just had a phone call from a Black Ferns selector. He told me I've made the group of forty they'll take to a training camp. From there, they'll pick the team for this year."

"That's amazing!" London said.

"Congratulations," Megan cried. "You've worked so hard. You deserve this."

"Well done," Jacey said. "When is the training camp?"

"I'm not sure. I haven't checked the information yet. Gary said he'd email it to me."

"Congratulations." Gerard kissed her cheek. "We're proud of you, but I'm not surprised by your selection. You've been playing well despite everything that's happening around you. And you're training, pushing yourself. You've made it so the selectors couldn't ignore you."

"I agree with everything Gerard said," Henry added. "You deserve this chance. A toast. To Maia and her continued success."

"Maia!" everyone chorused.

Maia smiled, her heart full of happiness and a sense of belonging she hadn't experienced since her parents died. She'd unconsciously been searching for this completeness that came from having a safety net. People who encouraged yet wouldn't hesitate to tell her home truths when she needed a kick in the backside.

A family.

Emotion kicked her, and happy tears flooded her eyes.

Henry moved closer, his frown only clearing when she smiled at him.

"I'm okay. Just happy. I haven't had this support before. Not for a long time."

"You have now," he said gruffly, drawing her close until his larger body surrounded hers and drew comfort around her. "You have now."

CHAPTER 30

The next morning, Maia pulled on warm clothes suitable for running.

Henry opened his eyes, the flash of gold making her smile. His hair stuck up, and he had a cute boyish look, offset by his slight frown. "What are you doing?"

"I'm going for a light run to warm up my muscles. Besides, I'm so excited, I can't keep still. I wonder if anyone else made the selectors' squad? I guess I'll find out this morning."

"Wait, I'll come with you. I worry about you."

"I'm capable of using good sense and running in safe places." She took a breath to control her irritation. Henry stressed if she was even a minute late or on her own. He meant well, but this overprotectiveness was wearying. "Stay in the warm."

"Don't forget you have someone harassing you. My job is to get you to your trials in one healthy piece. Besides, any time spent with you is worthwhile." Henry slid out of bed and stretched, his arms high above his head. He must've caught something in her expression, and he sighed. "You think I'm overreacting. Perhaps I am, but I can't stop until I know you're safe. I told you about Jenny. Her ex murdered her, and I couldn't stop him. I worry I might fail you in the same way, and I...I panic."

Maia stared at him. "You didn't fail Jenny. You were at a town event where everyone was having fun. The person who failed Jenny was the man who murdered her. Please remember that. I am taking care and doing everything right. Mostly I run with other people or in places that are well-frequented."

"Please. I understand what you're saying, but I like you."

"Aw, you say the sweetest things," Maia said, her gaze drawn to his splendid naked body. She fluttered her lashes. "Such a beautiful sight." There was *nothing* about Henry that suggested *old*.

"So you'll let me run with you and help you make the team? Excellent to hear," Henry said as he pulled on clothes.

"Okay. Okay. You've worn me down." Maia laced her running shoes, fizzing inside and having difficulty keeping still. Henry *liked* her. She was a lucky woman. "Even if I miss selection, I'll be closer to my goal. It's an opportunity to learn."

"Given your playing form, I think you're underestimating your chances. Stay healthy and uninjured, and you'll be a Black Fern. I want you to grasp your dreams, so I'm crawling out of a warm bed to run with you."

And to protect her, but she didn't say that aloud. She'd cut him some slack because this situation must be bringing back horrendous memories for him. Maia skipped across the room and kissed Henry on the cheek. "Thank you."

"You are welcome," Henry said and held out his hand. "Let's do this."

This set the strategy for her week. She was never alone. Megan and London dropped her off at her Dunedin training and picked her up again after doing the weekly shop. She'd showered at home, gladly escaping the disquieting atmosphere of the changing room because the selectors had only picked her and Jan to attend the training camp. Some were openly envious, and team tensions resurfaced.

Currently, she exercised with energetic boys and two girls. Despite the steep hill they were tackling, the kids chattered with each other, trading jokes and insults and scarcely puffing. They impressed Maia because she was feeling the burn and running out of puff.

A flash of black in her peripheral vision had her head swiveling. She blinked but didn't spot whatever had caught her eye. Must've been a rabbit or another animal. Henry had told her wild goats lived in this area.

"I see the obstacle course," one boy hollered.

The pace increased a fraction, and again, the kids amazed Maia. Levi had proudly told her their team hadn't lost a single game since they'd started training with her.

"I thought you might've turned back," Maia said, panting.

"No!" the boys and girls shouted in unison.

She grinned. "Let's see if the obstacle course sorts you out."

"Nah!" Levi boasted. "We're as fit as you."

They jogged down the hill and climbed the gate into the obstacle course paddock.

"Dad said they're gonna have another zombie run soon," a girl said. Her black ponytail bobbed up and down with each step while her green eyes flashed excitedly. "We could have teams of kids."

"Yeah," a boy shouted.

"I'm sure you could," Maia agreed as they approached the spaced tires. They'd done the course before. Twice, in fact, and it made a change from continually running. Maia loved the challenge of the obstacles as much as the kids. "Who wants to go first?"

"Me!" Everyone shouted at once.

Maia had experienced this before and had a strategy. "Today, the shortest person goes first. Line up in height order. I guess that means I go last," she said, laughing. "No photos of me messing up the obstacles, guys."

"Nah!" a short boy shouted, placing himself at the front of the line.

"We don't have a phone," Levi cried.

Despite their lack of height, the kids had a natural athleticism that they applied to each obstacle. She'd struggled with a couple. Never mind. Optimism spurred her onward. This time, she'd ace them all.

"Right," Maia said once the kids stood in a line. "Our last time over the eight obstacles was over an hour. Let's see if we can beat that today. Once I say go, I'll start everyone at five-minute intervals. Remember, if anyone is having trouble, ask for help. We're a team. Ready, steady, go!"

The first boy raced off like the wind. Five minutes later, the next kid—a girl—sprinted toward the tires and navigated them without hesitation. One by one, the kids started until she was on her own. Gleeful shouts rode on the wind, making her smile. These kids made training fun when, in the past, some days had been a grind.

Maia glanced at her watch and waited ten minutes before starting. Her legs were longer, and she should catch the kids easily enough. She sprinted for the first obstacle and ran through the tires, carefully placing her feet. She scanned the area, looking for the kids, but they'd scampered through the trees toward the next obstacles, and she grinned on seeing flashes of red, blue, and yellow in the distance. Their laughter floated toward her, and she ran with a broad smile.

The next challenge was a giant rope web pegged to the ground for the competitors to crawl beneath. Maia smiled ruefully. Her mature curves were not as suited to slithering along the ground beneath the woven obstacle.

It was slow going since her butt dragged along the rope barrier. She hit a muddy puddle, and frigid water soaked into her clothes. She bit back a curse, forcing her mind to tropical beaches and warm seas. It was her happy place when the frigid Otago chill nipped at her face and limbs.

Maia got stuck again and had to back up before progressing forward. At last, she clawed from under the webbing and jumped to her feet. She ran, steadily jogging up and down inclines.

She increased her speed to a sprint when she reached the flat and kept up this pace until she reached the next obstacle—a wall with a rope webbing. With a leap, she grasped the rope halfway up the wall and started climbing. Her warm muscles worked to haul her body upward. All those hours in the gym had helped her upper body strength, and right now, she was thankful for the habit of physical toil. At the top, she searched for the kids and spotted one or two running along the path through the trees. This wasn't the regular obstacle course route, but the water crossing wasn't safe during the winter, and Gerard had suggested dodging the trees, stones, and branches on the path was an acceptable contest.

Now that she'd spotted the kids, she thought she'd made up time and was catching them. She flung herself down the other side, ran along a gravel track, and down another incline before reaching the flat paddock. The native trees, on the other side, were her goal.

"Hurry, Maia is catching us."

She grinned, her competitive streak urging her to hurry.

The grass was spongy beneath her feet, and mud splattered up to coat her legs. Her close-fitting top clung to her skin with an unpleasant dampness as she raced across the paddock toward the trees.

The kids had gone silent, and she slowed to listen. She frowned because they were usually a noisy bunch. Were they playing a trick? Maia scanned the area and spotted nothing out of place.

The sun disappeared behind a cloud, and the cheer drained from the day. A shiver ran through Maia, but she forced herself to focus on her surroundings. The last thing she needed was an injury.

She entered the trees, and the temperature dropped. Fern leaves brushed her legs, the dampness soaking into the muddy fabric. She jumped over a fallen log and almost tripped over a rock. Her heart tried to leap up her throat, but she regained her balance after windmilling her arms.

"Crap," she muttered, slowing and testing her legs for signs of pain. A lucky escape.

Maia slowed again, deciding she could take the kids' ribbing. She'd rather their teasing than an injury. A blur of black and white had her screeching to a halt. She jerked, wary at the silence in the trees. No birds. Strange since she'd heard muted birdsong earlier.

Maia frowned. Was someone there?

"Are you kids playing a trick on me?" Her voice emerged with a quaver, and to her dismay, not a single child answered. Had she been mistaken, and they'd surged ahead?

Maia continued along the path. Now and then, she spotted a marker Gerard had placed to guide them through the trees. She picked up speed but took extra care with her foot placement when she reached a swampy part. Footprints showed in the muddy ground. The kids' mothers would undoubtedly curse her when washing the dirty clothes. She imagined smeared footprints in halls and entrances when the kids forgot to remove their shoes.

She'd been that child at one time.

The blow came out of nowhere. A tree branch. It clipped her arm, and pain radiated to her fingers. Then, a body blocked her way, and Maia lurched to a halt. She gaped and wondered if she was imagining things.

261

Chapter 31

"Amanda! What are you doing here?"

Amanda's usually smiling face twisted into an ugly mask. Her smooth hair was a mess of frizzy curls. "You fuckin' bitch. You've stolen everything from me."

Maia blinked, shock making her thought process sluggish while she struggled to connect the dots. "You...you..."

Amanda shrieked and wielded her stick like a sword, trying to gut her.

Maia ducked behind a tree. The branch whacked against the trunk, the whistling thump making her cringe. Too close. Dull pain radiated from her arm where Amanda's first blow had made contact.

"Amanda?" She meant business with that branch, and Maia had the kids to worry about. What if they returned looking for her? No! She'd try to de-escalate the situation and retreat.

Amanda broke into her frenzied planning. "You will *not* attend the Black Fern trials. I'm next on the list and will take your place."

"How do you know?" Cripes! This was jealousy? Amanda had natural talent—sure—but she didn't put in the hours. She'd smugly told them she enjoyed a social life. Maia hadn't commented then because Amanda's training opinions hadn't mattered to her. Maia had her plan and aimed for her end goal.

"My cousin told me I was close and just missed out." Bitterness coated Amanda's voice, a bubbling anger with a tinge of crazy. "This was my year."

"You don't train hard enough," Maia said, immediately wanting to recall her words.

Amanda snarled and thrust the branch at Maia, pure temper behind her lunge.

Maia scrambled backward, her heart racing. The kids. Hopefully, they'd kept running and arrived at the finish line. Maia didn't want any child injured by this unhinged woman.

She retreated, but Amanda trailed her, brown eyes full of craftiness.

Maybe Maia could get her talking. "Have you been following me?"

During the last week, her back had constantly prickled. Each time she'd turned around, she hadn't seen anyone. Had it been Amanda?

Amanda smirked, but her eyes lost some of the crazy.

"Have you been harassing me since I arrived? Have you been calling Henry and telling him he's a dirty old man?" Maia demanded, furious at the thought. She'd known someone was stalking her, but to have someone she knew hounding her...

A team member.

That made everything worse.

"You tortured those poor puppies."

Amanda shrugged. "My father gave them to my sister. A

263

present." Her lips twisted into a sneer. "They yapped. *Yap-yap-yap*, throughout the night, and they kept biting me. My sister spoiled them even when they chewed on my rugby boots. *Yap-yap-yap*. All the time. I sleep so much better now."

Maia gaped at her, scrambling to understand Amanda's despicable actions. Had she ever known this woman?

The stick slashed down again, whistling past her hip and knee. If she'd been a second slower... Before Maia could dodge again, Amanda stabbed with the stick. Maia wasn't quick enough this time, and the rough wood gouged her forearm. A grunt of pain escaped, and Amanda cackled.

"See if you can hold a rugby ball with a sore arm," she taunted. "You'll need your sugar daddy then because you won't have a career any longer."

The woman was crazy.

Maia backed up and almost tripped over a stump. The stick jabbed her upper thigh hard and fast. Pain streaked up her leg, and blood welled, soaking her leggings.

A sharp growl sounded to her right, and Amanda whirled.

Maia took advantage of Amanda's distraction and scrambled away, trying to distance herself. Every muscle ached, and her arm and leg throbbed in tandem. Amanda was strong. She was heavier than Maia and lifted incredible weights. Maia had always believed all-around exercise worked better, so she did endurance training and muscle building.

Another growl sounded, coming from a different direction.

Amanda turned. "What the fuck?"

A third and fourth growl sounded, each one closer than the last. Then, a wolflike howl broke out, prickling goosebumps across Maia's skin.

Amanda scooped up rocks and hurled them in the direction of the howls. A shriek of pain echoed through the clearing, and Amanda chortled, an unhinged laugh that scared the crap out of Maia. She limped a step, and a low moan squeezed free. The surrounding howls increased, and Maia gazed uneasily at the trees.

Was that a dog?

The animal edged closer, its amber eyes full of intelligence. No, a wolf. A yowl pierced the din. A chorus of howls and Maia dithered, unsure of where to run.

Amanda whirled back to glower at Maia. "How are you doing this?"

"Not me." Coldness seeped into Maia. She had to move. Somehow. Now, while Amanda remained distracted.

The cacophony crept closer, and Maia could have sworn she heard a deeper, louder howl echo from across the opposite hill.

"You bitch. You're not getting my team spot."

"Suppose I don't attend. There's no guarantee you'll get my place." Besides, she'd tell everyone who'd listen how Amanda had attacked her and destroyed her property. Surely Amanda didn't think she'd keep quiet? No, Maia *would* press charges.

A rock thumped into her shoulder, and Maia cried out. Immediately, eerie howls echoed around them.

Maia bit back a scream and staggered away. She blinked on seeing a black leopard, its brilliant green eyes focused on her. Black leopard? She blinked several more times, but no. She wasn't seeing things.

There was a black leopard, and it was slinking behind Amanda while the howls distracted the other woman. Maia could've sworn the leopard shook its head at her. No, two more black leopards were behind the first, creeping into a position behind Amanda.

A soft bark on her left had Maia jumping. A blond animal crept toward her, its golden eyes intelligent and full of caution. Maia swallowed hard but didn't make a sound. She could hardly believe it, but these animals were helping her. She pulled herself upright with the help of a slender tree. Unfortunately, the rattle of the leaves grabbed Amanda's attention.

"Stay right where you are," she snapped, hurling a stone at Maia. It barely missed.

Around her, the animals froze. The loud howl she'd heard in the distance sounded closer.

"What the fuck is this?" Amanda demanded. "You Doctor Dolittle?"

Maia had no answers.

A louder, deeper snarl ripped through the growls. Then a blur of black or brown darted behind Amanda.

Maia gaped. A dog.

An enormous dog.

No, it was a wolf.

And the canine was prowling toward Amanda with intent.

Maia swallowed hard. A distraction attempt would be the best idea.

"Call off your dog," Amanda shouted.

"Why?" Maia's eyes widened when she spotted a black leopard. The sleek creature was stalking Amanda from a different angle. Maia swallowed hard, her mind struggling to understand what she was seeing.

A roar sounded in the distance, and the wolf approaching Amanda howled in return. The eerie sound immediately bounced back. The wolf stared straight at Maia, its golden eyes alert. Maia could feel the animal's anger. It wasn't just the low, menacing growl directed toward Amanda, but it was in the animal's tense muscles and the calculated way it regarded the woman.

"Why is it so important for you to make the team?" Maia asked.

"My parents want me to do accountancy," Amanda spat. "My mother doesn't think rugby is feminine and thinks I should join the family firm."

Maia barked a laugh, the circumstances so near her own that she couldn't contain her reaction.

"It's not funny," Amanda snarled, her anger back.

She scooped up a rock and fired it so quickly Maia couldn't dodge. Fiery pain roared through her chest, the impetus of the throw dropping her to the ground. Amanda released a roar of triumph and surged toward her.

Maia didn't see what happened next, but the wolf growled. Amanda screeched—half surprised and half panicky. She crashed down, howling as her head struck a tree trunk. Immediately, the wolf pounced, grasping Amanda's arm in its mouth. It must've bitten down because Amanda screamed.

The black leopard stalked closer and stomped on Amanda's legs when she tried to kick. Maia's heart pounded, fear uppermost, yet the animals didn't divert their attention from Amanda. Several smaller animals crept from the trees. Maia tensed, but they swarmed her, licking and cuddling closer until her panic eased.

She had no idea what was happening, but the animals didn't seem a threat to her. She sank her fingers into the fur of a small black wolf.

"Henry, where are you?" a feminine voice shouted. That sounded like Laura.

"I'm over here!" Maia shouted.

Henry? Maia thought belatedly.

Amanda screamed suddenly and thrashed. Maia stared in shock as the two animals used brute strength to subdue her.

Laura appeared with Charlie on her heels. The cops took in the situation with one sweeping glance.

"Who is this?" Laura asked.

Charlie halted beside Laura before sidling around until he stood opposite the animals and Amanda. He didn't seem worried or scared, and Maia took her cue from the police officers.

"Amanda. She's on my rugby team. She... She admitted to stalking me and hurting the puppies. She's been calling Henry and trying to break us up."

"Liar," Amanda spat and kicked out with her leg. She got the wolf in the ribs, but the animal didn't release her. It growled and shook Amanda until she let out a pained screech. "Get your animals off me."

Maia limped toward Laura, her breath coming in harsh pants as pain raced up her leg. Pressure built at her temples, part relief and part stress. Had Amanda injured her badly enough to make her miss the trials? She shoved away panic. Something to worry about later.

The smaller animals had followed her, and each pressed against her, their presence bringing reassurance. Laura and Charlie had come. Amanda couldn't hurt her any longer.

A tear ran down her cheek, and Maia scrubbed it away. But the tears wouldn't cease, and her shoulders shook. One of the smaller animals near her let out a sharp cry, and the wolf and big cat immediately stared in their direction. Every muscle seemed to throb, and she wavered on her feet. Finally, she gave up trying to stand and sank to the ground. She closed her eyes and worked on controlling her emotions. She couldn't fall apart now.

"Maia," a soft voice said.

Maia's eyes flew open, and she started on seeing a naked Levi kneeling next to her.

"Did she hurt you?" he asked. "We signaled Henry as soon as we could."

Maia's gaze slid past Levi and the small leopards and wolves surrounding her. The giant wolf guarding Amanda was staring at her, his golden gaze intent as if he were listening.

Thoughts zipped through her mind, each more unbelievable than the next. This was the stuff of fiction. The things she wrote about in her fantasy novels.

Laura had mentioned Henry.

"Is that Henry?" she whispered to Levi, not taking her gaze off the wolf.

"Yeah." Levi sounded uncertain whether she should know this

information.

She quickly counted the animals pressing against her. If she included Levi in their number, her entire squad of youngsters surrounded her.

Laura and Charlie didn't seem concerned, behaving like they knew what was happening.

"Henry," Laura said in a firm voice. "Let Charlie put cuffs on her. We have to do this right."

"Let me go," Amanda said. "I haven't done anything. You wait until I tell my father what you've done. By the time he's finished, you won't have a job or money."

Neither Charlie nor Laura seemed cowed. Charlie pulled handcuffs off his utility belt and nudged the wolf aside. In seconds flat, he had Amanda cuffed and on her feet.

"What are you arresting me for?" Amanda screeched, fighting Charlie. She did an excellent job until the wolf grabbed her leg and tugged. The leopard circled to Amanda's other side and nipped her hand. Amanda yelped and staggered away. It was in the direction Charlie was trying to take her, so Maia assumed the leopard was helping.

"Henry, will you take care of Maia?" Laura asked. "I need to go with Charlie."

In answer, the wolf stalked past Laura, heading straight toward Maia. He'd looked massive standing over Amanda, but now he seemed enormous.

"Henry," Levi said. "We did exactly what you said."

The wolf nudged the boy, his gentleness and affection evident in the lick across the boy's cheek. The wolf growled, and Levi stepped away from Maia. He grinned as he closed his eyes, his brow scrunched as if he was concentrating hard. Seconds later, a faint glimmer shone around him, and he morphed from a grinning boy to a happy wolf pup right in front of her.

Her gaze shot to the adult wolf in time to see the animal change and Henry appear in its place. She covered her mouth with her palm, her eyes bugging wide as Henry kneeled beside her. Had he... She blinked hard, but no, Henry was still there, and Levi, the wolf, gave her a sly lick.

"Maia, are you okay?" Henry asked hoarsely. "When Levi signaled Gerard and me... Those were the worst moments of my life." He helped her rise with gentle hands. She wavered, shock doing a number on her knees, but he caught her against his body. His naked body.

Henry was a wolf.

Wolves and leopards surrounded her.

She wasn't seeing things.

The animals were not figments of her imagination; she knew them by name.

CHAPTER 32

Henry sidled closer to Maia, holding his breath. Each of his senses worked overtime, trying to read his mate. His nostrils flared, and terror tiptoed down his spine while he waited for a reaction. Levi whined, picking up on Henry's inner turmoil. Maybe he should've informed Maia earlier about his otherness, but the time had been inopportune. She'd been dealing with enough.

Amanda shrieked obscenities, and Henry glared at the protesting woman Charlie and Laura dragged away in handcuffs. Her pretty face contorted in another scream, and he took satisfaction in her disheveled appearance. The bitch. He and Gerard might've been too late if it weren't for the kids.

A shudder worked through him, a reaction to the close call. The woman's attack echoed the past so precisely. Jenny's ex had murdered her in this forest when she'd slipped into the trees for a quick toilet break while Henry waited for her. Despite the runners and zombies filling the paddock, no one had seen or heard a thing. He hadn't suspected danger until Jenny had failed to reappear, and he'd gone searching.

Gerard nudged him, and Henry shook away the past. He visualized his human form and flowed into his shift. It was time to see what Maia thought of his secret.

The kids loved her, and she'd let them close without panicking. He prayed there was room in her heart for him in both forms. London and Megan would help and share their stories because they understood the devastation he'd face if Maia rejected him.

Swallowing hard, he kneeled beside her. "Maia, are you okay?" he asked hoarsely. "When Levi signaled Gerard and me... Those were the worst moments of my life." He grasped her arms and lifted her to her feet. She wavered, and he balanced her while desperately assessing her reaction.

Her blue eyes were enormous in her pale, dirty face. The scent of coppery blood filled his next breath.

"Where are you hurt? Let me carry you to my vehicle."

"I can walk."

Henry tensed.

"Amanda can't see that she injured me," Maia said.

Henry assessed her in a quick visual sweep. He couldn't see blood, but the scent...

Levi must've shifted again because he said, "The angry lady hit Maia with the stick. She struck her arm and leg. Should've bitten her," he muttered. "She hurt my puppies and laughed about it. She is wrong in the head."

Another kid added their two cents. "The lady wanted Maia's place at the trials."

"Yeah," Sophia, one of Saber's twins said. "She's not even a good player. We watched the game where she hit the other lady. Why would you want her on your team if she lacks control?"

These kids knew about restraint. They learned early because

their safety depended on it, especially in this modern world of smartphones and instant communication.

Henry focused on Maia and found her watching him. Her silence tossed him into a sea of doubt. Anxiety. Was it shock at Amanda's behavior or terror at what she'd witnessed with him, Gerard, and the kids?

"How badly are you injured?" he asked.

"Nothing broken, but I have lacerations from not dodging fast enough. Bruises."

Henry relaxed a fraction. She seemed calm. Too calm.

His gut roiled, and he wasn't confident of what to do.

"Where are your clothes?" Gerard asked the kids.

Maia started at Gerard's deep voice and whirled, immediately grunting. Pain flitted across her face. "You, too?"

"Yes," Gerard said, glancing at him with sympathy.

He'd had to tell London, so he understood the anxiety riding Henry. What if Maia rejected him? What if she told the wrong people and endangered the shifter community? Amanda would tell everyone she'd seen wolves and leopards, but Laura and Charlie would handle that aspect. Everyone would think she'd hallucinated. The woman was deranged if she thought Maia's absence would secure her a spot on the team.

"Your clothes?" Gerard prodded.

"We had to change fast," Levi mumbled.

"Yeah, we heard the lady shouting," another boy said.

A girl's voice cut through the babble. Sophia, one of Saber's kids. "We ripped our clothes 'cause we were in a hurry. I'm sure Mum won't be too mad. It was an emergency."

Levi raised his chin. "Yeah," he said, nodding. "An emergency."

"Okay," Gerard said calmly. "Take me to your clothes, and we'll see what we can salvage. Mothers prefer you to think first and undress fast if necessary. Please remember that."

A flash of humor spurted through Henry at Levi's

long-suffering sigh. Given the circumstances, Megan and his dad wouldn't growl, but no doubt Jacey would spout words of wisdom. Henry had been the recipient during his boyhood. The lectures hadn't hurt.

"You ready?" he asked Maia.

She inhaled and released a slow breath. "Yes." She took a staggering step.

Henry guided her along the winding path leading through the forest. It was slow going, and he felt every one of Maia's pained winces and sighs.

Anger bubbled in him, the urge to swing at Maia's teammate. He'd heard enough to ascertain Amanda's warped jealousy.

But even so—he couldn't wrap his head around the twisted things the woman had done to terrorize Maia. He'd bet this wasn't the first time Amanda had stalked someone. Something to discuss with Laura and Charlie.

When they reached his vehicle, Maia wobbled. He settled her in the passenger seat, quietly grabbed his clothes, and dressed.

Gerard appeared, also dressed now and herding five naked kids. "Can you drop them at home? Megan and London will find clothes for them to wear."

Henry opened the rear door. The five kids piled into the back seat, chattering like boisterous birds. This had been an adventure, something out of the ordinary that they could tell their shifter friends. He caught Maia's frown but didn't comment. As soon as he dropped off the kids, he'd take Maia to Gavin because she was feeling Amanda's blows. He could still smell blood but couldn't see any on Maia's clothing.

The kids filled the silence, asking questions, which he answered truthfully. Yes, Laura would charge Amanda for the attack. No, nothing terrible would happen to them for showing their animal selves. No one would believe Amanda. Laura and Charlie would make sure of that.

Maia was listening closely, even though her head was back against the seat and her eyes closed. He hoped she understood no shifter would hurt her. They were the same people—hell, would she leave him and return to her house now that they'd captured her stalker?

He didn't want that. He wanted to keep her close. Keep her safe.

But he couldn't tell her any of that now—not when the kids were in the back seat.

Henry stopped in front of the family home. He texted Megan and told her Gerard would be home soon. He'd explain. "Tell your mum I'm taking Maia to Gavin," he said to Levi.

"Yes," Levi said before he and his friends sprinted to the house.

"They love you," Maia murmured.

"They love you, too," he replied because it was nothing less than the truth. "Are you okay?"

He didn't mean physically because it was easy to see her injuries bothered her. He meant mentally. How was she coping after learning she was living with shifters?

"You and the kids saved my butt." A noticeable shiver ran through her. "Amanda would've hurt me worse without your intervention. Right now, I'm numb. I can't wrap my head around the fact Amanda was responsible. She was friendly from the first day. Yes, she had a temper but never directed it my way."

Henry wanted to hug her, hold her, and tell Maia everything would be okay. It wouldn't—not for a while, so offering platitudes was no use. He set his vehicle in motion, backing up and heading toward Middlemarch.

Maia's eyes closed, but she wasn't sleeping. Henry glanced across at her, worry filling him as he felt her pulling away. Was it that he morphed into a wolf? Or was it something else?

Ten minutes later, he pulled up outside Gavin's surgery. Maia didn't move, and his worry increased as he rounded his vehicle to open the passenger door.

"Maia, come on. Let Gavin assess your injuries, and we can get you home."

She let him help her from the vehicle, placid in a way that wasn't Maia. Henry's worry increased, but he remained silent as he guided her to the front door.

It opened, and Gavin was there, his green eyes scanning Maia from head to foot in one visual sweep. "Charlie called and let me know you'd be coming. Bring her into the surgery."

Henry nodded. Charlie would've told Gavin that Maia knew about shifters.

Once they were in the surgery, and Maia sat, Henry squatted in front of her. "Can I remove your clothes so Gavin can see your injuries?"

Maia stood and raised her arms, grunting in frustration when she couldn't manage properly. Henry helped her to peel the clingy fabric over her head before tugging off her leggings. She winced and gasped when he pulled the fabric from her hip. The stench of blood combined with mud was more prevalent now. Blood trickled down her leg and plopped in spots on the tiled floor.

Gavin moved closer while Henry silently cursed, wishing he'd been faster getting to her. Her upper body bore bloody scrapes, and bruises were already forming against her creamy skin. It was her upper thigh that was the worst.

"When did you have your last tetanus shot?" Gavin asked.

Maia frowned. "I don't recall."

"I'll give you one now."

Henry held his breath, waiting for Maia to protest that Gavin wasn't a doctor, but she said nothing.

"What hurts most?" Gavin asked.

"Leg," she said without hesitation.

Gavin nodded. "Once I clean out the mud and wood splinters, it should heal quickly. When is your next rugby game?"

"This coming weekend," Maia said, frowning. "I have a rugby

camp the weekend after that."

"I doubt you'll be match fit by this weekend," Gavin said, using his usual honest assessment. "But you should be okay for light training by next week. If I were you, I'd tell your management. Be honest about your capabilities because you might worsen the injury if you try to play."

Maia nodded. "I refuse to let Amanda get away with breaking the law. I'll call my coach tonight."

"Can you move your arms?" Gavin asked.

Maia grimaced and did as he asked. She sighed, the sound coming from deep in her chest. "I don't get it. Amanda is a talented player. She could've gotten onto the team on her own merits. She didn't need to knock out the opposition."

"You're better," Henry said without hesitation. His entire family had seen that when they'd watched her play. "Which made you a threat."

Gavin moved around his surgery, collecting supplies. "Cleaning the wounds will hurt, but it's better than an infection."

Henry felt each wince and gasp as Gavin tended her wounds and wished he could've taken that pain for her. He wanted to howl on Maia's behalf. This wasn't fair. Although they'd caught Amanda, the woman might've done enough to derail Maia's selection.

At last, Gavin finished. He gave Maia a tetanus shot before telling her she could dress again.

Maia eyed her tight-fitting exercise gear with foreboding.

"I have a jacket in the vehicle," Henry said. "It will work until we get home."

"Thanks," Maia said.

"I'll give you antibiotics because your wounds were full of dirt," Gavin said.

Henry hurried and rushed back, relieved to find Maia speaking calmly to Gavin.

"Do you think I'll heal fast?"

"Not as fast as Henry or me, but you're healthy, and if you're sensible, you shouldn't have issues."

Maia's gaze shot to Henry. "You heal fast?"

"Yes," he said.

She gingerly stood to don the coat he offered her. It covered her to mid-thigh.

"If you have any concerns, call me," Gavin said. "Rest for a few days and ease back into your training."

"Thank you," Maia said.

"Thanks, Gavin." Henry plucked several bills from his wallet and handed them to Gavin. He frowned as Maia limped from the room and disappeared outside without waiting.

"She'll be fine," Gavin said. "Congratulations. She's a strong woman and perfect for you."

"Thanks," Henry said gruffly. Unfortunately, everything didn't feel fine. While Maia was talking to him, she wasn't *looking* at him. Should he have spoken to her earlier? Told her he had a dual nature. Fuck. He had no idea.

But he couldn't let her go. She was his mate, his other half.

She was his last chance of happiness.

CHAPTER 33

Maia climbed into the car, her muscles heavy. All she wanted was a shower and bed, in that order.

The other stuff...

It was challenging to wrap her head around how the family she lived with shifted into animals. Even young Levi. She wrote about fantastical stuff, thought about it, dreamed about it, and yet, this seemed different. Not that the family scared her. She liked every one of them.

Henry...

Heck, if the kids hadn't been present, things might've turned out differently. Amanda might've killed her.

The driver's car door opened and closed, and she swallowed hard. Henry...

"Maia, I'm still the same person who loves you. Perhaps I should've explained earlier, but selfishly, I wanted you to know me better. Don't get me wrong. I've always known you're my mate, but the age difference worked against us until now. You're a strong woman with goals and aspirations. It's taken this stubborn male a bit longer than you to understand that we might have years between us, but we're equals. We care for each other, and that is all that matters."

Mate?

Maia's brain seized on that info and refused to go further. She wrote about mates, read about them in other authors' books. She glanced at Henry and knew that her gaze was probing. But damn it, she wanted details.

More information.

Was this why she felt compelled to get closer each time she spotted Henry? Even as a child?

"Tell me about mates."

Henry started his vehicle. "In the shifter world, when a couple is perfect for each other, they're called mates. One completes the other, and no one else will do. To cement the bond, they'll bite each other here." He tapped a spot at the base of his neck. "In our case, because you're a human, I would do the biting. The wound will heal, leaving a slight scar and sensitivity to touch. It lets other shifters know you're claimed."

Maia pondered this. *Caveman, much?* "Do you howl and need to shift at full moon?"

"We all shift frequently, which means the full moon doesn't create problems. And yes, sometimes I howl to celebrate life."

Maia thought of the kids. "Are there lots of shifters in Middlemarch?"

"Yes," Henry said, glancing at her. "Right now, you need rest, but I'll answer any further questions tomorrow. You can also talk to London."

"London?" Maia asked.

"She's human. Also, Laura and Charlie. They have shifter mates, and you can speak freely to them. They've gone through this."

"What's that?" Maia asked, her tone sharp. She felt as if someone had pulled the ground from under her feet, and she'd fallen on her arse.

"Learning the person in their bed has dual forms," Henry said.

And with that, he backed out of the driveway.

Maia leaned back and closed her eyes. Discombobulated. A fantastic word to describe exactly what she felt. It wasn't disbelief because she'd seen the wolf and black leopard. She'd watched Henry and the kids transform.

"I'm out of sorts because I can't believe Amanda attacked me," she blurted into the heavy silence. "It's not that you turn into a wolf or that I'm living with animals." A giggle burst from her, a hairsbreadth from hysteria. Maybe she was worried about this discovery. She shouldn't be because they'd saved her, but she was shocked. "Sorry, that sounded insulting. I don't mean to offend anyone."

Henry gently squeezed her knee. "You have a right to your anger."

"I'll have to call Rose tonight," Maia said, cringing inside.

"What are you going to tell her?"

Maia frowned at the tension in Henry, slow to understand. "Oh!" she said when the truth slammed her sluggish brain. "I'll tell the coach the local police arrested Amanda for attacking and stalking me since my arrival in Middlemarch. Nothing else."

"Good," Henry said.

They lapsed into silence. Maia thought about the locals with dual forms, many of them kids. There was no way she'd place them in danger. *No way.* The kids had saved her. If they hadn't summoned help, anything might've happened.

Finally, Henry pulled up in front of his home. She hadn't considered demanding that he take her to her house, and that told her everything. She didn't fear Henry or the others and would never break their confidence. *Never.*

Henry mightn't openly display his emotions, but she loved him. With every small action, he showed he cared for her. Apart from the stalking aspect, moving to Middlemarch was an excellent decision she didn't regret.

Knowing Henry was a wolf shifter shed light on Levi's perplexing comments, propensity to howl, and other things that had struck her as odd. Yeah, none of this truth changed her everyday life. It was Amanda's actions that had Maia gritting her teeth. The betrayal.

"If I contact the Black Fern selectors and tell them Amanda attacked me and I'm uncertain if I'll be fit to take part in the trials, do you think they'll tell me not to bother?" Her biggest fear. Amanda might've scuttled her chances of obtaining her dream.

"My advice is to wait for two days. The worst bruising will appear by then, and the swelling should decrease. You'll know if you're capable of a hard training session."

"Yeah, makes sense."

"Come on," Henry said. "A hot shower will help to ease your muscles."

When he opened the front door, a loud shout sounded.

"They're home!" It was Levi, and the boy barreled around the corner, almost crashing into Maia. His two white puppies scrambled after him, barking in welcome. Henry scooped up his brother while bracing Maia. A sharp pain darted up her leg, but she bit back her gasp.

"Easy there, Levi. Sit," Henry said to the puppies. They obediently plonked their butts on the ground.

"What did Doctor Gavin say?" Levi demanded, his brown eyes full of concern.

Maia grinned at his cuteness. "I have stab wounds from the tree and cuts and bruises. Nothing broken."

"What about your trials?" Levi asked.

A pang of alarm darted her, and suddenly, she wanted to howl. Reaction setting in, probably. She attempted to swallow the knot in her throat before staring mutely at Henry.

"Is everyone home?" he asked.

Levi nodded enthusiastically. "In the kitchen."

"Give us a minute, and we'll talk to everyone together." Henry set down Levi, and his brother scampered away with the puppies chasing after him.

Now that she knew Levi morphed into a wolf, she could see it in his boisterous conduct, yet she'd suspected nothing. The adults had perfected their behavior after years of learning and intermingling with humans. It made her curious about other shifter types.

"Maia," London said the second they entered the kitchen. "Are you all right?"

"Sore. Bruised. No broken bones, but infection is a concern," Maia said. "Gavin thinks I'll be worse tomorrow when the stiffness sets in." She managed a reply without bawling.

"Your rugby trials?" Jacey asked, commiseration in his expression.

She swiftly glanced at Henry, who read her emotional turmoil and answered for her.

"We're giving it two days and will assess Maia's condition before she makes a decision."

Maia beelined for an empty barstool, scrambling onto it with a pained sigh. Once she'd situated herself, she discovered everyone watching her. "Sorry. I couldn't stand for a second longer."

"You should have a hot shower." Henry crossed to her side.

The adults and Levi continued to observe Maia.

"What?" she demanded finally. "Do I smell as well as look like a wreck?"

Henry rubbed her back in silent commiseration. "They're worried about your reaction to wolves and leopards roaming the

SHELLEY MUNRO

countryside."

"And a bear," Levi piped up.

"Shush," Megan said, a touch of reprimand in her voice.

"It surprised me, but Levi's chatter makes more sense now," Maia said. "As long as none of you intend to eat me, I'm good." She yawned. "I need to sleep."

Levi chortled. "We don't eat people. Burgers are much nicer."

"What he said," Megan agreed with a twinkle.

"Pleased to hear it. I'm partial to a meat pie, myself," Maia said.

"Gavin made her take pain pills and others to help ward off infection." Henry scooped her off the stool and strode toward his suite. "Levi, could you run ahead and open the doors for me?"

Levi sprinted away with his puppy entourage. A crash sounded as the first door whacked against the wall stop. The puppies barked in excitement.

"Without noise," Megan shouted.

Maia burrowed against Henry's warm chest. He smelled like home, and that prompted questions. Mates? Was that why she hadn't been able to stop thinking about him over the years? And while she felt comfortable with Henry and his family, would other shifters reject her? So many questions.

In his suite, Henry set her on her feet. "You're exhausted. I'll help you shower, and then it's into bed with you."

"No back scrubbing?" Maia asked.

"We'll have plenty of time for shower shenanigans," he said, "because you're going to marry me soon, and we'll live together here or at your place."

"Here," she said because she cherished having the others around.

"You'll marry me?" Henry asked, going still.

"You'll find out when you ask me properly," Maia said. "I'm too tired and sore to focus on the future. And I have questions."

"Noted," Henry said.

He helped her to disrobe and shower before settling her in bed.

After taking another of Gavin's pills, she drifted. Was it safe to take medication prescribed by a vet? She hadn't argued, and that told her, on some level, she trusted him. Gavin, a vet and doctor for those with dual natures, played a crucial role in this community. He'd helped her without hesitation, even though she might cause trouble for him. Gavin had done that for Henry.

That was her last thought before she slipped into a deep sleep.

When she woke, she tumbled from bed and groaned. Her leg throbbed, and every muscle screamed at her not to move. Impossible when the restroom was her goal.

Unaware of the time, she found herself alone. It was daylight outside. Maia struggled to the bathroom, tended to her needs, and switched on the shower. Warmth might help to loosen her whimpering muscles and at least get her moving. She needed to move without flinching since her coach would direct her to the team doctor for an assessment.

Maia dressed, but every move hurt, and the idea of running the length of a rugby field made her want to whimper. She wondered if Rose had heard about Amanda yet. Probably not. She reached for her phone and, without second-guessing herself, called Rose.

"Hello, Coach. It's Maia Jacobs." Maia hesitated over what to say and decided at the beginning. "Since I arrived in Dunedin, someone has been stalking and harassing me. My house suffered damage. My car. And then came the attack and my concussion. Yesterday, Amanda attacked me while I was on a training run. The kids with me got help, and the police took her into custody."

The line fell silent while she waited for a reaction.

"Rose, are you there?"

"Amanda attacked you?"

"She did."

"She phoned me last night and told me you assaulted her," the coach said, her voice emotionless. "She was upset and highly emotional."

Maia's stomach sank, and she clutched her phone more tightly. "That's not what happened. I can get the local police to contact you and corroborate my story. I intend to press charges. She injured me, and I won't be able to train on Wednesday. I hope I'll recover enough to attend training on Friday."

"Can you drop by this morning?" Rose asked. "I'll make a doctor's appointment for you."

"What time?" Maia asked.

"How about ten-thirty?"

"I'll be there," Maia said and disconnected. What the hell? Amanda had confessed and taken pleasure in telling Maia everything she'd done.

The bedroom door opened, and Henry entered carrying a tray.

"You're up," he said, setting the tray on a side table. "How are you feeling?"

"Sore. That's what woke me, I think. I had another shower, and that helped. Amanda rang the coach last night and told Rose I'd attacked her."

"She's still in Middlemarch, locked in a cell. I spoke to Laura ten minutes ago. Laura is waiting for transport to take her to Dunedin."

"Can she get out with bail?"

"Yes, but conditional on staying away from you."

"Kind of difficult if we're playing for the same rugby team," Maia snapped.

Henry raised his hands in silent surrender, and Maia pressed her lips together.

"Sorry. I'm frustrated and taking it out on you. I have a meeting with Rose at ten-thirty and a doctor's appointment right after."

"Can I drive you?" Henry asked.

"Thanks, I'd like that."

"Eat your breakfast, and do some gentle walking and stretches."

Yeah, that's what Gavin had recommended, even if she hurt.

He'd told her walking would help to ease her muscles.

"Thank you," Maia said, softening on seeing the perfect apricot-colored rose on the tray.

"Cup of tea?" Henry asked.

"Please."

They ate tea and toast together before walking to the kennels so Henry could release his dogs for a morning run. Now that she knew of his wolf heritage, the close dynamics with his dogs made sense. He was pack alpha.

Juno trotted over to Maia and rubbed against her legs. Maia winced but repositioned herself and petted the dog. The other dogs visited Maia, sniffing and brushing against her legs.

Henry stood beside her, smiling at the dogs' antics as they played together. "Sometimes, I'll shift and run with them. It's an excellent way to cement bonds, and I enjoy the rough and tumble exercise."

Maia smiled. "That must be nice. If we had children together, would they be like you or me?"

"Difficult to say. With the black leopards, the children always take after the shifter parent. With you and I, it could go either way. It depends if you have any shifter blood in your family tree." Henry slipped an arm around her waist and stared at her intently. "Would that bother you?"

Maia hesitated, thinking. "Are they born as human or shifter?"

"Always human."

"I guess that's okay," Maia said.

"That makes me happy. I might marry you."

"Still haven't asked me," Maia said. "And I still have loads of questions."

"I have answers whenever you're ready." Henry grinned, the boyish look suiting him. "I'll take you by surprise with a proposal when you least expect it."

"Deal," Maia said, cheering considerably at his willingness to address her queries. "You do that."

CHAPTER 34

Maia entered Rose's office at the appointed time, her gut bucking when she noted Cameron's presence. She managed a nod and sank into the last empty seat. She placed her hands in her lap and gripped them together.

Rose got straight to business. "Management says I must stand you down until we resolve this matter."

"What?" Maia's pulse hit a speed bump before taking off like a startled rabbit. "No."

Cameron shifted in his chair. "The management team states we had no problems before you started playing for us."

Maia gaped. "They're blaming me?"

Cameron merely eyed her with an impassive expression.

Maia got it, then. "They want me to drop the charges."

Rose gave a minuscule nod. "Amanda has bite wounds, cuts, and scrapes. She says you let your dog attack her."

"I don't own a dog," Maia snapped. "What about the police reports?"

Rose shrugged.

"Fine." Maia stood. She twisted too fast and winced at the pain that shot from her thigh.

"Maia, you have an appointment to see the team doctor," Cameron said.

"No," Maia said. "I don't have to do anything, not if I'm stood down."

Rose tapped her pen on her desktop. "It's a condition of your employment."

"And if I don't attend the appointment?"

"You won't get paid, and you'll give the management an excuse to cancel your contract," Cameron answered.

"Who is on the management team?" She'd scanned the names but hadn't recognized more than one or two. They'd seemed like distant figures, especially since she didn't have day-to-day contact with them.

Rose shrugged. "It doesn't matter. They pay your salary. You signed a contract and leave yourself open if you don't follow the terms and conditions."

"Fine," Maia gritted out. She didn't mention the Black Fern training camp, which was probably doubtful. If she didn't play, she couldn't impress. Amanda would win.

Life isn't fair. Her aunt's stern voice blasted through her mind, one of the few things her aunt had enforced on her that bore an ounce of truth.

"Anything else the management team said I should do?" The words burst from her and hovered near snide.

Rose's brows lifted. "You're to have no team contact, which means no training or games. They'll decide what will happen to you at the next board meeting."

"Which is when?" Maia clenched her teeth, refusing to show any weakness.

"It's next month. They met last week," Cameron said.

Maia reached the door without limping. Henry was waiting outside and stood immediately, obviously sensing her distress. She shook her head when he opened his mouth to speak.

"Not here," she said.

With her head held high, she exited the building. She allowed her shoulders to slump once she sat in Henry's vehicle.

"What time is your appointment?" Henry asked. "Do we have time for a coffee first?"

"Yes," she said. "I'm seeing that doctor at twelve-thirty."

Henry drove to the cafe they'd stopped at previously.

"Grab a seat, and I'll order the coffee," he said. "Do you want anything to eat?"

"No," she said, unsure she could even manage a coffee.

Henry joined her in minutes and took the seat opposite. "Tell me what happened."

So she did.

"Can they do that?" he asked, indignation coloring his expression.

"They pay my salary."

"Amanda has connections on the management team. They're covering for her."

"You think?" This emerged with more sarcasm than Henry warranted. "Sorry. None of this is your fault."

"What about your spot at the Black Ferns' training camp?"

"Neither coach mentioned the trials. Amanda told me she was next on the list. A reserve to go to camp if someone drops out. I can ring the guy who called me. He told me to contact him if I had problems. At least that way, I'd know my fate."

"God, Maia. I'm so sorry. I wish there were something I could do to help."

Maia reached across the table for Henry's hand. "You're on my

team, supporting me, and that's the best. I'll come back from this."
Somehow. If her team blacklisted her, other teams might refuse to hire her.

Either way, her dream had moved beyond her grasp. For this season, anyway.

Maia walked into the doctor's room at twelve-thirty, and the visitation didn't go as she'd imagined.

"We're worried about your mental state," he said, steepling his hands in front of his face.

"Pardon?" Maia said, unsure she'd heard correctly.

"High-performance sport is stressful. Not everyone makes the grade."

Her mouth fell open, shock making her faintly nauseous.

"Are you sleeping?"

Maia met his gaze despite her horror. She had to take care, or she'd increase her troubles. *Keep your temper. Answer calmly.* "Yes, I sleep well."

"Are you taking any drugs? Drinking more than usual?"

"No," Maia said firmly.

The bastard. He was in league with management and wanted her off the team. Her contract was clear on this point. She was to conduct herself in a proper manner.

"We'll do bloods. We can do them here," the doctor said.

Maia knew her rights, thankful that she'd read the contract carefully.

"Please provide a list of acceptable labs. I'll do it later this afternoon." There was nothing in her system that shouldn't be there. Gavin had assured her the drugs he'd given her were common painkillers.

"It would be a simple matter to do the tests now."

"I have another appointment," Maia said. "Sorry, but I thought this one would be the standard length."

The doctor made a tutting sound, and Maia ground her teeth

together. She should've let Henry come with her, but stupidly, she hadn't thought she'd require a witness.

"The list," she reminded him.

He grumbled but produced a list from his drawer. "We'll need the tests today," he said. "I want you to make an appointment to visit this doctor." He handed her a card.

"A psychiatrist?" Astonished he would want this, she gawked at him.

"Yes, it's a pity you have another appointment because I believe one of his patients has canceled."

Alarm bells peeled loud and clear. "Is there a list of accepted psychiatrists, too?" she asked.

"I believe so, but this man is on the list and in the same building." He smiled, a crocodile smile full of pretend charm and caring.

Maia forced herself to accept the medical lists and stood, offering a smile of her own. "Thank you. I'll make an appointment as soon as I can fit it into my schedule."

She left the doctor's office in a trance, starting when the receptionist called after her. "Miss Jacobs, we require payment today."

Maia halted, anger flooding her. They weren't even paying for this debacle. "Fine," she said. "I will require a tax receipt."

By the time she reached Henry's vehicle, she'd passed shock and plunged into fury. They were playing dirty, trying to force her hand. She loved rugby, and this would've been a disaster six months ago. It was horrific now, but she had Henry and his family for support.

"How did it go?" Henry asked.

"They want me to see a psychiatrist. Management has decided I have significant mental issues, but that's not the worst thing. The doctor wanted me to see the psychiatrist in his building."

"They're trying to force you to drop the charges."

"Yeah, and if I don't, they'll wreck my rugby career."

"Maia, I'm so damn sorry. There must be something we can do."

Maia exhaled. "The blows keep coming. The doctor gave me the list of team-approved medical labs and doctors. I'll get the blood tests done to prove I'm not on drugs."

"But what if your management tampers with the results?"

"They probably will," Maia said, "but I have to play their game while I'm under contract."

"Pick a lab, and we'll get the tests done. I don't know if it will help, but I'll stay with you, so at least you have a witness that the test was done."

"Thanks. I'll have to decide about the psychiatrist, too."

"Not right now," Henry said. "We'll do the blood tests. I'll ask Gavin if he knows any of the names on your list."

"Good idea." Maia closed her eyes and listened to Henry's conversation with Gavin on speaker.

"Hell," Gavin said. "Read the list, and hopefully, I know a name or two. Have them draw and test an extra vial of blood. Keep the results separate.

"Right, we'll do that," Henry said and started reading.

"That one," Gavin said, interrupting Henry. "I know the people there and went to university with one of them. A shifter. I'll call and let her know you're coming. Is it okay if I explain the circumstances?"

"Yes," Maia said, hope driving away the black cloud hovering over her head. "Do you know any of the people on the psychiatrist list?"

Henry read them off.

"That one," Gavin said, and a grin sounded in his voice. "I used to date that guy. We're still friendly and run into one another at medical conferences. He's not a shifter and unaware of the world, but he'll give you an honest assessment."

"Is there any chance they could falsify his report?" Henry asked.

Yeah, good question. She had no trust in the rugby club

management since it had become increasingly clear Amanda had inside contacts. None of the surnames matched hers, but something shonky was happening, and it wasn't in Maia's favor.

"Do you think that's possible?" Gavin asked, sounding surprised.

"The management team is trying to force Maia into dropping the charges against the woman who attacked her," Henry said.

There was a brief pause. "You could ask Tony to send you the report. I'm sure it's normal for patients to request a copy. Ask him."

"I'll do that," Maia said. "Thanks for your help."

"Any time," Gavin said before disconnecting the call.

"Your friends are amazing," Maia said.

"They're your friends, too," Henry said.

They'd accepted her, thanks to Henry. Learning about shifters had stunned her, and although she shouldn't, she was looking at them differently. They hadn't done anything to warrant this, generous with their help and support, and this contradiction was tossing her off balance.

Maia's phone rang, and she pulled it from her handbag. She didn't recognize the number and set it aside. It stopped ringing before giving her another alert. The voicemail had her stomach churning.

"It's the Black Fern selector. He wants to speak with me."

"Call him back," Henry said. "You'll only stress if you wait until we get home."

"What if—"

"The worst that can happen is they tell you not to come," Henry said. "If you don't have rugby commitments, we'll take a couple of weeks for a holiday in the sun. Either way, you'll have next year to make the team. You're a talented player, Maia, and you will make it."

She stared at her phone. Chances were the team management

had already spoken with selectors. They would've informed them she wouldn't be playing, that they'd stood her down. Heck, they'd cast her in the worst light possible.

Maia hit the call button and waited for the selector to answer.

"Maia, thank you for calling back," the man said.

"Sorry, I was driving," she said, lying without a blink.

"Your team management has contacted us and stated they've stood you down for discipline issues. We'd like to know exactly what you've done so we can proceed."

"Discipline issues?" Maia parroted.

Amanda was still messing with her, even though she was an innocent party. She glanced at Henry, and he nodded with encouragement. "It's true they've stood me down, but I've done nothing wrong. When I arrived to take up my rugby contract, I had problems. Someone tagged my house and let the air out of my vehicle tires. They tied a puppy outside, purposely hurting it, so I'd go outside to investigate. When I did, they struck me on the head. I suffered a concussion that had me off the field and on limited play for several weeks.

"That was the start of the nuisance pranks. I reported these crimes to the local police, who have been investigating. Yesterday, I went on a training run. I've been taking the young boys and girls from the local primary school with me, helping their team to train. We went over an obstacle course, and when we were running through the forest, Amanda, my teammate, attacked me. She wanted to injure me so I couldn't play rugby or attend your training camp. The young kids alerted adults working nearby, and the local police arrested her."

"I see," the selector said, his voice non-committal. "What happened next?"

"My coach called me into a meeting this morning and told me management was standing me down because I had attacked Amanda. They said if I dropped the charges, they might reconsider. They also instructed me to visit the team doctor." Maia issued a sigh because this was a nightmare. "Once I arrived at my appointment, I was told I needed to submit to drug tests and required a psychiatrist's report." She didn't mention the doctor pressuring her to use his clinic for the tests and use a psychiatrist in the same building.

"Do you have copies of the police reports?"

"I'm sure I could get them for you."

"Send them to the email address on the card I gave you," he said and hung up.

Maia scowled at her phone, frustration and acute disappointment making her chest ache. Her entire story sounded farfetched. She wouldn't believe it. "This is unfair. I have done nothing wrong."

"Sweetheart, I'm sorry. This isn't right, but I'm not sure what else to suggest."

"I could drop the charges," she said bitterly. "But I can bet that wouldn't go well for me either. They'll sideline me. I probably wouldn't get game time. They'd relegate me to water boy status."

"I'm so bloody sorry," Henry said.

Yeah, they were crushing her between a rock and a hard place. She'd bet they weren't standing down Amanda. Their team's convincing performance had secured them a spot in the playoffs.

"Next season, I'll have problems finding a team to sign me. No one will sign a troublemaker because the team management *will* bad-mouth me. I can't win, no matter what I do." Her throat grew tight, and she hung her head, every muscle in her body tense. Her stomach churned with nerves and disappointment.

Aunt Beatrice's whiny voice rippled through her thoughts again; this time, Maia imagined a victorious glint in her eyes. *"Life isn't fair, Maia. Remember that. Life doesn't owe you a thing."*

Maia snorted. That would teach her to try to one-up her aunt. Pettiness was a bad look, and she was paying for her attitude.

"I should sell my house and move back to Auckland."

"No," Henry snapped. "You can sell your house or keep it. I don't care, but you are not running back to Auckland. You are not leaving me. Hell! That didn't come out right. I love you. We're engaged to be married, and I want you at my side. You are *it* for me. If you want to play rugby for another team, I'll fully support you, but we are not breaking up. You hear me?"

"Half the people in Middlemarch heard you," Maia said, her heart instantly lighter. "I'm sorry. I'm feeling down and not thinking straight. When I started playing rugby and learned I had talent, I wanted to push myself and play at the highest level. It's disappointing I won't manage it this year, but I can try again. The game has given me purpose. I've done well and have to remember that."

"This decision doesn't mean you must end your rugby involvement. You love the game, right? So go into coaching or start a local team. Coach the school team. The kids love you already. You know, you could always speak with Megan. She used to be a sports reporter and was up for a top job. Her management replaced her with a younger woman. Megan ended up in Middlemarch to emcee a local tournament. She met Jacey and stayed."

"Truly?"

"Yes," Henry said as he turned into the driveway. "Ask her tonight. She'll tell you the story."

"And she writes books, like me."

"Another fortunate coincidence. All I'm trying to say is you have other options. Though not what you desire, these alternatives are solid. Plus, I'll have you here at my side, and we can talk about our wedding."

"And you still haven't proposed," Maia said, but the joke fell flat when it felt like she was fighting a losing battle, her rugby dream slipping from her grasp.

CHAPTER 35

Henry drove Maia to the appointment with Gavin's friend for her psych evaluation. On arrival, Maia asked if Henry could observe.

"Henry, you can sit over there but can't join our conversation. Can you do that?" The doctor grinned, but Henry could tell he meant it.

"Sure," Henry said. He'd hear their discussion without difficulty, anyway.

The consultation began, and Henry listened to Maia's calm, even responses with pride. No one in their right mind could accuse her of having problems. He and their friends knew this, and Henry thought Gavin's ex would say the same by the end of the consultation.

At the end of an hour, the doctor told her he could confidently give her a favorable report. He would email a copy to the rugby board and cc her.

"What did I tell you?" Henry asked.

"I wonder if they ask Amanda to jump through the same hoops."

Once they arrived home, Henry made a point of keeping Maia busy. She went to the local primary school and coached Levi's team. While she was there, the netball coach asked if she'd help to get her players fitter because the boys and girls in the rugby team sang her praises.

Later that night, Maia's phone rang while they were eating dinner.

"Answer it," Jacey said when she hesitated.

Maia's heart sank on recognizing the phone number. The selector. She steeled herself for bad news, closing her eyes seconds after she hit the button to accept the call. "Hello," she said, praying she could hold her emotions together.

"Maia," the man said, "I confirm you have a place at the upcoming training camp. Unfortunately, your team's decision to stand you down means no game time. That's problematic."

"Oh," Maia said, unsure where he was going with this. Luckily, she was healing well, and Gavin had expressed his satisfaction with her recovery.

"If you can find a local team to play for, we might give you a pass. Actually... Just a moment." Maia heard him speaking with someone before he came back on the line. "Come to the camp, and we'll talk more, but my friend coaches at Christchurch. They've had injury problems this season. Would you be interested in a short-term contract with them if we could set it up?"

Maia glanced at Henry, unsure how he'd take this, but he gave a definitive nod. "Yes, I'd be willing to do that."

"Excellent. The camp is in Wellington, and I'll email you the travel details."

"What about my current club? Won't they object?" she asked.

"Don't worry. I'll take care of that. Avoiding their training sessions and games is best for the foreseeable future. We don't want them to accuse you of leaking team strategy."

"Okay. Thank you." She hung up with a grin. "I'm attending camp!" Her phone rang again, and she pulled a face on seeing the number. She considered not answering, but that wasn't professional. "Hello, Maia speaking."

"Ms. Jacobs, this is Barry Curtis on the rugby board. We received your psych evaluation this afternoon and already have feedback from the team doctor. I'm afraid, given the results, we are terminating your contract as of today."

"P-pardon?" Maia said, shock giving her a one-two punch in the gut. There was nothing wrong with her mental state!

"You're not a suitable team player. Please return your uniform plus sponsored supplies in the next seven days, and you will receive your final wages. I'm sorry it came to this, Ms. Jacobs, because you're a talented player. Part of your obligation to the club is to show professionalism and be a role model for younger players coming through the ranks. We're not seeing that from you."

Maia remained silent because she was frightened of what she might say. She wanted to tell him what he could do with his team position and her views of the management team. She did neither.

"Did you hear me?" Barry asked.

"Yes," Maia said in a low voice.

"Well," he said. "We had such high hopes for you." He hung up, apparently finished with her and wiping his hands of the entire debacle.

"Maia," Megan said, her blue eyes full of sympathy. "This Barry Curtis is talking a load of bull crap."

"What did he say?" London asked, her eyes narrowed. "Maia is one of their best players."

"He told me I was unprofessional and setting a poor example for other players. Also, according to him, there was a problem with the doctors' reports."

"Gavin's friend gave you a copy," Henry said. "You're fine. Perfect."

"I know that. You know that, but they're pushing me out anyway," Maia said, not holding back her bitterness.

"The Black Fern selectors are still interested," Gerard said. "And the guy you spoke to has a contact in Christchurch. This might work out better."

"The Dunedin management will try to muck that up for me," Maia said, knowing this instinctively. Someone was protecting Amanda.

"They won't know straight away," London said, having caught up with the play despite not having shifter hearing. "Have you played Christchurch?"

"No, not yet," Maia said.

"Well," London said brightly. "They'll know when you run onto the field with the opposition."

"If everything falls into place. Besides, I'll have to find somewhere to live in Christchurch. That might not be simple."

"Ah," Henry said with a grin at Gerard. "That problem is easy to solve because our best friend lives in Christchurch. I'm sure he and Lisa have room for us to stay with them. We might have to work in exchange, but it should be fun."

"You'd go with me?" Maia asked.

"Security guard and boyfriend," Henry said. "Gerard and I have been considering casting a wider net for work. It won't hurt for me to investigate the possibilities while we're in Christchurch."

"Deal," Maia said, her heart lighter now that she might have a plan B.

One month later.

Maia jogged onto the field with her team, happy and determined to play well. She loped after her teammates—a captain and players who'd welcomed her without reservation. It took her time to relax and settle in because the Dunedin management had lodged a protest saying she couldn't transfer teams mid-season.

Luckily, the governing body had found in her favor. And since then, she'd focused on training, rugby, and writing. She and Henry had spent their weeks with his friends, Sam and Lisa, and managed two weekends in Middlemarch. They'd talked—a lot—and Maia was more comfortable with what she'd learned about shifters.

Maia and her teammates went through their warm-up routine while waiting for the opposition to arrive. They were finally playing Dunedin, and whoever won would progress to the semi-finals.

Amanda was on the team today, and Maia needed to engage in a sensible game. Stay out of trouble. Her team knew the situation and had promised to protect Maia from dirty play.

She had to do the rest herself and, hopefully, play the best game of her life. *No pressure.*

After the coin toss, the two teams ran into position. The referee blasted his whistle. Maia ignored Amanda and her furious glower but waved hello to Jan and Rebecca and received friendly greetings in return.

The Dunedin team took the kickoff, and Maia surged into action. One of her teammates caught the ball cleanly and ran forward. A hard tackle took her down, but she passed the ball to Maia, who flicked it onto her backline players. Maia dodged an oncoming player's tackle and sprinted after her teammates.

"You won't act so smug when I pulverize you into the ground," Amanda taunted in a low voice. "Your sugar daddy won't like you if you're broken."

Maia ignored the threat but watched for Amanda. The players on her team were fitter, which showed when they constantly ran the ball, keeping a fast pace.

Maia caught the ball and dashed toward the try line while assessing the opposition's field position. She ducked and weaved before passing to the halfback. The ball flew with precision along the backline, and their winger ducked inside an opposing player to score.

The tries kept coming, and frustration ramped up in the Dunedin team with lots of trash talk from Amanda and her closest friends. Jan and Rebecca avoided the drama and played well, but Maia's team rattled them.

When they started the second half, Maia let the insults and snarky comments roll off her.

"Let's go," her captain encouraged Maia and the others.

Their fullback caught the ball and rushed forward, dodging a tackle before passing to Maia.

"Go, Maia!" someone shouted from the sideline.

She raced forward, sidestepping once, twice, and tossing the ball to her teammate. Maia continued running, keeping up with the play of the ball.

The tackle came out of nowhere, and she hit the ground hard, the collision knocking the air from her lungs.

"Off the ball tackle, ref," someone from the sideline shouted.

The referee either didn't hear or hadn't seen because play continued. Maia picked herself up once the player hauled their body off hers. Amanda. *Of course, it was.* Amanda didn't check on Maia but raced away as if the illegal tackle hadn't happened.

Maia stretched gingerly. She was sore but uninjured. She ignored Amanda and threw herself back into the game.

Amanda charged at Maia when she had the ball, her expression one of rage. Maia couldn't avoid the tackle. The contact stole her breath and sent her flying. It was also too high—a dangerous tackle—and Maia saw stars when she struck the ground.

The referee's whistle blew, halting play. He trotted over to speak with the linesmen before returning and withdrawing a red card from his pocket.

Amanda argued with the referee before whirling to take a swing at Maia.

"Amanda," Jan said, her tone sharp and authoritative. "Stop. The referee has given you a red card. Get off the field so we can resume play."

Amanda's face twisted. "You are not the boss of me. Nothing wrong with my tackle. The ref needs glasses if he thinks I deserve a red card."

Maia's captain came forward and spoke to the referee. "There has been lots of play happening off the ball and trash talk."

"I'm aware," the referee said, waving his red card. "You made a dangerous tackle. Please leave the field, or I will call off the game."

"But it's not fair," Amanda snapped.

"Amanda," Jan said. "We can discuss this later with management and the coaches."

Finally, Amanda left the field, but only after several of her team murmured to her. Maia longed for Henry's shifter hearing to understand the conversation.

The last half an hour was fast and furious, with Maia's team running in four tries and their kicker converting each one. At the game's end, Maia was sore but still running freely, and for that, she was grateful.

Once the final whistle blew, Maia's team lined up to thank the opposition, but many of the Dunedin players walked off without acknowledging them. It was poor sportsmanship, and Maia was glad she no longer had an association with them.

Their team went into a huddle.

"Well done, everyone. We kept our heads and didn't let them needle us. We're in the next round," their captain ended gleefully.

"This is our best result in three years. All we need to do is work hard, and the title is ours for the taking."

"*Uh-oh*," one of their team said in warning.

Maia glanced to the right to see an enraged Amanda stalking toward them. Henry and Gerard were also heading their way, and Maia relaxed. Amanda couldn't do more than shout at her in public. It hadn't been Maia's fault Amanda had lost her temper, resulting in the referee sending her off the field.

"This is your fault," Amanda shouted, spittle flying and red patches of temper on her cheeks. "You enjoy making me look stupid."

"Think she's doing that all on her own," someone said.

Maia ignored the other woman. A red card meant a committee would look at Amanda's case and decide on disciplinary action. It was nothing to do with Maia.

Maia grinned at Henry. Her man. The more time she spent with him, the more she tumbled in love with the man. She took half a step toward Henry.

"Watch out!" someone shouted. A teammate.

Maia jerked, feeling a presence beside her. She whirled and barely missed the punch Amanda threw at her.

"What's going on?" It was a female reporter for the local paper.

"Nothing," Maia said.

"She's lying," Amanda howled. "She stole my place on the team."

"I play for Christchurch," Maia said, hoping Amanda wouldn't swing at her again.

"Duck!" Henry shouted without warning.

Maia dropped, and Amanda tripped over her, the force of the blow she'd aimed at Maia throwing her off balance.

"Doesn't look like nothing to me," the reporter said.

Maia scrambled away from Amanda and joined Gerard and Henry, trusting them to tell her if Amanda tried to strike her again. She relaxed when she spotted Amanda's teammates and the assistant coach. Maia watched Amanda struggle to run after her, but Cameron manhandled her toward the changing rooms.

"What can you tell me about the bad blood between Maia and Amanda? Didn't they used to play on the same team?" the reporter asked, shoving a microphone at Maia's teammates.

"I have nothing to say," one said.

"Time for a shower," another said.

En masse, her team left without commenting. The reporter glanced at Maia but must've thought better of trying to get a soundbite from her.

"Do you need to do any promo stuff before you leave?" Henry asked.

"I'll check with the coach," Maia said. "I'll introduce you."

"Amanda is digging herself a deeper hole," Gerard said, his green eyes full of concern. "Surely they'll punish her this time."

"She'll get herself arrested again," Maia said. "I refuse to accept her crap."

"Maybe you should take out a restraining order, so she's breaking the law if she comes near you," Henry said. "Your teams won't meet again, so she can't say the restraining order would stop her from playing rugby."

Gerard snorted. "She's doing that by herself. What did she think she'd achieve by attacking you in public?"

"She wasn't thinking," Henry said. "The woman has a temper and sees red instead of commonsense."

"Coach Riley?" Maia said on reaching their head coach. "This is my boyfriend Henry and his business partner Gerard. Is there anything I need to stay for?"

He shook hands with Henry and Gerard before turning to her. "You did good, missy. Great game. Still can't believe those idiots kicked you off their team roster. Their loss. My gain," he said, his broad grin revealing a missing eye tooth. "We have the hospital visit next week. Other than that, it's our usual training schedule. Have some fun." He waggled his finger at her. "Not too much, though. I need you fighting fit for our next game. Things have become serious."

"Yes, coach," Maia said.

She, Henry, and Gerard wandered off to join their family and friends who'd come to see her game. Levi sprinted over with his best friend. Both boys gave her an enormous hug. Everyone was staying with Sam and Lisa before traveling to Dunedin. Henry and Maia would remain with them until the season's end.

"Amanda!" a man roared.

Everyone, including Maia, turned toward the shout.

"Whoa," Maia said, staring at the gun Amanda aimed in their direction.

"Levi. Scott. Behind us now," Jacey said. "Everyone else, back up slowly."

Sam and Gerard melted into the background while Henry shoved her behind him.

"Henry," Maia said, his name a soft protest.

"A bullet won't hurt me as much."

"You've taken everything from me!" Amanda screamed.

Where had she bought a gun? Guns weren't a common commodity in New Zealand.

"Back up slowly," Jacey instructed those behind them.

"Pay attention," Amanda screamed. The gun fired, punctuating her order.

"What do you want?" Maia called, wincing as a thunk sounded behind her, followed by a metallic reverberation.

"For you to get the hell out of my life," Amanda screeched.

Maia noticed the reporter sidling closer, intent on a story. Maia wanted no part of this drama.

"Amanda, put down the gun," Cameron shouted. "This isn't the way to solve your problems."

"You're right," Amanda called. "I'll shoot her, then she won't be an issue." Amanda prowled closer while everyone around Maia backed to safety.

Without warning, Amanda darted forward, but Gerard and Sam glided behind her. They exchanged hand signals before they tackled her. Amanda jerked, loosed a screech. The gun fired. A woman shrieked.

The reporter. She dropped to the ground, holding her arm and screaming hysterically.

"She shot me," she howled.

Sam and Gerard pinned Amanda's bucking body, Gerard taking the gun away.

Jacey spoke on his phone. "Yes, they've secured the woman. We need an ambulance and the police. A stray bullet hit a spectator."

"You okay?" Henry asked.

"Yeah. I'm thinking Amanda won't get bail. If she thinks I won't press charges, she needs her head read," Maia snapped, thankful for Henry's friends. *Her friends,* too, now that her shock about shifters and learning most of her friends were dual-natured had dissipated.

"The cops have arrived," Jacey said. "Plenty of witnesses. That will help."

"Is the reporter okay?" Maia asked.

"The bullet nicked her arm," Lisa said. "A doctor is with her."

"Thank goodness," Maia said. "This might truly be over now."

CHAPTER 36

She'd been wrong.

The media attention after the attack drove her crazy, and it made her thankful she was in Christchurch rather than Middlemarch. Reporters followed her, popping from behind trees and cars, asking intrusive questions, and making her life miserable. Something she could've done without on finals day.

"Out of the way," Henry growled, using his elbows when a reporter wearing an arm sling shoved a microphone in Maia's face and fired questions like a machine gun.

"Move back," Gerard said in a hard voice, his usual smile and easygoing nature absent while in security mode.

Maia spied their team changing room door with relief, eager to get out of the spotlight and relax. Her strides lengthened. She needed her best game today. Her very best effort. Although she had nothing to prove, pride compelled her to want a win today. Did it make her petty if she wanted to rub the noses of the Dunedin team's management group in the dust? Probably.

"You okay?" Henry jerked her away from the barrage of nosy press questions.

"I'd hoped the reporters would find another story to amuse them," Maia said.

"Rugby is the national game." Gerard kept his voice low. "Two women slugging it out makes for salacious reading."

"I didn't do anything," Maia snapped.

Gerard's impish wink didn't mollify her.

"Stop teasing my girl," Henry said.

They reached the dressing room door.

"We'll wait outside until the team is ready to leave," Henry said.

"Thanks." She was ready to take ten minutes to chill and run over the game plan.

Maia pushed inside to excited chatter, the scent of liniment, and women braiding their hair. She sucked in a ragged breath and grasped for calm.

"Maia, I'll braid your hair for you," Jill, their captain, offered.

It was a new team ritual, started after they'd made it to the quarter-finals. They'd kept winning, so the braiding continued.

Maia nodded, her butterflies massing. Nerves were invaluable, but she veered on the edge of panic because not one of the team's set plays popped into her head when she focused on their game plan.

It didn't help that the Black Fern selectors were revealing their team selection tonight. After the debacle with Amanda, they'd postponed their announcement. They didn't want the franchise dragged into the public mess Amanda had caused. Several of her team had attended the training camp with Maia, so the tension was palpable. Everyone wanted to play the game of their lives.

"I see that sexy man of yours is hovering outside," another of her team said.

Maia suppressed her instinctive wince. That was another thing that bothered her. Henry had gone into super protective mode and refused to let her go anywhere alone. Despite her attempts to talk to him, he insisted his responsibility was to keep her safe. She loved him. She did, but he was smothering her, and if he didn't ease up soon, she'd explode.

Maia said none of this, however. "He worries, and the press isn't helping. They won't leave me alone."

"Take your hands off me," a woman snapped.

"Ah, yes. The reporter that got shot," Jill said, cocking her head to better listen.

"Ma'am, this is the team dressing room and not available to outsiders," Gerard said in a placating voice from the other side of the door.

"Who said?" The reporter sounded much closer.

"The team manager," another voice said. "Please escort her to the exit."

"My pleasure," Gerard said.

"You can't do this," the reporter protested.

"We can," the manager said. "It's an important game today, and you're interrupting my players' preparation."

Gerard must've propelled the reporter away because her protests grew fainter.

The door opened, and Penny, their assistant coach, poked her head inside the dressing room. "Everyone decent? James wants a word before you head out to warm up."

Jill tied Maia's braid and glanced around. "All safe."

And it was true. They were ready to run onto the field.

James, Penny, and their manager entered the dressing room, and silence fell.

"Everyone knows the game plan. You've worked hard and deserve your place in the final. I want you to go out there, do your best, and enjoy the moment. You've already gone further in the competition than we have before, but I think you can shock this Auckland team. Remember that. They might have a home-team advantage, but we have fans, too," James said.

"We know you'll each give one hundred and ten percent. You always do," their manager said. "But I want you to know that whatever the result, we are proud of your accomplishments. We couldn't have asked for more of you."

"Except you want us to win this game," someone quipped.

"Yeah, no pressure, Coach," another player said.

Laughter filled the dressing room, easing the tension.

James grinned. "We're doing this for Maia and the other prospective Black Ferns. We want them to show well for the selectors."

"Yeah," their winger yelled, pumping her fist.

"Right," their manager said. "Squeeze together, and we'll take a quick photo to post on our social media."

Five minutes later, they jogged down the tunnel into the stadium to the crowd's roar. Maia ran at the rear with Henry and Gerard beside her. Henry grasped her hand and kissed her hard before she exited the tunnel.

"I love you, Maia, and I'm proud of you," he said, his eyes glinting golden, which she now knew was his wolf.

"Have a great game, Maia," Gerard said, giving her a brief hug. "We'll be watching and cheering."

Family.

That got Maia straight in the heart because it was something new. She'd stayed with the team the previous night, but London and Megan called to wish her luck. She'd spoken to Jacey and Levi, who was beyond excited that he and his team were attending the game. Emily and Saber had texted her while Isabella, Leo, and Kian were in the stadium crowd. Isabella had told Maia she expected a personal recommendation of her services since she'd done a fantastic job of whipping Maia into shape.

Yeah, this support gave her all the feels.

"Crush them," Henry said, and after a last kiss, he released her.

Maia ran onto the pitch, ignoring the flash of cameras and the increased volume from the crowd. She and her team warmed up at one end of the field, the Auckland team at the other. Before Maia knew it, the whistle to start the game blew. She put on her game face and threw herself into the play. Her first touch of the ball eased her nerves, especially since she caught it and passed safely.

After a tough battle, they were leading by three points at half-time.

James was pleased. Maia could tell, although he wasn't effusive about it.

"You have them rattled," he said. "Their coach will urge them to plug the holes in their backline, so this is the plan."

It was an excellent plan, and Maia's team followed his instructions when they grabbed the ball in the second half. They took the Auckland team by surprise, and they were slow to regroup. Two converted tries later, Maia thought they had a solid grip on the game. But they kept plugging away, their fitness helping them to keep the pressure on their opposition.

Maia snapped up the ball from a loose pass and galloped toward the try line with minutes left on the clock. She dotted down and, seconds later, found herself crushed in the middle of a team hug.

Their fullback missed the conversion goal, but it didn't matter. They kept the Auckland team in their territory, not allowing them room to maneuver or get near their scoreline.

The final siren wailed. The game was theirs. Players hugged Maia before they lined up to shake hands with the opposition team. The crowd applauded, and Maia noticed her Middlemarch friends cheering loudest of all. She waved at them before speaking with the Auckland opposition players, trading a few friendly words and shaking hands.

An inner sense made Maia's attention stray to the crowd. A man jumped the barrier, sprinting in their direction. He held something in his hand. She squinted and quickly backed up.

"Maia," Henry said with sharp urgency, appearing behind her. He grasped her arm and shoved her behind him while Gerard blocked her when she tried to stand beside Henry.

The man kept sprinting toward them, and the other players noticed.

"Is that a gun?" one asked.

Every player ran in different directions, pushing and shoving. Some shouted in alarm.

Maia peeked between Henry and Gerard and glimpsed security men giving chase.

"He's got a gun," Henry said, his muscles tense.

"Any idea who he is?" Gerard asked.

"I don't recognize him," Maia said.

"Where are you, bitch? You can't hide. She's on remand, and it's your fault."

Maia's stomach sank. "Do you think he's related to Amanda?"

"That'd be my guess," Henry said evenly.

Neither he nor Gerard took their eyes off the man.

"Stop hiding!" the man shouted. "Bitch, you've ruined my dreams."

Maia was tired of this. She darted around Henry. "Here," she snapped.

The man fired his weapon.

"No!" Henry shouted and dived, pushing Maia and covering her with his larger body.

"*Oomph,*" Maia grunted on hitting the ground. Henry jerked, still acting as her shield, and Maia panicked when liquid soaked into her clothes.

"Henry. Henry!"

He moved, grunting as he lifted off her.

"You're bleeding." She glanced frantically for Gerard, but he was helping the security men contain the assailant. The man struggled violently, and it took three to overpower him.

"That bitch had it in for Amanda. She was jealous of my daughter," the man howled.

"Doesn't mean you can shoot her," Gerard snapped.

"Henry." Maia ignored the shouts, petrified that he'd hurt Henry. He meant everything to her. She tore at his shirt, attempting to locate an injury. "Where are you hurt?"

"Paint gun," Henry said. "Winded. Let me breathe."

She paused. "You're not shot?"

"No."

Maia sagged against him, holding him tightly until she could breathe again without terror taking her out at the knees. "My life flashed before my eyes," she whispered, still clutching Henry. "It was a life without you, and I hated what I saw. Henry, will you please marry me? Life is short. Unpredictable. I don't want anyone else. I want you. So please marry me and put me out of my misery."

"You don't mind that we're different?" he murmured, his large body tensing again when the man continued hollering. "That I'm older?"

"I adore your wolfish ways, and age is just a number. Like you said, we're equals. A partnership, and that's perfect for me. For us." She honestly didn't care that everyone she lived with, apart from London, could morph into an animal. They were a devoted family, and they embraced her, accepting her into their group with affection, laughter, and care because Henry loved her. "I love everything about you, Henry, and have instinctively trusted you since I was twelve. Please marry me."

"Yes." And he drew her into his arms and kissed the stuffing out of her.

Gradually, she noticed cheers and catcalls from her fellow players and the Auckland team they'd played.

Henry pulled back, his expression impassive, but his brown eyes glowed, and he didn't fully release her.

Jill grinned at Maia. "Now that the police have Paint Gun Man in custody, could we get on with the prize-giving?"

"Of course," Maia said in a nonchalant air. But she glanced at the security men who had the interloper contained.

"That *is* Amanda's father," Henry said. "Gerard and I investigated him. In his youth, he was a talented rugby player, but a severe injury in a vehicle accident meant he couldn't play professionally. From what we can gather, he passed his talent on to Amanda and insisted she fulfill his dreams. She snapped under pressure, and it appears that the stress of her arrest was too much for her father."

"That's sad," Maia said, watching her team as they lined up to receive their medals. "My aunt was forceful in her opinions and tried to coerce me into following her instructions. I know what it feels like, but why didn't Amanda speak to her mother or an outsider if she hated playing rugby so much?"

"They're waiting for you," Henry said, giving her a tiny shunt. "But to answer your question, I think she bought into her father's dream. Maybe she thought he'd love her more if she did as he asked."

"Makes sense," Maia said, pecking him on the cheek before jogging away to join her team.

Henry rose from the restaurant table where they'd had a celebratory dinner and held his hand out to Maia. "Would you like to walk around the waterfront?"

"I want to go," Levi said.

"Let your brother go with Maia," Megan said. "We'll walk after we eat our dessert."

Henry sent Megan a grateful smile before leading Maia outside. Despite his deep affection for his family, he craved time with Maia. He didn't want to live alone, frightened something might happen to her as it had to Jenny. Maia had told him she'd prefer to spend time with him and enjoy every moment given to her.

His woman was brave and wise.

He'd been holding himself apart, too terrified to fully live and love again because of something that might happen. He no longer wished to live in fear. Jenny hadn't deserved to die, but he had to take a chance and keep living. Fate had given him this opportunity and placed Maia in his path.

"Where are we going?" Maia asked.

"I thought we'd cross the pedestrian bridge and walk to the Wynyard Quarter. We can stop for a drink if you want." He also wanted to give her the ring in his pocket and make their engagement official. While Maia was with her team, doing interviews and taking photos, Henry went ring shopping. The instant he'd seen the ruby-and-diamond ring, he'd known it was perfect for Maia.

He savored her hand in his, just being with her without glancing over his shoulder or worrying about someone shooting at them. A ferry nudged into its berth while a bus full of commuters lumbered down the road.

"I'm proud of you. You played well today. The Black Fern selectors would be crazy not to pick you for their team."

Maia's phone rang, interrupting. "Talk about coincidences. It's the selector."

"Answer it."

"Maia Jacobs," she said, and Henry caught her trepidation.

"Maia, I'll keep this short because I have a long list of people to call, but we'd like you to play for the Black Ferns."

"Really?" Maia said.

"Really," the selector said, laughing. "Your play has impressed us, especially since we know you've had background drama. We'll email you the training details and our program for this year. Okay?"

"Yes. Thank you so much!"

Henry heard both ends of the conversation and squeezed her biceps in silent congratulations.

Maia hung up in a daze, her grin slowly widening and excitement spreading over her face. "Henry, I did it. I made the team!"

"You did. They'd be fools if they ignored you because you're a fantastic player." He hugged her hard, pressing her firmly against his chest and breathing in her scent. His mate. He was a damn lucky man.

After a long moment, he pulled back and fumbled in his pocket. He opened the green box and extended it to her. "Maia Jacobs, I am crazy about you. Please accept this ring to make our engagement official."

"Henry." She held out her hand.

He pushed the ring onto her finger with a sense of satisfaction. "I love you, Maia. Thank you for persevering and making me realize I was an idiot. My life is so much better with you in it."

"Aw, Henry." Maia smiled at him, one of her big, bright smiles that always made him feel at peace. It shone in her eyes and lit his world. Maia accepted his grumpy arse and made him a better man. A better wolf. He held out his hand, and she took it as they continued to meander along the waterfront, savoring the sea air, the city noises, and the lights.

He had his dream woman, his lady, by his side. Life couldn't be better.

Living the dream!

CHAPTER 37

W hen she and Henry returned to the hotel, they found London, Gerard, Jacey, Megan, and Levi loitering in the lobby.

"Did she say yes?" Levi demanded.

She exchanged a glance with Henry and extended her left hand. Megan and London pounced, seizing her to study the ring.

"It's beautiful," London said, hugging Maia. "We knew Henry was gaga about you, and this would happen eventually, but I'm so glad you're joining the family."

"What she said." Megan embraced Maia. "Have you discussed wedding dates?"

"Not yet," Maia said. "It will depend on my game schedule. That was my other news. I made the team. They called me while we were walking."

"Congratulations," Jacey said, his blue eyes full of happiness.

He and Gerard hugged her, as did Levi.

"Will you still have time to train with us?" Levi asked.

"When I'm at home," Maia said.

"Yay!"

"Maia and I will discuss wedding dates, but it will be soon," Henry said.

Maia agreed. As she'd told Henry, life was too short to waste time.

"We should have a celebratory drink," London said.

"Tomorrow night when we're at home," Henry said firmly. "Maia and I want alone time."

"Why?" Megan asked innocently, but her blue eyes danced with pure devilry.

Henry growled, and Gerard laughed.

"Stop teasing the boy. We'll meet you for breakfast at eight and need to be at the airport at ten," Jacey said, chuckling. "Good night, and congratulations."

Henry took Maia's hand and whisked her to the elevator and their room.

Finally, he closed the door behind them. "Alone at last."

Maia felt herself beaming at him. "I'm so happy, Henry."

"Want a nightcap?" he asked, winking. "I'll get it while you peek at the info the Black Ferns sent you."

Maia plucked her phone from her shoulder bag without hesitation, thankful Henry understood she'd want to see the upcoming schedule. "We have a tour of the UK and Ireland," she said, speed-reading. "I'll be away most of November and the first two weeks of December."

Henry handed her a glass of Scottish whisky containing three ice cubes. "We knew that would be a possibility. We can still talk every day."

A wave of love engulfed her. "Henry, I appreciate your support." And she meant every word. Some women who'd attended the training camp didn't have backing from their partners or families, making playing rugby difficult. One woman's partner had given her an ultimatum—him or rugby. She'd chosen rugby.

"We could get married as soon as you get home." He handed her a glass. "What do you say to a Christmas Eve wedding? A summer wedding with the ceremony outside and our friends and family in attendance."

Maia didn't hesitate. "Yes, that gives me time to consult Caroline about a dress before I go, and you can take care of the rest." She grinned. "What do you think?"

Henry sipped his whisky, not giving her much of a reaction. "I can do that and can consult with you. Megan and London will help."

"I trust you implicitly," Maia said. "Surprise me."

"That's settled then," Henry said, drinking the last of his whisky in one mouthful. He set his glass aside and prowled toward her. "Our wedding is on 24th December."

"It's a date," Maia said.

Henry plucked her glass from her hands and set it on the coffee table, still serious but not grumpy. She could see caring combined with anticipation stamped into his features. "We have other things to take care of now."

"What might they be?" But she'd guessed, and pleasant nerves stirred in the pit of her belly.

"My wolf is out of patience and wants to claim you. It's the only way you'll get away on your tour. I don't mean that to sound like a threat, either. It's... It's my primal side. But I don't want to force this on you either. We can wait until you're ready. *Somehow*."

Maia met his gaze without hesitation. "I adore all of you. I love your human sensibilities and the sharp edges of your wolf. It's what makes you Henry. You're not forcing me to do anything since I'm with you one hundred percent."

Relief swept across his features. His warm breath puffed against her neck before he swept her off her feet and carried her to the bed. He set her in the middle of the mattress and grinned.

"My, Mr. Anderson." Maia fluttered her eyelashes at him. "What big teeth you have."

He snorted. "Yes, I'm your big, bad wolf, and don't forget it."

"You forgot, handsome. You scrub up well."

"Thank you. Your little red dress is sexy, but you'll look better out of it."

Maia fluttered her lashes again. "Thank you, kind sir. I love you, Henry. You know that, right? I get that occasionally you still wonder if we're doing the right thing because I'm younger, but think of the adventures we can have together."

"Starting right now," Henry said, shrugging off his jacket and setting it aside on a chair. He sat to slip off his leather boots and socks. Maia watched with interest when he stood again, unbuttoned his steel gray shirt, and tossed that on top of his jacket. He yanked on his belt, and it slid free of his black trousers. Soon, his trousers joined the pile, leaving him in his tight-fitting boxers.

Maia's brows rose. "Surely, you're not stopping there?"

"I find my willpower lacking with you."

"Oh?"

"Tease." Henry hauled her to the edge of the bed. At his urging, she stood and turned to present her back. Henry's warm hands slid down her zipper, and he helped her lift the dress over her head.

"Sexy underwear," he said, running a calloused finger along the shoulder strap of her black bra.

She turned to him, studying the face of the man, the shifter she loved. "You told me that when I was dressing."

"And unfortunately, we were in a time crunch."

They exchanged a grin.

"We're not in a hurry now," she pointed out.

Henry tilted his head, his brown gaze meeting hers. "My wolf is impatient. He sees this as the start of our official mating. If you have any doubts at all, now is the time to tell me because—"

Maia placed her fingers over his mouth, exasperation giving way to understanding. Henry had no doubts about her, and London and Megan had told her if you found a mate, that was it. No divorce. Not if it was a true mating. "Henry, this is the last time I will say this. I fell for you when I saw you during the school trip to visit your dogs. I didn't understand then because I was so young. But after that, I measured every man I met against you. When I started writing, I used a pen name. Do you know what name I used?"

He shook his head, his gaze still on her.

"Henrietta M. March in salute of you and Middlemarch. You have always been with me, and it was you who drew me back once I secured my rugby contract. I have no doubts. We're going to explore life and have children in the future. We'll grow together and be happy. So happy. Do you understand?" Maia sucked in a breath, realizing that she hadn't breathed through that rant. And it had been a tirade because Henry needed to understand.

He cocked his head. "Henrietta M. March?"

She stomped over to her phone and pulled up her website to show him.

"Huh," he said. "You told me you wrote fantasy. When I have time to read, I like action thrillers and mysteries. Henrietta March." When he met her this time, his eyes were more golden than brown. "You've always been mine."

"And now he gets it," she murmured.

"Maia." The passion and love in his face and the amber flashes in his eyes stole her breath. "Mine."

"And now he gets it," she repeated.

"Yeah, I'll admit I pushed you from my mind because you scared the hell out of me. I'm a male and can be stubborn—if you haven't noticed. But once you came back, you made it impossible to ignore you. I wanted to protect you. Still do."

"I'm fine with that as long as it works both ways."

Henry nodded and embraced her. His mouth claimed hers, and there was a new relaxed air between them. Henry had asked her to marry him, but he'd still held a niggling doubt about her age. It seemed she'd put his last fears to rest, and happiness spilled from him. The same joy that filled her.

He lifted and resettled with her on the bed without parting their lips. Tenderness took over until their kiss became more heated. More passionate. He dispensed with her underwear and his and stroked her arms and hips with his rough hands. He kissed the curves of her breasts and pushed her legs apart with his muscular thigh.

"Henry." Maia touched and caressed, her hands wandering as she savored the firmness of his muscles, reveling in their differences.

He held her gaze, and she smiled, spotting his wolf now that she knew he was part of Henry. "I love all of you, Henry. Every part of you. Can I bite you, too?"

Henry shivered, and she took that as a yes. Excitement bloomed in her because she quite liked the idea of claiming him in this way.

He cradled her head and rolled until she sprawled on top of him. Her pulse rate jumped, and she grinned down at him, her hair falling across his face. She leaned low to skim her lips down his neck and purposely nipped the cords. Henry moaned, tensing beneath her.

"You are prodding the wolf, sweetheart," he said, his voice gravely low.

"Yes," she agreed, holding back her grin. This man was everything to her. Strong. Loving. Protective, yet he knew her well enough to understand she needed her dreams. She gave him more teeth at the spot where his neck met his shoulder, and his entire body shuddered. His hands tightened on her shoulder and hip.

"Maia," he said, his voice harsh now.

Before she could speak, he grasped her firmly, and seconds later, she was beneath him, pinned to the mattress. His hands roamed her body with greater purpose. His lips claimed hers, and this kiss was possessive, passionate. Consuming. Maia held on tight, desire a tidal wave rushing through her until she became lost in a sensual haze. The sharp nip of teeth on her neck had her jolting, but the initial pain rapidly receded when Henry lapped the spot with his tongue.

Sensation flared, and the atmosphere in the room thickened with expectation. Her expectation. Henry's expectation.

"Not yet," Henry said.

Maia laughed. "Promises. Promises."

Henry halted her teasing with a kiss. He cupped one breast and tugged her nipple. The quick bite of pain settled between her thighs, and she stirred restlessly. Henry intended to tease until raw need drove her to plead with him to hustle.

But she could reciprocate. She nuzzled his neck, and he growled. She hid her grin at the wolfish tell and wriggled beneath him. The rumble intensified. He lifted his head to glower at her, but her grin merely widened.

"One day," he threatened.

"One day what?"

"I might forget I'm a gentleman and spank you."

"*Ooh*, kinky."

Henry scowled and pinched one of her nipples. Hard. Maia jumped, digging her fingernails into his shoulders. He shuddered, his breath emerging in harsh pants.

"I wanted to go slowly and make this memorable."

"Every time with you is remarkable." It was the truth.

"In that case." Henry reached under the pillow and pulled out a strip of condoms he must've stashed earlier. He opened one and deftly rolled it onto his shaft.

Anticipation shimmered through Maia, and given the devilish

quirk of his lips, he knew it. With a throaty groan, he stole a kiss as he roughly parted her legs. She eagerly arched beneath him, but he took his time, his scorching glance raking her body. It was like a physical touch, and her breathing grew ragged.

"Henry." It was a complaint and drew low laughter from him.

"I love you, Maia."

"I know." Everything inside her turned mushy. "You show it every day."

This time, their kiss was slower and full of tenderness. Henry guided himself into her and pushed home with one unhurried stroke. Her breath caught at the sense of fullness. The rightness.

Henry withdrew slowly and filled her again. She wrapped her legs around him and lifted into his next stroke.

His kiss was tender, and desire rippled through her, each of his thrusts driving her need higher. He trailed kisses across her jaw and down her neck. She gulped in a breath, sensing he'd bite her soon. It was barbaric, yet equally thrilling. She already belonged to Henry, and this would be a physical badge of ownership.

He sank into her with an even stroke, going deep and skimming her clit. She hissed at the shards of bliss firing to life. He nipped her, and the sharp pain darted to coalesce with the stirrings of pleasure.

Henry palmed her left breast and pulled back to fill her again while nibbling her neck. The constant physical stimulation had sensations sizzling through her.

"Henry," she whispered.

He seemed to understand because he quickened his pace, his thrusts becoming erratic as he bit down. Maia had wondered if there would be pleasure in this private celebration between mates because biting sounded painful. The enjoyment factor was way more than she'd expected. She gasped and went liquid deep inside. She pulsed around Henry's cock, and his next stroke into her set off fireworks. He bit harder, the initial pain of his teeth morphing into indescribable pleasure.

Henry groaned as she pulsed around him. He thrust once. Twice and groaned again. He licked the spot where he'd bitten her, and reaction surged in her. This slice of pleasure was deeper, and Henry's shallow thrusts intensified the sensations. Her breath whooshed out, lazy satisfaction filling her.

She kissed Henry's shoulder before sliding her mouth closer to his neck. Instinctively, she bit until tasting blood. It wasn't repulsive, not when Henry shuddered in her arms, his gasp carrying a hint of shock.

She understood because a connection snapped into place between them. She'd already felt like Henry was her other half, but this was more. There was an intensity, a sense of belonging that deepened between them.

"Maia," Henry said, a slight tremor in his voice.

"Yes," she said simply, telling him with her reply that she felt what he did and understood the mate bonds in a way she hadn't earlier. They were meant to be together. She gave a lazy lick over the area where she'd bitten him, eliciting a groan from Henry.

"Wow," he whispered reverently. "We're mates in every sense of the word now. I'm a lucky wolf."

"I think we're both lucky," Maia said softly, sleepily kissing him on the shoulder.

Henry parted their bodies and rolled off her to deal with the condom. Upon returning, he climbed into bed beside her and drew her close.

"Gerard and Jacey told me mating was intense. I didn't understand until now."

"Me neither. You told me what to expect but didn't mention the emotional connection that snapped into place."

"I didn't know."

Maia cuddled closer, sleepy and contented. "I love you so much, Henry, and I can't wait to marry you. I feel as if I've waited for years."

"We've both waited," Henry whispered, but Maia was half asleep.

She was with the man she'd always wanted, the man who was perfect for her in every way, and she couldn't be happier.

Thank you for reading **My Grumpy Wolf**. Would you like more of Henry and Maia? Subscribe to my newsletter (https://dl.bookfunnel.com/k0p0tbnug1) and receive a free copy of **I Do**, a short story featuring Henry and Maia's wedding day.

ALSO BY SHELLEY

Middlemarch Shifters
My Scarlet Woman
My Younger Lover
My Peeping Tom
My Assassin
My Estranged Lover
My Feline Protector
My Determined Suito
My Cat Burglar
My Stray Cat
My Second Chance
My Plan B
My Cat Nap
My Romantic Tangle
My Blue Lady
My Twin Trouble
My Precious Gift
My Grumpy Wolf

Middlemarch Gathering
My Highland Mate
My Highland Fling
My Elusive Mate
My Valiant Princess
My Highland Wedding
My Highland Billionaire

Middlemarch Capture
Snared by Saber
Favored by Felix
Lost with Leo
Spellbound with Sly
Journey with Joe
Star-Crossed with Scarlett

House of the Cat
Captured & Seduced
Claimed & Seduced
Merry & Seduced
Stranded & Seduced
Seized & Seduced
Hunted & Seduced
Festive & Seduced
Betrayed & Seduced
Enticed & Seduced

Dragon Investigators
Blue Moon Dragon
Blood Moon Dragon
Black Moon Dragon
Snow Moon Dragon

ABOUT SHELLEY

USA Today bestselling author Shelley Munro lives in Auckland, the City of Sails, with her husband and a cheeky Jack Russell/mystery breed dog.

Typical New Zealanders, Shelley and her husband left home for their big OE soon after they married (translation of New Zealand speak - big overseas experience). A twelve-month-long adventure lengthened to six years of roaming the world. Enduring memories include being almost sat on by a mountain gorilla in Rwanda, lazing on white sandy beaches in India, whale watching in Alaska, searching for leprechauns in Ireland, and dealing with ghosts in an English pub.

While travel is still a big attraction, these days Shelley is most likely found in front of her computer following another love - that of writing stories of contemporary and paranormal romance and adventure. Other interests include watching rugby (strictly for research purposes), cycling, playing croquet and the ukelele, and curling up with an enjoyable book.

Visit Shelley at her Website
https://shelleymunro.com

Join Shelley's Newsletter
https://shelleymunro.com/newsletter